PRAISE FOR RHYS BOWEN'S
IN FARLEIGH FIELD

Winner of the Left Coast Crime Award for Best Historical Mystery Novel and the Agatha and Macavity Awards for Best Historical Novel

"Well-crafted, thoroughly entertaining . . ."

—*Publishers Weekly*

"The skills Bowen brings . . . inform the plotting in this character-rich tale, which will be welcomed by her fans as well as by readers who enjoy fiction about the British home front."

—*Booklist*

"In what could easily become a PBS show of its own, Bowen's novel winningly details a World War II spy game."

—*Library Journal*

"This novel will keep readers deeply involved until the end."

—*Portland Book Review*

"*In Farleigh Field* delivers the same entertainment mixed with intellectual intrigue and realistic setting for which Bowen has earned awards and loyal fans."

—*New York Journal of Books*

"Well-plotted and thoroughly entertaining . . . With characters who are so fully fleshed out, you can imagine meeting them on the street . . ."

—Historical Novel Society

"Through the character's eyes, readers will be drawn into the era and begin to understand the sacrifices and hardships placed on English society."

—Crimespree Magazine

"Instantly absorbing, suspenseful, romantic and stylish—like binge-watching a great British drama on Masterpiece Theatre."

—Lee Child, *New York Times* bestselling author

"*In Farleigh Field* is brilliant. This is magnificently written and a must read."

—Louise Penny, *New York Times* bestselling author

PRAISE FOR RHYS BOWEN'S
THE TUSCAN CHILD

A *New York Post* Must-Read Selection

"Pass the bread, the olives, and the wine. Oh, and a copy of *The Tuscan Child* to savor with them."

—NPR

"Readers who enjoy World War II historical fiction and rural Italian culture will appreciate this story by a master of her genre."

—Library Journal

"The alternating narratives keep the story moving along, and the pastoral setting is transporting."

—Booklist

"Besides being an action-packed story that is intense and haunting, Bowen also brings to life the setting where the reader can smell the cooking scents, see the brilliant olive groves, and hear the Italian chatter."

—*Crimespree Magazine*

"This novel is well plotted with characters that are so compelling, with their attributes and flaws, that the reader can almost feel as if they had sat down and shared a glass of *vin santo* with them."

—Historical Novel Society

"The interwoven mystery is expertly crafted and unravels at a pace that will keep readers guessing until the end. This is an overall enjoyable trip to the Tuscan countryside and readers will be reluctant to leave this charming and intriguing place."

—*RT Book Reviews*

"*The Tuscan Child* presented me with a conundrum—didn't want the book to end, yet I couldn't put it down. Best read with a glass of Chianti beside a roaring fire. Brava Rhys Bowen—brava!"

—Jacqueline Winspear, *New York Times* bestselling author of the Maisie Dobbs historical mystery novels

THE
VICTORY
GARDEN

Tell Me, Pretty Maiden

In a Gilded Cage

The Last Illusion

Bless the Bride

Hush Now, Don't You Cry

The Family Way

City of Darkness and Light

The Edge of Dreams

Away in a Manger

Time of Fog and Fire

The Ghost of Christmas Past

ROYAL SPYNESS MYSTERIES

Her Royal Spyness

A Royal Pain

Royal Flush

Royal Blood

Naughty in Nice

The Twelve Clues of Christmas

Heirs and Graces

Queen of Hearts

Malice at the Palace

Crowned and Dangerous

On Her Majesty's Frightfully Secret Service

THE
VICTORY
GARDEN

RHYS BOWEN

Text copyright © 2019 by Janet Quin-Harkin, writing as Rhys Bowen
All rights reserved.

Published by Lake Union Publishing, Seattle

www.apub.com

Amazon, the Amazon logo, and Lake Union Publishing are trademarks of Amazon.com, Inc., or its affiliates.

ISBN-13: 9781542040129 (hardcover)
ISBN-10: 1542040124 (hardcover)
ISBN-13: 9781542040112 (paperback)
ISBN-10: 1542040116 (paperback)

Cover design by Shasti O'Leary Soudant

Printed in the United States of America

First edition

This book is dedicated to Linda Myers in celebration of our 35 years of friendship. Linda was my choir director at St Isabella's Church, and we shared some great choral moments together. She has also been one of the biggest fans of my books. She is now moving away. I will miss her. Also a special dedication to Susan Charlton, who lends her name to a principal character in this book. I should point out that Susan is neither old nor haughty! She is a wonderful person and does a great deal of good. And, as always, my grateful thanks to Danielle Marshall and the whole team at Lake Union, who make working with them such a joy.

CHAPTER ONE

The Larches, Near Shiphay, Torquay
Devonshire
May 14, 1918

To Miss Clarissa Hamilton, Field Hospital 17, British
Forces, France

My dear Clarissa,
   Thank you very much for your long letter. I am in
awe of the matter-of-fact way you recount such dangers
and horrors. Who would have thought that you, who
shrieked at seeing a mouse in our dormitory, would have
turned out to be so fearless?
   And you have every right to scold me. I know I prom-
ised to write to you regularly, and I have failed miser-
ably in that task. It is not that I am lazy—nor have I
forgotten you, you can be sure of that. You are never out
of my thoughts and prayers. It's just that I find my own
life here in the countryside so sadly lacking compared to
the excitement and danger that you face daily. In truth, I

have nothing to write about, and I am ashamed to admit it. While you are there amongst the trenches in France, tending to the wounded, being shelled by the enemy, here I am, safe and secure in my English country village, doing nothing more for the war effort than taking some of Mummy's scones and rock cakes to the wounded soldiers in the convalescent home and trying to convince myself that the presence of a young lady will cheer them up.

The rhythmic clickety-clack of a lawnmower made Emily Bryce cease her writing and glance out of her window. Old Josh was pushing the mower over a lawn that already appeared to be immaculate. Her gaze swept the full length of the garden to the rhododendrons and azalea bushes, now in full springtime bloom, surrounding the bottom of the lawn with brilliant pinks and oranges. The apple trees in the kitchen garden were also white with blossom. Her parents seemed to take it for granted that their grounds would look perfect, not appreciating how lucky they were to have a gardener who was well beyond the age to be called up to fight. Their smooth and comfortable life had not changed one bit, apart from . . . She sighed and turned her attention back to the letter.

How I wish that I were with you, in spite of the awful conditions and danger that you write about. I even think I could face a few rats and bad rations to escape from the tedium of my daily life. My parents still keep a tight rein on me, and in spite of my constant entreaties will not let me do anything more useful than those convalescent home visits (well chaperoned by my mother!). Remember that song about 'only a bird in a gilded cage'? That is me. As you well remember, Mummy had made it her sole purpose in life to make a good match for me (preferably with a title!). If there had been no horrid war, she would have moved mountains to have had me presented at court. Now there are no balls, no hunts—in truth, no eligible young men to be found any longer—she has become bitter and resigned. She wants me out of her sight and yet will not let me escape.

I realize that this desire to keep me cocooned has something to do with Freddie's death. They have taken it awfully hard. He was Father's pride and joy, you know. A first at Oxford and destined to become a barrister and then a judge, like Father. Yet he survived for less than a week at the front in Ypres.

She paused again, staring out across the garden, breathing in the scent of newly mown grass mingled with the bonfire Josh had started behind the sweet peas. Safe, familiar scents. Scents of home. *How stupid it is that we are raised to keep our feelings to ourselves,* she thought. *How ridiculous that I can't even tell my best friend the truth, that Freddie's death has shattered our family.* She remembered her father as quite jovial before the war, and her mother, while a born snob, had occasionally shown a softer side. Now it was as if they had both locked themselves away, her father silent and remote, prone to outbursts of anger, and her mother critical of everything. Sometimes she could sense them looking at her, and she was sure they were wishing it was she who had died and not Freddie. *Oh Freddie,* she thought. How could she write that she had taken it awfully hard, too? That after three years his death was still a raw wound. He was her big brother. Her protector. She still remembered it as if it were yesterday: her last term at school, right before the house tennis matches. Being summoned to the headmistress's office, standing there in her tennis skirt, clutching her racquet and wondering what she had done wrong. The headmistress instead taking her hand and sitting her down before she gave the bad news. To have her headmistress, normally so terrifying, being kind and gentle with her was too much. It was the only time she had allowed herself to cry.

3

Emily glanced down at the paper. The pen had dripped a blob of ink, and she blotted it hastily before dipping into the inkwell again.

> *So I can understand why they were so adamant about my not joining you in the volunteer nurse brigade, but not why they won't let me seek any kind of useful employment. Bad things are hardly likely to happen to me in a volunteer centre, sorting old clothes or rolling bandages in Torquay, are they? I wouldn't even mind working as a volunteer nurse at the convalescent home. At least I'd be doing something useful. I am dying of frustration and loneliness here, Clarissa. I want to be useful. I want to do my bit, so that Freddie's death was somehow not in vain. I know I shouldn't be complaining when I have such an easy life, but*

"Emily?" Her mother's strident voice echoed up the staircase. "Where are you, child? I told you we would be leaving at ten thirty on the dot. Come along. We can't keep the young men waiting. Best foot forward."

Emily put down the pen. The dreaded visit to the convalescent home. The letter would have to wait. It was not that she disliked visiting the wounded officers. Actually, she would have quite enjoyed it if she had been alone. It was following her mother through the wards, watching her playing at Lady Bountiful and not being allowed to interact with the young men herself that she found so frustrating. She stood in front of the mirror, twisting her ash-brown hair up into a hasty bun, jabbing in hairpins in the hopes of holding it in place before cramming her blue straw hat over it. Critical grey eyes stared back at her. Too thin. Too tall. Too angular. Then she grimaced at her reflection, grabbed her gloves and hurried down the stairs. Her mother was standing by the front door, looking resplendent in lavender silk with a matching dyed ostrich feather in her hat. *Far more suitable for a garden party than a convalescent home visit,* Emily thought. Florrie, the maid, stood beside her, her arms piled high with cake tins.

"Where have you been?" Mrs Bryce demanded. "I haven't seen you since breakfast."

"I was writing to Clarissa," Emily said. "I received a letter from her in the morning post, and she chided me for not writing back."

"She is still in France?"

"Yes."

"Working in a hospital there?"

"Not exactly. A makeshift tent near the front. It sounds rather awful."

Mrs Bryce shook her head. "I still can't understand why her parents let her go. A girl from a good family like that. What were they thinking to have her exposed to those conditions? It's a wonder her mind doesn't snap."

Emily shot her mother a glance, went to say something, then thought better of it. "She wanted to go, Mummy," she said instead. "She was determined to go. You know Clarissa—she likes to get her own way, and she can be quite forceful when she puts her mind to it."

"Well, you can thank your lucky stars that we were more sensible than her parents and kept you from such horrors."

Emily saw her mother looking her up and down. "Is that what you plan to wear?" she said.

"Is there something wrong with it?" Emily retorted. "It doesn't reveal too much flesh, does it?"

"On the contrary. It's just rather plain, that's all. We should remember that we are going with the purpose of cheering up these young men—making them remember that there is a better world waiting for them after the war."

"If they are still here after the war," Emily said, then instantly regretted it.

Her mother frowned. "No time to go and change now. Here, pick up that platter from the table, and then we must be on our way. I told Matron I'd be there at eleven, and you know I am a woman of my word."

Emily followed her mother out of the front door. Florrie brought up the rear of the procession. Emily thought privately that it was a bit excessive serving wounded servicemen with silver tongs from crystal dishes, but her mother had maintained that there were standards to be upheld, even in wartime. "It is a home for officers, after all," she had said. "It is good to remind them that the old standards of civilization still exist."

They walked down the raked gravel drive, out of the main gate and down the lane, between high banks on which a few late bluebells were still blooming. It was a perfect spring day. A pigeon was cooing in an oak tree above them, and somewhere in the woods a cuckoo was calling loudly. The adjoining property had belonged to an elderly colonel and his wife. They had moved to a hotel in Torquay and turned over their house to the government to be used as a convalescent hospital for wounded officers.

It is indeed a lovely setting, Emily thought. Surrounded by fields and copses, the upper floors giving a glimpse of the distant sea—exactly the right environment to heal the mind as well as the body. Most of the men she had seen there had physical wounds, some rather terrible—blinded and burned by mustard gas, missing limbs—but others had minds that had broken with what they had seen and endured. She had overheard a nurse complaining about how noisy it was at night when so many men shouted out in terror from nightmares or sobbed like babies.

A maid opened the front door, and they were admitted to the cool marble entrance hall.

"Matron is expecting you, ma'am," the maid said, bobbing a curtsy. "She invites you to take a cup of coffee with her in her study."

"How kind." Mrs Bryce nodded graciously. "I look forward to joining her after we have done our first round of visits." A selection of cakes was arranged on the platters, and her mother went off like a ship in full sail, with Emily trailing behind.

"Good morning, gentlemen. A selection of my home-made baked goods to cheer you up and remind you of your own homes," Mrs Bryce said as they entered the first ward. "Oh yes, do try the iced bun. An old family recipe, you know."

Since her mother had never baked anything in her life, Emily tried not to smile. This was a room of those further along in their rehabilitation. They sat in armchairs or on chaises with rugs over their knees and regarded Emily with interest.

"Stay a while and talk to us, you adorable creature," one of them said, holding out a hand as Emily passed.

Emily was quite willing to do so, but her mother intervened. "Come along, Emily. We haven't time to dilly-dally. There are all those wards upstairs to be visited."

"But you don't need me to follow you around," Emily said. "Why don't I take a tray to different rooms and that way halve the work for you?"

He mother frowned and waited until they were in the hall again before replying. "It isn't seemly for a young girl to visit a room full of men unchaperoned."

Emily had to laugh. "Mother, I don't think I'm in any danger from a room full of crippled soldiers. Besides, you saw them—they wanted me to stay and talk. They need cheering up."

"Emily, keep your voice down. I do not expect you to argue with your mother where we can be overheard."

The grandfather clock in the hall began to chime eleven. Mrs Bryce turned and handed the platter to Emily. "I'd better go up and have that cup of coffee with Matron. I don't like to keep her waiting too long, so I suppose we will postpone the rest of the visits. You had better remain down here for the moment. I don't think you were included in the coffee invitation with Matron. Take this platter and fill it with a good selection of cakes, then bring it up to me in about fifteen minutes. Come straight up the stairs. I don't want you wandering this place alone."

"No, Mother." Emily sighed. She glanced at Florrie and they exchanged a grin. After they had arranged the mixture of iced fairy cakes, rock buns and cream puffs on the plate, Emily waited in the cool quiet of the front hall, listening to the distant murmur of male voices, until what she thought was a suitable amount of time had elapsed. Then she lifted the platter and headed up the curved staircase.

As she came to the top of the first flight, she heard raised voices. Then a male voice said, quite distinctly, "Aw, bugger!"

"Such language. Behave yourself, Flight Lieutenant Kerr," said a booming woman's voice. "Just lie still. I'm not going to hurt you."

"Not going to hurt me? It's about time someone taught you how to change dressings without ripping off half a patient's skin," replied a man's voice with a strange accent.

Curiosity drew Emily to the open door. The man lay on a narrow bed, the large figure of a nurse looming over him. He was the most handsome man she had ever seen. He had unruly red-blond hair and a tanned, outdoor look to him quite unlike the pale English young men Emily was used to. She hadn't realized that she was standing and staring until suddenly he looked up past the nurse and spotted Emily standing there. She had no time to shrink back out of sight. His eyes lit up, and to her embarrassment he winked at her.

"I'm doing my best, Lieutenant," the nurse said. "You have to understand that changing burn dressings is not an easy task."

"Not with sausage fingers like yours," he replied. "You ought to let that young lady volunteer do it for you. Look at her dainty little hands. I bet she wouldn't skin me alive."

The nurse spun around to see Emily standing there, red-faced. "This young lady is only a visitor," she said, "and would no doubt be horrified at your language. And for your information I qualified at one of the best London hospitals and have changed thousands of dressings."

"Old cow," the man muttered.

"What did you say?"

"I said, 'Okay for now,'" he replied, looking up at her innocently. Emily turned away, pressing her lips together, afraid she'd burst out laughing.

"Don't go," the young man called after her. "Come and talk to me. I haven't seen a pretty face in months."

"I'm afraid I have to take these cakes up to Matron's room," Emily said, conscious of the nurse glaring at her.

"You're not even going to share your goodies with poor wounded blokes like us?" he asked. "We're the severe cases, you know. All flyers."

"You're not severe, you're all hopeless," the nurse said, "and I've no doubt that the young lady will be back with cakes for you when it's your turn. But only if you behave yourselves."

"We'll all be as good as gold, Nurse," he said, and he shot Emily a grin as she turned back to look at him.

The nurse followed her out into the hallway. "I must apologize, Miss Bryce. He's Australian, you know. No sense of propriety or decorum, as far as I can see. We've just received several of them into this ward. All members of the Royal Flying Corps—aviators, brave boys. Personally, I think they need their heads examined, flying in the sky with a craft that is essentially held together with paper and string. So I am trying to give them more leeway than I would in normal circumstances—knowing what lies before them, I mean."

When Emily looked at her curiously, the nurse moved closer and lowered her voice. "The life expectancy of a pilot in the Royal Flying Corps is six weeks, Miss Bryce."

"Ah, there you are," came her mother's voice. "We wondered where you had gone. I hope you haven't disregarded my wishes and been frat-ernizing with the young men."

"No, Mother, I came straight up the stairs at what I thought was the right time," Emily said.

"Well, come along then. Let's start with the rooms at the back," her mother said. "We have a lot to get through before lunchtime, and your father will be home for luncheon today."

Emily glanced back at the open door, but she could no longer glimpse the cheeky Australian. She gave a sigh and went to join her mother.

CHAPTER TWO

As if encouraged by the news from the front lines that a victory might finally be within sight, the weather turned unusually warm and sunny. Mrs Bryce served the first strawberries and cream on the lawn and persuaded Josh to outline the tennis court and put up the net, just in case tennis partners could be found.

"I've been thinking, Emily," she said. "If the weather remains this favourable, we may just hold your twenty-first party outside—lanterns in the trees, ice creams, violins by the fountain . . ."

"Mummy, I don't need a twenty-first party," Emily said. "It wouldn't be right to celebrate while so many people are suffering and mourning. Besides, who could I possibly invite? Every young man I knew has been killed and most of the young women have moved away or married."

"I expect your father can rustle up some suitable dance partners." Her mother tossed her head in the way that indicated she didn't like being crossed. "And there are certainly enough families around here to whom we owe a favour or two. The Warren-Smythes, for example. Their daughters will be home from school, and Aubrey can come down from the city."

"Mummy!" Emily rolled her eyes. "Aubrey Warren-Smythe must be almost thirty and is as dull as ditchwater. And there really must be something wrong with him if he hasn't been called up yet."

"I gather he has weak ankles," Mrs Bryce said seriously.

Emily swallowed back a giggle, then she said, "I really don't want a party made up of people to whom Daddy owes a favour."

"You must still be in touch with old school friends who are available to attend," Mrs Bryce said. "What about that girl whose cousin was a viscount?"

"Daphne Armstrong? Now married to another viscount," Emily said.

"Splendid. We'll invite them then. That will certainly make the Warren-Smythes sit up and take notice, won't it?"

"Mother! She was never a close friend, and I haven't spoken to her since we left school. Can we just forget about the party?"

"Absolutely not. My mind is made up. I had always planned to have my daughter come out properly into society. I had expected her to be a debutante. And since that option has been denied you, the very least I can do is to give you a twenty-first party."

Emily could see there was no point in fighting. "I'll go and see if any more strawberries are ripe before the birds find them," she said, and set off with a basket across the lawn, through the shrubbery to the kitchen garden. She had just bent down to pick strawberries when she heard noises amid the rhododendron bushes that separated the Bryces' property from the convalescent home next door. She looked around, expecting it to be Josh, but he was weeding the borders beside the drive. She backed away. There were sounds of blundering and undergrowth being trampled. It sounded like some kind of large animal. Then she glimpsed a figure—a man was pushing his way through the hedge that separated the Bryces' home, the Larches, from the adjoining property. *A tramp,* she thought, *come to steal our fruit.* She waited as the man eased his way between rhododendron bushes and then she demanded, in a loud voice, "What do you think you are doing, trespassing on private property?"

The man spun around at the sound of her voice and almost lost his footing as he stepped into a newly turned bed. He had to grab on to a nearby branch to steady himself.

"Aw, stone the crows. You nearly gave me a heart attack," he said. He emerged from the shadows, and Emily recognized him as the Australian who had winked at her.

"Oh, it's you," he said, his face lighting up with a beaming smile. "My little vision from the other day. So you *are* real. I thought the morphine was making me hallucinate. And to think you live so close by."

"Yes," Emily said, no longer able to be indignant as he was smiling at her. "And you are trespassing," she added. She was conscious that she was perspiring, and that she was dressed in a simple cotton frock that revealed too much shoulder.

"I didn't mean any harm, and I didn't think anyone would mind," he said. "They had us parked outside in bath chairs like a lot of old fogeys and I couldn't stand it a moment longer. When there were no nurses around, I got up and sneaked off. I've been dying to take a closer look at this place. I can see a bit of the grounds from my window, and it all looked so perfect, so unreal . . . that green, green grass and all those roses. My word, if my mother saw this, she'd think she'd died and gone to heaven."

"You like roses, do you, Flight Lieutenant?" Emily asked.

"I was thinking of my mother. She tries to grow flowers, especially roses, but she never quite succeeds. Where we live, there's only about six inches of rain a year. Not enough for a proper garden, but she keeps on trying. If she could only see this, I bet she'd just break down and cry."

"Where do you live exactly?" Emily asked.

"What we'd call Back of Burke," he said, "meaning the outback. Middle of nowhere. The far western part of New South Wales. The closest town is Tibooburra, and that's not much of a place."

13

"And what does your family do out there?" She realized she was sounding like her mother.

"We're farmers."

"Farmers? How can you farm with so little rain?"

He grinned. "We run sheep."

"Sheep? Sheep can exist with no grass?"

"There's a little grass. Not green like this around here, but enough to keep a sheep alive. We can only run about one sheep per acre though."

"One sheep per acre?" Emily tried to grasp this. "Then how many sheep do you have?"

He frowned, thinking. "I'm not quite sure. Maybe twenty thousand or so."

"Twenty thousand? Then you have twenty thousand acres?"

"More than that. We have land that's not much good for anything as well."

"You must be miles from your nearest neighbour then."

"About fifty."

"Fifty miles?"

He nodded, grinning at her incredulous face.

"Isn't it terribly lonely? What happens if you have a medical emergency?"

"We take care of it, or we die. You have to be pretty self-sufficient if you live like us. We do our own blacksmithing, sheep shearing, you name it."

"Golly," was all Emily could find to say.

"And in answer to your other question, yes, I guess it is a bit lonely for my mother. It was all right when we nippers were at home. I've got two sisters. Then we all were sent off to school and my sisters stayed on in the city—one is a teacher and the other got married and has a kid of her own. My mother didn't want me sent off to school. I was her youngest, you see. Her baby. But Dad insisted. He needed his son to be properly educated to take over the station one day."

"Station?"

"What we call our farms. Sheep station."

"I see." She nodded.

"So my mum took it hard when I was sent to school. And she took it even harder when I enlisted and sailed for Europe. Then I was at Gallipoli with the Anzacs."

"I hear that was frightful," Emily said.

"My word. It was a massacre," he said. "I was one of the few lucky ones, and I decided it was a mug's game being a sitting duck on a beach, so I signed up for the Royal Flying Corps. Well, that's what it was called when I joined it. Now we're the Royal Air Force, so I'm told."

"Did you know how to fly?"

"Actually, no, I didn't, but I can drive pretty much any vehicle, and I figured I'd take to it quite easily. They were desperate for any bloke who was mug enough to try, and I took to it like a duck to water."

"What's it like to fly in an aeroplane?" Emily asked.

"Oh, it's amazing. You feel so free and light—just like a bird. And you look down on the land below you and it looks like toy farms and houses." He gave a chuckle. "Only you don't look down much because you never know which direction the enemy is coming from. And when they do come, it's a fight like no other. You swoop, you bank, you dive, and all the time shooting at each other until one goes down in flames."

"How horrible." Emily shivered.

"Oh no. If it has to be war, then this is about as good as it gets. At least it's a gentleman's war in the air. Warrior against warrior. If you go down, you go down with honour after a good fight."

Emily didn't know what to say to this.

"Look," he said, "I can't go on talking to you if I don't know your name."

"It's Emily. Emily Bryce. What is your name, Lieutenant?"

"My name is Robbie Kerr, although at home most people call me Blue."

"Blue?"

"On account of my red hair."

"Now you're making fun of me," she said, feeling herself flushing.

"Oh no. In Australia, blokes with red hair are always called Blue."

"Then it sounds like a silly place."

"Oh no." He shook his head this time. "It's a bonzer place. Plenty of land and sunshine, and nobody cares if you're a duke or a chimney sweep. But out where we live, it's no place for a woman, really. No hat shops or beauty parlours or even other women to talk to. That's why I wanted to see this garden . . . to finally have something positive to write to my mum about. All she's heard is bad news so far. Gallipoli, and then being shot down in France . . ." He was staring out past her, across the lawns. "So I thought I'd describe these flowers. She'd like that."

"You're a good son."

"I try to be," he said, giving her a mischievous grin.

"But should you be up and walking around?"

"Probably not. They're worried about my burns getting infected. The plane caught on fire, see. Oh, and I broke my leg."

"Then you definitely shouldn't be walking around. Aren't you on crutches?"

"Yeah, but I left them on the other side of the hedge."

"Robbie, you should go back at once. You're supposed to be resting."

"No, I'm supposed to be using that leg. They've given me exercises to do. Just not squeezing through hedges. So can I see you again?" he asked. "You're the first good thing that's happened to me in a while. All I'm faced with is dreadful old battleaxes like that Nurse Hammond."

"You called her an old cow."

He grinned. "So I did. Sorry about that. The pain makes me forget my manners sometimes."

"It was nothing to do with pain. You enjoyed needling her."

He gave a sheepish smile. "Aw yes, well . . . I have to do something to cheer myself up, don't I? Been lying in a bloody hospital bed for too long."

"Please go back before you're found to be missing, Robbie." She reached out and touched his arm. "I don't want you to get into trouble, and I certainly don't want you to re-injure that leg."

He stood looking down at her. She hadn't realized until now how tall he was. "So when can I meet you again?"

Emily made a face. "My mother would have a fit if she saw us here. She's very prim and proper. And we haven't been introduced."

"Introduced?" He looked amused.

"Oh yes. In polite society, I'm not supposed to talk to anyone unless we're properly introduced."

"And you thought Australia was a silly country?" He chuckled. "At least we can talk to anyone we want to. The prime minister or a swagman."

"I agree, it is rather silly," Emily said. "We have so many rules here—which fork to use and where to seat people at the dinner table, but all that stuff matters to people like my mother."

"Not to you?"

"I haven't had a chance to escape yet and try out the real world beyond home. I've been cooped up here for the whole war, dying of frustration, dying to do something—volunteer, do my bit."

"So why haven't you?"

Emily chewed on her lip. "My parents. They won't let me go. They are worried that something will happen to me." It sounded silly when she said it. Weak. Pathetic. "My brother was killed, you see," she added, trying to explain. "And my parents . . ."

"They were worried they'd lose you, too."

"Yes."

"I suppose I can understand that. My mum was really upset when I said I was joining up."

"But that's different. You were going a long way from home, going to fight. I only want to find some useful volunteer work in a town."

"Then perhaps they are worried about unsuitable young men and you being brought up so sheltered." His eyes were holding hers. "Not realizing that unsuitable young men were lurking in your own bushes."

Emily laughed. "It's ridiculous, isn't it?"

He shrugged. "I suppose no parents want their babies to leave the nest. So what are you going to do about it?"

"Until now, I've played the devoted daughter. My father made me promise to take care of my mother; not to do anything to upset her any more. But it's gone on long enough. I'll turn twenty-one soon, and then I'm free to make my own decisions, so I'll make my escape."

"Good on yer," he said. "You have to find the courage to take your life into your own hands. So where will you escape to?"

"I'm not sure yet. I'd rather like to volunteer as a nurse, like my friend Clarissa."

"Oh, good idea," he said. "Volunteer here. I'd like you as my nurse. I'd get better a lot quicker, I'm sure. And we wouldn't have to be introduced. So when can we meet, before you turn twenty-one?"

Emily felt her pulse quicken. It had been so long since a young man had looked at her in this way, especially a man like Robbie. Had a man ever looked at her like that, she wondered? Then a picture flashed into her mind. A boy with red hair and light blue eyes, not unlike Robbie, and also deemed unsuitable by her mother. A boy who had been killed at the front a month after Freddie. And she had promised herself never to feel anything for a young man again. She tried to sound measured and in control as she answered. "I do have to walk past your hospital to go to the nearest pillar box. And I do write letters to my best friend."

"So if I happened to be near the gate at a certain time . . ." He gave her a knowing grin.

"At eleven o'clock, say?"

"That would be good. After morning rounds. They'd approve of my taking a gentle stroll up the driveway."

Emily beamed at him. "All right. Eleven o'clock then. Now please do go before my mother sees you."

"Rightio," he said. "See you tomorrow then, Emily." He reached out his hand to touch her, then thought better of it. "You're the first good thing that's happened to me in quite a while."

And me, too, she thought, as she watched him disappear between the rhododendron bushes.

She walked back to the house with a smile on her face.

"Where have you been?" Her mother was in the front hall, adjusting the flower arrangement on the side table, as Emily came in through the front door, slightly breathless. She glanced down at the empty wooden basket in Emily's hand. "I thought you went to pick strawberries."

"They weren't quite ripe," Emily said. "I thought I'd give them another day or two."

And she walked past her mother and was conscious of her critical stare as she went down the hall towards the kitchen.

CHAPTER THREE

Dear Clarissa,

I finally have some news. I've met a fascinating chap. He's an aviator with the Royal Air Force and he's Australian. He's quite different from any boy I've met so far. He says what he thinks, completely oblivious to any of our conventions, and he's obviously very brave, but he came to see our garden to have something uplifting to describe to his mother, who tries to grow flowers in the most inhospitable place. Isn't that sweet? And he's awfully good-looking, too. I'm sure my mother wouldn't approve of him, so we're meeting in secret, which of itself makes life a little more spicy.

My mother is in full planning mode as my twenty-first birthday is next month. I don't suppose you have any leave coming to you, do you? Mummy wants to invite all sorts of awful, snobby people—like Daphne Armstrong, because she's married a viscount! So it would be lovely to have you there for moral support. Also because I haven't seen you for over a year, and I'm dying to hear everything. I'm thinking of signing up myself after I turn twenty-one, so you can give me all the grim details.

Emily finished the letter, put a stamp on it and went downstairs, to find her mother sitting at the small Queen Anne desk in the morning room. She looked up, frowning.

"I don't know where to find a band these days," she said. "I might have to put out feelers in Plymouth, or even Exeter. There are those old men who play at the Grand Hotel in Torquay . . ."

Emily gave a despairing laugh. "Mummy, they are at least ninety, and they play Strauss waltzes."

"Nothing wrong with a good Strauss waltz. But I agree, they are a trifle doddery. Ah well. Perhaps I'll send Daddy on the quest. He's got the assizes in Exeter next week."

The ormolu clock on the mantelpiece started to chime the hour, making Emily look up. "I'm just off to post a letter to Clarissa," she said. "Anything you want posted?"

"Not today, dear. And when you come back, we need to finalize a list of people to invite."

Emily tried not to break into a run as she went up the drive and then hurried down the lane. She didn't see him at first as she approached the gate, and felt absurd disappointment. But as she looked towards the house, she saw him coming, walking slowly with the help of crutches. He spotted her and tried to hurry. Emily held up a hand. "Take your time or you'll trip."

He was quite out of breath when he reached her, with beads of sweat on his forehead, making her realize how much this simple walk was hurting him. "Sorry about that," he said. "I had to wait for the doctor's visit. They were concerned about one of my burns not healing properly."

"You probably dislodged the dressing when you climbed through the hedge," she said.

"Could be." He smiled at her.

"Are you still in much pain?"

"All the better for seeing you." He gave her a reassuring smile, then looked around. "Let's go under the trees over there, where we can't be seen. I don't think anyone would mind us chatting, but word might get back to your mother."

"Good idea," she said, and walked slowly beside him. "My mother has launched herself into planning my twenty-first party. I told her I didn't want anything special, and I feel it is wrong to hold a big celebration when the country is still at war and so many people are suffering, but she's determined. She wanted me to be presented at court, you know."

"My word," he said. "I didn't realize you were royal or something. Should I call you 'Your Highness'?"

Emily laughed. "We're not royal. We're not even aristocratic. My father is the son of a vicar and rose to become a judge. My mother is solidly middle class. Her father was a bank manager. But she has grand ideas. She was set on my marrying a title."

"And you?"

"I'm set on marrying for love. There was one young man I was rather keen on, when I was eighteen. But he was killed in Flanders, the same week as my brother."

"War's a bugger, isn't it?" he said. "All the mates I started out with are gone. And now most of the boys I flew with." He said it in the most matter-of-fact way, as if it were something quite expected.

She felt a shiver of alarm. "You won't have to go back, will you? Not after all your injuries. Won't they send you home to Australia?"

"But I want to go back. I have to. Aeroplanes are making a difference. We're actually winning at last. I have to do my bit."

"But you've already done more than your bit." She said it more vehemently than she had intended.

He smiled at her. "Don't worry about me. I live a charmed life. God doesn't want me and the devil won't have me."

"Don't speak that way, please."

"You don't want to get too fond of me, Emily. I'm unsuitable, remember." He finished the phrase lightly and gave her a wink. "Anyway, the war's going to be over soon. That's what everyone's saying. And as soon as I'm released from duty, I'm going back to the farm, to work with my dad."

"Do you want to do that?" she asked cautiously. "Now that you've seen more of the world? You told me I should find the courage to live my own life."

He was frowning. "Oh, but I want to. It's a bonzer life. All that open air and freedom to do what you want, and I've got grand ideas for making things better. I'm going to have an aeroplane shipped from here. Think what we can accomplish with that! Check the waterholes and for broken fences, fly someone to a hospital, even go and visit a neighbour. My word. An aeroplane will change everything. I might even ship more than one and teach other blokes to fly." He looked so animated, but then his smile faded. "But like I said, the outback's no place for a woman, especially not a woman who is used to fancy things."

They chatted for a few minutes longer, then Emily realized she shouldn't stay out too long.

"See you tomorrow?" Robbie asked. "Same time?"

Emily nodded. She almost skipped like a small girl on her way to the pillar box. It was no good Robbie saying that she shouldn't get too fond of him. She already was.

After that, she managed a few minutes with him every morning, and even the dreaded visit to the convalescent home with her mother was made sweet by knowing that she would find an opportunity to slip away and see him. Each time they talked, she sensed his enthusiasm for his life in Australia and his closeness with his family. His mother had played games with her children, taught them to read, sung them to sleep. Emily couldn't ever remember sitting on her mother's knee, and certainly not being sung to sleep.

"And my dad," he continued. "He and I used to go out riding together every morning. He came out from England as a young bloke, you know. Come out from a town, with no skills, nothing, worked as a farmhand, saved his money and built our place up from scratch. And he loves the land the way I do. He's excited like a little kid when he sees a flight of galahs."

"Galahs?" she asked.

"Pink cockatoos," he said. "Pretty birds, but a bloody nuisance. They'd strip the wood off the porch if you let them. But when you see a flock of a thousand of them landing at the waterhole . . . my, but that's a lovely sight. I'd love to show you . . ." He broke off, as if he might have gone too far. "So did you just have the one brother?" he asked.

Emily nodded. "Yes. He was four years older than me. There was a sister in between, but she died of diphtheria when she was a baby. So now it's just me."

"So you can understand why they want to hang on to you, can't you?"

She nodded. "I suppose so. But I can't be cooped up forever. In my mother's day, a girl stayed home until she was married. But that can't happen any more, can it? How many girls will never marry because there are no young men coming home?"

"Then you have to stick up for yourself and do what you want."

On another occasion, he asked, "What would you have done if there hadn't been a war? Apart from getting married, I mean."

Emily gave him a shy smile. "My teachers at school said I had a good brain and wanted me to go to university, but my mother thought it was a silly idea. She said too much education was not good for women. They needed to know how to run a home and a family, and being educated only made them discontent. I'm afraid she's hopelessly old-fashioned in her ideas."

"Would you have wanted to go to university?" he asked.

Emily considered this. "I'm not sure. I don't think I'd have wanted to be a professor or even a teacher. I told you I'd like to try being a nurse. I don't know whether I'd be any good, but at least I'd know I was doing something worthwhile."

"You're chatting with me. That's something worthwhile," he said. "Raising a poor, wounded bloke's spirits. I count the minutes until you come every day, Emily."

"I do, too," she said. "You're certainly raising my spirits, too, Robbie. My mother noticed it yesterday, but of course she got it wrong. She thought I was excited about my upcoming party."

"You're having a party?"

"My twenty-first. My mother's in a full planning frenzy." She hesitated, wondering if she could find a way to invite Robbie. An image swam into her head of dancing with him, his arms holding her tightly. "I should be getting back," she said. "The dressmaker is coming round for my fitting. I'll see you tomorrow."

But dry and summery spells never last long in England, and the weather broke that night with a vengeance, with driving rain and gale-force winds. There was no question of going out for a walk. Mrs Bryce revised her party plans to include an option for an indoor event. She also revised down the numbers as it became evident how few young people were available.

"We can't have a party with so few men," she said. "I have twenty girls who have accepted, but only four men, and two of those are still schoolboys."

"We could invite some of the officers from the convalescent home," Emily said, as if the idea had just occurred to her. "You said yourself the other day that there are some well-mannered chaps amongst them."

"Now, that's not a bad idea," Mrs Bryce said. "Some of them are ambulatory and fit enough to dance, and the others can sit and make polite conversation. As soon as this rain abates, I'll have a little talk with Matron and see which young men she thinks will do."

They went on their weekly visit to the convalescent home in the motor car because the weather was still so unsettled.

"I must speak to Matron about letting some of the young officers attend your party," Mrs Bryce said. "I'm sure she can't object. We'll send a motor car around for them."

As she disappeared towards Matron's room, Emily darted quickly to see Robbie. He was sitting up in bed, writing a letter.

"Hey, Robbie, wake up. Here comes your young lady," one of the men further down the ward called out.

Robbie looked up, startled, then his face broke into a big smile. "My word, aren't you a sight for sore eyes," he said. "I was just writing to my mother and telling her about you. I was trying to describe you, but I couldn't get it right."

"How about elegant, sophisticated and dazzlingly beautiful?" she said, her eyes challenging him.

"All of the above, naturally."

This made her blush. "Look, Robbie, I wanted to invite you to my party next week."

"I don't think your mother would want me there, would she?"

"I want you there, and besides, I've squared it away with Mummy. We were horribly short of young men, so I suggested we should invite some of the officers. She's up with Matron now obtaining permission."

"I might not know how to behave—speaking to people I haven't been introduced to and that sort of thing."

"Rubbish, you'll be fine. I'll tell them your parents are big land owners in Australia, which is true. Around here, we're very impressed with people who own big farms."

"Can I bring a couple of my mates?" he asked. "I'll need a bit of moral support."

"Anyone would think I was inviting you to an expedition to a lion's den," she said. "Look, if you don't want to come to my party, I'll understand, but I'd really like to have an ally there myself amongst all the dreadful bores that Mummy has invited."

"All right," he said, after a pause. "I guess I can suffer anything to be with you."

"What are the names of your friends?" she said. "I'll go up to Matron now and tell her I want you added to the list."

A wary look came over his face. "I don't think she has the highest opinion of us, from what she's heard from the nurses."

"Then I'll send the motor for you myself if necessary," Emily said. "And I'll tell my mother that you are coming. It is my party after all."

"That's my girl." Robbie beamed. "Learning to show some spunk. I like that."

"You're teaching me bad habits," she said.

"Not at all. I'm teaching you how to survive in a difficult world. You can't be under your parents' thumb forever. You have to take charge of your own life now you're going to be twenty-one."

"Too right," a voice from the next bed chimed in, making her realize that their whole conversation had been overheard by the entire ward.

CHAPTER FOUR

By the day of the party, the weather had changed again. For two days before, there was brilliant sunshine, making them worry that it was too good to last. Weather in the West Country tended to be especially changeable. But the day itself dawned fine and bright. Tradesmen's vans arrived with provisions and extra chairs and tables for the garden. A dance floor was erected on the side lawn. Lanterns were strung in the trees. Extra girls were hired to help cook and to wait at table. Mrs Bryce was a bundle of nerves, flitting from one setting to the next, double- and triple-checking anything that could possibly go wrong.

Emily found that she was torn between excitement and dread. It was her big day, after all, and she wanted it to be special, but she was also afraid it wouldn't live up to her dreams. And if Robbie could be there, that was all that mattered. The party was due to begin at eight. At six o'clock, a taxicab pulled up outside the house. Emily had been with her mother in the dining room, debating the arrangement of food on the buffet table. They looked up at the sound of tyres crunching on gravel.

"Now, who could that be as early as this?" Mrs Bryce said. "Not a tradesman's van. Surely it's not a guest who has the time wrong? Oh Lord. And neither of us dressed yet."

Someone was emerging from the back door of the cab—someone in a nurse's uniform. Emily gave a little squeal of delight. "It's Clarissa!" she shouted, and rushed to the front door. Her best friend stood there looking rather pale, her dark hair shorn into a bob and her brown eyes seeming larger than ever in that white face, but she opened her arms and rushed to embrace Emily.

"You sly thing!" Emily exclaimed. "Why didn't you tell me you were coming? When you didn't respond to my invitation, I feared that you couldn't get away."

"My dear, I didn't know myself that I was coming until yesterday," Clarissa said. "We were waiting for replacements who didn't arrive, and there was no way I could leave without them. But then, at the last moment, a lorry with two new doctors and three new nurses appeared. What a godsend. And the sister in charge said that I could be spared, as long as I came straight back. So I only have three days. This evening with you and then up to my parents tomorrow. And I have to warn you that I've nothing suitable to wear. I was sure you'd have something . . ."

"You're so right. My mother had two different dresses made for me, as the weather has been so changeable. Now they'll both be put to good use, although I hope it won't be too big for you. You've lost an awful lot of weight."

"The result of little sleep, little food and too much worry, I suspect. We work twelve-hour shifts, day or night, and at the end it's impossible to sleep. Sometimes there are bombardments going on nearby, and one knows it's only a matter of time before the next load of wounded are brought in."

"I think you're frightfully brave," Emily said. "I'd really like to volunteer, but I wonder if I'd have the nerve for it."

"I asked myself the same thing," Clarissa said. "Oh, trust me. There were so many times during the first weeks that I said out loud, 'What in heaven's name am I doing here?' But you get used to it. You'd be amazed how quickly one gets used to horrors. And at least I know I'm doing some good. I know that some poor chap didn't die because of me, and that's worth every sleepless moment."

"Golly," Emily said.

The taxicab driver had unloaded Clarissa's small suitcase and was standing patiently, waiting to be paid.

"Oh, I'm frightfully sorry." Clarissa fished for her purse and paid him, obviously tipping him handsomely because he saluted her.

"And you want me back here at nine o'clock tomorrow morning, Nurse?"

"That's right. Thank you."

"Come and meet Mummy and see all the preparations," Emily said. "We've enough food to feed the five thousand. You wouldn't think there was a war on or rationing. Cook has worked wonders, and the farmers around have been terribly generous. And we have our own strawberries and raspberries . . ."

She picked up Clarissa's suitcase, slipped her arm through her friend's and led her towards the house.

"Mummy, look who has just arrived," she called.

Mrs Bryce had clearly been hovering. "Clarissa, my dear, what a surprise," she said. "Don't you look important in that uniform. But why didn't you tell us you were coming? We haven't made up the spare bedroom. I'll have to get Florrie on to it right away."

"Oh, don't worry about me, Mrs Bryce," Clarissa said as she shook her hand. "I'm used to sleeping anywhere these days. I've even slept on an operating table when it wasn't being used."

"Good heavens. I heard of some of your adventures from Emily. They sound quite harrowing. Your poor parents. They must be worried sick."

"Actually, I believe they are quite proud of me," Clarissa said. "Daddy is a doctor, after all. He's glad I'm following in his footsteps."

"But you won't do this sort of thing when the war ends, surely?"

"I might. I'm quite good at it. And I can't picture myself just sitting at home and doing embroidery after this."

"You mean working? Holding a job?"

"I think quite a lot of women will be holding a job after the war ends, Mrs Bryce. We've lost so many men. Women will have to fill all manner of jobs."

Mrs Bryce laughed uneasily. "You see women as bricklayers and steeplejacks, do you, Clarissa?"

"If necessary. If the country is to get up and running again."

Mrs Bryce shook her head as if trying to digest this. She walked across the hall and rang a bell. Florrie appeared. "Florrie, Miss Hamilton has arrived. Can you see that a room is made up for her?"

"Yes, Mrs Bryce," Florrie said. "Do you want me to finish putting out the spoons for the ice creams first?"

"Don't worry, Mummy. Clarissa and I will take care of it. I can make a bed, you know," Emily said.

"But you should think about getting ready. And poor Clarissa is no doubt hungry. We shall not be eating until after nine. Why don't you take her down to the kitchen and see if Cook can find something for her?"

"We'll take her bag up to my room first," Emily said, and started up the stairs. Once in the room, she sank on to the bed. "Goodness, but I shall be glad when this is all over," she said. "As you can probably see, Mummy has turned this into a big production number—all the stops pulled out. It's a wonder she hasn't brought down the London Symphony Orchestra to play."

Clarissa sat beside her. "So do tell. Any nice chaps coming?"

"Maybe." Emily gave an excited little smile. "We've invited some of the officers from the convalescent home. And one of them will be my Australian. So hands off him."

Clarissa gave her a long hard look. "Are you really smitten? Is that wise? Won't he go home to Australia after the war?"

"Yes, he plans to."

"And would you want to go with him?"

"I don't know. He hasn't asked me yet. In fact, he's said several times that it's no place for a woman. Where he lives sounds a bit grim, but he has lots of bold ideas about making life better there. It would be a challenge—something I'm itching for at this minute." She lay back and sighed. "I can't tell you how awfully boring and frustrating it's been here. Every attempt to do something useful has been thwarted. My parents simply won't let me out of their sight. It feels as if my life has been put on hold all this time. You know how we talked at school about travelling, seeing Europe, doing something exciting. And you have, although not in the way you planned. And I've done nothing whatsoever. So now that I'm twenty-one, I finally mean to play my part, and they can't stop me."

"You plan to join the Voluntary Aid Detachment, do you? Become a volunteer nurse like me?"

"I've been thinking about it. I'm rather scared about doing what you do—seeing the blood and all that death, but if you can do it, so can I." She hesitated. "But I don't think I should go out to France. My mother couldn't handle that."

"My mother does," Clarissa said. "In fact, she's jolly proud of me."

"Yes, well, your mother didn't lose her only son, did she? They worshipped Freddie. They thought the sun shone out of his head. I probably shouldn't be telling you this, because they don't want anyone to know, but my mother had a mental breakdown after he died. She was in a sanatorium for three months. And since then, she's . . . well, she's cold and hard, as if she never wants to feel anything again."

"I'm sorry, Emmy," Clarissa said. "But they certainly need nurses here at home, too. Let me know when you're ready and I can put you in touch with the right people. Now, I suppose we'd better get cracking if you are to be looking your best when your guests arrive."

Emily jumped up and went across to the wardrobe. "So this is the dress I'm not wearing tonight," she said, and held up a shimmering pink gown.

"But it's lovely," Clarissa said. "Why don't you want it?"

"I like the other one better." Emily produced a royal blue dress in the Grecian style. "I think it's not so little-girly, and the royal blue suits my colouring better. The pink will show off your dark hair perfectly. In fact, you'll have the officers swarming around you like bees around the honey pot."

Clarissa laughed. "You are funny," she said. "But I can see the blue will be perfect with your fair hair. So let's go and find some food to keep the wolf from the door, and then we'll change, shall we?" She reached out her hand and took Emily's. "I can't tell you how lovely it is to be here. Almost like a dream, really. I mean, look at this room: all pink and white, and your bookcase with all those marvellous books. God, do you know how I long to have time to read again? And those sweet dolls sitting on the shelf. When I'm lying on my cot in the middle of the night and the sky is lit up with exploding shells, it's hard to believe there are still places like this in the world."

"You don't have to go back, Clarissa. You've done more than your share," Emily said.

"I must go back. I've signed on, just like any man who enlists. I can't quit until they discharge me." She stared past Emily, out of the window and across the broad expanse of lawn. "Besides, I'm good at what I do. I can help save lives."

"I'm really proud of you. No, more than that. I'm envious of you. You're leading your own life. You're doing something worthwhile. I've always loved this room, too, but right now it feels like a prison. I can't wait to get away."

"Do you remember our attempts to escape at school?" Clarissa asked, laughing.

"That time we tried to climb down the drainpipe and got stuck halfway? Matron was furious, wasn't she?" Emily laughed, too. She took Clarissa's hands. "I'm so glad you're here to help me get through this. Oh well, let's face the music, shall we?"

CHAPTER FIVE

The first guests started arriving around eight. Emily was positioned on the front steps with her parents on either side of her, greeting arrivals. As she smiled and nodded and thanked people for coming, her eyes kept straying down the driveway. Josh had been dispatched to pick up the officers from the convalescent home. She saw the Daimler pulling up for a second time and four young men got out. She broke away from her parents and ran down to Josh. "There will also be three Australians, Josh. Make sure they are picked up, please."

Josh frowned. "I was told seven young men. And this makes seven."

"It may be that the matron did not approve of sending the Australians, but I've invited them. Could you please go back and find them?"

"Anything for you, Miss Emmy. Especially on your big day." He gave her a big grin and put the motor car into gear.

Emily was trapped by Aubrey Warren-Smythe when the Daimler returned. The young men who emerged were all on crutches. One had burns down one side of his face. Emily went over to them. "Oh, I'm so glad you've come."

"You look lovely." Robbie's eyes lit up when he saw her. "We almost didn't get here. We were told that we were not well enough to venture out in public yet." A smile spread across his face. "I think that was an excuse because Matron didn't think we'd be right for your little do. Too rough and ready, eh, boys?"

The other two nodded. "But where are my manners?" Robbie went on. "Emily, may I present Jimmy Hammond and Ray Barclay. Jimmy's from Queensland and Ray is from Melbourne, where the people are almost as toffee-nosed as here."

"Just because we're not savages like you, Kerr," Ray Barclay said, shaking Emily's hand. "There are some civilized people in Australia, you know."

"And who have we here?" Mrs Bryce came to join them. "More officers, I see."

"Mummy, these three lieutenants are all aviators, from Australia."

"Aviators? How terribly brave," Mrs Bryce said. "But should you be out and about with your injuries?" She glanced down at their crutches and bandages. "Matron said she was only sending over young men who were almost ready to be released."

"I invited them, Mummy. They are far from home and need cheering up. Besides, they are fighting for a country that isn't even their own. They deserve a treat."

"Very well." Mrs Bryce nodded. "Please feel at home, gentlemen, but do be careful with those crutches. There are steps, and we will be on the lawn later. Oh look, Emily. It's Colonel and Mrs Hetherington just arriving." And Emily was taken off to meet the next arrivals.

After that, the evening passed in a blur. Emily noticed that Clarissa was indeed surrounded by the officers. Emily had a hard time avoiding being cornered by Aubrey, who insisted on telling her long and complicated stories about the banking world in London. When she finally broke away and went to find Robbie, she came upon the three Australians standing beneath a large painting that hung in the drawing room. It was a portrait of a man on a horse, his hair in long cavalier curls.

The Australians were chuckling when Emily found them. "I wonder if he went to sleep with curlers in his hair," Jimmy was saying.

"No, it's a wig," Robbie answered. "They wore wigs in those days."

"Rather him than me," Ray said. "He looks a proper fairy, doesn't he?"

Emily noticed her mother standing in the doorway. Mrs Bryce frowned, then turned away. "You should probably be careful what you say." She put a finger to her lips, glancing around. "Mummy's really proud of that painting. She likes to hint that he was an ancestor. Of course, he wasn't. She bought it at an estate sale."

"Yeah, you two," Robbie said. "Behave yourselves. No more making fun of the pictures."

Supper was announced. Emily led Robbie and the others into the dining room. "You won't be able to carry plates," she said. "Why don't you find seats outside and I'll see that food is brought to you. What do you think you might like?"

"My oath, this is some spread," Ray Barclay said. "We haven't seen food like this since we left home. At the hospital, it's mainly stodge with a tiny sliver of meat occasionally. Or pies made out of potato and veg. Is this how people live around here, or just posh people like you?"

"Oh no. We've been on rations ourselves," Emily said. "It's just that so many friends were generous for the party. A local farmer sent us the ham, and another one two-dozen eggs, and we grow the salad stuff in our own kitchen garden. Now what would you like—a taste of everything?"

"What's that?" Jimmy went over to a dish in the shape of a big fish. It was pink and shiny and decorated with sliced olives. He dipped his finger into it and popped it into his mouth. "It's fish paste," he said with distaste.

"It is salmon mousse," Mrs Bryce said in a cold voice, appearing in the doorway behind them. "We were fortunate enough to acquire a piece of salmon from Fortnum and Mason in London."

"Mousse? Is that like a Scottish mouse?" Jimmy asked, not seeing Emily's warning frown.

"No, it's that thing with big horns," Ray chimed in.

"I'm not exactly sure how it is made," Mrs Bryce said, her voice now clipped. "But it is one of Cook's specialties."

With that, she swept off. Emily showed them to their seats and brought them plates before filling her own and coming to sit beside Robbie.

"Sorry," he muttered. "I can't keep a rein on my friends when they've had a bit to drink. I think they upset your mum."

"She's easily offended," Emily whispered back.

Clarissa came up to them. "Save me two seats, will you? I'm getting plates for me and for Lieutenant Hutchins." She blushed a little. "He's from Berkshire and his father plays golf at the same club as Daddy. Isn't that amazing?"

Emily smiled. It was turning into a good evening after all.

After supper, the band was playing beside the dance floor. Emily's father came up to her. "I think it's only right that I claim the first dance with my daughter." He held out his hand to her and led her on to the floor. "You're looking very lovely tonight, my dear," he said as they began to waltz. "Very grown-up suddenly. It's hard to believe our little girl is now a woman." There was a catch in his voice. Emily thought it was the first time he had spoken to her with any emotion for a long while.

"Thank you, Daddy." She smiled up at him.

"I think the party is going well, don't you?" he went on. "Your mother was in a frightful state about it, wasn't she? Between ourselves, I was a little worried it was a bit much for her. But now I think it was a good idea, don't you? It's given her something to celebrate at last."

Emily nodded.

They danced in silence, then he said, "So are you enjoying yourself?"

"Immensely," she said.

"Fraternizing with the officers, I notice." He gave her a wink. Then his face became sombre. "If I were you, I'd keep my distance until this wretched war is over. Only leads to heartbreak, my dear. You fall in love and then they are killed. You've already lost a beloved brother, so my advice to you is to keep your heart locked well away until peacetime. And from what we hear, that won't be long, now that the Americans have joined the fray."

Emily nodded and said nothing. As soon as the dance had ended, she made her way to where Robbie was sitting. He stood up as she approached. "I regret that I can't ask you to dance with me. I used to be quite a dancer before the war. We only had kangaroos to dance with and they aren't too fussy."

Emily laughed. "We could take a little stroll," she said.

"Rightio." He grabbed his crutches. They weaved their way through the crowd until they were beyond the light of the lanterns. Music floated out across the lawn.

"A grand party you have here," he said. "No expense spared."

"I'm their only remaining child, and this is the closest they'll get to presenting me formally into society."

"So you're supposed to find a posh husband tonight, right?"

"My father just warned me in quite the opposite direction. He told me not to fall in love until the end of the war because life is too precarious."

"So are you going to obey? Lock yourself away in an ivory tower until the war is over?"

"I don't think I can," Emily said. "I've already lost the key to that tower."

They stood looking at each other, then he rested his crutch under his shoulder, took her chin in his hand and kissed her. That first kiss was a mere brushing of the lips, but then he pulled her closer and the kiss was long and demanding. As they broke apart, each a little breathless, Emily turned to see her mother standing at the edge of the crowd, staring in their direction.

"I suppose I'd better go back to my guests," she said shakily.

The last guest left at two in the morning. Emily flopped down on to the sofa. "My feet are killing me," she said to Clarissa.

"Mine, too, but it was worth it, wasn't it? What a lovely party. And Ronald is going to write to me."

"Ronald?"

"Lieutenant Hutchins I told you about. And we'll see each other when we're both safely back home. Isn't that amazing?"

"I'm so happy for you." Emily studied her friend's face, now no longer pale and drawn.

"And what about your Australian?"

"He kissed me. It was wonderful."

"Emily?" Mrs Bryce came into the room. "It's time poor Clarissa went to bed. She should be getting some rest before she returns to France. Off with you, young lady."

"I'll come up and unhook you," Emily said.

Emily's mother restrained her. "Just a minute. I want a word with you." Her face was like stone. "Those uncouth Australians you invited to the party—what were you thinking, child? And did it not occur to you to ask our permission first?"

"One of those Australians is my friend, Mother. He asked to bring his mates with him. I agree; they were a bit boisterous. I'm sorry."

"They are quite of the wrong class, Emily. Absolutely unsuitable. I saw you with that boy. Don't think I didn't."

"Mummy, he's just different, that's all. His parents own a large property in Australia. Over twenty thousand acres."

"I understand that cowboys in America also have lots of land, but that doesn't make them the sort of cultured people one would want to fraternize with. They were boors, Emily. Utterly uncivilized. So you can put any notions in that direction out of your head. Your father and I forbid you to see him again."

Emily opened her mouth to say she was now twenty-one and could do as she pleased, but thought better of it. This was not the right moment for a big scene. Without another word, she stalked out of the room and up the stairs.

CHAPTER SIX

Clarissa left in the morning, having given Emily details on whom to contact about joining the volunteer nurses brigade. After she had gone, Emily sat at her desk, pen in hand, but she hesitated to write the letter. If she had to go up to London for training, she wouldn't see Robbie again. It was going to be hard enough to slip away and visit him after last night. She knew that her mother was vindictive and manipulative enough to ask Matron to have him transferred to another facility right away.

Then an idea struck her—wherever he was transferred, she would volunteer as a nurse at that hospital. She didn't have to go to the front, like Clarissa. Surely nurses were needed at home, too. She had to grin at her own bravado.

Her suspicions proved to be right. A few days after the party, Mrs Bryce took to her bed, claiming complete mental and physical exhaustion. Emily seized the chance to hurry next door to see Robbie. She found him sitting outside in the sunshine amongst a row of bath chairs, his face showing concentration as he tried to weave a raffia mat.

"Look who's coming, Rob. Mind your manners," one of the men called. Robbie looked up, then put down the mat and attempted to stand.

"Stupid waste of time," he said, indicating the project. "What do I need to plait raffia for?"

"I suppose it's to keep you busy, and out of mischief," Emily said.

He smiled at her, but there was a guardedness in his smile that she picked up on straight away. "Hold on. Let me get my crutches, and we'll go for a walk," he said.

"Will Matron approve?" she asked.

"I don't care," he said. "I'm not going to be here long anyway."

"You're not?" They started to move away from the other men, into the shade along the side of the building.

"No, I'm being transferred in a couple of days," he said. "To the naval hospital in Plymouth. I'm told it has better opportunities for rehabilitation to get me up and walking again."

"Oh, I see." She stood looking at him. "Why the naval hospital when you're with the air force?"

"We're not big enough to have a hospital of our own yet, I suppose. And Plymouth is a navy town and the hospital's supposed to be the best."

Emily tried not to let her disappointment show. "Well, I suppose that is good news in a way, isn't it? Better than wasting your time here weaving mats."

"Yes," he said, "if I could really believe this was all arranged for my own good."

"You think my mother might have had something to do with it?" she asked.

He frowned. "You know something about it?"

"No, but I suspected she might do something like this. I got a long lecture after you left about your being unsuitable and that I was forbidden to see you again."

They passed beyond the building, walking in silence, heading for a rose arbour. When they reached it, they sat on the wooden bench, the heady scent of pink roses all around them.

"She's right, you know," he said at last. "I am quite unsuitable. So maybe this is all for the best, Emmy. You shouldn't fall for me. I'm a bad prospect. My chances of surviving until the end of the war are not good, and if I do, then I'm heading ten thousand miles away from your home. I couldn't expect you to follow me there, not to lead the sort of life I'm used to. Not so far from your family. It would break their hearts." He paused. "So maybe it's good that I go away now and we remember each other fondly. I'll carry your picture in my head when I'm flying over enemy lines. I won't ever forget you."

"Don't talk like that, please, Robbie. Of course I'm not going to forget about you. I care about you, you know. I'm not going to give up without a fight. Plymouth isn't the end of the world. It's only an hour on the train. I'll come and visit you there. I told you I was determined to find some sort of useful work. And my parents really can't object any longer. Now that I'm twenty-one, I'm supposed to offer my services to the country. I was thinking I might try to volunteer as a nurse at your naval hospital."

He looked concerned. "You wouldn't really want to be a volunteer nurse, would you, Emmy? It's not the sort of thing you've been used to. They'll have you carrying bedpans and taking off bloody dressings."

"My friend Clarissa, whom you met at my party, had the same upbringing as I. We were at a posh girls' school together. But now she's working on the battlefield in France, in the worst possible conditions—rats and mud and awful wounds—and she's thriving on it. So you see, it is possible."

"I still don't think—" he began.

"What's the matter?" she demanded. "You don't think I'd be able to handle it? Or are you hinting that you don't want to see me any more?"

He winced. "You know that's not true, Emmy. I can't tell you how I feel about you. But it's because I care so much that I want only the best for you. A happy life. The sort of life you deserve."

Emily put her hand over his. "Let's take it one day at a time, shall we? Let's enjoy the fact that we're both alive and you're here right now and see what the future brings us."

"Rightio," he said. He grimaced and looked out beyond Emily. "Oh, stone the crows. There's Nurse Hammond. I'll catch it for running off like this. Look, I don't want to get you in trouble with your mum. You slip off through the hedge. You can get through where I did that time. Behind that big oak. And I'll go and face the music."

"All right." She gazed at him with longing, impulsively reaching out to stroke his hair back from his forehead.

"You didn't mind it when I kissed you the other night?" he asked.

"Mind it? It was wonderful. I still think about it."

"That's good." He gave a fleeting grin. "Because it was pretty special for me, too." He gave her a little shove. "Go on. Stay hidden until I get to the nurse, then run for it."

He came out of the arbour and started to hobble back towards the building. "Sorry, Nurse," he called. "I had to stretch my legs. I was getting a terrible cramp from sitting in that chair."

"A likely tale, Flight Lieutenant Kerr."

"No. Fair dinkum. And I wanted to see the roses. Did I tell you my mum tries to grow roses at home?" His voice died away. Emily waited until he was walking back with the nurse, then she darted across the lawn and squeezed through the hedge.

By the end of the week, he had gone. Emily decided the time had come to make her own move. She raised the subject at the breakfast table. Her mother had emerged from her bed, looking pale and listless.

"Now that I'm twenty-one," Emily said, "it's time I did something useful. I'm supposed to report to the local volunteer headquarters."

"I certainly hope you are not contemplating doing anything foolish like enlisting in the VAD like Clarissa?" Her mother's voice was taut.

"I promise I'm not going to volunteer for overseas work, Mother," Emily said. "I'll stay right here in Devon for now, but I can't sit at home being idle any longer."

"Yes, good idea. I'll drive you into Torquay if you like," her father said. "I believe they have a recruitment office there. They'll find you something to keep you busy."

"I hardly think they'll have many volunteer opportunities in a small town like Torquay," Emily said. "What would they want me to do—act as a chambermaid in one of the hotels? Walk elderly colonels along the seafront promenade? No, I really feel I should go to one of the bigger towns like Exeter or Plymouth. So if you'd be good enough to drop me at the station, Daddy."

"I'll be going into Exeter tomorrow if you want to wait," he said.

"No, thank you. I'd rather get moving as soon as I can," she said. "I've been wasting my life for so long . . ."

"If only you'd paid more attention to one of the young men at the party, maybe you'd find yourself with a wedding to plan," her mother said bitterly. "I've told you that Aubrey Warren-Smythe was quite smitten with you, and you couldn't even give him the time of day. He has a good job, good prospects . . . he may not be the best-looking young man in the world, but you could do worse."

"Mummy, he has weak ankles, remember?" Emily said. "Besides, I'm in no hurry to get married. I want to see a bit of life first. I went straight from boarding school to the middle of a war. I've never had a chance to travel, to spend time in London, to go to a play in the West End, even. I know those things won't be possible until the war is over, but at least I want to gain some feeling of independence. You do understand, don't you?"

"In my day, a young woman never needed to be independent," Mrs Bryce said. "She was under the protection of her father until a suitable husband was found for her. That way, she was always safe."

"Maybe I don't want to be safe and protected," Emily said. "And remember what Clarissa was saying—after the war, women will be called upon to do men's jobs. I should gain some experience."

"The girl is right, Marjorie," her father said. He reached across and patted his wife's hand. "You can't hang on to her forever, old thing. I see no harm in her doing some kind of suitable volunteer work. Go to the recruitment centre with my blessing then, Emily, and see what they have available." Emily could not believe how easily they had capitulated. It was as she went up the stairs that she heard her father saying, "I think a job is an excellent idea, Marjorie. It will take her mind off that Australian chap, and who knows, she might well meet someone we'd approve of. A local boy."

She dressed in a sombre blue linen suit with white gloves and a white hat. Her father dropped her at the station, but instead of taking the train to Exeter, she went in the other direction, to Plymouth. As the fields and woods flashed past her, she tried to remember when she had last been on a train alone. She had travelled to school and back, but in the company of a mistress and other girls. A rush of excitement shot through her. This was a first step. A small one, but one in the right direction. With any luck, by the end of the day, she'd be working near Robbie as an independent woman.

When she alighted from the train at Plymouth railway station, she was given directions to the Royal Naval Hospital. It was a long walk, she was told, but she could catch a bus or take a taxi. She opted for the bus, and soon found herself standing at the entrance to the hospital, gazing in awe. She had expected a building like other hospitals she had visited—grim and square and featureless. This was a series of elegant Georgian buildings spaced around a square of lawn. It was vast and quite intimidating. As she stood there, wondering which of the buildings she should approach, a group of nurses came towards her across the green. They wore crisply starched caps and dresses, and their capes blew out in the breeze as they walked. Emily approached them.

"Excuse me, but could you tell me where I should go if I wanted to become a volunteer here?"

"Are you a nurse?" one of them asked.

"No, not yet. I'd like to become one."

"We're all navy nurses here," another said. "Members of the Queen Alexandra Royal Navy Nursing Service. I'm not sure they'd take you now, with no nursing skills. It wouldn't be worth training you if the war's going to end soon."

"But what about ward maids, helpers? Surely you must have those," Emily said.

"Yes, but it's frightfully menial work." The nurse gave Emily a worried frown. "However, you should go and speak to the sister in charge. She'll set you straight. Over in Trafalgar—that building at the end. Her office is just off the main hall, on the right. I'd take you, but we're due on duty, and our sister is a real cow if we're a minute late."

Emily thanked them and headed towards the building they had indicated. She found the office with no trouble and was soon facing a distinguished-looking older woman—not unlike her former headmistress at school.

"And what can I do for you, young lady?" she asked.

"I'd like to volunteer my services," Emily said.

"As what?" The voice was clipped, but the expression not unfriendly.

"As a nurse, I thought originally, but I've just been told that your nurses are all members of the Queen Alexandra Royal Navy Nursing Service."

"That is correct. Do you have nursing training?"

"I have no training in anything," Emily said. "But I'm willing to learn."

"How old are you?"

"Twenty-one."

"And what have you been doing since you left school—if you went to school, that is?"

"I did go to school. I went to Sherborne. But since then, I've been doing nothing. Stuck at home, knitting socks and gloves for the troops and taking teacakes to the local convalescent hospital."

"Both admirable occupations, but why stuck at home?"

Emily chewed on her lip. "We live out in the country, for one thing. But the truth is that my parents did not want to let me go. My only brother was killed at the start of the war, during his first week in Ypres. My parents were both devastated and thus terrified to lose me."

"And what has changed now?" the sister asked.

"I've just turned twenty-one. They can no longer stop me." She took a step towards the desk. "I want to do my bit, Sister. I've been dying to do something useful. Can you not find a place for me?"

"I'd really like to, my dear." The sister paused. "But the truth is that we have a full complement of volunteers at the moment. We have local girls—sailors' wives, you know, wanting to keep busy rather than worry. Also refugees from Belgium—peasant women who are used to hard work and don't mind scrubbing floors and washing bedpans."

"I wouldn't mind," Emily said. "Truly I wouldn't."

"I commend your attitude, but we really can't use you, I'm afraid. Have you been to the local recruitment headquarters?"

"Not yet. I came here first."

"Why so insistent on working in a hospital?"

"I have a school friend who is a nurse on the front lines. She started off as only a volunteer. Now she's helping in the operating theatre."

"Well, they were desperate in the early days. Good for her. And you want to show her that you have her spunk? Or do you feel that you have a true calling to the profession—because if you are truly sincere, I can write a letter for you to our training hospital in Portsmouth."

"Thank you," Emily said, "but I think I'd like to stay close to home. I'm all my parents have now. I wouldn't like to desert them completely."

"Then I suggest you go to the volunteer headquarters and see where you are needed."

"And do you know where it is located?"

"In the Guildhall on the Royal Parade. Ask anybody. They can direct you there. It's a longish walk, but it's a fine day, isn't it?" She stood up and held out her hand. "Good day to you, Miss . . ."

"Bryce," Emily said. "Thank you, Sister."

As she came out of the building, she stood looking around her. Had Robbie been moved here yet? If so, which building was he in? She didn't think it was wise to ask after him at this moment—it might make it too obvious why she was here.

The day was a warm one, and Emily felt quite flushed and sticky by the time she came to the imposing building on the Royal Parade. She was directed upstairs to a disappointingly small and cramped office and faced a middle-aged woman—the sort who usually run Women's Institutes and garden clubs.

"Want to volunteer, do you?" she boomed. "Splendid. We could use able-bodied girls like you."

"I was hoping to volunteer at the Royal Naval Hospital," Emily said. "But I went there and they have no need of more volunteers. I'm willing to try anything."

"That's good," the woman said, "because what we really need is land girls."

"Land girls?" Emily sounded surprised.

"Women's Land Army," the woman went on. "We're in desperate need, actually. There are no men to work in the fields and the early crops are ready for harvest. As you must know, last year's harvest was a complete failure, and if we don't do something soon, the country won't be able to feed itself. We might win the war, but end up starving. That's not what we want, is it?"

"No, it isn't," Emily agreed tentatively.

"So we're recruiting young women to work on the farms. Anything the farmer needs—harvesting crops, milking cows, making hay. It's hard work, but rewarding, knowing that you are feeding the country. So what do you say?"

This was so far from what Emily had been anticipating that she couldn't answer right away. She had dreamed for so long of playing her part, nursing the wounded like Clarissa—but working in the fields like a farm labourer? And out in the country somewhere, far from Robbie? It seemed like going from one prison to another. And yet she had wanted to do something useful, and this seemed to be where she was needed.

"Would I be stationed in this part of the world?" Emily asked. "Because my parents are nearby."

"Of course. We have a training centre near Tavistock, and after that, you'd be sent to a farm somewhere in South Devon."

I'd have days off, she thought. *I'd be close enough to go and visit him. And it might be rather a lark to work in the fields with other women . . .*
"Then I'm happy to volunteer," Emily said.

"Splendid." The woman stood up and shook her hand violently. "You'll not regret it. We give you a uniform, you'll get training, and we pay you fifteen shillings a week. That goes up to twenty shillings when you become skilled. You'll be lodged at the training centre, which is on a farm outside Tavistock, and after that, you'll stay at the farm you are sent to. I'll find the forms for you to fill in and then you are all set."

She opened a filing cabinet, then looked up. "Just one thing. Once you sign up, you can't just quit when you feel like it. You are part of the country's forces as much as if you had joined the army. I want to make that perfectly clear."

"I understand," Emily said. She sat at a nearby table and signed.

CHAPTER SEVEN

Emily waited until they were at the dinner table that evening to give her parents the news.

"So how was your excursion into town today?" Mr Bryce asked as he reached for the soup tureen. "Did you find yourself a suitable volunteer job?"

"Yes, Daddy, I did."

"Well, what is it?" her father said impatiently. "Spill the beans. Don't keep us in suspense."

Emily took a deep breath before she said, "I'm going to be a land girl."

There was a horrified silence.

"A land girl?" Mrs Bryce said at last. "And what exactly is that?"

"A member of the Women's Land Army, Mother, as I'm sure you know perfectly well."

"You'll be working in the fields like a common farm labourer?" Mrs Bryce's voice was now shrill. "Did they not have any more suitable jobs?"

"I'll ask colleagues in Exeter," Mr Bryce said, nodding to his wife. "I expect I can find you some kind of office work, or even teaching in a school."

"But I don't want to be stuck in an office, filing and making tea. And they need farm workers, Daddy," Emily said. "The country is liable to starve if they don't find women to work in the fields. I'm able-bodied."

"But you are a gentlewoman. They meant that they need lower-class girls. Girls who are used to that kind of drudgery," Mrs Bryce said, as if she were talking to a simple child.

"They don't care how nicely we speak, Mummy. They are desperate. Anyway, I've said yes. I start training on Monday."

Mrs Bryce glared at her husband. "Say something, Harold. Tell her that we utterly forbid her."

"You can't forbid me. I've already signed up."

"Your father will go to the office and tell them that you made a mistake. You didn't realize what you were committing to. He'll tell them that he's found you a more appropriate situation for a girl of your class."

"No, Mummy. You don't understand. I have enlisted, just as if I were in the army or navy. I am officially part of our forces. I'm afraid there is no going back."

"This was an extremely unwise move on your part, Emily," Mr Bryce snapped. "Absolutely thoughtless, and as you can see, quite distressing for your mother."

"You should be proud of me, Daddy. I'm finally serving my country, and out of concern for you, I elected to stay at home and not volunteer abroad like Clarissa."

Her father had now risen to his feet. His face was beetroot red. "Be proud of you? My daughter, a field hand? A peasant girl? I don't care what you signed. You can go right back tomorrow and tell them that you have changed your mind."

"I'm sorry, but I'm not doing that. In fact, I'm rather looking forward to it," Emily said. "Besides, you can't stop me. I've turned twenty-one. I can now make my own decisions."

"May I remind you that you are still dependent on us for money?" Mr Bryce bellowed. "You don't have a penny in the world or a roof over your head apart from this house."

"Actually, I'll be given room and board and paid a small wage each week," she said. "Oh, and they provide a uniform." She softened her tone. "I don't want to hurt you, either of you, but you have to let me make my own way. I won't be in any danger. I'll be fed and looked after, and I'll be doing a valuable service. And when the war is finally over, then we can talk about my finding a job that you consider more suitable."

Mr Bryce ladled leek and potato soup into his bowl. "Well, you've made your bed, young lady. Now you lie in it. No calling for us to rescue you when you find you can't face another day of back-breaking toil, or you're out in freezing rain with chilblains."

"Actually, Daddy," Emily said, accepting the tureen when it was passed to her, "I think it might be a lot of fun."

"And where will you be stationed? Did they tell you that?"

"I'm being trained near Tavistock and presumably sent to a farm in South Devon. I won't be too far from home."

After the meal, she heard her parents talking. Her mother was still inclined to be weepy, but her father said, "It could be worse, Marjorie. At least she'll be safely away from men and well supervised. And it's not as if she's going to be in danger. And the war should be over soon, so you'll have her home again."

"I suppose you are right," came her mother's tearful reply.

Relations with her parents were frosty as Emily packed a bag and left on Monday morning. Her mother hardly said a word, and almost refused to lend her a suitcase to carry her things. Her father did agree to drive her to the station. For a while, they drove in silence, then he said, "You realize this is an act of pure selfishness on your part, and ingratitude after all we have done for you. We sacrificed to send you to a good school. We wanted the best for you. And now you have broken your mother's heart."

Emily swallowed hard to keep her temper in check. "What would you have me do, Daddy? Stay at home quietly until we all realize that there are no suitable men coming home from the front for me to marry? And you can watch me become a bitter and lonely spinster?"

Her father cleared his throat. "No, of course not. I understand you want to spread your wings a little, make your own way in the world. But a more fitting position could have been found for you. I'm sure one of the solicitors I work with could find work for you in his office, or one of the families we know would welcome you as a governess."

"How is being a governess in any way superior to being a land girl?" Emily could hear her voice rising now. "A servant to a family we know? How could Mother hold her head up high knowing her daughter was a servant?"

"A governess is more than a servant, Emily."

"Only by a little. She is a prisoner in the schoolroom. She takes her meals alone, shunned by the family. Besides, I have already made up my mind. I have volunteered, and there is nothing more to be said."

"As you say, there is nothing more to be said." Her father snapped the words. "Well, I'll be interested in how long you can stick it."

They pulled up outside the station. He hauled out her suitcase, put it on the ground and drove away without saying goodbye. Emily felt a fleeting moment of panic, watching him go, but then she took a deep breath and went to buy her ticket.

As the train took her away from home, she felt an absurd sense of elation. For the first time, she'd be free. This opinion changed within half an hour of reporting in at the railway station in Tavistock, where a bus was waiting to transport the women to the training centre. There were eleven other women of various ages. They assessed each other shyly while murmuring polite how-do-you-dos as their names were called. An Irish girl with bright red hair looked around the group. "Well, don't look so gloomy, all of you," she said, laughing. "It's not a funeral we're going to, you know."

There were grins as they boarded a waiting bus. Emily sat next to a girl who looked ridiculously young. She sat hunched over, staring down at her hands as the bus revved up and drove off.

"I'm Emily," she said. "What's your name?"

"It's Daisy, miss." The voice was scarcely loud enough to be heard.

"You don't have to call me miss. We're all the same now, you know."

"Sorry, miss, but I've been in service all my life, and you're clearly from a good family, so it wouldn't seem right."

"All your life?" Emily chuckled. "You don't look much more than twelve."

"I've just turned twenty, miss. That's the youngest you can be to join up. But I've been in service since I was twelve. And my mother before me with the same family. She was head parlourmaid, and then she married the groom. I was born above the stables, and when I was twelve, I went to work in the big house."

"Where was that, Daisy?"

"Moorland Hall, up near Okehampton."

"Did your parents mind you going away from home?"

"My mother died a couple of years ago." Daisy looked up now. She had a soft, sweet face surrounded by wispy, light brown hair. "And my dad, well, he doesn't care. He's hardly ever noticed I exist. He's a little too fond of the drink, if you must know the truth, miss. But the family keeps him on because he's so good with the horses."

"I see." Emily looked at her with pity. "And the family didn't mind?"

"It wasn't up to them, was it?" Daisy said, for the first time sounding defiant. "They couldn't stop me, although the housekeeper did say she couldn't guarantee there would be a place for me when I came back." She looked down at her hands again, encased in black cotton gloves. "I saw how hard my mum worked all her life, and I made up my mind that I wanted something better for myself. So when I heard that they were looking for land girls, I thought I'd take my chance." She looked up at Emily, studying her with interest. "But how about you, miss? You surely didn't have to be a land girl. You could have got yourself a proper job in the town if you'd wanted to work."

"I could have, but I heard how desperately they needed women to work in the fields, and frankly, I wanted to escape from my home. My mother is desperate to marry me off. And she's forbidden me to see the young man I like again. He's in the naval hospital in Plymouth—not too far on my day off. So this suits me splendidly."

Daisy actually laughed. "You're quite a card, miss."

"Do call me Emily, please."

"All right. Emily then. So why doesn't she approve of your young man?"

"He's Australian, for one thing. He doesn't know the right way to behave in our sort of society. He thinks it's silly that you can't speak to someone unless you've been introduced. You must know how it is. Who sits next to whom at a table. Which fork to use."

"I know all those little things are important to your kind of people. I've had to polish the silver—all those knives and forks. And I had it drummed into me that I must never be seen by the family when I light the fires."

"You had to light the fires?" Emily asked.

Daisy nodded. "I had to be up at five. Get the copper started to heat the bathwater, then take the coal up to all the bedrooms and get the fires going before anyone wakes up."

"Goodness," Emily said. "No wonder you were so anxious to escape."

"Those coal scuttles were ever so heavy, miss. I'm thinking carrying sacks of potatoes will be no trouble at all for me."

The remark made Emily pause. Would she be required to carry sacks of potatoes? What if she was not strong enough for the tasks? What if they sent her home because she failed to measure up to their requirements? Well, she decided. She'd just have to make sure that she didn't fail!

CHAPTER EIGHT

The bus had left the town behind and now drove through country lanes with hedges on both sides. Contented-looking cream-coloured cows looked up from their grazing as they passed. Then they turned in between granite gateposts and pulled up outside a square, grey stone farmhouse. Emily climbed down from the bus, conscious of the mud beneath her feet. She hoped the uniform included shoes, or hers would soon be ruined.

When the last girl had alighted from the bus, a woman came out of the farmhouse and brought them to order with a blast of her whistle. She was dressed in a khaki uniform jacket and skirt with a green armband attached and a badge on her rather ample chest. She reminded Emily instantly of her least favourite teacher at school.

"Attention, ladies," she called in a voice that betrayed a lifetime of giving orders. "Welcome to the training centre, where you will learn how to become a useful member of the Women's Land Army. You have enlisted to serve your country, and for this, your country thanks you. I am Miss Foster-Blake. I am the superintendent here, and I will be in charge of you until you are sent out to farms in the area. You will take your orders from me and from your instructors and do exactly what you are told at all times. Is that clear?"

"Yes, ma'am," came a few muttered responses.

"I said, is that clear?" she repeated.

"Yes, ma'am," they shouted back this time.

"When you hear this whistle, you drop what you are doing and you come running," she went on. "When I call your name, you will proceed into the farmhouse, where you will be kitted out with your uniforms. You will then go straight up to the dormitory, select a bed and change into your uniforms as quickly as possible. You will then report downstairs, where you will be briefed and given your schedule. Is this clear?"

"Yes, ma'am," they chanted.

"I will now call your names," Miss Foster-Blake said. "As your name is called, you will march briskly into the house. Alice Adams."

A thin, scrawny woman glanced around nervously, then scurried into the house.

"Emily Bryce." Emily was about to follow when the woman stared at her and asked, "Are you related to Judge Bryce?"

"He's my father," Emily said, blushing as she felt all those eyes on her.

She waited for the woman to say that this was not a suitable place for her and she should return home, but instead she said, "I am also a justice of the peace, and our paths have crossed several times. A fine man. Make sure you do him proud."

"Yes, ma'am," Emily muttered, and hurried after Alice Adams.

As her eyes adjusted to the darkness of the farmhouse interior, she saw that a trestle table with piles of clothing had been set up along the length of a large room. Two women, already dressed in the khaki uniform of the Women's Land Army, stood behind it.

"Take one of each as you move along," one of the women said.

"What about sizes?" Alice Adams asked.

"There's one size in most things, except boots. Then it's small, medium or large. You'll have a belt and an elastic waist in the bloomers. Get cracking."

Emily followed her, picking up the khaki tunic, matching bloomers, a jersey, a mackintosh, a floppy felt hat and knee boots. Then she was directed up the stairs to a room on their right. Alice stood inside the doorway, looking around. It wasn't a large bedroom to start with, and now three sets of bunk beds had been crammed into the space. There was a similar room behind it for the other six women.

"One of the good things about being at the top of the alphabet," Alice said, grinning at Emily. "We get to choose beds first. Away from the window and the draught, I think, don't you? Unless you want to slip out at night, that is. And a top bunk. You don't want to find you've got a heavy girl above you, making the whole thing creak and groan."

Emily hadn't considered this. "Oh, you're right," she said, and commandeered the top bunk beside the one Alice had chosen.

"I'm not sure how we get down in the middle of the night if nature calls," Alice said. She had a strong cockney accent, quite unlike the soft and slow Devon burr that Emily was used to.

"There's a sort of ladder," Emily pointed out.

Alice reacted to her cultured, upper-class voice. "Hark at Miss Hoity-Toity," she said. "What are you doing here in a place like this? Shouldn't you be at the fox hunt or the palace or something?"

"Shouldn't you be in Whitechapel or Shoreditch?" Emily retorted.

Alice threw back her head and laughed. "Quite right. You got me there. I'm far from my home turf, ain't I? If you want to know, I came down here with my husband, Bill, on our honeymoon before the war. I thought I'd died and gone to heaven. All the gardens and the sea and the fresh air. Lovely, it was."

"Where is Bill now?" Emily asked as she removed her jacket and hung it on the row of pegs.

"Dead. That's where." Alice looked up from unbuttoning her cotton frock. "He copped it a couple of years ago at the Somme. He managed to stay alive for two whole years, but just before he was due to come home on leave, he was gassed. They brought him home, but he didn't stand a chance. Lungs were shot, you see."

"I'm so sorry," Emily said.

"Well, it's not like he was the only one, was he?" Alice shrugged. "I reckon every family has got a story like mine to tell."

"We lost my brother right at the start," Emily agreed. "So you decided to come back here where you had happy memories."

Alice nodded. She stepped out of the frock and hung it beside Emily's jacket. Then she picked up the bloomers and laughed. "How about this, eh? We get to wear trousers. And you know what? I ain't wearing no corset no more. If we're going to work like men, we want to breathe properly." She glanced at Emily. "'Ere. Help me unhook this." Emily obliged, feeling embarrassed and awkward at touching another woman's body. Alice didn't seem to mind. She whipped off the corset and waved it around as more women entered the room. "How about this, girls? Freedom at last. Come on—off with them."

Four more women had come into the room. They laughed, but the Irish girl shook her head. "I'm not risking my figure," she said. "I'm proud of my seventeen-inch waist, I am. And I aim to keep it."

"Suit yourself, love," Alice said. "You'll regret it when we're doing back-breaking work in the fields."

"Do you think it will be back-breaking?" one of the young women asked nervously. She was a slight little thing with a perpetually frightened, rabbit-like look.

"I don't know," Alice said. "I went down to Kent to pick hops in the summer when I was a girl. That wasn't too bad. A lot of fun, actually." She stuck out her hand. "I'm Alice, by the way. And this is Emily."

"Ruby," the frightened girl said. "I'm away from home for the first time. I'm not sure how I'm going to handle it."

"Me, too," Daisy said. "We'll look out for each other. I'm Daisy."

"Maud," a larger woman said, sticking out a meaty hand and giving Daisy's a hearty shake.

"And I'm Maureen," the Irish one replied.

Emily had turned away as she removed her dress, feeling horribly self-conscious of her lace-trimmed slip compared to their well-worn undergarments. Should she take off her corset, too? The others seemed to have no hesitation about removing theirs, giving whoops of delight as they twirled them in the air. Then she remembered how much she had hated wearing it when her mother took her to be fitted for one when she turned eighteen. "You'll thank me for this later when you retain your girlish figure," her mother had said, although her own figure was anything but girlish.

She fumbled with the hooks.

"'Ere, hold on a mo, love," Alice said, and her calloused fingers freed Emily in seconds. Emily smiled self-consciously as she whirled her corset with the others. Their noise had attracted some of the women from the other room.

"What's going on in here then?" one of them asked, poking her head around the door.

"This. That's what!" Alice replied. "We've made a stand for freedom. No more corsets if they want us to do a man's work."

"Good idea!" the woman said. "Come on, girls. Let's do it, too."

Emily stepped into the bloomers and adjusted the elastic around the waist, then buttoned the tunic. They felt coarse and heavy. She was going to be weighed down when she put the boots on. A small wave of panic went through her. What had she let herself in for?

"Are you sure this is all right?" Ruby asked, glancing down nervously at the pile of corsets on the floor. "Won't our insides all rattle around or fall apart?"

"God didn't make corsets, love," Alice said. "Women survived without them for a few thousand years. I feel better already, personally."

They hadn't quite finished dressing when the whistle sounded, and they had to scramble to do up buttons and hurry downstairs. Rows of chairs had been set up in a back room with a blackboard in front. Miss Foster-Blake stood there.

"Splendid. You all look the part now. Right. Straight to work. How many of you have been a member of the Girl Guides?"

A couple of hands were raised. "Well done," Miss Foster-Blake said. "Your skills will prove useful. I myself was captain of a troop before the war. And how many of you have worked in agriculture in any way?"

Again, a couple of hands went up.

"Doing what?"

The big-boned girl from their room said, "My dad was a farm-worker, miss. We used to help pick the crops during the summer."

"Then you will be a great asset to us—Maud, isn't it?"

"Yes, miss."

"And who else?"

One girl had picked apples. Another older woman had grown veg-etables in her own garden. As they went around the room, Emily was feeling more and more inadequate. It seemed they had all done some kind of physical work, except for the Irish girl with the red hair. It turned out Maureen was a dancer at a show on the pier in Torquay and was ambitious to make her name in show business. "I'd be in London now if it weren't for that cursed Kaiser," she said. "On account of him, all the theatres are closed. Still, this should keep me fit."

They were then given their schedule. Up at dawn for milking instruction. Breakfast at eight. Planting and harvesting practice until lunch. An hour's rest after lunch, then haymaking and animal care until six. Supper at six thirty and free time until bed at nine.

"It's like ruddy prison," Alice muttered during a tea break. She had latched herself on to Emily. "Working on the chain gang."

"Why did you come?" Emily asked. "You could have volunteered in London."

"I wanted to do my bit to defeat them Hun bastards—pardon my French—so that Bill's death wasn't for nothing," Alice said. "And I read in the paper how we might all starve if there weren't women to work on the land. That and I couldn't afford the rent no more. Not on a widow's pension. So I thought, why not? What have I got to lose? At least they pay us and feed us here, don't they? What about you, ducks?"

"I've been wanting to do something useful for ages," Emily said. "I've been dying of boredom at home. But my parents wouldn't let me go. Now I've turned twenty-one so they can't stop me. I really wanted to volunteer as a nurse like my friend, but it seems they have enough nurses and not enough land girls. Also my young man is in hospital in Plymouth. That's not too far."

"A sailor, is he?"

"No, he's an aviator in the Royal Air Force. He brought back his aeroplane in flames rather than parachute down behind enemy lines."

"Blimey. That takes some guts. So will he go back to flying when he's recovered?"

"I rather fear he will," Emily said. "I just pray the war ends before they release him from hospital."

"And then you'll get married?" Alice asked.

Emily paused. Would she really marry Robbie if he asked her? Would she be prepared to travel to the outback and live miles from the nearest person?

"We'll have to see about that," she answered.

CHAPTER NINE

Perry's Farm
Near Tavistock, Devon
June 18th, 1918

My dear Clarissa,
As you can see from the address above, I have done it! I have escaped from my gilded cage! Not quite as dramatically as you, I'm afraid. They were not in need of local volunteer nurses, and when it came to it, I was not prepared to go to Portsmouth for proper nursing training. I had to admit to myself that I was scared as to whether I could handle what you have to go through. And, truth be told, I didn't want to be so far away from Robbie, who is now in hospital in Plymouth. I haven't had a chance to visit him yet as we haven't had a day off, but I've written to him with all the news and I hope to go on Sunday.
 So I've become a land girl. Can you imagine? It is awfully hard work. I've got blisters all over my hands, and we are bossed around by a woman who was a former Girl Guide captain and reminds me of Miss Knight at

school. You know how frightful she was. Well, this woman is worse. One of my fellow recruits said, "It's like being in the army!" To which another replied, "Why do you think it's called the Women's Land Army?" And we all laughed.

There is a really good spirit amongst the women. We are a motley crew—mostly from humble backgrounds, except for one middle-aged woman whose husband was an accountant. The poor fellow was called up on his fortieth birthday—killed right away, like Freddie. It's so sad, isn't it? Almost all the girls have had some sort of loss—brothers or sweethearts, even one father. In spite of the fact that they have very different backgrounds from mine, I really like them. There's one really flashy Irish girl and one who complains about everything, but on the whole they are good-natured. We have to get along well because we are all crammed into bedrooms together. You should hear the barnyard noises at night! Oh, and we have cold water to wash in. As you can imagine, there is not much bathing done, and the personal hygiene after a day in the fields leaves a lot to be desired. But I am learning to get used to farmyard odours of various kinds!

So far, we have tried to milk a cow (without much success), learned about the dangers of pigs—they can kill you if you are not careful! We also learned not to stand behind a horse (common sense, that one). One girl had hysterics when we had to feed chickens. She thought they were attacking her when they were only trying to get at their food. She fell over and they swarmed all over her. You should have heard her screams! Up next is ploughing and haymaking, which seem more serene occupations. And then, at the end of four weeks, we are sent to a farm.

*I do hope all is well with you. Are you seeing fewer
casualties? Has Lieutenant Hutchins written to you?
Oh dear. The whistle sounds. I must report for duty.
Love from your friend,
Emily*

That evening, her sense of obligation got the better of her and she wrote to her parents, a polite and formal note letting them know where she was and that she was flourishing on hard work and fresh air. On Sunday, she hitched a ride on a farm cart to the nearest bus stop and made her way into Plymouth.

"Well, look at you," Robbie said, beaming as she entered his ward. "Aren't you looking the picture of health? Outdoor life agrees with you."

"It does," Emily said. "Although I'm afraid I shall never look pale and delicate again. I've got quite a sunburn, on my arms, too. But you're looking better yourself."

"I am," he said. "They are making me do all kinds of exercises."

"I hope you're behaving yourself here," she said sternly.

He glanced at the other men in the ward and laughed. "I'm being as good as gold, aren't I, mates?"

"You? You're a royal pain to the nurses." The man in the next bed chuckled. "You should see how he winds them up, miss."

"They don't allow any nonsense," Robbie said. "They run a tight ship here, as they say. Very military. No answering back."

"Are you allowed out?" she asked.

"What, off grounds? I shouldn't think so, but I'm encouraged to walk. Hand me those crutches, although I'm told I'm to give them up in a few days."

Emily did as he asked, and they walked side by side down the long corridor.

"This hospital is enormous," Emily said. "All these buildings."

"Ah, do you know it was built like this deliberately, with different buildings far enough apart so that infectious diseases wouldn't spread from one to the other. It's very advanced, this place."

It took a while to help him down the stairs, but then they were out on the central green. Seagulls wheeled overhead, crying, and the tang of the sea was in the air. In the distance, Emily glimpsed the blue water of the estuary.

"It's a nice place, this," she said. "I can see that people would recover here."

"I haven't really had a chance to see the sea properly yet," he said. "It's a novelty to me, you know, having grown up so far inland. But I've enjoyed getting a good view of it from the air. Maybe later they'll let me wander around and we can go to a headland or a beach."

"That would be very nice," she said. "I'm fond of the sea myself. We only live six miles from Torquay, but we rarely went to the seaside. My mother has an aversion to sand."

"My word." He laughed. "She wouldn't do well where I come from. The wind blows red dust over everything. It's quite a challenge to keep the place clean. My mum does a good job."

"She must work very hard," Emily said.

"Oh, she has a servant and a couple of Abo girls to help out."

"Abos?"

"Aborigines. Native women, you know. They are good workers, our two. And their husbands are terrific stockmen."

They stopped at a bench and sat there, side by side. Robbie slid his hand across and took hers.

"Robbie!" she exclaimed. "People might see."

"I don't care," he replied. "You're my girl, aren't you?" He turned to look at her. "You are my girl?"

"Of course I am," she said.

As she smiled at him, she felt a jolt of excitement. He had warned her not to get too fond of him. So what exactly did he mean by his question? That she was his girl for now, or was he suggesting something more? It didn't matter, she thought. At this moment, she was sitting beside him, his hand holding hers, and that was good enough for now.

Emily managed to see Robbie the next two Sundays of her training. She noticed a vast improvement every time she visited, and realized with a sinking heart that the time would soon come when he would be sent away. As his strength returned, he was allowed to leave the hospital grounds, and he walked with Emily first through the town and then out to the headland, where they sat watching the navy ships entering the harbour. A stiff breeze blew in their faces, laden with the tang of salt. The sea beyond was dark blue, speckled with white breakers.

"This would be a perfect spot to build a house, wouldn't it?" she asked, sighing with contentment. "Imagine pulling back the shutters to see that view every morning."

Robbie was quiet as they walked home, and Emily realized she had not been tactful. He was going to go home to Australia, to a dusty farm far from the ocean, and she had to make up her mind whether she'd give all this up to follow him—if he asked her, that was.

The end of the training period was fast approaching. Some of the girls had learned to milk a cow successfully. Others were still unable to squeeze out a drop. The large Maud was so heavy-handed that the usually placid cow lashed out with a kick. Emily watched that back leg with trepidation when it was her turn, but to her delight, she ran her hand down the udder and was rewarded with a stream of milk shooting into the bucket.

"Well done, my dear," said the old farmer who was instructing them on animal care. "You've got a nice, light touch. The cows appreciate that."

She was less adept at steering a plough behind a team of Clydesdales. It required so much stretch to hold the shoulder-high handles that it was beyond most of the girls, especially the shorter ones.

"What wouldn't I give for a long hot bath," Maureen said as they sat outside the farmhouse on a warm evening. "Every bit of me aches after wrestling with that plough."

"I've never had a long hot bath in my life," Daisy said.

"Never had a bath?" Mrs Anson asked. She was the older middle-class woman who had grown vegetables and whose accountant husband had been called up to military service on his fortieth birthday. She didn't seem at all bitter about this, nor that she had lost a safe and respectable way of life.

"We servants had to share bathwater," Daisy said. "Being the lowest of the maids, it was always cold by the time it got to me."

"How disgusting." Mrs Anson wrinkled her nose. "I must say, I'd appreciate a good soak in a tub, too, Maureen."

"You wait till we're sent out to real farms," Susie, the girl who had picked apples, said. "Now we're just trying our hand at things. There, we'll be working non-stop all day."

"Trying to cheer us up, are you?" Maureen said. "You're a proper ray of sunshine."

Emily studied the group with interest. The work was hard and new for all of them, but nobody was really complaining. Ruby, the one who was attacked by the chickens, had never left home before. She missed her mum, and Emily had had to comfort her through a couple of tearful episodes. Maureen missed men, she said. She hoped there might be some strapping farm boys on the farm she was sent to.

"Don't be silly," Alice said. "There are no strapping lads any more. That's why we are doing this. We'll all just have to get used to there not being men around."

"Bite your tongue! No men around? I'll go bonkers," Maureen said. "What would life be without a good kiss and cuddle?"

"I suppose it is something we'll all have to face," Mrs Anson said quietly. "How many thousands have died already? There certainly will not be enough men to go around."

"Then I'll be off to the colonies," Maureen said. "Good healthy lads out in Australia and Canada, eh?"

"Let's just win the war first," Mrs Anson said. "The news isn't too good, last time I heard. A new offensive by the Jerries, so it seems. They're not going to give in."

"I thought we were supposed to be winning!" Maureen said angrily. "They were saying it would be over as soon as the Americans arrived."

"Let's hope and pray it will be over soon," Mrs Anson said.

"Amen," came a soft voice from one of the girls.

At the end of their third week, they were summoned unexpectedly after lunch by Miss Foster-Blake.

"I've news for you, girls," she said. "I'm afraid your training is going to have to be cut short. We've a local farmer who has a new potato crop ready for harvest and nobody to work the fields, so I'm sending you out. We need to get those potatoes picked before they are spoiled in the rain. There will be a farm wagon coming for you in the morning." She looked from one face to the next. "I expect you to work your hardest. No slacking off. I'm dividing you into two teams, each with a team leader who will make sure you all do your share. Understood? Mrs Anson, you will be one team leader, and Miss Bryce the other. Do not let me down."

The reality of what she had signed up for hit Emily when she saw the field of potatoes. Row after row of mounds topped with straw that needed to be dug up and the potatoes picked into baskets. She really wished she had not been made a team leader. She had timid little Ruby, clueless Maud, Maureen, Alice and Daisy in her squad. Originally, she set Maud, who was big and powerful, to digging out the plants with the fork, but Maud was also not the brightest, and Emily soon realized that the digging required finesse so that the fork didn't spear the potatoes. So then she tried Daisy, who, although slightly built, was strong, and she proved remarkably adept at lifting the plants loose from the soil with minimal damage. The rest of them were down on hands and knees, scraping the potatoes free of dirt and dropping them into baskets. It was back-breaking work, bent over for hours, then carrying the heavy baskets to fill sacks, which were then loaded on to a farm cart. The farmer didn't seem particularly grateful that they were saving his crop. He complained they weren't working fast enough and seemed to enjoy observing them and pointing out they were missing the smallest potatoes.

"I'll shove him in the next sack, so help me," Maureen muttered as he walked away.

By the time they were taken back to the training centre at night in the back of a jolting farm cart, they were too tired to do anything but flop into bed.

"Talk about a baptism of fire." Mrs Anson looked almost grey with exertion. She stumbled, but Emily caught her.

"Are you sure you're all right?" Emily asked her. "Is this too much for you? Because we can tell Miss Foster-Blake."

"No, I'm fine," Mrs Anson said. "Just not used to it, that's all. Neither are you. But I'm not going to give up. My husband must have felt the same way when they put him through army drills. I'm doing this in his honour."

She's brave, Emily thought. *They are all brave.*

The next morning, they awoke to the sound of rain drumming on the roof above.

"Would you look at that!" Maureen said. "Makes me quite home-sick for Ireland."

Alice gave a disgusted snort. "You must be the only person who is delighted to see rain."

"Not delighted. Just homesick," Maureen said.

"We won't have to work in that weather, will we, miss?" Daisy asked.

"I'm afraid there's a van already waiting outside," Emily said. "We do have mackintoshes." She tried to sound cheerful, but she felt as disheartened as they did as they boarded the van.

The field had turned into a sea of mud. They picked the potatoes with freezing fingers while the rain lashed at their faces. At lunchtime, they staggered to the shelter of a barn, where they gratefully drank cups of tea provided by the farmer's wife. She looked at them with understanding. "I imagine it's a bit of a shock to you, isn't it?" she asked. "Farm life takes a bit of getting used to. It will be better when the sun comes out."

They wolfed down great hunks of bread and cheese and pickled onions to go with the tea, then trudged out into the rain again. After several hours of more labour, Emily was staggering to the edge of the field to deposit her basket of potatoes. She slipped and slid in the mud and almost went down. She had been concentrating so hard on not falling that she had kept her eyes on the ground ahead of her. When she looked up, she saw two figures standing under umbrellas, watching her.

"Emily!" Her mother's voice echoed out across the field. "Just look at you. What a disgrace. Covered in mud and hauling potatoes like a peasant. If your grandparents could see you now, they would be appalled. Put that basket down instantly and come with us."

"I'm working, Mummy," Emily said as she reached them and deposited the basket on the trestle table. "I can't leave. I'm in charge of my girls."

"It's all right," her mother said. "Daddy has arranged things with your supervisor. Miss Foster-Blake. He knows her, apparently. So it's all squared away."

"What is?" Emily asked. She started to tip the potatoes into the waiting sack.

"You're leaving this fiasco. Daddy's arranged a proper job for you with a solicitor in Exeter."

"You'll board with his family during the week and come home to us at weekends," her father said. "Mr Davidson says he'll even train you to use a typewriting machine. That will be a useful skill, won't it?"

Emily fought to stay calm. She was conscious that the other women were observing her with interest. "You have no right to interfere like this, Daddy," she said. "I'm over twenty-one, able to make my own decisions, and I'm staying on here. I'm needed. If these potatoes aren't picked, they'll rot, and the country is already desperately short of food."

"A job that any low-class girl could be doing and should be doing," Mrs Bryce said. "But not someone who was reared for better things. You surely can't tell me you'd rather be toiling in the rain and mud than helping a solicitor in a safe and dry office?"

"I can't say it's particularly fun at the moment, but on the whole, yes, I am enjoying it. And I'm performing a valuable service for my country."

Mrs Bryce gave an exasperated sigh. "Say something, Harold. Tell her to come with us immediately."

"I will say something." Mr Bryce frowned. "If you persist in disobeying your parents, then you are on your own. If it's your life, then you lead it. You will no longer be welcome at our house."

Emily took a deep breath to calm her rapid heartbeat. "Very well." She held his gaze, chin stuck out defiantly. "If that's what you want. But I will not be bullied or dictated to. I'm not a child any more, and I'm prepared to make my own way and my own mistakes if necessary." She looked up as Daisy staggered towards her with a full basket. "Over here, Daisy. Here, let me help you. Get the sack."

"Come, Marjorie. You're getting wet, and we are wasting our time," Mr Bryce said.

Her mother hesitated, turned to leave, then swung back again. "It's that boy, isn't it? That Australian. I know you're still seeing him against our wishes. We checked with the hospital he was sent to. He's the one that's put these rebellious ideas into your head."

"No, Mummy. The ideas were already there. I just had no way to implement them before," Emily answered as she held open a sack to receive potatoes.

"Then good luck to you, that's what I say," Mrs Bryce said. "I hope you will enjoy living in squalor in the depths of Australia."

With that, she stalked off, her dainty shoes slithering in the mud.

Emily noticed her hands were trembling as she held open the sack. She felt as if she might be sick. They were her parents, after all. Her home. A place where she had once been loved and protected. She fought back the temptation to call after them, "I'm sorry. I didn't mean it. I love you." But saying those things would mean giving up Robbie, giving up this work, and she knew she wasn't going to do either.

CHAPTER TEN

Crammed together in the back of the van on the way home, the other girls crowded around Emily.

"Was that your mum and dad?" Maureen asked.

Emily nodded. She had been in shock and close to tears ever since the encounter. She didn't dare herself to speak or she was afraid she might cry now.

"They were certainly going at you, weren't they?" Alice went on. "What was all that about?"

Emily took a deep breath. "They had come to take me away," she said. "They think this kind of work is beneath me. They'd gone behind my back and arranged to have me released. They'd even found me a job in a solicitor's office."

"And you didn't take it?" Maureen asked. "Are you out of your mind, my girl? A good job in a nice dry office and maybe a lawyer husband in your future?"

Emily had to laugh at this. "Mr Davidson is seventy if he's a day, and yes, I suppose it would have been a good job in many ways. But I'd already agreed to do this and I'm not letting anyone down."

"Good for you," Ruby said. "We'd miss you if you went away."

"She looked like a right old cow, your mum, if you don't mind me saying so," Alice said. She put a hand on Emily's shoulder. "Don't you worry, love. You've got us now."

Miss Foster-Blake was waiting for them when they arrived back and were taking off their muddy boots and sodden mackintoshes in the mudroom behind the farmhouse. "Well done, ladies. A tough day's work and you came through admirably . . ." She broke off when she saw Emily. "I didn't think we'd be seeing you again," she said. "Your father pulled strings for you."

"Strings I chose to ignore," Emily said. "I made a commitment here. I'm not backing out of it, whatever my parents want."

To her surprise, Miss Foster-Blake smiled. "Well done. That takes spunk. And duty and loyalty. I like that. You'll do well in life, Miss Bryce." As Emily headed into the house, she called to her, "Oh, and a letter came for you today. From your young man, I believe."

Emily ran up the stairs and snatched up the envelope from the table. Robbie wasn't as good at writing letters as she was, but each note from him was precious to her.

My dear Emmy,

I have some news. I was going to say good news, but you probably won't think that it is. I have been certified fit to go back and join my squadron. I leave on Monday. So this will be the last time we'll see each other for a while. I'm really hoping we can spend the whole day together on Sunday. Do you think they would let you get off work early on Saturday and you could come into Plymouth and we could have the evening together then? I know there are boarding houses close to the hospital where wives and sweethearts stay when they come to visit. I could arrange to put you up in one of those. Let me know right away and I'll get things arranged.

I can't wait to see you, my darling girl,
Your Robbie

Emily sat on a bottom bunk, not moving, staring down at the letter. She knew it was inevitable that this was going to happen, but after a day of physical exertion and the horrible scene with her parents, it was one thing too many. She felt tears welling in her eyes and tried to squeeze them back. She had never cried in public before. She pressed her hand to her mouth, then looked up as Alice came into the room. "Good news, love?" she asked. Then she saw Emily's face. "Oh no. It's not bad news, is it?"

"It's my sweetheart, Robbie. He's been in hospital, and now they've certified him ready to go back to his squadron in France. This will be the last chance I have to see him."

Alice put a bony arm around her. "You have a good cry, my love. That always helps."

"I'm not a very good crier, I'm afraid." Emily attempted a smile. "But I'm so worried for him, Alice. At the convalescent home where we met, the nurse told me that the life expectancy of a flyer was six weeks."

"He's survived this long, hasn't he? With any luck, the war will be over before you know it."

"Oh, please God, I hope so," Emily said.

She splashed cold water on to her face so that Miss Foster-Blake would not see she had been crying and went to find her. She was in the small office going over paperwork.

"Next batch of recruits due to arrive on Monday," she said, looking up as Emily entered. "Only seven this time. Not enough, really. Still, I expect we'll muddle through. Did you want something?"

"I have a special request," Emily said. "Would it be possible for me to get off a little early on Saturday and go into Plymouth? You see, my young man is about to be discharged from the hospital there and sent back to France. It will be the last time I see him for a while. So then we'd have Saturday evening and Sunday together."

"Saturday evening or Saturday night?" Miss Foster-Blake asked sharply. "I don't think that would be a wise move, Miss Bryce. You have your reputation to think of."

"Oh no," Emily said, blushing. "It's not like that at all. Robbie is still in the naval hospital. He said he'd fix me up with one of the boarding houses where the wives and sweethearts stay. He's a very respectable person, Miss Foster-Blake."

"Your parents didn't seem to think so. They told me he had been a bad influence on you."

"My mother doesn't like him because he's Australian. He doesn't care a fig for our petty conventions, and he's not the sort of match she would have made for me. But he's a good person."

"So you plan to marry him after the war and go to Australia with him?"

"He hasn't asked me yet." Emily felt herself blushing. "But if he does, I think I might say yes."

"Where does he live in Australia? In one of the cities?"

"No, on a big farm in the outback. A sheep station, he calls it."

"Think about it very carefully, won't you? Thousands of miles from home and a life of drudgery. None of the things you are used to, I'd imagine. No nice shops, theatres, educated people to talk to. And a harsh climate."

"I know. He's done everything he can to put me off. He's even told me it's no place for a woman."

"There you are then. At least he's honest."

"But these last weeks have proved to me that I can cope with hard conditions. And I really think I love him. What if he's the one I'm meant to be with? The one I'll be happy with?"

Miss Foster-Blake stood silent for a moment. "You're a sensible girl, Miss Bryce. I expect you'll do the right thing. Very well, I give you permission to leave at four and be back by Sunday evening."

"Thank you, Miss Foster-Blake." Emily beamed. "You don't know how much this means to me."

"I do know in wartime we have to take any sliver of happiness that is offered to us," the woman said. "Now go and clean yourself up. You're still covered in mud."

CHAPTER ELEVEN

By Saturday, the weather had cleared up, and a fresh breeze was blowing in from the sea as Emily hitched a lift into Tavistock and then took the train to Plymouth. Robbie was waiting downstairs in the hospital foyer, dressed in his uniform, his hair slicked down. He looked different from the boy in the dressing gown with the unruly hair, and she was reminded of the evening at her party.

"You made it," he said, holding out his hands to her. "I was afraid that old battleaxe of yours wouldn't let you go at the last minute."

"She did give me a warning against unsuitable young men with evil designs," Emily said, laughing.

"And how do you know I don't have evil designs?" he retorted.

Emily felt herself blushing. "Because I know you," she said.

"Too right. I'll always treat you with respect, Emmy. You're a quality girl. You deserve only the best," he said. "Right then. Let's deposit your bag at this guest house, shall we? It's not much to look at, but the blokes tell me they take good care of you there. The navy lieutenant in the next bed said he put his wife up there when she came to visit."

"I'm sure it will be fine," Emily said. "After sleeping six to a room in the most uncomfortable bunks that creak and groan every time one turns over, I'm sure it will be like heaven."

He went to take her bag.

"You don't have to do that. I can manage," she said.

She watched a frown cross his face. "Emily, I'm certified fit to fly a plane," he said. "I can carry an overnight bag, I promise you."

They set off together. Robbie slipped his hand into hers. She looked up to give him a little smile. He still walked a little stiffly, she noted, but he was making a supreme effort to stride out. As they approached the harbour, they could see fishing boats bobbing in the water in a wide estuary. Green fields came down to the banks on the far side, and as they watched, a ferry left the far shore, coming towards them. It was a peaceful scene, as if war were only a nasty rumour, far away.

"Here we are." Robbie led her to a house in a terrace that faced the water. Across the front was painted "Seaview Guest House."

"I've checked it out," he said. "It's nothing fancy, but it's clean."

The landlady was all smiles when Emily was introduced. "A local girl, are you? He said you were from Devonshire yourself."

"I am. Near Torquay."

"Fancy that. I've a sister who lives in that part of the world. And this young man is all the way from Australia. Left his homeland to come and fight for us. I call that noble, myself. Now, if you'd like to see your room . . ."

She started up a steep and narrow staircase, moving with surprising agility for one of considerable bulk. She opened a door to reveal a tiny room with nothing more than a single bed, a chest of drawers with a mirror on it and a washbasin against the wall. As Robbie had said, it was nothing fancy, but clean.

"Bathroom down the hall," the landlady said. "Breakfast at eight. Cup of tea whenever you've a mind for it. And I lock the front door at ten."

They thanked her. Emily left her overnight bag and followed Robbie down the stairs.

"You must be hungry," he said. "I thought we'd get a bite to eat and then maybe go to the cinema. A real date for a change."

"I'd like that." She smiled at him. "I hardly ever go to the pictures. It's a real treat."

"I asked your landlady about where to eat," he said, "and she told me of a place that does the best fish and chips. I know it's not what you're used to, but it's wartime, isn't it? There aren't many cafes open, and when they are, they serve the most disgusting muck."

"Robbie," Emily said, laughing. "Do you know what I'm used to these days? A great hunk of bread with cheese and a pickled onion for my lunch and a big vegetable stew for supper. That's what I've been living on. Fish and chips sounds heavenly."

The cafe was situated by the docks, looking out over the water. Late sunlight still sparkled, painting the scene with a rosy glow. Inside, it was not at all fancy, but it did have red-and-white-checked tablecloths and a small vase of flowers on each table. They sat in the window, facing each other. Two large mugs of tea were brought, and then two huge plates of cod and chips with a plate of bread and butter.

"Stone the crows," Robbie said. "This is more food than I've seen since I left home. And fish and chips is quite a novelty for me. You don't find fish where I come from."

"It's a novelty for me, too," Emily said as she popped a chip into her mouth.

"What do you mean? You live here. You can eat it all the time."

"I can't remember the last time I had it. On holiday once in Cornwall when I was quite small, I remember. It's not the sort of food my mother thinks suitable. Working-class fare, you know."

He chuckled. "Oh right. Not like the salmon mouse."

"It's mousse, as you very well know!" She slapped his hand, laughing.

His eyes held hers, and she felt a shiver at the way he was looking at her.

"So tell me," he said, "what did you do with yourself all that time stuck at home?"

"Nearly went mad," she replied. "Actually, I came home from school when we got the news that Freddie had been killed, so we were in full mourning for six months. Black dresses, no callers, no music, nothing. It was silly, really. Freddie would have found it silly. As if any amount of mourning could bring him back."

"And then?"

"It took me a long while to get over his death—longer than I would have thought. I think I must have been in a state of shock, or depression, I suppose. None of the things I'd grown up to expect would happen after school—balls and parties and meeting young men."

"So you didn't meet any blokes before me?"

Emily blushed. "There was one young man. He was one of Freddie's friends from Oxford and came to be a clerk for my father. He was rather handsome. He looked a little like you, actually. He came to stay a couple of times."

"What was his name?"

"His name?" She laughed. "Sebastian. A frightfully upper-class name."

"So he was one of your lot? Good family and all that? Your mother must have encouraged that one."

Emily laughed, remembering. "Oh yes. She did. I was quite smitten, and I think he quite liked me, even though I was much younger. But it never went anywhere. He got his call-up papers, and shortly afterwards, we got the news that he'd been killed in action. I was just beginning to get over Freddie's death. This was the final straw, you know. And after he died, I decided I was not going to feel anything for anyone again because I'd only lose them." She looked away, staring out of the window. A fishing boat with red sails was leaving the harbour. The failing sunlight made those sails glow like blood. They sat in silence. Then she said, "After that, there didn't seem much point in anything." She gave a long sigh. "I wanted to find work, to keep busy and do something useful, but my mother was terrified of losing me, so they wouldn't let me out of their sight."

"Have they come to terms with your working in the fields?"

"Absolutely not," she said. "They tried to remove me. It was horrible, Robbie. An awful scene in front of everyone. And my father said if I chose to disobey them, I need not bother to come back home ever."

"My word," he said. "That's harsh talk. But I bet it was spoken in the heat of the moment. He didn't mean it."

"I don't know," she said. "Maybe. He does tend to explode in anger these days. The way I feel right now, I don't want to go back to them. I don't want my life to be dictated by other people."

"So you're not going to be under your husband's thumb?" he asked, his tone lighter now.

"Certainly not!" she replied.

There was a pause while each of them considered where this conversation might lead and the implications of it.

"So what picture is playing at the cinema?" Emily asked.

"We have a choice. There is *Tarzan of the Apes* at the Gaumont and *Salomé* at the Regal."

"Oh, I think *Tarzan of the Apes*, don't you?" she said. "*Salomé* would be rather too intense, and I don't want to see John the Baptist's head being cut off."

"Rightio," he agreed. "Although I was looking forward to that dance of the seven veils."

Her eyes challenged his. "All the more reason to see *Tarzan*," she said.

He laughed.

They managed to finish every morsel on their plates and followed it with a jam roly-poly and custard. Feeling horribly replete, they set off again, hand in hand. The world was now bathed in pink twilight. Swallows darted past them, seagulls swooped overhead, crying plaintively, and from the estuary beyond came the mournful hoot of a tug-boat. Emily sighed with contentment. *I must remember every detail of this evening,* she thought.

They paid to enter the cinema and Robbie led her up to the balcony and then to the back row. "I have to confess my evil intent," he whispered as they took their seats. "It doesn't really matter what film is showing. I wanted the chance to put my arm around you in the dark, and kiss you properly with nobody to see us. You don't mind, do you?"

"Of course I don't mind." She gave him a little smile. "Who knows when we'll have the chance to do this again?"

The theatre lights went down and the organ began to play. Advertisements were shown, and then several cartoons and a newsreel. They were hardly aware of the cartoons, but when the newsreel started, the music became sombre and military. This made them stop and look up to see the words on the screen: "German Offensive on the Marne."

"The Germans, under Ludendorff, have launched a new offensive on the Marne."

"It's a good thing I'm going back. I'm needed," Robbie said. "They don't have enough planes or pilots."

"But I thought we were finally winning," Emily said. "I thought victory was in sight."

"I think this is a last desperate attempt by the Germans to slow the inevitable, cause as much harm as possible before they have to surrender," Robbie said. "They must realize their cause is hopeless."

"Shhh! Quiet," came a voice from the seats in front of them.

Robbie looked at Emily and they grinned. He slipped his arm around her again and she rested her head on his shoulder. It felt wonderful, even though the brass pips on his epaulette dug into her. She looked up at him, and he started kissing her.

"A rather silly film, don't you think?" he asked as they walked home, his arm around her shoulder. "Swinging through the jungle and saying, 'Me Tarzan, you Jane'?"

"I thought he looked rather good in a loincloth," Emily replied.

"I didn't realize you had eyes for other men." He gave her shoulder a squeeze.

"There's a lot you still don't know about me," she replied. "I might not be the nice, respectable girl you like at all. I might have dark and secret thoughts. I might have a terrible temper. We know so little about each other, Robbie. We've only seen the good sides of each other."

"It doesn't matter," he replied. "I only know that you're the girl for me. I knew it the moment I spotted you peeking around the door of that hospital room."

They reached the guest house front steps. "I'll say goodnight then," he said. "I better not kiss you. That old woman is probably watching through the net curtains. But I'll come for you in the morning, after breakfast, all right? And we can have the whole day together."

"What shall we do?" she asked. "Do you have anything special in mind? A picnic?"

"Better than that," he said. "One of the doctors at the hospital has become quite a mate. He's got a boat, and he's offered to take us out for the day. I thought that would be a different sort of thing to do, seeing as the only boat I've ever been on was a bloomin' great troop ship." He paused, looking down at her. "That is all right with you, isn't it?"

"I don't know if I get seasick," Emily said. "I've never tried."

"Oh, we're not going out to sea," he said. "Just cruising up the river, I think."

"In which case, it's a lovely idea."

"See you in the morning then, my darling," he said. "Sweet dreams."

He gave her a civilized peck on the cheek. Then he opened the front door for her and blew her a kiss as he closed it behind her. Emily stood in the front hall, smiling.

CHAPTER TWELVE

In the morning, Emily came down to the smell of bacon frying.

"Good heavens!" she exclaimed as the landlady brought in a plate of bacon, eggs and fried bread. "Where did you manage to find bacon?"

"Ah, I've got a nephew who owns a farm." The old lady smiled. "He sometimes manages to find a bit of bacon that's not going to the government. And my sister keeps chickens."

Emily ate with delight. She had just finished when Robbie arrived. "Was that bacon I smelled?" he asked.

"It was. Bacon, eggs and fried bread. Heavenly."

"And all I had was lumpy porridge," he said. "Are you ready? The weather looks nice and fine for our outing."

It does, Emily thought. *Maybe too fine. Not a cloud in the sky.* "Let's hope it stays that way," she said. "The local people here would say, 'Fine before seven, rain by eleven.' Do you think I should take my mackintosh, just in case?"

"The boat has a cabin, so I'm told. Let's take a risk, shall we?" He took her hand again. It felt more natural this time. She glanced at him and gave a happy little smile.

They reached the harbour and saw a tall grey-haired man waving at them. Robbie waved back, and the man came towards them. "I've brought her to the steps," he said. "She's all ready to go."

Emily looked down at a teak motor launch. It had an outdoor seating area and then two steps down into a little cabin.

"Very nice," she said.

"Emily, this is Doctor Dawson," Robbie said. "Doctor, this is the young lady I've been telling you about."

"The land girl, right?" The doctor smiled at her.

"At this moment, yes."

"And how are you finding that? Hard work?"

"Very. But it's quite good fun working with the other women."

"Good for you. I'm afraid we're throwing your young man out of the hospital. He causes too much trouble, you know." There was a twinkle in his eyes. "So go and enjoy yourselves today. Make the most of it. If you take her upstream, there's a good pub on the Cornish side. The Three Bells. They make a decent pasty for lunch."

"You're not coming with us?" Robbie asked.

"Much as I'd like to, I have been called in for an emergency," Dr Dawson said. "I'll show you how to work the controls. It's quite simple. You can fly a plane. You'll pick it up in an instant." He went ahead of them down the steps, then held out his hand to Emily. "Watch your step near the bottom. They are rather slippery with seaweed. There's quite a tide here." He took her bag, then helped her aboard. While he explained the controls to Robbie, Emily went into the cabin. It had a tiny galley with a sink and cupboards, a fold-out table and bench and at the back a bunk built into the bulkhead with just enough room above it to crawl in. It was well designed and delightfully cosy, Emily thought.

"I wouldn't take her out to sea if I were you," she heard the doctor saying as she came back up the steps. "She's quite seaworthy, but navigation with waves and current is a little more tricky."

"Oh, don't worry, Doc. I think we'll be quite happy pottering around on the river," Robbie replied.

"I'll leave you to it then," the doctor said. "If you tie her up on one of these rings when you return, I'll take her out to her mooring later."

He gave a friendly wave and climbed the steps, leaving Robbie and Emily alone.

"Let's give it a try then, shall we?" Robbie asked. He sounded a little nervous. He stood at the controls and started the motor. It made a satisfying pop-pop noise. "Untie the rope, please, Emily," he said. Emily reached out and unwound the thick rope. Once it was inside the boat, Robbie pushed the throttle forwards and the boat moved away from the dock.

"Piece of cake," Robbie said, grinning at her.

They moved out into the estuary at a sedate pace. "I'm tempted to see how fast she'll go, but I suppose I'd better not," Robbie said.

"Don't you dare. My hat will blow away," Emily called back, putting her hand up to hold on to her wide-brimmed straw hat.

They started out heading towards the sea, cruising past the battlements of the old town. Then, just when Emily was feeling a little nervous that they might actually be heading for the Channel, in spite of the doctor's warnings, Robbie turned the boat at the breakwater and lighthouse. They crossed the estuary, admiring the view back to the town of Plymouth, perched on its headlands, and the Royal Navy ship sailing from the harbour. Then they made their way slowly up the river. There were houses on the banks, but soon they were replaced with fields and copses. Only the occasional cottage was nestled in a hollow, or here and there a magnificent home with manicured grounds coming down to the water and a sleek yacht moored at a jetty.

Emily stood beside Robbie, enjoying the gentle breeze in her face.

"I could take to this," he said. "I wonder if we could put in a lake at home."

"Not with six inches of rain, you couldn't," she replied, laughing.

"A pond then. We have stock ponds—billabongs, we call them. And it would have to be a very small boat."

They both laughed at this, then Robbie grew sombre again. "You take all this for granted, don't you?" he said quietly. "These houses and green fields and gardens."

"I suppose I do," she said. "They are all I've ever known."

She waited for him to say something else, but he was silent, staring ahead as he steered the boat. Then he said, "I want you to know that I'll cherish these last two days together, Emmy. I'll never forget one minute."

"Last two days *for now*, Robbie," she corrected. "We'll see each other again as soon as you come back from France."

"Yes," he said slowly, "but then I'll be heading back to Australia."

She wanted to say, "But I'll come with you if you ask me," but that sounded too forward. Perhaps he didn't want to marry her.

He cleared his throat. "That bloke you liked. The one who was killed?"

"Sebastian?"

He nodded. "Did you love him?"

She gave a sad little laugh. "Robbie, I was eighteen. He was a handsome young man, probably six years older than me."

"So he didn't ask you to wait for him?"

"I had a schoolgirl crush on him. He did kiss me once, but I don't think he saw me as anything more than Freddie's young sister. But I was devastated when we heard he had been killed."

"It's a bloody stupid war," he said. "I watched all my mates getting mown down at Gallipoli. I was only spared because a great big bloke fell on top of me. I was drenched in his blood."

She touched his hand. "I'm so sorry."

"I'm not. Well, I'm sorry for that poor bloke. But I'm still alive."

He was silent again, and Emily felt a shiver of uneasiness. Robbie wanted to know if Sebastian had asked her to wait for him. Maybe he had also asked a girl back in Australia to wait for him. Maybe Emily was just a girl to cheer him up when he was so far from home. But as she sneaked a glance at him, she was sure that he did care about her. Maybe that was why he looked so troubled now. Either he was unsure which girl he really loved and wanted or he was trying to find a way to say that, after today, it would all be over between them.

As they progressed upstream, the river narrowed. They passed under an impressive railway bridge.

"The Royal Albert Bridge," Emily said, trying to switch to less threatening topics. "We learned about it at school. Built by Brunel."

"Impressive." He nodded.

At last, they came to the pub the doctor had told them about. Thick woodland sloped steeply down to the river, and the only building in sight was nestled at the water's edge with a jetty beside it. The sign swinging outside said "The Three Bells." It was white-painted, with trestle tables set on the small lawn, on which a child was playing with a dog. A motor car was navigating the steep road down to it, and people were seated at one of the tables, enjoying drinks on a fine day. Robbie cut the motor and they managed to navigate to the jetty. He clambered out and they tied up.

He has taken to it easily, Emily thought as he held out his hand and helped her out. She admired the grace of his movement. His wounds were indeed healed and he was ready to go back to his aeroplane. She pushed the thought to the back of her mind. She would not think about it today. Today, they were having a lovely time, and it was as if the war were far, far away.

They took their seats at a bench along the wall.

"What's that we have to order?" Robbie asked.

"Cornish pasties. They're very good, and we are in Cornwall now."

Robbie shook his head. "It's amazing how quickly you go from one county to the next in England. In Australia, we'd be travelling all day. Okay, so pasties it is, and a beer to go with it?"

Emily hesitated about drinking beer. "I've never tried it," she said. "At least, no more than a sip of my father's. I didn't like the taste."

"Maybe you should stick to cider then," Robbie said. "Come to that, I'd better stick to cider, too. I haven't had a beer since I was first in hospital. It might go to my head."

He came out with a tray holding the pasties and two big glass mugs. "That's a lot of cider," Emily said warily.

"It's a hot day. We're both thirsty." He put the cider down beside her. They ate the pasties with appreciation. The pastry crust was crisp and flaky, and inside was a mixture of warm vegetables and meat. The cider was sweet and fizzy and went down easily.

"I feel quite sleepy," Emily said as they sat in the sun after the meal.

"Me, too. That cider had quite a powerful effect," Robbie replied. "Let's get back in the boat and find a quiet little backwater where we can take a nap."

They cast off successfully and glided further upstream. Here, the river split into several side channels. They picked one that looked inviting. Trees came down to the banks, and there was no sign of human habitation.

"This will do nicely," he said. "We don't want to go too close into shore or we could get tangled up in those trees." He threw the anchor out over the side. Emily started down the steps into the darkness of the cabin, holding on a little unsteadily as the cider was definitely now making her woozy. She unpinned her hat and then flung herself down on the bunk with a sigh of contentment. Robbie followed her and crawled on to the bunk beside her. She was horribly conscious of his closeness. Then he said, "Emily. I want you to know that you're a grand girl, but I can't ask you to marry me. You know that. I couldn't do it to you. I won't do it to you. I couldn't take you away from all this."

"You haven't tried asking me," she replied. "I might say yes."

"But you wouldn't know what you were getting into," he said. "I told you when I met you that it's no life for a woman where I come from. Especially a woman who is used to all this." He shook his head firmly. "No. I won't do it. We'll have the memory of today." He leaned towards her and kissed her tenderly. "But I want you to know that you are the most wonderful girl I've ever met. I do love you."

"And I love you, too," she replied. She wanted to scream, "Don't be so stupid! Ask me to marry you," but she couldn't bring herself to do it. A small voice whispered that perhaps he was only making excuses and he didn't want her as his wife.

He put his arm around her. She was conscious of his breathing. After a while, she realized he had fallen asleep. She closed her eyes and soon she drifted off, too.

CHAPTER THIRTEEN

It was an ominous rumble that woke her. She had no idea where she was. She tried to sit up, bumping her head on the deck above and making her cry out in pain. Robbie murmured in his sleep but didn't wake. The rumble came again. She eased herself off the bunk and made her way across the cabin and up the steps to the deck. This wasn't easy, as it was somehow at a strange angle. When she reached the open air, she understood why. While they had slept, the tide had gone out, and the boat now lay tilting to one side in the mud of an almost-dry creek. The sky overhead was heavy with dark clouds, and a rumble of thunder came again in the distance.

"Robbie!" she called as she hurried down the steps to him. "Wake up. We're stranded here."

He also bumped his head as he tried to sit up, and let out a profanity. Then he saw her standing there and apologized.

"Sorry about that. I forgot where I was. My word, I've got a headache. That cider must have been extra strong." He saw her face. "What's the matter?"

"Come and look." She directed him up on to the tiny deck.

"Crikey!" he exclaimed. "Well, that's a rum do, isn't it? I didn't think there would be tides this far up a river."

"What are we going to do?" she asked.

"Nothing much we can do," he replied. "We'll just have to wait for the tide to come in again and float us free."

"But that could be hours. I have to be back by seven."

"Your boss lady will just have to understand, as will the people at my hospital. We didn't mean to get stuck here." He put a comforting arm around her shoulder. "Don't worry, my love. We're safe. All we have to do is wait it out."

The moment he uttered those words, the heavens opened, and they scrambled back to the shelter of the cabin before they were drenched. Hail bounced off the deck and thudded on the roof of the cabin. Lightning flashed, followed by a loud crack of thunder. The storm was rapidly approaching them. Then, without warning, there was a blinding flash and a crash of thunder at the same time. A tree on the bank nearby went up in a sheet of flame.

"Stone the crows," Robbie muttered. "We are sitting ducks out here."

"Don't say that." She grabbed on to him. She could feel herself trembling.

"It's all right, my darling," he said softly, wrapping her in his arms and nuzzling at her hair. "I won't let anything bad happen to you, I promise."

"How can you promise?" Emily found herself near to tears. "You can't stop a storm, and if it's going to . . ." Another huge clap of thunder exploded overhead. Emily gave a gasp of fear and buried her face in his chest. "Hold me tight, Robbie."

As she looked up at him, his mouth crushed down on to hers. Then he was half-carrying her across the cabin and on to the bunk. His hands were on her body and she felt herself responding, not knowing what was happening but wanting it to go on. She felt the weight of his body on hers, his lips pressing hungrily at her mouth. She was only vaguely aware that he was lifting her skirts.

Afterwards, they lay together, holding each other tightly as if they each were the last safe object in a world turned crazy. Robbie was the first to speak. "I'm sorry," he said, propping himself up on his elbow to look at her. "I'm so sorry, Emmy. I don't know what came over me. I didn't mean to. I promised myself that I wouldn't let this go too far."

"It's not your fault, Robbie," she said shakily. "I didn't exactly stop you, did I? I must have wanted it as much as you."

"Are you all right?" he asked.

"Apart from being in a dangerously tilted boat, stuck in the mud in the middle of the thunderstorm, I'm just fine, thank you," she said.

He burst out laughing. "You're such a great girl, Emily. And I've just realized something. I can't live without you. I know that now. I've tried to make myself think that I could walk away and leave you to a good life here, but I can't. I'll stay here in England after the war if you tell me to. I'll do whatever you want."

"You could ask me to marry you first," she said, smiling at him now.

He looked around. "I'm not exactly in a position to kneel," he said, "and I don't have a ring to give you, but will you marry me?"

"Of course I will. And you don't have to worry about staying in England. I'll come with you to Australia. I'll follow you wherever you want to go."

"You will? What about your parents, your family?"

"My father just made it clear to me that if I stayed on as a land girl, I was no longer welcome at their house. So that makes me think I'm free to go where I want, and as long as I'm with you, I don't care where it is. It will be a great big adventure."

"Too right," he said, beaming at her. "A blooming great adventure." He took her face in his hands and kissed her, tenderly this time. "Mrs Robbie Kerr, eh?"

She nodded.

"First thing I have to do is find you a ring. I don't know how I'm going to do that when I have to ship out first thing tomorrow morning, but I'll do it somehow. We'll get married, and when I'm finally demobbed, I'll go back to Australia first and make everything nice before I send for you."

"You don't have to do that. I'll come with you."

"No, you won't. I'll be going home on a troop ship with a thousand other blokes. You'll come out on a proper P&O liner. And I'll be waiting for you at Sydney Harbour. And we'll have a honeymoon by the ocean."

"How wonderful," she said. "I can't believe this is happening."

"Me neither." He looked out past her. "Oh look, the storm seems to have passed over. It's no longer raining so hard. Now all we have to do is wait for that tide to come back in."

It wasn't until after seven o'clock that the water had risen enough to float the boat off the mudbank. By then, the rain had stopped, and the setting sun flooded the scene with glowing light. Emily propped open the mirror in her compact and tried to make her hair look respectable again. She smoothed down the creases in her dress before joining Robbie at the controls.

"Let's hope it will start or we really are up the creek," he said. They exchanged a grin when the motor started nicely. They hauled in the anchor and eased forwards.

"Can you make it go faster?" Emily said.

"I think this is it, I'm afraid." He tried moving the throttle, but it responded only with a measured chug-chugging. And as they approached the mouth of the river, there were boats on moorings, making navigating around them a challenge. It wasn't until nine that they pulled up at their original dock. It was almost dark. There was no sign of Dr Dawson, nor of anyone else.

Emily helped Robbie tie up the boat securely, then they climbed the slippery steps. At the top, Emily stood, biting her bottom lip. "I'm not sure what to do now," she said. "Even if I can still get a train back to Tavistock, I won't be able to hitch a ride back to the farm tonight. And I certainly don't want to spend the night on Tavistock Station."

"We'd better see if that guest house has room to put you up again," he said.

Emily hesitated. "Robbie, what about the expense?"

"Don't worry about that. I have plenty of back pay coming to me. Three months in a hospital and I've hardly touched a penny. Besides, money is one thing you won't have to worry about in the future. My family is quite well heeled, you know. Wool is a prosperous commodity. You won't lack for anything. And if I buy that aeroplane I've been talking about, then I'll fly you to the nearest ocean whenever you want."

Emily laughed. "Oh Robbie. It all sounds like a lovely dream, doesn't it?" Then her smile faded. "But for the present, I think I'm going to be in big trouble. You, too."

"Nonsense. They'll understand I had trouble with the boat. I've been a good boy the rest of the time. Haven't tried to sneak out like some of them." He slipped his hand around her waist. "And your old battleaxe will understand, I'm sure. It wasn't our fault. We didn't know about tides and mudbanks."

Emily nodded. She wished she could be sure. They walked together to the Seaview, where the landlady had a good laugh about their predicament. "Mercy me," she chuckled. "Did you not know that the tide leaves those upper reaches dry? Did you not ask yourself why there were no other boats up there?"

"Robbie's from a place that's hundreds of miles inland," Emily said. "He's never driven a boat before. And I've certainly never been up this river."

"Well, no harm done, is there, apart from missing your train home," the old woman said. "And as it happens, your room is still vacant. What time do you want breakfast in the morning?"

"Oh, I'm afraid I must leave long before breakfast," Emily said. "I must catch the first train out or I'll be in even bigger trouble."

"Then I won't charge you for breakfast," the woman said. She looked fondly from Emily to Robbie. "In fact, you know what? I won't charge you at all. And if the young man had a mind to stay the night as well . . . I might not even notice."

They laughed uneasily, but Robbie said, "Kind of you, missus, but I'm overdue back at the hospital. Just take good care of my fiancée, will you?"

"Fiancée, is it now?" she asked.

"It is. We're getting married as soon as the war's over."

"Let's pray that it's very soon," the old woman said quietly. "Too many young lives have been wasted in this stupidity. God bless you, my dears."

Emily walked with Robbie a little way down the street. "I can't bear to say goodbye," she said. "Please take care of yourself. No heroics. Don't take on any dangerous missions you don't have to. And write to me."

"I will, whenever I get a chance, I promise. You take care of yourself, too. And I'll send you that ring as soon as I can. Maybe they make good rings in France." He looked at her tenderly, then tilted the brim of her hat back and kissed her.

"Goodbye, my darling," he said.

Emily blinked back tears as she watched him vanish into the night.

CHAPTER FOURTEEN

Miss Foster-Blake eyed her coldly as she came towards the farmhouse. "And what do you have to say for yourself, young woman? I thought I could trust you, or I would not have let you go in the first place. A fine example you are setting for those girls who are not of your class."

"I'm so sorry," Emily said. "We went out on a boat, you see. And we didn't know that rivers are tidal. We got stuck in the mud for hours in an awful thunderstorm, and by the time we made it back to Plymouth, I realized I would have no way of getting a ride to the farm."

"A good excuse for spending the night with a young man." Miss Foster-Blake was still glaring at her.

"No, absolutely not," Emily replied. "He put me up at a guest house and he went back to the hospital where he is being treated. He was also really worried that he'd be in trouble."

"I see." Her expression had softened a little. "Well, I suppose you can't be expected to know about tides."

"The doctor who owns the boat was supposed to be coming with us," Emily said, "but he had a last-minute emergency. Otherwise, there would have been . . ." She broke off in mid-sentence. Otherwise, Robbie would not have made love to her and asked her to marry him. One small thing and her whole world had changed. She tried to keep the repentant look on her face and not to smile.

"I don't expect you've had breakfast," Miss Foster-Blake said. "Well, go and grab some bread and jam, and then get into your work clothes while I find a way to ferry you out to your colleagues."

Alone in the bedroom, Emily changed out of her crumpled clothes and put on her uniform. Robbie would already be heading to Dover and across the Channel. She managed to put on a cheerful face as a van deposited her at the potato field. Her fellow land girls broke off their work as she appeared.

"Here she is at last," Maureen called out. "The sinner returneth! Staying out all night? And I thought you were pure as the driven snow."

Emily felt herself blushing. "If you really want to know, we were out in a boat in a thunderstorm and we got stuck in the mud," she said. "By the time we made it back to the harbour, it was too late to catch a train, so my young man put me up in a guest house—"

"Sure he did." Maureen nudged Ruby who was standing next to her. "They spent the night in a hotel. You hear that, Ruby?"

"It wasn't like that at all," Emily said, her face bright red now. "He took me to the guest house and then he went back to the hospital. And today he's on a train heading back to France."

She swallowed hard, worried that she might cry.

"Watch your tongue, Maureen," Alice said sharply. "Can't you see the poor girl is upset? Her bloke's going back to the front. Never you mind, love." She put an arm around Emily's shoulders. "Come on. We've got plenty of lovely taters to take your mind off him!"

Emily looked at her and grinned. "You're wicked," she said.

"But at least I made you smile," Alice retorted. "So you had a lovely time, did you?"

"Absolutely perfect." She took a deep breath. "And what's more, he asked me to marry him."

"You're engaged?" Daisy asked excitedly.

Emily nodded.

"Hearty congratulations, Emily," Mrs Anson said. "I am so pleased for you."

"But don't he come from Australia?" Alice asked.

"He does. And we'll be going back there after the war."

"All the way to Australia?" Ruby looked terrified. "My, but that's so far. And all them kangaroos and things."

"It doesn't matter. I'll be with him," Emily said. "Not long now, so Robbie told me. He gets the latest news from the navy. That German offensive—it was just a desperate last attempt to stop the Allies' advance. He reckons it will all be over before Christmas."

"Saints be praised for that," Maureen said. "Four years of our lives wasted."

"So many men's lives wasted," Mrs Anson said quietly.

"Here comes old Crosspatch," Daisy warned. "We'd better be working or else."

They returned to their harvesting. The rain had made the red soil even heavier, and they had to take turns digging out the plants with the big fork.

"I never thought I'd want to milk cows or look after pigs, but after this, it seems like a piece of cake," Daisy commented as she lifted a plant free and the rest of the girls squatted to pick the tiny tubers.

"Cows have to be milked at five in the morning," Alice pointed out.

"Ah, but I'm used to that," Daisy responded. "Always up at five in the big house." She moved closer to Emily. "So where do you think your wedding will be? At your home here in Devon?"

The full memory of the quarrel with her parents came back to her. Her mother would never agree to her marrying Robbie—that was obvious. "No, I don't think so. I've no idea. We'll take that one step at a time."

"Did he give you a ring?" Maureen called.

"It was all rather sudden," Emily said. "He hadn't intended to propose to me. He didn't think I'd want his life in Australia. But then he said he couldn't live without me. So he didn't have a ring ready. He's going to try and send me one, but I don't know how that will be possible at the front. We'll just have to wait until he comes back. But that's fine."

However, two days later, a small package arrived. It was waiting with the rest of the post on the hall table when they came in from the fields. The rest of the women crowded around Emily. "Go on. Open it!" voices urged. Emily would rather have opened it in private, but she could not disappoint them. Inside was a letter.

> *My own darling girl,*
> *We stopped in Dover between the train and the boat. Some of the blokes took the chance to pop to the nearest shops for cigarettes. I didn't have time go to a proper jewellers', but I saw this in a pawn shop window, and I thought it would do until we can choose a real ring together.*

Emily opened the small box. It was a small gold band with a row of tiny inset rubies. Emily's fingers trembled as she took it out and put it on. The women gave sighs of happiness.

"Isn't it pretty?" Emily held it up to show them.

"You've got a good bloke there, Emily, love," Alice said.

"You don't know how I'm wishing that would happen to me," Maureen said dreamily. "I think I'll have to come out to Australia to visit you and you can introduce me to his friends."

"We're going to live out in the middle of nowhere on a farm," Emily said. "I don't think you'd find it much fun."

"Well, maybe not a farm. I'll have had my fill of farming by the time this is over. How many more potatoes can there be in the world?"

"It might be something worse after this," Maud said gloomily.

"What could be worse than digging up potatoes all day?" Maureen demanded.

"Mucking out pigs?"

They nodded agreement.

"I heard that we'll be done here by the end of the week," Mrs Anson said.

Emily slipped off to their room. She sat looking at the ring on her finger, then she took it off, put it in its little box and tucked the box under her pillow. She wasn't going to risk wearing it in the fields.

Perry's Farm
Devon
August 8, 1918

> *My dear Clarissa,*
> *I'm sorry I haven't written for a while, but we've been worked so hard that I've had no time to breathe, let alone write. By the time we come back to the farm after twelve hours working in the fields, we are almost too tired to eat the stew or meat pudding that's waiting for us, and we fall asleep instantly after.*
>
> *But luckily we have dug up our last potato and moved on to something new. We are haymakers! We are learning to use a scythe, which looks terrifying. One wrong sweep and we cut off our feet at the ankles! Then we have to rake, bundle and bring the bundles to the haystack. The farmer does the actual stacking. He's much nicer than the last grumpy man, although he does get a good laugh out of our pathetic attempts at scything.*
>
> *And I've good news I've been dying to share with you. Robbie asked me to marry him and I said yes. We'll get married as soon as he is out of uniform and I'll go out*

to him in Australia. And in answer to your unspoken question: no, my parents do not know, nor would they approve. They have made it quite clear what they think of Robbie. It is a terrifying thought that I'll never see them again, but I had to choose, and I chose a man who loves me.

You'll have to be bridesmaid of course. Or maybe we can have a double wedding when you marry your Lieutenant Hutchins. Does he write to you faithfully? Robbie isn't the best correspondent, but I can quite understand that he can't tell me what he is doing, and post from the front lines doesn't always get through safely to England.

So I am counting off the days, and I bet you are, too. One of the girls has acquired a Brownie camera and has taken snapshots of us haymaking. When they are developed, I'll send you one so that you can see what a brawny farm girl I have become.

Do take care of yourself,

Your friend,

Emily

CHAPTER FIFTEEN

The haymaking coincided with a dry spell. The work no longer seemed hard after the baptism of fire with the potatoes. The women laughed and sang as they worked. The farmer's wife and daughters appeared with pasties and jugs of lemonade. Alice, who had been to the music halls in London, sang them all the cheeky songs of Marie Lloyd.

"Oh, you don't know Nellie like I do, sang the naughty little bird on Nellie's hat."

Daisy and Ruby were shocked, but the others chuckled and joined in the chorus, even Mrs Anson, who certainly hadn't heard such things before. Emily realized that she had seldom felt so happy before. Her happiness was perfect every time a note arrived from Robbie. As she had said to Clarissa, he wasn't much of a letter writer, but at least the notes were positive. He was being trained to fly a Vimy bomber, which was much bigger than the small fighter planes he'd flown before. He'd taken to it instantly, he said, and he was thinking it would be the perfect aeroplane to take back to Australia to carry cargo and passengers.

When Emily lay in bed, she pictured herself in an empty red landscape, waving to Robbie as he flew off in his aeroplane. Would she worry about him? Would she be lonely? Doubts crept in, but she pushed them aside. She'd be Mrs Robert Kerr, and that would be enough.

When the hay was all gathered and successfully stacked, and as there was no rain in sight, the farmer held a party. There was cider, and sausages were cooked on a bonfire. They sang in the firelight "Keep the Home Fires Burning" and "Pack Up Your Troubles in Your Old Kit Bag."

"I wonder where we'll be going next," Daisy said to Emily as they rode back to the training centre in the back of a van.

"I don't know." Emily thought about this. "It's getting towards the end of the season, isn't it? I wonder what they'll do with us when winter comes and nothing grows."

"Send us home, most likely," Daisy said. "They won't want to pay or feed us when there's no work. Oh Lord, I don't want to go home. Do you?"

Emily couldn't say that she didn't have a home to go to. "We'll think of something," she said. But in bed that night, she lay staring at the ceiling. What if the war went on and it was another year before Robbie was released from service? Where would she go? What would she do? Her parents would hardly be likely to take her back.

The next morning, they waited to hear their fate. Miss Foster-Blake came in while they were still eating porridge at breakfast.

"The farmer tells me he was satisfied with your work, girls," she said. "Most satisfied. Well done. I am proud of what you have accomplished, and you should be, too. And as we have no requests for your service for the immediate future . . ." She paused.

"We're going home?" Ruby asked excitedly.

"No, Ruby, you are going to make good use of that time with extra training. You never completed the course, so there were items that were not covered. The handling of sheep, for one thing. And methods for improving the quality of the land . . ."

A sigh could be heard amongst the women.

"She means dung spreading," Maud muttered.

"Be ready to report for duty in twenty minutes," Miss Foster-Blake added. Then, in a quieter voice, "Emily Bryce, I'd like a word with you."

Emily's heart leapt into her throat. What had she done wrong? And then, worse than that: she'd had news about Robbie. She could hardly make her feet follow the woman across the room. When they were outside in the hallway, Miss Foster-Blake turned to her. "We have had a rather unusual request, Miss Bryce. Do you happen to know Lady Charlton?"

Emily reacted with surprise. "Lady Charlton? I'm afraid not."

"I thought you might move in the same circles."

"Much as my mother would love it," Emily said, "we do not mix much with titled people."

"No matter," Miss Foster-Blake said. "As I said, we have had a request. Lady Charlton owns an estate not far from here, at the edge of Dartmoor in the village of Bucksley Cross. Her gardeners all enlisted in the army, leaving the grounds to run completely wild. She wondered if we could spare any of our land girls to bring the estate back to its former state. I thought of you, naturally. You are a good worker, a quick learner, and you know how to behave with a person of her class. So I'd like you to select two girls to accompany you—girls you know will work hard and conduct themselves well."

"Alice and Daisy," Emily said immediately.

Miss Foster-Blake raised an eyebrow. "I'm surprised at your choices. Not Mrs Anson, with whom I presume you have more in common?"

"Alice and Daisy have nothing," Emily said. "They need to be needed."

"Ah. Very wise." She nodded approval. "I see you are growing into a leader like your father, Miss Bryce. Very well. Alice and Daisy it shall be. Go and fetch them, and have your bags packed in half an hour. Lady Charlton will be sending a motor car for you."

"Will we be staying there then?" Emily asked.

"You will. I gather there is a cottage on the estate where you will be housed, and you will take your meals at the big house. When you arrive, the handyman will show you where you can find the necessary implements for your work. So work hard and do us credit, Miss Bryce."

"Don't worry, we will," Emily said. She went in to fetch Alice and Daisy. They followed her, mystified.

"'Ere, I ain't finished me porridge yet," Alice said. "It will get cold."

"No time for that now," Emily said. "We have a new assignment. We're going to work on the estate of a titled lady."

"Just us?" Daisy looked back at the rest of the group, still eating.

Emily nodded. "Miss Foster-Blake wanted to send me, and she asked me who I'd like to take with me."

"And you chose us?" Daisy's pinched little face lit up.

"I did, because you're both good workers and because I get along well with you."

"That's real nice of you, Emily," Alice said. "You're a proper toff, you are. So we're going to swan it with the aristocracy, are we? Blimey."

"Don't thank me until you've seen it," Emily said. "It might be awfully hard work."

"What can be so hard about tidying up a garden?" Alice chuckled. "She doesn't grow potatoes, does she?"

A well-worn Daimler motor car arrived in front of the farm about twenty minutes later. The rest of the girls crowded around as Emily, Daisy and Alice loaded their bags on to the board at the back, where an elderly chauffeur strapped them on.

"Some people have all the luck," Ruby said. "There you lot will be, living in a swanky house and eating good food while we're stuck here shoving around a lot of sheep and doing muck spreading."

"We're being housed in a cottage, Ruby," Emily said. "And we'll be estate workers—no different from farm workers, except no sheep."

The others laughed.

"There might be a handsome footman," Maureen said. "Emily's snagged her beau, but you could do worse, Daisy!"

"No, thank you," Daisy said. "I've had my share of big houses and their dramas. I wouldn't mind marrying a country boy—if any of them come home, that is."

They fell silent, considering this.

Then Maureen managed a laugh again. "If they don't, then you'd all better come with me to Canada—hook ourselves up with big strong lumberjacks, eh?"

"I'm thinking of going to Canada," Mrs Anson said, making them all look at her in surprise. "I've a sister out there, and there's nothing for me in England once the war is over."

"In you get," the chauffeur said, eyeing them with distaste. "You can't keep Her Ladyship waiting."

The others waved as the motor moved away. They drove along country lanes between fields of sheep and cows until the great curve of Dartmoor rose in front of them, its smooth, bleak hills punctuated with rocky outcroppings and weathered stands of Scots pines, sculpted by the winds. But before they reached the moor, they turned into an impossibly narrow lane, bordered by high hedgerows. They crossed a rushing stream on an old granite pack bridge. A memory stirred in Emily's head—a family outing up to Dartmoor, to a place that looked a lot like this. She had been four or five at the most. Freddie had been ten. She, always the adventurous one, jumping ahead on stepping stones over the rushing stream, missing her footing and falling into the swiftly flowing water. And instantly her big brother had been beside her, sweeping her up, carrying her to safety. She closed her eyes to shut out the pain, and when she opened them again, there before them was the village.

"Blimey," Alice said.

"It's like something from a picture book," Daisy agreed.

Emily's spirits rose. The village nestled at the edge of the moor. A great sweep of hill rose behind it, and there was a group of wild ponies silhouetted against the horizon. The village itself was built around a sloping green with a weathered Celtic cross in the middle. On one side of the green was a row of thatched cottages, on the other a pub called the Red Lion, with its sign swinging in the breeze. And at the far side of the village was a church with a tall square tower. The lane continued behind the cottages, between two granite posts and up a curved driveway to a large grey-stone house. The facade was free of adornment, apart from a front porch. A Virginia creeper climbed up one side, its leaves already turning blood red. Scots pines at the rear protected the house from the Dartmoor winds. And around it was a wilderness of land—an overgrown lawn, tangles of shrubs, herbaceous borders high with weeds.

"Blimey," Alice said again, only this time she didn't sound so enthusiastic.

Emily nodded. "I can see we're going to be kept busy here."

At the sound of the motor, the front door opened and a frail-looking old lady came out. She was dressed head to toe in black, with a high collar and a beaded shawl over her dress. On her head was a black lace cap, and she leaned on an ebony cane. As Emily had time to observe her, she decided she wasn't as frail as she looked. Her expression was of extreme haughtiness and disdain.

"Ah, there you are. I wondered if there had been an accident or something. It's not much more than five miles, is it?" Her voice matched her haughty expression.

"They weren't quite ready," the old man said. His voice, on the other hand, had a strong Devon burr to it. "And it took a while to get their bags loaded on."

"No matter," the woman said as they climbed out of the back seat. "I am Lady Charlton. Welcome to Bucksley House. I trust you are going to return my grounds to their former glory."

"We'll do our best," Emily and Alice muttered in unison.

"Splendid. Now, Simpson will show you where we keep the tools of your trade, and then he'll drive you and your bags down to the cottage. You'll install yourselves and then get right to work. Is that clear?"

"Yes, my lady," they all muttered. In spite of her diminutive size, Emily found her quite intimidating.

"This way, ladies." The old chauffeur led them around the house to a cluster of outbuildings. There were stables, now no longer used for horses. One now served as a garage for the motor car. And at the end of the row was a tack room. Inside was an ancient lawnmower and a rack of assorted shovels, forks, hoes and rakes.

"I reckon that grass is going to need to be scythed before you can mow it," the old chauffeur said. "I doubt you young ladies have ever used a scythe!" And he chuckled.

"As a matter of fact, we've just come from haymaking," Emily said. "We are pretty handy with a scythe."

"Well, blow me down," he said. "I'd help out, only my rheumatics makes it hard for me to do much these days. But I've been doing what I can for Her Ladyship, since all the menfolk went away and it were only me."

"You're the only man what's here?" Alice asked.

He gave a grunt. "That's me. Chauffeur, handyman, boot polisher—you name it, I do it. Should have retired years ago. I'm seventy-seven now, but I can't leave Her Ladyship in the lurch, can I?"

"It's very good of you, Mr Simpson," Emily said.

He looked at her with interest. "And good of you, too, miss, if you don't mind my saying so. Girls of your class aren't meant to work in fields."

"But I'm quite enjoying it, Mr Simpson," Emily said. "Better than sitting at home doing nothing."

"I'd agree with that," he said. "My wife thanks the good Lord every day that I'm out of the house and not under her feet." He nodded at them. "Come on then. Get back in the motor, and I'll drive you down to the cottage. 'Tis a fair walk."

They bumped down a rutted track that ran behind a kitchen garden. There were vegetables and various fruit bushes growing. "I tries to keep the kitchen garden growing so Her Ladyship has something to eat," he said. "There used to be plenty coming from the home farm. Ten men working on that, there were, but now they've all gone to the war, apart from the farm manager and a couple of boys, so they are down to just a few cows and chickens these days."

They had come to the bottom of the estate, close to the church and a weathered stone school building. Simpson got out to open a gate and they were back in the lane.

"Here we are," he said. "Cragsmoor Cottage. It ain't pretty, but it will keep the rain off your heads."

This was not like the thatched cottages they had seen beside the green. It was a square stone building, like a child's drawing of a house: two small windows on either side of a front door, its paint peeling. It was surrounded by a high stone wall and an overgrown garden.

"Come on then, get your things," Simpson said, and he unlatched the straps on the back board. They opened the front gate and walked between high bushes to the front door. It opened with an ominous creaking sound. Inside felt cold and damp. They stood looking around them.

"I'll leave you to it then." Simpson started to walk away. "Don't dilly-dally too long. Her Ladyship expects you to get straight to work. You can pick up your bedding when you come up to the house for your dinner."

"Dinner?" Emily asked. "Are we not going to be fed at lunchtime?"

The old man chuckled. "Only posh folks like you call it luncheon. To us, it's our dinner, isn't it? I'll be off then. You know your way back."

"I was going to say I've seen worse, but I really haven't," Alice said.

"It really is pretty grim, I must admit," Emily agreed. They were standing in what had been a living room. There were a couple of rickety wooden chairs, a table covered in a faded woven cloth and a big stone fireplace. The floor was slate tile. There were dark oak beams across the low ceiling, and tattered net curtains hung in the window. At the back was a tiny kitchen with a cast-iron stove, a copper and a sink, and on the other side was a bedroom with an old brass bedstead. An impossibly steep, narrow staircase led up to an attic, of which one end had been partitioned off into a small bedroom. The other side was an open storage area with no proper floor and various bits of broken furniture lying about. The bedroom ceiling sloped down, so that it was only possible to stand upright in the middle of the room. A small window on the side wall looked out over the village.

"I don't like to say it, but there's no bathroom and no lav," Daisy said, coming up the stairs behind the other two.

"There's a copper in the kitchen," Alice said cheerfully. "We can heat water in that to wash with, but no lav? Maybe it's outside."

They went to look, and it was—an afterthought tacked on to the house beyond the back door.

"I won't fancy going out here at night," Alice said. "I hope they have jerries."

"Jerries?" Emily looked confused.

"Chamber pots, love," Alice chuckled. "I don't suppose you've ever had to use one with nice indoor plumbing, but the rest of us, we're used to jerries."

"Goodness," Emily said, thinking of having to use a chamber pot with other women in the house.

"Well, we'd better get to work, or I think that old lady will have something to say," Alice said. "Come on. Let's face the music."

They walked back up the hill.

"What should we start on first?" Daisy asked.

"I think it had better be the lawn," Emily said. "It's been fine weather for a while, so the scything and mowing should be done while the grass is dry."

"I wasn't any good at scything," Alice said. "Nearly took me blooming feet off a couple of times."

"Daisy was, weren't you?" Emily said. "She got the hang of it right away."

"Yes. I wasn't bad, was I?" Daisy blushed at the praise.

"Right, Daisy, you scythe, and we'll rake and bundle, and then we'll take turns with the mower. I rather think it will take two of us to push it. It looks awfully heavy."

It was indeed hard work trying to push the mower. Simpson told them that he had oiled it, but even so, it took two of them to propel it over a lawn choked with weeds. They worked solidly for a couple of hours, and by the time the church clock had struck twelve, they had mowed a patch of lawn at the front of the house.

"I wonder what time dinner is," Daisy said. "I'm awful hungry."

"Let's go and see," Emily said. She led the others towards the front door and rang the bell. It was opened by a thin little woman with a sharp, foxy face and sandy hair now streaked with grey. Her small dark eyes darted nervously.

"Yes, what do you want?" she demanded.

"We wanted to know if it's time for our lunch yet," Emily said. "We're the land girls who have come to work for Lady Charlton. We were told we'd be taking our meals at the big house."

"I know who you are," the woman said. "And you've got a nerve, showing up at the front door. You go round the back to the tradesman's entrance. I'm not having you traipsing in mud across my nice clean floors."

"Oh, I'm sorry," Emily said, flushing at this onslaught. They made their way around the house to where a door had been opened for them.

The woman was standing there. "Make sure you wipe your feet properly," she said. "Mud scraper's to the left."

"We don't actually have much mud on us," Emily said. "It hasn't been raining and the grass was quite dry."

"Hark at Miss Hoity-Toity there," the woman said. "Well, come on in then. I've put bread and cheese out for you on the kitchen table."

"Are you the cook?" Emily asked, trying to appear friendly.

"I am Mrs Trelawney, the housekeeper," the woman said. "These days, I also cook for Her Ladyship myself, and take care of her. We're down to one maid, Ethel, and she's getting on in years, too. But it's only Her Ladyship in the house, so most of it's closed off."

"Pleased to meet you, Mrs Trelawney," Alice said. "I'm Alice Adams, and these two are Daisy and Emily. And we appreciate you getting a meal for us."

This seemed to do the trick. The expression of hostility softened a little. "I've no doubt it's hard work out there," she said. "I think we might have a bit of pork pie to go with the cheese, and some good pickled cabbage, too, that I put up before the war started."

The meal was washed down with a big stoneware mug of tea.

"And we need bedding for the cottage," Emily said. "Do we get that from you?"

"I'll see what we have to spare in the linen cupboard and have it out by the time you come for your supper at six," Mrs Trelawney said. "Make sure you come here nice and prompt because I have to serve Her Ladyship her dinner at seven thirty, and I don't want you under my feet then."

"If I was the old lady, I wouldn't want to live with her," Daisy muttered as they went back to work. "She's got a face that could curdle milk."

"She wasn't overly friendly, was she?" Emily said. "You'd think she'd welcome company, stuck there alone all day."

They went back to the scything and mowing, and by six o'clock they had made good progress on the front lawn. Their supper was shepherd's pie and runner beans from the kitchen garden, followed by rice pudding. They were all feeling comfortably full by the time they went down to the cottage carrying sheets, blankets and pillows.

"Why don't you take the room upstairs," Alice said. "I expect you'd like a bit of privacy."

"So I'll be the first to know if the roof leaks?" Emily teased.

"Not at all," Alice retorted. "Me and Daisy is used to sharing a bed, so it won't bother us."

Emily went upstairs to make her bed. The cottage had a sad, neglected feel to it, and this small room with its sloping ceiling felt especially cold and damp. There seemed to be a draught coming from the window, and there weren't even any curtains here. No lamp either. When night fell, she'd have no means of light at all. "I'll need to ask for a candle tomorrow," she decided. She started to make the bed, taking care not to bang her head on the sloping ceiling. As she moved around to the other side of the bed, she glanced out of the window. The village was bathed in setting sunlight. It looked like a picture postcard. Nothing moved around the green. It struck Emily how empty it seemed.

She put on the pillow slip and folded down the sheet. The mattress felt hard and lumpy. Emily sighed, and for a moment, a memory of her comfortable bedroom with its pink silk eiderdown flashed into her mind. She turned her gaze back to the room. Apart from the bed, there was no furniture at all. Not even a table to put a lamp or candle on. Hoping to find something she could use, she came out of her little bedroom and crossed the landing to the storage area. At the entrance, she hesitated. It was dark, dusty and musty, and she could see cobwebs festooned from the beams. The window at the far end was covered in more cobwebs and let in little light. Her bedroom window had faced the setting sun. This one faced the hillside, and twilight was fading fast. "Come on," she said to herself. "It's only a few cobwebs." And she forced herself to pick her way amongst the discarded objects. There was not much in the way of furniture. A cracked water basin, an old school desk, a torn lampshade—everything broken beyond repair. Hardly encouraging. She recoiled in horror as she saw a ghostly figure standing in the corner. She almost retreated, her heart pounding. Then she made herself go forwards and laughed out loud when she pulled off an old sheet and found a hatstand beneath it. At least she'd have somewhere to hang her clothes. As she went to move it, her hand brushed a cobweb. She stumbled, pitched forwards and put out her hands to save herself. Dust rose in a cloud, and she found that what had stopped her fall was an old trunk. That would do to put a candle on at least. She attempted to lift it and found it surprisingly heavy. Her heart beat fast as she squatted to open it. The latch was rusted, and it took a lot of jiggling before it flew open. It was full of books. This struck her as surprising—the last thing she expected to find in what had surely been a labourer's cottage.

Emily dragged the trunk out on to the landing, where she could examine its contents properly. She picked the books up one by one: Dickens and Tennyson, a history of England, as well as the sort of holy stories handed out as Sunday school prizes. Someone with education had lived here once. Then, she caught sight of an old brown-leather volume with no title. She pulled it out and opened it to find it was a journal, handwritten in tiny fading copperplate script.

The light was starting to fade. She carried the journal over to the window and attempted to read the writing.

From the Journal of Susan Olgilvy, July 10, 1858
In the Village of Bucksley Cross, Devonshire

> *I have done it. I am officially the schoolmistress of the village of Bucksley Cross, Devonshire, installed in my own little cottage at the edge of Dartmoor. There are thatched cottages on the other side of the green, a church with a tall,*

square tower and a public house that looks quite invit-
ing (although I am sure that ladies do not venture into
a public house, especially not spinster schoolmistresses).

The chairman of the parish council personally
escorted me across the green to my small, grey stone cot-
tage with a slate roof, set amid a rather overgrown and
neglected garden.

"I think you'll find everything you need here, Miss
Olgilvy," he said. "The ladies of the parish have made sure
the house is comfortable and well-furnished, providing
items from their own households when necessary."

"You are very kind," I replied, but now as I stand
alone in my tiny living room and look around me, I have
to admit that his definition of well-furnished is a far cry
from my own.

CHAPTER SIXTEEN

Emily went to find the others. "Look what I've found," she said. "Someone's journal from long ago. Isn't that interesting?"

"It's bad luck to read someone else's diary," Daisy said, regarding Emily with horror.

"Really? I never heard that," Emily replied.

"That's what Rose told me when we shared a bedroom at Moorland Hall and I peeked into her diary. She said she'd read her sister's diary and then right after she caught scarlet fever and nearly died. And sure enough, I spilled a pail of water all across the floor and got into terrible trouble for it."

"But this is from eighteen fifty-eight. The person is probably dead by now."

"All the same, it's private, isn't it?" Daisy said.

"Then why did she leave it here for anyone to read?"

"Maybe she died," Alice said.

Emily stared down at it, feeling suddenly awkward. "All right. I'll put it back," she said.

"So what are we supposed to do now?" Alice asked. "It's only eight o'clock, and I ain't ready to go to bed yet."

"There are some books upstairs," Emily said. "Come and see if there's anything you might like to read."

"I ain't a big one for reading," Alice said. "I gave that up when they kicked me out of school and sent me to work in the garment factory. Oh, I know how to read the newspaper headlines, but that's about it."

"Oh, you're missing so much, Alice," Emily said. "Books are wonderful. You can get transported away by a good story. If we're living in a place like this, we can read about Paris or a tropical island and feel like we're there."

"You can read to us, maybe?" Alice suggested.

"We can take it in turns, to improve your reading." She looked across at Daisy, who was now shifting uncomfortably from one foot to the other. "I can't read, Miss Emily. I never learned."

"Then I'll teach you. It will give us something to do in the evenings before it gets too dark. You won't go far in life if you can't read, either of you."

"You're right there," Alice agreed. "When Bill was called up, I tried to get a job, but there weren't much for someone like me with no education. Only the factories. I got a job for a while in a munitions factory, then there was this explosion and a lot of girls were killed and I thought, 'I'm not staying here like a sitting duck,' so I quit."

"Shall we choose something to read now?" Emily asked.

"All right," Daisy said. "You choose for us." She went to sit down on one of the chairs. There was a loud snapping sound. The leg broke, and Daisy was catapulted on to the floor.

"Are you all right?" Emily asked, laughing, as they hauled her to her feet.

"Only embarrassed at looking like a fool." Daisy joined in the laughter. "Lucky I'm wearing bloomers or I'd have shown my underwear. I hope the beds don't give out on us during the night."

"What a dump!" Alice exclaimed. "You'd think they could find somewhere a bit better to put us, wouldn't you? If they are down to one maid, wouldn't there be servants' rooms in the big house?"

"I suppose one doesn't put outside staff in the inside servants' quarters," Emily said.

"That's right," Daisy chimed in, still brushing the dust from her skirt. "My dad was the groom and we lived above the stables. And the gardeners lived in their own cottages. And they were never allowed inside the house at all. That's the way it's done."

"Sounds ruddy stupid to me," Alice said. "You wait till the communists take over, like in Russia. They'll put ten families in houses like that one."

"Golly," Emily exclaimed. "Do you really think the communists will take over in England?"

"Probably not," Alice conceded. "We're too sensible here, aren't we? Apart from going into a war that makes no sense for anybody. Declaring war because a ruddy archduke was shot in some piddling little country somewhere. It's not as if anyone was trying to invade us."

"I agree," Emily said. "I think it was all a ghastly mistake, but once it started, nobody would back down."

They stood in silence for a moment. Outside, they could hear the rooks cawing as they returned to their nests in the big pine trees behind the vicarage.

"You know what I want to do?" Alice said with sudden determination. "I want to go down to the pub."

"The pub?" Emily sounded shocked. "Can ladies go to a public house?"

"It's wartime, love. I don't think the rules apply any more. Come on. I need cheering up, and I need to get out of this dreary hole. Let's go and meet people and have a drink."

They set off down the lane, crossing the village green to the pub on the other side. The "Red Lion" sign glowed in the last rays of sunlight.

They pushed open the heavy oak door and stepped into a low-ceilinged room filled with the sweet scent of pipe tobacco. The walls were panelled in oak, now almost black with generations of smoke. There was a big fireplace on one wall decorated with horse brasses around it. There were similar oak benches around the walls and several glass-topped tables. Two old gentlemen were sitting at a table in the far corner, both smoking long clay pipes. One of them was Simpson—the other looked even older than he did. They looked up, frowning, as the women came in.

"Good evening, ladies. What can I do for you?" A woman was standing behind the bar. She had a round face with hair pulled back into a bun, and she was smiling at them.

"We're the land girls come to help Lady Charlton," Emily began.

"I know who you are, my dears," the woman said. "Simpson here has been telling us all about you, and how one of you is a proper toff, too. So what will it be?"

"I wouldn't say no to a gin and lime," Alice said.

Emily had never tried gin, and tried to think what a respectable girl should ask for in a pub. At least she knew she liked cider. "A half-pint of cider, please," she said.

"And me, too," Daisy chimed in.

"Right you are, my dearies," the landlady said.

The old men were still staring.

"Should we go through to the private bar, do you think?" Emily asked. "We don't want to upset your regular customers."

"Regular customers indeed," the landlady said. "We don't get no customers these days, apart from the old geezers here. All the men have gone, haven't they, including my husband. He didn't have to go, silly old bugger." She gave a despairing chuckle. "He were thirty-five, but he said, 'I've got to do my duty, Nell. England expects me to do my duty,' and off he went, leaving me to run this place alone."

"Is he still alive?" Emily asked cautiously.

A spasm of pain crossed her face. "Still alive, all right," she replied, "but only just. He's lost one leg and his lungs are destroyed, and he's still in some hospital near London. I don't know if he'll ever come home, to be frank with you. I try to get up to London to visit him when I can, but it's not easy. I can't leave the pub, can I? It's not making much money these days, but it's the only income I've got." While she talked, she pulled two half-pints of cider and then measured out a gin and lime. "But then, I'm one of the lucky ones, so they tell me. Mrs Soper up at the forge and Mrs Upton at the shop, they've both lost their menfolk. The Reverend Bingley's son was taken. And Mary Brierly's son, which was a hard blow, her being a widow." She pushed the drinks towards them. "There you go, my dears. Get those inside you and you'll feel a lot better."

They carried their drinks to the nearest table and sat down. The landlady came to join them, a glass of beer in her own hand. "It's not often I get someone to talk to these days. Those two over there ain't got two civil words between them. And the rest of the women—well, we're raised not to go near the demon drink, aren't we? Most of them are scared to be seen in a public house. Or too overworked to have the time, or the money. More's the pity. I'm losing money hand over fist, and I'm fair worn out, too." She paused and took a generous swig of her beer. "And this used to be such a lively place before the war. My husband used to say, 'We've got a little gold mine here, Nell.' Lots of day-trippers and ramblers in the summer, and all the farmhands from hereabouts. Now I wonder if things will ever get back to normal." She seemed to realize she had been talking too much and held out her hand. "I'm Mrs Lacey, by the way. Nell Lacey."

"Alice Adams." Alice held out her own hand. "And these two are Emily Bryce and Daisy Watkins."

"You're not from these parts then," Mrs Lacey said, picking up on Alice's cockney accent.

"Me? No, I'm from London."

"My word. That's a powerful long way from home. How do you like it here?"

"I like it just fine, apart from that cottage we've landed in."

"Cottage? Where did they put you then?"

"The witch's place, that's the one," called Simpson from the far table.

"She never put them in there! What was she thinking?" Mrs Lacey looked alarmed.

"The witch's place?" Emily asked. "Is that what it's called?"

Mrs Lacey looked uncomfortable. "Don't pay no heed to him. It's been empty for a long while, that cottage, on account of no one wants to live in it. Some say there's a curse on it, but I don't believe that for a minute. It used to be where they housed the schoolmistress before they built the new school about twenty years ago and Mr Patterson came to be schoolmaster."

"Only women have lived in that cottage, and they all come to a bad end," the other old man said, looking up from his pipe. He seemed to relish spreading that information.

"They have not all come to a bad end, Mr Soper. Don't go putting ideas like that into these ladies' heads."

"What about that Goodstone person? She died, didn't she?"

"Yes, but that was TB. Anyone can catch TB, can't they? Nothing to do with the cottage."

"And don't forget about the witch," he added, waving his pipe at them.

"Well, I grant you that," Mrs Lacey said. She turned back to Emily. "One of them was hanged as a witch long ago."

"Well, that's cheerful, I must say," Alice said.

"Oh, you'll be just fine," Mrs Lacey said, attempting a big smile. "You're only here for a few days, aren't you?"

"How long does it take for the curse to kick in then?" Alice asked.

Mrs Lacey threw back her head and laughed. "You're a rum one, aren't you? That's what we need around here—someone to cheer us up."

Darkness had fallen by the time the three of them walked back to the cottage. There was no moon, and the cold light of the stars did little more than hint at the dark shapes of buildings and trees. A wind had sprung up, a cold one sweeping down from the heights of the moor. Branches creaked and danced above them.

"I hope we can find our way back to the cottage," Daisy said. "It's terrible dark, isn't it? Listen to that wind."

"We'll find our way all right, don't you worry," Alice said. "But we're a daft lot, aren't we? We should have left the box of matches where we could find it. Now we'll have to scrabble around in the dark before we can get a lamp lit."

"Are there any matches?" Emily asked.

"I can't say I remember seeing any," Alice said. "Oh well, it looks like we'll be feeling our way in the dark then."

"I'll ask for some matches and some candles in the morning," Emily said. "There's no light at all up in my bedroom, and I don't know how I'm supposed to make it up and down the stairs."

"Use the jerry, love. Ain't there one under your bed?"

Emily hadn't looked. "Maybe."

"You don't want to try tackling them stairs at night. You'll break your ruddy neck," Alice said.

They reached the cottage door. Its opening creak now sounded unnaturally loud and ominous. They closed it with some difficulty, pushing against the wind.

"You won't get much reading in tonight," Alice tried to joke. "Take them stairs carefully, won't you?"

Emily felt her way across the hall and up the stairs, reluctant to leave the others so far away. She heard them talking and giggling as they got ready for bed, banging her head more than once on the ceiling. Then she undressed and climbed in between her own icy sheets. The wind rattled at her window and moaned down the chimney. Witch's cottage. Only women have lived here, and every one of them came to a bad end. The words echoed around inside her head.

"This too shall pass," she said. "It's only for a week or so, and then Robbie will be coming home and I'll be with him in sunny Australia." And she pictured herself lying in bed beside him, the sweetness of his kisses, the way he had made her feel when they had made love.

In the morning, she would write to him and tell him about the cursed cottage and the visit to the pub, and he would laugh when he read it.

CHAPTER SEVENTEEN

The wind had not died down by morning. It blustered, hitting them full in the face as they made their way up the path to the big house. Mrs Trelawney let them in, saying, "Come in quickly, and close the door, or my bread won't rise properly."

She didn't bother to greet them, and Emily got the feeling she resented the extra work. She ladled out three bowls of porridge, which seemed to have become the standard breakfast fare everywhere they went, but there was also a jug of cream to go with it, and sprinkled with brown sugar, it was quite palatable. Then there was toast and marmalade and plenty of tea, so they felt ready for the day when they went to work.

"I don't think we want to try and push the lawnmower around in this wind," Emily said. "Maybe we should start on the flower beds beside the drive." They brought out hoes and forks and started digging up weeds. They had been allowed to grow unchecked, and it was hard to sort out the flowers that struggled to grow between them. Rose bushes had sent out long suckers that now tangled with bindweed. Emily muttered as thorns dug into her hand. She picked up a pair of shears and cut back the rose. Then she decided that the only thing to do was to prune it right back and let it start over. She had just snipped off a stem when she heard a voice behind her.

"You, girl! What are you doing?" Lady Charlton was standing there, today wearing a woollen shawl over her black dress. She peered through a lorgnette at the rose bush. "You are ruining my roses."

"I'm sorry," Emily said, "but the roses are so tangled with the weeds that this seemed the only way to tackle things."

"That's no way to prune, young woman."

"We're doing our best," Emily retorted. "None of us is a trained gardener. Before this, we've only been digging up potatoes and cutting hay. If someone can show us, we'll be happy to learn how to prune properly."

Lady Charlton blinked with surprise then frowned as she was aware of Emily's upper-class accent. "And who are you, exactly?" she asked, peering at Emily through the lorgnette. "Not a land girl, surely."

"Yes, I am," Emily said. "My name is Emily Bryce."

"Good gracious," Lady Charlton said. "I thought the land girls would be all farmworkers' daughters."

"Not in the least," Emily said. "One of us is from London, Daisy is a servant from a stately home and I myself am the daughter of a judge. And amongst our squad there is a dancer from a show on the pier, a well-spoken middle-aged widow and only two girls who were in any way connected with agriculture before."

"I stand corrected," Lady Charlton said. She raised the lorgnette she wore around her neck and studied Emily. "Emily Bryce, you say?"

"Yes, my lady," Emily replied.

"From these parts? I don't recall running into a Bryce."

"My family lives near Torquay," Emily said.

"You say your father is a judge?" The old lady continued to study her. "What does he think of his daughter becoming a land girl?"

"Not very much." Emily grinned. "But I've actually been quite enjoying it."

Lady Charlton nodded, as if she approved. "Then I appreciate your coming to help with my poor garden. As you can see, it is in desperate need. You've settled in all right, have you? Is the cottage comfortable?"

"I wouldn't call it comfortable, I'm afraid," Emily said.

"What did you expect, the Ritz?" The haughty tone returned.

"No, Lady Charlton, but it would be nice to have some furniture that doesn't break when we sit on it. There are only two old chairs, and one of them collapsed. Apart from that, there is almost no furniture at all."

"I see," Lady Charlton said. "I have to confess I haven't visited the place in many years, but I always seemed to remember it was furnished. Come to think of it, I don't think anyone has lived in it for quite a while. Tell Simpson what you need, and he can round up things that are not in use here."

"Thank you, that's kind of you," Emily said. "And some candles, please. It was quite alarming having to go to sleep in utter darkness."

"I assumed Mrs Trelawney would have taken care of such things. I did let her know you were coming. Tell her what you want."

Emily didn't like to say that getting anything out of Mrs Trelawney would be like wringing blood from a stone. Instead, she murmured, "Thank you," and went back to work.

When Lady Charlton had gone, the other two came up to Emily. "Well done," Alice said. "I heard you telling her a thing or two."

"Simpson is going to find us more furniture," Emily said, "and Mrs Trelawney will give us candles."

"Not without a fight, I expect," Alice said.

By the end of the day, the front beds were cleared and the rose bushes pruned back. As they stood to eye their accomplishments, Emily glanced up at the house. Lady Charlton was standing in the window and nodded her approval.

Later on, they had just finished a bowl of mutton stew with dumplings when Lady Charlton appeared at the kitchen door. They all rose to their feet.

"Continue with your dinner, please," Lady Charlton said. She looked at Emily. "I was wondering if this young woman would care to take a glass of sherry with me when she has finished her meal."

"It's very kind of you, my lady," Emily said, feeling horribly awkward because the others had not been asked.

Alice, as usual, sensed this. "Don't you worry about us, love. We'll see you back at the cottage later."

Feeling the others' eyes upon her, Emily followed Lady Charlton through to the main part of the house, along a draughty hallway and into a large drawing room. A sofa and several Queen Anne chairs were arranged around an enormous granite fireplace in which a fire was burning, even though it was still summertime. A tray with a sherry decanter and two glasses had been put on a low table in front of the fire.

"I know it's an extravagance to keep a fire burning in summer," Lady Charlton said, "but the rooms are so vast in this place, and I feel the cold at my age. Do sit down."

"Thank you." Emily perched at the edge of one of the chairs.

Lady Charlton handed her a glass. "I'm intrigued. What made you decide to become a land girl?"

"I felt I should do what I can to help the war effort," Emily said.

"Hardly a normal occupation for one of your class."

"I wanted to volunteer as a nurse, but they didn't need any more volunteers. They did need land girls."

"What did you parents think of this? They surely can't have approved?"

"They did not." Emily had to smile. "Quite the opposite. They did everything they could to bring me home again."

"But you dug in your heels and stood up to them. Well done. One should make one's own decisions in life."

"I agree, but my parents do not," Emily said. "I'm afraid a great rift has come between us."

"I'm sure they'll relent when this nonsense is all over and you can return home."

"I don't think they will." Emily pressed her lips together, trying not to show emotion. "They do not approve of the man I'm going to marry."

"A rascal, is he? Or not of our class?"

"Not at all. He's a good man. Kind, funny. And his family is quite wealthy. But he's Australian. He doesn't believe in the whole class distinction thing. He doesn't play by our rules. He thinks they are silly."

"And your parents disagree?"

"Oh yes." Emily had to smile now. "It's a pity, but I'm going to marry him, whatever they say."

"You've turned twenty-one?"

"Earlier this summer." *How long ago it seems,* she thought. *Another lifetime.*

"Then I suppose your life is in your own hands, and you are free to succeed or fail on your own terms."

"I wouldn't call marrying Flight Lieutenant Kerr failing," Emily said. "Surely marrying the man one loves is the highest achievement in life?"

"Not all would agree with that. It doesn't always bring happiness to move too far from where we are planted."

"So you would not have left your home for a man you loved?"

"I didn't say that," Lady Charlton replied. "I am merely spouting conventional wisdom. Not everyone has to live by convention, like your Flight Lieutenant Kerr."

A log settled on the fire, sending up sparks.

"You live all alone here, my lady?" Emily asked, changing the subject away from her.

"I do." Lady Charlton sighed. "My husband died ten years ago. He was a good man. A fine man. He threw himself into every activity with enthusiasm. He travelled the world. He was a great collector. And when we inherited this house, he took an active role in the running of the home farm—improving breeding stock, lambing, you name it, and he wanted to be part of it. Well, he was present at a lambing one dreadful spring night. He came home soaked to the skin, caught pneumonia and died. Such a waste."

"I'm so sorry," Emily felt obliged to say. "And you had no children?"

"One son. James. He was a career military man. Officer in the Grenadier Guards. And he had one son as well. My grandson, Justin. He wanted the boy to enlist at the beginning of the war when he turned eighteen, but the boy refused. He said he thought wars were wrong and solved nothing. His father was furious with him. There was a terrible shouting match and the boy walked out. We haven't heard a thing from him since. But we were told that he did do his duty when he was called up, and was sent off to France. However, we have no idea what happened to him. His body could not be found after a particularly fierce offensive, so either he was blown to pieces or he chose that moment to desert. We can only pray it was the former."

"You'd rather your grandson was blown to pieces than escaped?"

"If it meant dishonour, yes. If he deserted and is recaptured, it would mean the firing squad. So yes, I pray he was killed doing his duty."

"And your son?" Emily asked.

Lady Charlton stared into the fire. "My son died in the first year on the Somme, leading a charge over the top. He was buried with full military honours."

She continued to stare into the fire, her face like stone, but her back straight and proud. Then she looked across to Emily. "You must come and take sherry with me every evening you are here. I will welcome the company. Mrs Trelawney has no conversation except for complaints. If I hear about her rheumatics one more time, I feel I shall scream."

Emily laughed. "I would be delighted to take sherry with you, but I feel a little awkward about it, since my companions are not invited. I wouldn't like them to think that I am getting special treatment."

"Do you not believe they would feel ill at ease in a room like this, speaking with someone like me?" Lady Charlton asked. There was a glint of humour in her eyes.

"I suspect you are right, Lady Charlton," Emily agreed.

"Then put it to them that they are welcome to join you if they'd like to. I will wager they will refuse."

The old lady proved to be right.

"Not me, thanks," Alice said, shaking her head violently when Emily extended the offer. "You wouldn't catch me sitting with that old tartar."

"Nor me," Daisy added. "I'd be terrified I'd spill something or say the wrong thing."

"Don't worry about us, ducks," Alice went on, seeing Emily's embarrassment. "Daisy and me will take ourselves off to the pub and have a nice chat with that Mrs Lacey. You're welcome to your sherry with the grand lady in the grand room and having to be so frightfully posh." She put on a fake aristocratic accent.

And so Emily sat with Lady Charlton after their supper the next evening. She learned that Lady Charlton had travelled with her husband for the first twenty years of their marriage, living in Switzerland and as far away as Egypt, India and Mesopotamia, until he inherited the title and house from a distant cousin and had come to be lord of the manor here.

"Sometimes I have cursed that cousin for dying," she confessed. "Until then, we had an exciting life. We thought we couldn't have children, but then James was born to us quite late in life. My husband sent him to boarding school in England at a very young age, insisting it was the right thing to do for boys of our class, but I was really sad that he never saw his parents. So in a way I was glad when we were compelled to come home."

"I long to travel," Emily said. "I am so excited about the journey out to Australia."

"I never had a chance to visit Australia," Lady Charlton said. "I should like to have done so. Now I only visit places when I read." She looked up suddenly. "Do you enjoy books?"

"I do, very much," Emily said.

"Then let me show you our library." Lady Charlton got to her feet. "Come with me."

She led Emily along the long hallway through a door at the far end. Emily gasped. The walls were lined with leather-bound volumes. Dust motes danced in the slanting rays of the setting sun. Around the floor were display tables.

"My husband was a great collector," Lady Charlton said. "He collected everything from Egyptian artefacts to butterflies." She walked over to one of the tables and ran her hand lovingly over the glass.

"If you would like something to read while you are in residence here, feel free to borrow a book from my library."

"Oh no, I don't think I would want to take one of these beautiful books down to the cottage," Emily said, embarrassed at the thought of coming into this lovely room in her muddy uniform. "And I've discovered some books for me to read."

"Really?"

"Yes, I found an old trunk with books in it."

"Oh. An old trunk. Of course." She nodded as if this made sense. "I'd forgotten."

"I plan to teach Daisy and Alice to read. They won't get anywhere in life if they can't."

"You look out for each other. I like that," Lady Charlton said. "I have a feeling that we women will need to support each other in the years to come. We will have no menfolk to take care of us."

Emily returned to the cottage, armed with candles and a box of matches, to find no sign of the other two. She sat on her bed in the fading light and wrote to Robbie in pencil. It was easier than trying to juggle pen and ink. She told him all about the house, about Lady Charlton and the library and the cottage. *We were told it was cursed, and it does have an uneasy feeling to it, but we're only here for a few days and none of us has turned into a frog yet.* She tried to make every sentence funny and light so that he'd smile as he sat on his bunk near the enemy lines.

The other two women came home after dark, delighted to find Emily reading, lying on her bed with a candle on the old trunk.

"Candles!" Daisy exclaimed. "I'm so glad we don't have to fumble around in the dark no more. I have to confess I was a bit scared last night with that wind and all. It didn't sound natural, did it? If Alice hadn't been beside me, I'd have been a nervous nelly."

"And speaking of Nellie," Alice said. "We got along like a house on fire with Nell Lacey. She's a good sort, you know. Worried sick about her husband, but don't complain. None of them do. We met Mrs Soper from the forge, and she's lost her husband and doesn't know what she'll do and who will take over as blacksmith. She has sons, but not near old enough to wield the hammer in the forge. But you know, in spite of everything, we all had a good laugh."

"I'm glad you had a good evening," Emily said, noting their animation.

"We did. Sorry you weren't with us. So you survived your sherry party then." Alice looked at her with pity. "Brave of you."

"She's lonely," Emily said. "She's lost everybody she loved. She has no one." She hesitated, then added, "Do you mind if I take sherry with her every evening after our dinner? I said I couldn't spend too long with her because I want to start teaching you to read better."

"We don't mind, do we, Daisy?" Alice said, giving Daisy a nudge. "Give me a gin and lime and a good natter rather than a sherry any time."

That night, Emily lay in bed, watching the flickering light of her candle play on the ceiling. It was a warm, still evening with no breeze, and sweet scents drifted in through her open window. She could hear Alice and Daisy still talking and laughing downstairs. *It's not so bad here after all,* she thought.

CHAPTER EIGHTEEN

When the three women returned from their work the following day, they found the broken chairs had been replaced with three sturdy ones. There was a rug on the floor and another oil lamp had been provided.

"Thanks to you for getting along so well with the old lady," Alice said. "This place is starting to look quite homely. If we're here much longer, we'll have a sofa and an aspidistra and pictures on the walls."

"I wish we had some more clothes," Emily said. "This uniform needs a good cleaning. I'm getting tired of wearing it, and I feel uncomfortable sitting on Lady Charlton's nice furniture in it."

"I wonder how much longer they'll be needing us as land girls," Daisy said. "I mean, we can't do much in the field during the winter, can we?"

"And from what they are saying at the pub, the war won't go on much longer," Alice said. "The Germans are in complete retreat. Mrs Soper reckons they'll want to make peace before the end of the year."

"Thank God," Emily said, smiling. Robbie would be back, and they'd get married, and she'd have a whole new life to look forward to. She had a sudden idea. "You two should come out to Australia with me," she said. "I've heard it's a wonderful life out there. Plenty of food and sunshine and not enough women to go around."

"We might just take you up on that," Alice said. "I can't see myself going back to the Smoke. Not after this. You don't know how people live there—like rats, all crammed together in dark little streets. That's no way to live, is it?"

"And I'm not going back to Moorland Hall, whatever I do," Daisy said firmly. "Not if it was the last place on earth."

"Was it as bad as that? Worse than digging potatoes?" Emily asked.

Daisy nodded. "It wasn't the work I minded. I was brought up to work hard. It was the master."

"He was unkind?"

"No," Daisy said angrily. "He couldn't keep his hands off the servants. He had his way with one of the maids, Millie, and when she was in the family way, they sent her off somewhere. And then he started looking at me. And one morning, I had to carry the bathwater into his bathroom and he was there, naked. And he grabbed me. I managed to get away, but I'm not going back."

"Of course you shouldn't. Dirty old bastard," Alice said angrily. "Don't you worry, Daisy. Me and Emily will make sure you're looked after. We won't desert you."

"You're such good friends," Daisy said, her eyes tearing up. "I never had good friends before. This has been a proper blessing to me."

On Sunday, there were eggs for breakfast, and they went to church in the village. The church was surprisingly large for the size of the population, and light filtered in through old stained-glass windows. Emily looked up at the saints smiling down at them. The church smelled of old furniture polish, candles and the flowers in vases on the windowsills. She felt a moment of great peace as the tinted light surrounded her, as if it were a personal blessing. Afterwards, they met the Reverend Bingley, who shook their hands and welcomed them officially.

Luncheon was a big meal, a fish pie and marrow in a white sauce. Mrs Trelawney looked more disapproving than ever. "Imagine a Sunday lunch without a roast," she said. "No joint of beef, no leg of lamb or pork. Instead, a bloomin' fish pie! It's an insult, that's what it is."

"It's a very delicious fish pie, Mrs Trelawney," Daisy said quietly. "I really like it."

"Well, I've done my best with what is at hand," the cook conceded. "And there is a good apple pie to follow, from our own apples, mark you."

After lunch, the weather was fine and bright, and they walked up on to the moor. Alice cried out at the sight of the wild ponies appearing on the ridge above then galloping off as the women approached. The heather was in bloom, and the hillside glowed magenta and purple. When they had climbed a way, they stood, looking back. The village, nestled in its hollow, looked like the wooden toy village Emily used to play with. Smoke rose from some of the chimneys. Around it, a patch-work of fields, divided by hedges or stone walls, stretched away into the distance, dotted with white sheep and cream-coloured cows. Far off, they could see more villages, a town and then the haze that crept inland from the sea.

"This is the life, eh?" Alice said. "You don't know how much better I feel now I'm not breathing in all that smoke and dust. I used to wake up every morning coughing. My mum died of bronchitis or something like it. Coughed all the time. I wish I could have brought her here."

"I like it, too," Daisy said.

Emily was looking around, taking in every aspect of the view—the green of the fields and woods, the purple of the hillside, the white dots of sheep. *In Australia, there will just be red earth,* she thought. Would she miss this green and pleasant land? Then she thought of Robbie, his arms around her, making her feel safe and loved. *It will all be worth it,* she told herself.

After a simple cold supper, they walked down to the village.

"Don't you have to join the old lady for sherry?" Alice asked her.

"It's my day off," Emily replied. "I think I'm free to do what I want." All the same, she felt a pang of guilt that Lady Charlton might be sitting all alone, waiting for her in the big empty house.

The pub was shut on Sunday, but the women of the village had assembled on the village green, sitting on the benches below the Celtic cross. Some of them were knitting. Several small children were chasing each other with squeals of delight. The two old men were sitting apart, smoking pipes. Bats flitted through pink twilight. It was a perfect rural picture, Emily thought, until you realized there were no men there, no boys older than about twelve. They were introduced to the women—the shopkeeper and the wives of several farm labourers—and Alice introduced Emily to Mrs Soper, the blacksmith's wife. These women already seemed to know a lot about them, thanks to Alice and Daisy's nightly pub visits.

After a few polite words, the women reverted to local matters. Whose brother or son had come home; whose had not.

"What about your man?" Nell Lacey was asked. "When is he getting out of that hospital?"

"Not for a while," Nell said. "They have to make a wooden leg for him, and his lungs have to improve before they'll let him out."

"When do you plan on going up to London to visit him again?" one of the younger women asked.

Nell frowned. "Who would run the pub if I left? We have to make a living somehow, don't we?"

"At least you have a man who'll be coming home," the blacksmith's wife said bitterly. "What about me? I miss my Charlie something terrible. And it's not just missing him and learning to live without him, is it? I want to know how I'm expected to carry on without him. Who is going to shoe the horses and mend the farm implements? That's what I want to know."

"I know, Mrs Soper. I've been thinking the same thing. Mine may be coming home eventually, but how am I going to take care of him?"

Nell Lacey asked. "I am already run off my feet without having to nurse him in between manhandling the barrels."

There was an awkward silence.

"Are there no men left in the village?" Emily asked. "Apart from the two over there?"

"There's the reverend," the blacksmith's wife said. "But he and his missus keep themselves to themselves, except when she's organizing something for charity. And then there's Mr Patterson at the school. But he don't mix much, do he? Not a great one for conversation."

"So you're living in the cottage, are you?" one of the women asked. "How are you liking it?"

"It's not too bad," Alice said. "Not exactly like home, but we're surviving."

"Have you seen any ghosts yet?" the woman persisted, giving her neighbour a dig in the ribs.

"There aren't any ghosts, Edie. Don't go scaring them like that," Nell Lacey said.

"Of course there are ghosts," the woman went on. "Don't they say that woman runs screaming over the moor? That one that was hanged for being a witch?"

"That's just an old wives' tale," Nell said.

"Well, that's what we are, old wives, isn't it?" the woman said, chuckling.

"No we're not. We're widows, most of us, aren't we?"

Again they lapsed into silence.

"How are you getting on with the old lady then?" The young wife broke the silence, holding a squirming toddler on her lap. "I find her terrifying."

"Emily here gets along with her just fine," Alice said. "She's invited to take sherry every evening."

"Ah well, she would, wouldn't she," Nell Lacey agreed. "She'd want to be with her own kind."

"She must miss her menfolk," the young wife said. "I miss my Johnny something terrible."

"She only has herself to blame, don't she?" Nell Lacey said angrily. "They sent that poor boy to his death."

"The grandson, you mean?" the same young woman asked.

"That's right. Master Justin. As sweet and kind a boy as you'd ever meet. And when he told his father he didn't believe in the war and he wasn't going to fight, well, nobody listened to him. His father was furious, and his grandmother said she was disappointed in him, and between them they made sure he was called up and his request to be a conscientious objector was turned down. Off to the front he went, and that was the last anyone heard of him. Blown to pieces by a grenade, that's what they reckon."

"And the old lady's son is gone, too," someone else commented. "Although he was a different kettle of fish. Hoity-toity like the old lady. Always was a priggish little boy, right from the start. Sent off to some posh boarding school, and when he was home, he wouldn't play with us because we were beneath him, right, Peggy?"

The blacksmith's wife nodded. "Died just the same, didn't he? Buried with full military honours, so they say. But that doesn't bring him back, does it? And now the old lady rattles around that big place and has nobody."

They sat in silence as the sun dipped behind the horizon and a cold wind sprang up.

After a couple of weeks, they had made good progress on the grounds. The lawns around the house had been mown, the front beds cleared of weeds. Some of the larger rhododendron bushes had been cut back. One day, they came in for their midday meal to find a pony and trap outside with a man standing beside it.

"I've been sent to find you young ladies by that Miss Foster-Something," he said. "You're wanted back with the other land girls right away."

"Oh." Emily felt a rush of alarm. Were they about to be disbanded, sent home? In which case, where should she go? Where could she go? "We'd better go and tell Lady Charlton that we are leaving," she said.

"You go. You're teacher's pet," Alice said. "I might nip down to Nell at the pub when we collect our belongings."

Emily went in by the servants' entrance as usual, and didn't like to pass through the swing door unannounced. "Would you go and find Lady Charlton, please, Mrs Trelawney?" she said. "I have to speak to her."

"What's this about?" the housekeeper asked sharply.

"We've been summoned back. We're leaving."

"Oh." The woman couldn't control the smirk that crossed her face. "She will be sad. I'll tell her."

"I'd rather tell her myself, if you don't mind."

"She's in the library, I believe. You know where that is, don't you? She took you there once." There was clear dislike in her voice. *She's jealous,* Emily thought. *She's jealous because Lady Charlton has enjoyed talking to me.*

"Thank you," she said. "And thank you for your delicious meals." Then she pushed open the door and made her way down the main hallway. Another door was open, and she saw that the room was shrouded in dust sheets. The hallway could do with a good sweeping, too, she noticed. There were cobwebs around the light fixtures. She knocked before entering the library. Lady Charlton was standing, lost in thought, staring down at one of the display tables. She looked up in surprise when she saw Emily.

"These are things that my husband brought back from India," she said. "Such fine workmanship, and do you know that gold and silver objects are weighed and sold by the amount of precious metal there, not by the fine craftsmanship. Isn't that strange?"

"I'm sorry to disturb you, Lady Charlton," Emily said. "But we have to leave. We are being called back to join the other WLA members."

"Oh dear." Lady Charlton looked annoyed. "I have been enjoying our little chats."

"Me, too," Emily said. "You have so many fascinating stories."

"They say the war will be ending soon," Lady Charlton said. "And you will marry and go out to Australia."

"Yes, I hope so, very soon," Emily said.

"Will you write to me?" the old woman asked. "I never reached Australia. I'd like to read a first-hand account of your impressions."

"Yes, I'd be happy to."

"And your account of the voyage out. We made that voyage, my husband and I, as far as Singapore once. I found it most interesting—apart from the part when I was seasick in the Bay of Biscay." She smiled.

"I had better go," Emily said. "The trap is waiting for us." She held out her hand. "Thank you for your hospitality."

"Not much hospitality, I'm afraid. I now regret putting you up in a labourer's cottage. I thought you'd all be farm girls, you see. I had no idea—"

"No, it was fine, honestly," Emily interrupted. "I actually came to enjoy it. It's been neglected for a long time, I can see that, but I imagine it could once have been quite cosy."

"Yes." She nodded, and as Emily went to leave, she called after her. "Wait. I should like to give you a little present."

She went over to one of the shelves and took from it a round, brass object. "My husband's compass," she said. "He took it everywhere he went. I'd like to know that you have something to guide your way."

"Oh, but I couldn't . . ." Emily flushed with embarrassment. "Not your husband's."

"He has no need for it any longer. Neither do I," Lady Charlton said. "May it guide you well, as it did my dear husband."

She put the compass into Emily's hand. It felt surprisingly heavy. Emily looked down at the needle, swinging and pointing away from the house. "Thank you. I will treasure this," she said.

She joined Alice and Daisy, who had put away their garden tools. "We'll need to go down to the cottage to collect our things," she told the driver. "It might be easier if you meet us in the lane behind the row of cottages. The path down the garden is horribly rutted, and I don't know if the trap will fit through the gate."

"Right you are then, miss," he said. "And don't you ladies hurry yourselves unduly. That Foster woman, she don't know how long it would take to find you, do she? So I might just pop across to the village shop for the newspaper and a smoke while you are packing up." And he gave them a wink.

They walked down the hill.

"I'm sorry to leave now," Alice said. "I was getting quite used to it here. I wonder where we're off to next. I do hope it's not pigs. Pigs scare me."

"Or cows," Daisy added. "Cows are bigger. And they have horns."

Alice looked at Emily. "You're awful quiet. Don't tell me you're sad to be escaping from your sherry with the old girl?"

"I am, actually," Emily said. "But I was just wondering what I'd do if we find out we're to be going home. I don't seem to have a home to go to."

"We'll work it out. Don't you worry." Alice patted her shoulder.

Emily stood in the attic room, watching stripes of sunlight on the sloping ceiling. She put the last of her toiletry items into her bag, fastened it and gave a sigh as she descended the steep stairs. The pony and trap appeared, and the carter helped them on to the long seats at the back, then handed up their bags. Then he clicked his teeth and the pony set off at a lively trot. They passed the village green, over the packhorse bridge and away. The sun shone down on them, and the trap swayed with a gentle rhythm. Emily closed her eyes.

She opened them when she heard Daisy say, "Oh no."

"Oh no what?" she asked. Then she saw they were holding the newspaper that the carter had bought. They looked at her with stricken faces.

"What is it?" Emily asked again.

Silently, Daisy passed the newspaper across to her. On the front page, one of the headlines read, "Fearless Flyer Crashes Doomed Plane in Field to Save Village." Emily didn't need to read on to know that it was Robbie.

CHAPTER NINETEEN

The news had apparently reached the farm before they did. The other women were waiting and helped Emily down from the trap, murmuring condolences. Miss Foster-Blake came out.

"Emily, my dear. We are all so sorry," she said. "You've had a terrible shock. Come inside and have a glass of brandy."

She led Emily away as though she were a little child and sat her down. It was a complete re-enactment of the scene with her headmistress, the unexpected gentleness from one who had been so strict and severe. Emily felt a big gulp come up into her throat. She tried to swallow it down, but it escaped as a heaving sob. She put her hands to her face and burst into tears.

"I should never have loved him," she gasped between sobs. "If I hadn't loved him, he'd still be alive."

"What are you talking about?"

"Every time I've loved someone, they have died. It's as if I've cursed them with my love."

"Well, that's nonsense, and you know it," Miss Foster-Blake said. "At least you can console yourself by knowing you made his last weeks happy. He died knowing he was loved. Not everybody can say that. And he died doing a noble deed. He gave his life for others. You should be very proud."

"Proud?" Emily looked up, brushing tears from her face. "I don't want to be proud. I want him alive. I read the article. It said he had time to bail out, but the plane would have crashed on to a village full of people. Well, right now, I wish he had bailed out and killed someone else instead. Why did he have to be so bloody noble?"

Miss Foster-Blake didn't even react to the strong language. "You're distraught, my dear. Here, take a sip of the brandy, and then we'll decide what to do next."

She put the glass to Emily's lips like a child and made her drink. Emily gulped, then gasped as the fiery liquid went down.

"Now," Miss Foster-Blake said, "I think the best thing for you would be to go home. Go to a place where you can be taken care of and cherished. You'll need time to grieve and to heal. I'm discharging you early."

"No." Emily shook her head. "You don't understand. I can't go home. My father told me that if I disobeyed him, I was no longer welcome at their house."

"People say a lot of things they don't really mean. I'm sure your parents will change their minds when they see their child in such distress," Miss Foster-Blake said. "Any parent would. I'm sure they have wanted the best for you all along."

"They didn't want me to marry Robbie," Emily said. "Now my mother will gloat and say it was all for the best, and I couldn't stand that."

"So you'd rather stay on here?"

Emily nodded. "I want to work so hard that I don't have time to think. And these women are my family now."

"As you wish," Miss Foster-Blake said. "But my offer still stands. I will send Jenkins to the doctor and have him prescribe a sleeping powder for you today, at least."

Emily allowed herself to be led up to her bunk and tucked in like a small child. As soon as she was left alone, she retrieved the little leather box from under her pillow. She took out the thin gold band and slipped it on to her finger. "Mrs Robbie Kerr," she whispered. The sleeping powder arrived and did the trick. She slept for twelve hours, not hearing the other women come to bed or rise early the next morning.

When she opened her eyes, it was to a rainswept sky that echoed her mood. She retrieved the article in the newspaper. "Brave Australian flying ace, Robert Ferguson Kerr of New South Wales." She kept reading it over and over, as if in doing so she might read a different outcome, that in spite of his plane going down in flames he managed to survive. But the article never changed. He was dead. Gone forever. She would never see that cheeky smile again, never hear that deep Aussie voice saying, "You're my girl."

Miss Foster-Blake poked her head around the bedroom door. "Ah, you are awake. Come and have a good breakfast. The farmer has supplied us with eggs."

Emily sat at the oilcloth-covered table and dipped a finger of toast into a boiled egg, but she found it hard to swallow. Miss Foster-Blake looked at her with sympathy. "You don't have to go back to work right away," she said. "Take a few days off. Go into Tavistock or Plymouth—"

"No!" Emily said more violently than she had intended. "You don't understand. I have to work. I have to work so that I don't have time to think."

"I do understand," Miss Foster-Blake said. "We lost two of my nephews—they were brothers—within a week of each other. Such bright, fun-loving boys. I know a little of your pain. All I can say is that you are amongst friends here. Although I still think that you should be at home. I can easily arrange for it—"

"No," Emily said again, and this time remembered her manners to add, "thank you. Please do not write to my parents or tell them about this."

"They will see it in the newspapers, I'm sure. Your young man was quite a hero. He saved lots of lives." She looked long and hard at Emily's face, noticing the defiantly stuck out chin. Then she sighed. "But I respect your decision." She put a hand on Emily's shoulder. "When you have finished your breakfast, you shall come and help me with paperwork. They are sending us new recruits."

"What will you do with them?" Emily asked. "Isn't the growing season almost over?"

"Winter vegetables to be planted," Miss Foster-Blake said. "And some of these girls will train in forestry. Sawing up fallen trees and lopping off dangerous branches. That sort of thing."

The women returned from their work, red-faced from the wind and soaking wet.

"Blimey, I thought I'd be blown away out there," Alice said.

"What were you doing?"

"We're picking apples, love. I was up a ladder, throwing them down to the ladies below, and there was this ruddy great gust of wind. If I hadn't clung on to the tree, I'd have been a goner."

"She does exaggerate," Ruby said. "The tree was scarcely taller than us."

The others laughed, and Emily tried to smile. She looked around. "Where's Maureen?" she asked.

"Oh blimey, you didn't hear about her?" Alice glanced at the others.

"What happened?" Emily asked.

"She sneaked out without permission and went into Plymouth to meet a sailor," Ruby said with great glee. "And Miss Foster-Blake caught her climbing in through the window in the early morning. Dismissed her on the spot. Sent her packing."

"So where did she go?" Emily asked, wondering what she would have done in the same circumstances.

"Home to Ireland, so I believe. She was asking for trouble, that one, wasn't she? Always after the boys."

"I, for one, will miss her," Alice said. "She was always cheerful, wasn't she? Made us laugh."

I'll miss her, too, Emily thought, and the unfairness of the situation struck her. Maureen had done what she had done—stayed out all night. But Miss Foster-Blake had believed Emily to be a good girl and Maureen to be a bad one. She had accepted Emily's excuse even though—Emily felt her cheeks flushing—she and Robbie had done what Maureen probably had not. And the memory of that sweet, passionate moment flooded back to her. *I will never lie in a man's arms again,* she thought.

The next day, she awoke with the others as early morning sun streamed in through the window. She sat up, reaching for her toilet bag, and then it all came flooding back to her. Moving like an automaton, she grabbed her bag and stumbled after the others into the bathroom. She found it impossible to swallow more than a mouthful of the stodgy porridge, and was hardly aware of lining up with the others as they climbed on to an old wagon to be taken to the apple orchard. The wagon had been used for dung, and the women were crammed close together. Emily found the smell, coupled with the unwashed odour of the women, to be overwhelming. She leaned out as far as she could, gulping in the fresh, cool breeze. *I would be better off at home,* she thought in a weak moment. She pictured her pink and white bedroom, the lace curtains, the sweet smell of roses wafting in through her window. And long soaks in a big bathtub, and lots of dresses hanging in her wardrobe and dainty shoes to wear. She had almost convinced herself that she wanted to go home, until she pictured her mother's triumphant face. Her mother telling her that she was better off without Robbie and now she could look for someone more suitable. No, that could not be borne.

The apple picking was pleasant enough, although the weather was turning colder. They wore jerseys under their tunics. The jerseys were made of coarse wool and itched terribly, but it was better than being cold.

"What wouldn't I give for a nice soft silk blouse or a good fine-wool jumper," Mrs Anson confided to Emily as they worked together, putting apples into baskets carefully without bruising them.

Emily glanced at her. "How long had you been married when your husband died?" she asked.

"Sixteen years," she replied.

"You had no children?"

"We were not blessed with any, I'm afraid, although I should have loved a big family. I was an only child."

Emily paused, then asked, "How long did it take you to get over—"

"My husband's death?" She shook her head. "One never gets over it, my dear. There will always be a hole in my heart where he used to be, but one comes to terms with it. You tell yourself that you are just one of many. So many other wives and mothers and sweethearts are feeling the same pain. You just have to get on with life and hope that eventually the pain will dull a little. And it does. I can think of my husband quite fondly now, remembering good times. Time is the only healer."

Emily nodded and went back to work.

The weather brightened, and the apple picking became a pleasant occupation. After the best apples had been selected, the ones with bruises or defects were also put into baskets to be made into cider. When the last tree was stripped, Emily felt a shiver of fear that they would be told they were no longer needed. And then what? What would she do when the land girls were disbanded? Where would she go? Clarissa had said that women would need to take over men's jobs when the war ended. If she went to a big city—Bristol or even London—would she find a job and be able to support herself? The idea was alarming, but at the same time exciting.

I'm an educated girl, she thought. Her teachers had urged her to go on to university, but then the war had come and Freddie had died, so university had become impossible. But a job in an office, or even teaching in a small school. They would be possible, surely?

But the apple picking was not their last assignment. Miss Foster-Blake looked stern when she addressed them at supper that night. "I'm afraid I have a real challenge ahead for you. A nearby farmer is readying his fields to plant winter crops, mainly onion sets, but also cabbages and beetroots. The fields will need to be ploughed first."

There was a collective groan. None of them had had much success with ploughing.

"Will he supervise?" Mrs Anson asked. "Does he have a tractor?"

"He has a team of horses, but he can no longer do the ploughing himself as he has come home from the front with compromised lungs. He will advise."

"A fat lot of good that is," Alice said. "That ruddy plough was almost as big as me."

"Perhaps this one will be easier," Emily said.

"I don't mind doing the ploughing," Maud said. "I'm the biggest one here, and the strongest, too."

"Good for you, Maud," Miss Fraser-Blake said.

The girl looked absurdly pleased, as if nobody had ever told her she was good at anything before.

They set out for the farm. It was close to the edge of Dartmoor, in a bleak and treeless situation. The women were silent as they climbed out of the back of the van. Wind swept down from the heights.

"I wish we'd remembered to wear our mackintoshes," Mrs Anson muttered to Emily. "This wind goes straight through the tunic, doesn't it?"

"It's certainly cold for September," Emily agreed. "But as soon as we try pushing that plough and planting onions, I imagine we're going to be warm enough."

The farmer met them and led them to a team of massive Clydesdales, standing impatiently in front of a plough. He was a big-boned countryman, a Clydesdale himself rather than a thorough-bred, but his face betrayed that he was in pain, and he wheezed when he spoke to them.

"Good of you to come, ladies," he said. "I were worried we'd never get the fields planted this year and we'd all starve come spring. I've got four little 'uns at home, and I hate to be letting my family down."

"We'll do our best for you," Mrs Anson said. "But we have to warn you that we're not all farm girls. We've had little training and experience."

"Don't you worry, my lovey," he said in his rich Devon accent. "You get them onions and cabbages in the ground and I'll be happy as a sandboy."

He led the plough out to a fallow field. Maud took one handle. Emily looked around at the others. "I suppose I'm the tallest," she said. "I should take the other handle."

They set off. The horses were doing the pulling of the old cast-iron plough, but it was still hard to steer it and keep a straight furrow. Emily's heart was thumping and she gasped for breath. *Why did I volunteer to do this?* she asked herself. *It's really too much for me.*

"Are you all right?" Maud asked when they came to the end of the first furrow and stopped to take a breather. "You look a funny colour."

"I'm not feeling too well," Emily said. "I think that rabbit stew last night upset my stomach."

"I can manage on my own," Maud said.

"Of course you can't," Emily replied. "It's almost too much for two of us. I'll be all right. I didn't fancy much breakfast this morning, so I'm probably just hungry. Come on, let's get going again. It looks like rain."

They started back again across the field. Other women were already breaking up clods, hoeing up weeds and raking the turned furrow smooth.

"Nice work, ladies," the farmer called to them. "I know that old plough is a bit of a bugger to steer. I meant to get me one of them fancy tractors after the war. Now I'm not sure we can even keep the farm. My oldest boy is only ten. I'll have to wait a while until he's big enough to help with the big chores, although they're all good little helpers in their way. My wife, too, bless her."

Emily wanted to say that she'd had enough, but she couldn't.

"Should I take over for one of you?" Daisy asked.

"No, I can keep going," Maud said, "but I don't know about Emily here. She doesn't feel too well."

"I'll be all right," Emily said. She started off down the third furrow. There was a strange singing noise in her head. Lights flashed in front of her eyes and her legs buckled under her.

CHAPTER TWENTY

When Emily opened her eyes, she was in a strange kitchen, sitting with her head between her knees. As she sat up, she saw children staring at her with fascinated, worried expressions. A woman with a fresh, friendly face was standing over her. "Here, my love," she said. "Have a cup of tea. That ploughing were too much for you. I told Bert that he couldn't expect young women to do the job, but it were our only chance to get the fields planted, see."

"I'm so sorry." Emily tried to sit up. "I just haven't been feeling too well. If I can drink the tea and maybe have a piece of bread I'll be all right again, ready to go back to work."

"You'll certainly do no such thing," the farmer's wife said. "I can see you're from a good family, not brought up for hard work like we are. I told Bert that I'd try to handle the ploughing, but he didn't want me to, seeing as I'm in the family way again. I always feel terrible the first few months—dizzy, off my food, can't stand the smell of cooking . . ."

Emily stared at her. Dizzy, off her food—was it possible? Why had she been so naive that she had never considered it before? But it was over a month since she and Robbie . . . and during that time, she had not had a return of the little monthly visitor.

I'm pregnant, she realized. *I'm going to have Robbie's baby.* She felt a fleeting moment of elation—that the baby would be something to remember him by—before reality and panic set in. What was she going to do? Where was she going to go? If she went home, what would her parents say? She sat, sipping at the big blue-and-white-striped mug of tea, trying to calm her racing thoughts. She couldn't tell anybody. They would only have a few more weeks at the most before they were dismissed for the winter, and then she'd decide what to do next.

The farmer's wife wouldn't let her leave the kitchen until the others came in for their midday meal. Then she ladled out big bowls of split pea soup, which the others ate with relish. Emily couldn't stand the smell and only pretended to eat.

"What's the matter?" Alice asked.

"I think I must have some kind of stomach grippe," Emily replied. "Something I ate."

"I'm not surprised, with what we've been fed recently. I wish we were back with Mrs Trelawney's cooking again. I'd even face the old lady and that cold, damp cottage for a big helping of her shepherd's pie."

Emily's stomach churned at the mention of shepherd's pie, but she found herself thinking of Lady Charlton and the cottage. Yes, she had been happy there.

After they had finished their meal, Emily was feeling better, and went outside to work with the others. She opted to plant the onion sets, bending to press them into the moist ground. She felt quite well again, and wondered if perhaps she had been wrong after all. Maybe it was some kind of stomach upset and she was getting over it. That evening, she ate a hearty meal of steamed meat pudding and cauliflower, followed by stewed rhubarb and custard, and fell asleep easily enough.

The next morning, she had to rush to the lavatory, where she threw up last night's meal. This confirmed her suspicions. She didn't know much about having babies, but she had overheard one of their friends complaining about morning sickness and how she felt right as rain by midday.

I have to know, she decided. But she could hardly leave the other women to do the work. She did her share all week, and then on Friday afternoon they were released early. The farmer was pleased with their progress and said he'd take them into Tavistock to give them a chance to do some shopping or have a cup of tea at a cafe. They were all pleased about this, although it was too bad there was no cinema in Tavistock, and they couldn't go all the way in to Plymouth. Once there, they split up, some to the haberdashers for new handkerchiefs, some to the chemist for sweet-smelling soap.

"Where are you off to?" Alice said to Emily as the latter tried to slip away. "I'll come with you."

"I thought I'd go to the bookshop," Emily said. "I don't have anything to read."

"When do we ever get time to read?" Alice demanded.

"Saturday and Sunday are coming up and I've nowhere to go."

"In that case, I think I'll see what Daisy and Ruby are doing," Alice said. "You wouldn't catch me dead in a bookshop."

The moment Alice had headed after the disappearing girls, Emily slipped around the corner and located a building with a brass plate saying, "D.M. Packer, MD." She let herself in to find an empty waiting room. A worried-looking woman, who was probably the doctor's wife, appeared and looked surprised to see her. "How did you get in?"

"The front door was unlocked," Emily said. "Isn't this the doctor's surgery?"

"It is, but surgery hours are not until six this evening."

"Oh." Emily looked crestfallen. "So is the doctor out on his rounds then?"

"He's just come back after morning rounds and is taking a late lunch," the woman replied. "If you'd like to leave your name and come back later . . ."

"I can't." Emily felt close to tears. "I'm with the Women's Land Army, and we are being picked up in an hour's time. I just hoped that . . ." Her voice trailed off.

The woman's expression softened. "I could see if he might spare a moment if the problem is not too complicated. We're very grateful for all that you ladies are doing, keeping the farms going around here. Wait one minute."

Emily waited. Then another door opened and the woman said, "The doctor will see you, my dear. This way."

The doctor shared a worried expression with his wife. He was in late middle age and looked tired. Emily felt guilty that she had disturbed his lunchtime rest.

"I'm so sorry to take you from your luncheon," she said.

"I'd pretty much finished. You just disturbed my after-meal pipe." He managed a smile. "And I should be rationing myself. Tobacco's hard to get anyway. Now what seems to be the problem?"

"I'm wondering how soon you can tell if you are pregnant?" Emily felt her cheeks burning.

"You think you might be in the family way?" he asked. "We can't tell for sure until we can actually hear a heartbeat, but I'd have a pretty good idea after about six weeks. How far along do you think you are?"

"About six weeks," Emily confirmed.

"Right. If you take off that tunic and hop up on the table, I'll take a look at you."

Emily did so, squirming in embarrassment as she took off her outer garments. The doctor gave her a thorough examination that was even more embarrassing. "Any symptoms?" he asked. "Nausea? Dizziness? Vomiting?"

"All of the above," Emily confessed.

"And tender breasts?"

Emily put her hand to one and reacted with surprise. "Yes, as a matter of fact."

"And they seem bigger than normal?"

"I think so."

He smiled then, making him look a lot younger. "Then, my dear, I think it's fairly conclusive." He glanced down at her hand that still wore Robbie's band. "Is your husband serving abroad? I take it he was home on leave."

"He's dead," Emily said bleakly. "He was in the Royal Air Force. A pilot. His plane crashed."

"I'm very sorry," the doctor said. "So it's up to you to make sure that a healthy baby carries on his name, right?"

Emily nodded, too full of emotion to speak. The child would not bear Robbie's name. But at least she knew the truth now. All she had to do was decide what happened next.

She came out to see Alice waiting on the high street. She waved when she saw Emily. "Where did you get to?" she asked. "I popped into that bookshop and they said they hadn't seen you."

"Oh, I just wandered around," Emily replied.

Alice frowned. "Is there something you're not telling me?" she asked. "You've been acting strangely. Of course, I can understand that you're still dealing with your man's death. I know it takes a while to come to terms with that. I couldn't think about my Bill without an actual physical pain in my heart for the longest time. So I do know what you're going through."

"You don't know it all, Alice," Emily said. She took a deep breath. "I've just seen the doctor. I'm going to have a baby."

"Ah." Alice nodded. "I wondered as much. I heard you chucking up your breakfast. Well, that's a bit of a bugger, isn't it?"

Emily had to laugh at her choice of language. "More than a bit of a bugger, Alice. It's the worst thing that could happen. I have no idea what I'm going to do next."

"Go home to your folks, that's what I'd say."

"But you don't know my parents." Emily shook her head violently. "My father already told me I was no longer welcome at home when I disobeyed them and stayed working in the fields."

"I'd give it a try anyway, duck," Alice said. "I don't believe any parent would leave their child in the lurch when something as bad as this has happened." Then she wagged a finger. "You know what? Tell them you and Robbie got secretly married. They won't approve, but at least it will be more respectable."

"I couldn't lie to them!"

"It might make things easier. Tell everyone you were secretly married. Just call yourself Mrs Robbie Kerr. So many men are dead, who's to know the difference?"

"I don't know." Emily hesitated, chewing at her lip. "My father is the sort who would contact Somerset House and demand to see the wedding certificate."

"They might find it easier to go along with the lie, for the sake of respectability," Alice said. "Are you going to tell the other girls?"

Emily shook her head. "I can't. Especially not Miss Foster-Blake. She'd despise me. So please don't say anything."

"You'll have had some of them putting two and two together and making four if they've heard you in the lav throwing up," Alice said. "And the fainting."

"I suppose so. But we haven't much longer, have we? If I can just keep going until we're released for the winter, then I'll have time to work out what to do next."

"Miss Foster-Blake said we will have a free weekend coming up after we've finished the planting," Alice said. "Why don't you go home then, test which way the wind is blowing, you know? See if you'd be welcome or not. I'm betting they'll welcome their only daughter home with open arms."

"If only you are right," Emily said.

Alice put a tentative hand on Emily's arm. "And if not, we'll be here for you."

Emily nodded, swallowing back tears. Until recently, she had never allowed herself to cry. Now tears were always just below the surface.

CHAPTER TWENTY-ONE

Autumn came on with a vengeance. Leaves turned to yellow, then brown, and soon they swirled in the wind. Luckily, the ploughing was done and the last of the winter crops planted.

"Well done, girls," Miss Foster-Blake said. "You can be proud of what you have done for these farmers and for England. Not long now, I suspect, before we are given permission to send you home, at least for the winter. And with any luck, the war will be over when the spring comes, and we can all return to our normal lives."

An old bus took those who were going home to the station. Alice and Daisy were staying behind, as were some of the others. Ruby was in tears at the thought of seeing her mum and dad again. Emily felt something akin to panic. She still didn't know if she was doing the right thing in going home. How could she tell her parents the truth? What would they say? She had no idea. She alighted from the train at Torquay station and caught a bus to her parents' village. It was a grey, blustery day, and the wind swept her along as she walked up the lane to her house. As she passed the convalescent hospital, she heard the sound of men's voices and laughter. She peered through the gate. Some of the patients were having an impromptu football match. One had a bandage around his head, another an arm still in plaster, but they were playing with enthusiasm. As she stared down the gravel drive at the front of the house, she saw a figure crossing the lawn—a redheaded man on crutches. An absurd hope leapt in her heart. He hadn't died, just been badly wounded. She opened her mouth to call out his name, but he turned to look in her direction and she saw that it was a stranger.

She made herself keep walking until she pushed open the front gate of her parents' house and started up the perfectly raked drive. Old Josh came around the side of the house, pushing a wheelbarrow. "Well, it's never Miss Emily! Welcome home," he said. "My, but you're looking smart in your uniform."

"Not really, Josh," she said. "The uniform is in sore need of cleaning. I've worn it for the past three months."

"Ask Mrs Broad to take care of it for you," he said. "Your mum and dad will be so surprised to see you. I reckon they both miss you a whole lot."

"I hope so," she said. Instead of opening the front door, she rang the bell. Florrie answered it, and her face broke into a beaming smile.

"Miss Emily. It's you! What a treat. Come on in."

"Who is it, Florrie?" came her mother's strident voice from the drawing room.

"It's Miss Emily, come home to us at last," Florrie called.

Emily's mother emerged, paused in the doorway and stood looking at her. Emily sensed her indecision, as if she wanted to rush forwards and embrace her daughter, but she wasn't going to give that daughter the satisfaction of knowing she had been missed. Instead she said, "So, you've returned to the fold, have you? Expecting a warm welcome?"

"I didn't quite know what to expect, Mummy," Emily said. "But I had a couple of days off, so I thought you might like to know how your daughter was faring."

"So you're not home for good then?"

"No, I have to be back on Monday morning," Emily replied.

Her mother still stood poised in the doorway. Then she said, "Well, I suppose you'd better come in. Florrie, you may bring us some tea. And tell Cook to see if she can rustle up some meat. I don't suppose Miss Emily has had a decent meal in months."

"Actually, we've been eating quite well," Emily said as she followed her mother into the sitting room. "Lots of stews. And plenty of rabbit."

"Rabbit? How disgusting."

"Well, they are a pest on the farms, so we're doing everyone a favour by eating them," Emily said. "Rabbit stew really isn't bad."

"Well, I can assure you we will not be reduced to rabbit tonight." She sank into one of the armchairs.

"Where's Daddy?" Emily asked as she perched at the edge of the sofa, looking out on to the garden. "Not working on a Saturday, surely?"

"No, he went for a walk to buy the newspaper," her mother said. "The boy delivered the wrong one. We've a new newspaper boy. The other one volunteered at sixteen. I suppose he thought he was doing something brave, not foolish. And this one is not very bright. He should know that a family like ours would never take anything except the *Times*." She gave Emily a withering look. "And speaking of newspapers, we read about that Australian you were keen on. I warned you, didn't I? I said he'd come to a bad end."

"Hardly a bad end, Mummy." Emily swallowed back her anger and forced her face to stay calm and composed. "He died a hero, saving a whole village."

Mrs Bryce gave a patronizing smile. "My dear girl, that is all just war propaganda. That's what they always say—he died a hero. He died instantly and didn't suffer. All lies to make everyone feel better, feel that this ridiculous war has been worth something." Her voice cracked with emotion, and she put a hand up to her mouth. "I'm sorry. Stupid of me. I still miss your brother. So does Daddy. Such a stupid waste." Then she composed herself. "But for you it's all for the best, isn't it? I mean, you could never have taken a chap like that seriously, never gone to live in

Australia. They say the war will be over soon and the young men will be coming home. We can start making plans for you. Maybe a sort of late season in London?"

"Mummy, did it never occur to you that I might want to make my own way in life and not marry a man of your choice?" Emily heard her voice rising now. "Besides, how many men will actually be coming back? And in what condition? Certainly not what you'd call a good catch!"

She looked around as Florrie came in with a tea tray. "Heavens," Emily said. "What dainty little cups. One forgets. I'm used to great big pottery mugs these days. And slices of bread the size of doorsteps."

She helped herself to a biscuit and savoured the delicate taste. As she looked across the room and out to the manicured lawn of the garden, she thought how strange it was. She had taken this life for granted. In truth, she had longed to escape from it, longed to know what the real world was like. But now that she was about to face the grim reality of that world, to find out if she would be an outcast forever, she longed to return here, to a place of order and beauty and safety. At this moment, she decided she'd even be willing to put up with her mother's judgemental ways. But what would her mother think about the baby? Would she worry what her friends might say? Could Emily really pull it off to make the world believe she was a war widow, just like so many others? She stole a glance at her mother's self-satisfied face, her hair twisted into a perfect chignon at the back of her head, a string of pearls at her throat.

"Goodness, child, we'll be having luncheon soon," Mrs Bryce said as Emily helped herself to three more biscuits.

Emily couldn't tell her that they were necessary to combat the nausea that was threatening. Instead, she said, "Mummy, I haven't had a treat like this for several months. And we work so hard that we're always hungry."

"Working in the fields like peasants! I saw you, covered in mud and filth. I have never been more ashamed."

"Ashamed? That my work is feeding people in cities who would otherwise starve? Would you be ashamed if I was like Clarissa and was covered in blood from saving soldiers' lives?"

Mrs Bryce flushed. "There were other ways you could have served your country. Dignified ways, proper for a girl of our class. You could have taken the place of a missing man in that solicitor's office."

"I did what was needed when I signed up," Emily said, "and in spite of the hard work, I've enjoyed it. I've enjoyed the camaraderie of the other women, and the feeling of accomplishment when we complete a task."

"You will presumably want to come back home when the war ends and you are released from duty?" Mrs Bryce asked stiffly. From the tone of her voice, Emily couldn't tell whether her mother was hoping for a positive or negative answer to this question.

"It depends on several things," Emily said. "Mainly on whether you and Daddy would welcome me back."

"You upset your father and me with your ungrateful disobedience," Mrs Bryce said. "I have been a bundle of nerves, worrying about you; worrying about that Australian you insisted on seeing. I don't know how I feel now. Of course you are my daughter, and as such I shall always feel an obligation towards you. But I don't know if I want a headstrong girl constantly fighting against my wishes and suggestions, constantly ignoring her parents' advice when they know better."

"I see," Emily said.

"Do you want to come home? To go back to your old life here, in your parents' home?"

"I'm not sure yet," Emily said. "I may not be released from service for quite a while. I don't suppose the men will return overnight, and so many have been lost. They may need the Women's Land Army to help with the crops for some time to come."

"So you see a future for yourself working in the fields then?"

"I am not thinking beyond one day at a time, Mummy." Emily got to her feet. "I think I'll go up to my room and see which of my clothes I might want to take with me."

"Take with you? For what occasion? Do they have a fieldworkers' ball? Or tea dance?" And she gave a brittle laugh.

"I am heartily sick of the uniform, that's all," Emily said. "It is stiff and heavy and not that warm on cold days. I'd welcome wearing something different on a day off."

She left the room before her mother could ask her anything more. Once up in her room, she stood, taking deep breaths to calm herself, letting the tranquillity of the soft colours wash over her. It would never work, would it? If she came back here, she would have to live with her mother's scorn every day. She'd be told what a scoundrel Robbie had been to take advantage of her. "Now do you see why we tried to protect you?" her mother would say triumphantly. Could she endure it? She gave a big sigh. There might be no other choice.

She opened her wardrobe and ran her hands over the delicate silks and soft woollens. How many of them would she ever wear again? She went across to her writing desk and stared out of her window. There, in the bushes—that was where Robbie had first come into the garden. She pictured it clearly, his strawberry blond hair in rakish curls, the way his eyes lit up when he saw her. It seemed impossible to believe that he'd never smile at her again. A stiff breeze blew up, sending leaves flying from the trees and leaving behind dead and bare branches.

When she came downstairs again, her father had returned home. He had already been told that she was in the house. He was sitting in his armchair in the drawing room, the *Times* open on his knee. His face had that stern but just look on it that Emily was sure he practised for addressing people in his court.

"So the penitent has returned, tail between her legs, eh?" he said. "I told your mother you'd be back soon enough. She's been quite upset these last months, you know. Extremely upset. And now you want to carry on as if nothing has happened—all water under the bridge, is that it?"

"No, Daddy," Emily said. "I only came home because I have two days' leave and I thought you might want to know how I've been faring."

"I see. Then you are not home for good?"

"Not at the moment, no." She took a deep breath. "We have not been discharged yet."

"Well, you will be soon enough." He wagged a finger in her direction. "That devil the Kaiser is on the run, and we're going to make him pay for what he's put us through. It will all be over in a month or so, you mark my words. And then I suppose I can see if there might be a job for you with one of our acquaintances. I can quite understand that a bright girl like you doesn't want to spend her life at home waiting for a husband who might never show up these days."

Emily didn't know what to say. Her father took her silence to be submission. "I expect your mother will be glad to have you home again. Dashed lonely for her. Only her charity work to keep her going."

The gong summoned them to the dining room, where they were served a clear beef broth with croutons, followed by steamed plaice with a parsley sauce. After months of stews, it tasted heavenly. But the atmosphere at the table was still decidedly frosty. Her father slurped his soup, getting a disapproving glance from his wife. Otherwise, there was silence.

"So what news from your friends and acquaintances, Mummy?" Emily asked eventually, finding the silence overwhelming. "Any good news?"

"I can't say that there is," Mrs Bryce said. "Well, the Thomas boy has been invalided out and he's home, so that's a relief to Myrna Thomas. But he might have shell shock, which will be worrying."

"Shell shock," her father said in a disgusted tone. "I don't believe in this shell shock. It's just an excuse to get out of fighting. Something no doctor can detect during an examination."

"I heard from a nurse that some of the patients cry at night at the convalescent home," Emily said. "There must be something wrong with them."

"Weaklings, that's what. Brought up too soft. Pampered by doting parents. Your brother would never have given in to shell shock, I can tell you that."

There was another awkward pause. "And what about the Morrisons? Do you see them these days?"

She detected a hesitation, an awkwardness. Mr Bryce cleared his throat. "I suppose you'll hear about it eventually, so I might as well tell you. Mildred Morrison has been a very stupid girl. She's going to have a baby, can you imagine. No husband, I have to tell you."

"Phoebe Morrison is dying of shame," Mrs Bryce chimed in, "but I always said the girl had a flighty look to her, didn't I? They should never have sent her to that progressive school. All that interpretive dance and those play readings. It's not good to fill a girl's head with too much of that stuff. But I never thought she'd go completely off the rails like that."

"What's going to happen to her?" Emily found it hard to say the words.

Mrs Bryce shrugged. "They've sent her away, naturally. To one of those homes, one gathers. I mean, the scandal would ruin them. No one would ever want to do business with her father again. And if they are lucky, she can return to the fold, and her parents can claim she was off doing war work."

"Only the cat is already out of the bag," Mr Bryce added. "If you know, Marjorie, then probably the whole world knows."

"You are not insinuating that I'm a gossip, are you?"

"Of course not, my dear. I am merely saying that whoever told you has told other people, and you know the way word spreads in rural places like this."

"Anyway, I shall have to cut them from our social list," Mrs Bryce said.

"I don't know why they've been so lenient with the girl," Mr Bryce snapped. "Her father should have shown her the door, cast her out completely. That's what I would have done."

"And what will become of the child?" Emily asked, proud of the way she was staying so composed.

"Adopted, one presumes," Mrs Bryce said. "Or else an orphanage. The Morrisons certainly won't want anything to do with it."

Emily looked down at her plate, at the now-congealing white sauce, and swallowed back bile. She felt as if she could vomit at any moment. Well, Alice had told her to see which way the wind was blowing, and now she knew. It was not in her direction.

Emily wasn't sure how she got through the rest of the day. She stood in the pleasant sunlight of her room, taking in every little familiar aspect: the silk eiderdown that she used to snuggle under at night; the picture of a Swiss lake on the wall; the dolls still sitting on a shelf, observing her with their stiff, haughty expressions. How could she possibly choose what to take with her? How did you pack a whole life into a small suitcase? *Be practical,* she told herself. *Only things you really need.* She spent the afternoon in her room, going through her wardrobe and drawers and wondering which items she could wear in the future. She realized her fashionable dresses were all made to wear with a corset. Even without a spreading waistline, she doubted she could ever fit into them again. But she chose a serge two-piece and a couple of plain dresses that could be altered, as well as petticoats, stockings and warm jackets. Then she looked at her bookcase and ran her hand over the dear, familiar titles from her childhood. Of course, she couldn't carry books with her.

But she would take her jewellery. She had been given some nice pieces for her twenty-first, and had inherited a couple of family pieces, too. She might have to sell them one day. She took them out of the jewel case and tucked them into the toe of her slipper.

She wondered if her parents would send her things on to her if she ever found herself settled somewhere. She realized now that she could never tell them. She'd have to make some kind of excuse. Another kind of war work that was sending her abroad—to Belgium or France, maybe, to help with the repatriation of refugees when the war ended. Yes, that would do nicely. And she'd be moving around. She'd write when she could.

But she couldn't say that lie to their faces. Instead, she played the dutiful daughter all through the dinner of steak and kidney pie, which she found horribly rich. The thick red gravy and pieces of kidney were almost impossible to swallow.

"Lost your appetite, have you?" her father asked. "I should have thought work in the fields would have given you a healthy appreciation for food."

"Oh, I've been eating lots, Daddy," she said. "It's just that I've never liked kidneys, and now I've been working on farms and have seen animals slaughtered, I'm afraid it's rather put me off."

"Absolute nonsense. Kidneys are good for you. Lots of iron. Eat up."

She forced herself to chew a few bites, then hid the rest under her cabbage. The apple crumble and custard went down more easily, and the glass of port after the meal did settle her stomach a little.

The next morning, she made the excuse of having to meet the other women at the station to get a ride back to their hostel. She had asked Florrie to bring down a suitcase from the attic and she carried this with her.

"What's this?" her father asked as she carried it out to the motor car. "Planning for a long stay?"

"No, Daddy. Just some of my own clothes for days off and some of my books that I miss reading. It's awfully boring in the evenings."

"I imagine it would be. I can't see that those farm girls would have much in the way of conversation. Still"—he patted her knee as he climbed into the car beside her—"it will all be over soon, won't it?

And I'll start fishing around for a proper job for you. You should definitely learn to operate a typewriting machine. Lady secretaries will be in demand, I suspect. And after your stint in the fields, you shouldn't find the typing too taxing."

They pulled up outside the station.

"Goodbye, Daddy," Emily said, and kissed him on the cheek. She stood watching as he drove away, then she followed the porter out to the platform.

CHAPTER TWENTY-TWO

When Emily arrived back at the farm and was carrying her suitcase upstairs, Miss Foster-Blake appeared in the hallway below her. "A word with you, please, Miss Bryce, when you have deposited your things."

Emily's heart lurched. What could she have done wrong? She was back in good time. She had had permission to go. She deposited her suitcase under the bunk, hung her mackintosh and hat on the peg and stuck the hairpins back in her hair before going downstairs.

Miss Foster-Blake was sitting at her desk in the little room that served as her office. She motioned Emily to pull up a chair. "You had a pleasant visit home, I take it?"

"A little strained, if you want to know," Emily replied. "My parents still make it clear that they do not approve of my disobeying them."

"So what will happen when this assignment concludes?" Miss Foster-Blake asked. "Will you return home and be the dutiful daughter?"

"I . . . I'm not sure yet," Emily replied. "I am not sure what I am going to do."

"I know, Emily," the woman said quietly.

Emily looked up in horror.

"Alice told me," she went on, "and before you blame Alice, it was I who confronted her and wheedled the truth out of her. I suspected, you see. I've seen girls in your condition before. Those early morning rushes to the lavatory. That time you fainted."

Emily sat silent.

"I want you to know that I am not judging you. God knows you loved the young man. He intended to marry you. And so many young women have found themselves in your condition. I only want to help, Emily."

Emily looked up in surprise. The tone was so unlike the brisk sergeant-major demeanour she associated with Miss Foster-Blake. "I don't know what to do," she said.

"Did you tell your parents?"

"Fortunately no. They were talking about a girl of our acquaintance who finds herself in a similar condition, and their vitriol about her made it quite clear how my news would be received. They'd never forgive me."

"So what do you propose to do?"

"I have no idea." She stared down at her hands. "Absolutely no idea."

"Then maybe I can help," Miss Foster-Blake said. "I have a friend who is on the board of governors of a home for girls like you. It's in Somerset, in the hills, away from everywhere. And it's run by nuns. You can keep working here as long as we are in operation and then go there until the child is born."

"And what happens to my baby?" Emily asked.

"The nuns will find a suitable adoptive family for it. You can return home and nobody will ever know."

"But you don't understand," Emily said. "I am not going to give up my baby. I loved Robbie Kerr, and this child will be all I have left of him. I don't care what it takes or what I have to do, but I am not going to give it up."

"But, my dear, please think logically. You have your whole life ahead of you. Such a bright future. What can you do if you are hampered by a child? How will you pay to feed it? Who will look after it when you work, and work you most certainly will."

"I don't know," Emily said. "I don't know anything except I will not give it up. On the train back here, I wondered if I should go out to Australia. Maybe Robbie's parents would like to meet their grandson, and might welcome me, too."

"And if they don't? If they don't accept the child is their son's?"

"Then I find myself some kind of employment in Australia. I can say I'm a war widow there."

"You certainly can't travel in your condition," Miss Foster-Blake said. "And how will you pay for your ticket?"

"I brought my good pieces of jewellery with me," Emily said. "I can sell those if I have to."

"I urge you to think this through carefully. Society is not kind to unmarried mothers. You don't have friends or relatives who might take you in?"

"My school friends have either married or are volunteering themselves. My best friend is a nurse in France." She hesitated, wondering how Clarissa would accept her news. Surely Clarissa would not be shocked, after all she'd seen and been through. "Apart from that, it was always my parents' friends. And no relatives, apart from aged great-aunts who would be just as disapproving as my parents."

"Then at least you should go to St Bridget's home until the child is born. After that, you will have some serious decisions to make. I can't say that I envy you."

Emily stood up. "I thank you for your concern," she said, "and for trying to help, but I have to think this through for myself. I'll let you know what I decide." In the doorway, she turned back. "And please, I'd rather the other women didn't know."

"Of course not," Miss Foster-Blake said. "It's up to you to tell them when you are ready. But I think you'll find they are all on your side."

She went to her bedroom and climbed on to her upper bunk, where she sat, hugging her knees. Should she write to Robbie's parents? Would they want to know about Robbie's child? He had said he was telling his mother about her, but what exactly had he said? What if they thought she was just some girl he'd met, pleasant but not one he particularly cared about, and with no proof that the child was his? And as Miss Foster-Blake had said, she certainly couldn't face that long sea journey alone in her condition, not knowing what might lie at the end. She'd wait until the baby was born, she decided, and then send Robbie's parents a photograph. The absurdity of this struck her—that she should somehow have the money to have a photograph taken.

She was about to lie down when she noticed a letter on her pillow from Clarissa. She tore it open and read swiftly down the page.

> *You would expect that things might be winding down, now that the German operation has moved to the south and there is the last big push, but we are as busy as ever with an outbreak of influenza. The Spanish flu, they are calling it, and it is particularly aggressive. Grown men, healthy men catch this flu and are dead in a couple of days. The doctors are bewildered, and there seems to be little we can do to save these patients. I pray to God that it doesn't reach England.*

The letter went on, with Clarissa wanting to know more about Robbie, how he was doing and what were her wedding plans.

> *If I'm to be a bridesmaid, please put me in blue. It goes so well with my eyes.*

The absurdity of this was too much for her. She closed her eyes to squeeze back tears. Could she write to Clarissa and tell her the truth?

Then she decided Clarissa was someone she could tell. But not yet. Not today, when she was still overwhelmed with emotion. However her parents had behaved, they were her parents—and in spite of everything, she loved them. She knew she was walking away from the house she had grown up in, the security of her childhood. There would be no one to take care of her again.

She was still lying on her bunk when she heard footsteps coming up the stairs. She looked up as a strange woman came in. Her hair was in a sleek dark pageboy bob with a straight fringe, and she was wearing red lipstick. Emily looked again, then sat up in surprise.

"Alice?"

"How do you like it?" Alice put her hand up to her hair. "We decided, since we were wearing bloomers, we'd go the whole hog and get our hair cut. Daisy and me went into the hairdresser in Tavistock yesterday, and then we went to the chemist and bought some lipstick and rouge."

"You look marvellous. So glamorous," Emily said.

Alice's face became serious again. "How did it go at home then?"

"It didn't," Emily replied. "It was awful, Alice."

"You told them then?"

"I didn't get a chance to. They launched into this long tirade about a friend's daughter who is in the same condition as me. They said the most awful things. My father said if it were his daughter, he'd show her the door, cast her out . . ." Her voice quivered. "So I packed up some of my things and I left."

"I'm sorry, love," Alice said. "You've gone through more than a human should bear. But don't you worry, we won't let you down."

"But what will we do when we leave here, Alice? You don't have a place to go, do you?"

"I've got a little put by," Alice said. "Not much. And I've relatives in London, but frankly, I've already decided I'm not going back there. So I've had a chance to think this past couple of days, and you know what I'm thinking? I liked that little village we were in. I enjoyed Nell Lacey's company, and she's struggling to run that pub on her own. So I thought I might offer my services. She doesn't have to pay me, but she can offer me a roof over my head, and I'll help her with the pub and taking care of her husband when he comes home."

"Oh," Emily said, trying to be glad for Alice, but realizing that this plan did not include her. "That's a splendid idea, Alice."

"It need not be forever," Alice said. "Just until the world returns to normal." She looked at Emily. "You could come, too. I bet a pub has to have spare rooms."

Emily shook her head. "No, I couldn't. I'm not being a burden to anybody. I have the pay that is owed me that I haven't touched, which would take care of my board and lodging for a while, and I've some jewellery I could sell, but I don't want charity."

"How is it charity for a friend to want to take care of you?" Alice asked sharply.

"You would be tainted with my shame," Emily said.

"That's bloody nonsense and you know it. Anyway, you tell people you're a war widow. Nearly everyone is. No one will even question it. The subject of your young man didn't come up during the week we were there. You'd be quite safe."

"No, I told Lady Charlton all about him, and how we were going to marry and move to Australia. She gave me a compass as an early wedding present. So if she knows, Mrs Trelawney knows, too. And if Mrs Trelawney knows, she's probably told the whole village."

"Don't you believe it, love. They don't like that Mrs Trelawney down in the village. They think she's spiteful and gives herself airs."

Emily stared out of the window. It was a bright day, and puffball clouds raced across the sky. She remembered the view when they had stood together on the moor, how hopeful everything had seemed, how perfect the village had looked lying in its hollow. And her thoughts went to the little cottage.

"There is one thing I could do," she said slowly. "I could ask Lady Charlton if I could live in the cottage in return for continuing to work on her garden. It doesn't seem she'll have any gardeners returning from the war, so I can be useful."

"You'd rather live in that poky place than in a room in the pub?"

"Yes, I would," Emily said. "Only I'd have to tell Lady Charlton the truth first. It would be up to her to decide."

"Well, at least we'd be close by and I could keep an eye on you. Make sure you were eating properly," Alice said. "And I could help you get that place spruced up again. It needs a lick of paint, a good scrubbing and new curtains."

"Yes," Emily said. "I believe it could be quite nice."

Daisy came into the room and beamed when she saw Emily. "Oh, you're back," she said. "Did you have a lovely time with your folks? And what do you think of my hair?" Her bob was shorter than Alice's, and it bounced when she twirled. "It feels so free and light. My dad's going to kill me when I go home. But then I'm not sure I'm going home again. I'm certainly not working at that place."

"You should come with Emily and me to the village," Alice said.

"What village? When?"

"When we're kicked out of this," Alice said. "I'm going to see if Nell Lacey wants help at the pub and Emily's going to move into the cottage."

"That cottage? The haunted one?" Daisy looked worried. "Why?"

"Because I want a place of my own, Daisy. A place where no one knows me."

"Why would you do that?" Daisy was frowning. "You've got a nice home to go to."

"I haven't. I can't go home any more. I'm going to have a baby."

"Blimey," she said, picking up Alice's favourite swear word.

"Please don't tell the others yet."

"Oh, I won't. How awful for you. But at least you're not going to let them send you to one of those homes. I've heard about them. Terrible places, and they won't even let you see the baby after it's born."

"No, I have no intention of going to any home," Emily said. "Somehow or another, I'm going to make this work for me and my baby."

"And you think the old lady will let you live in her cottage?" Daisy asked.

"I have no idea. I'll have to see, and if not, then I'll think again, but I'd like it there, and I'd like to be near Alice in the pub."

"And what about me? You can't leave me behind," Daisy said. "I want to go where you go."

"Maybe one of the other women will want a helper," Alice said. "Mrs Upton in the shop, or Mrs Soper at the smithy."

Daisy had to smile. "I don't see myself as a blacksmith," she said. "But I do know how to be a housemaid. Old Lady Charlton only has that one maid, Ethel, and she's old and short-sighted, isn't she? I've seen the dust in that place."

"But I thought you didn't want to go back into service," Alice said.

"I don't, but I think I'll go where I'm needed for now. And I'd be close to the two of you."

"Rightio," Alice said, clapping her hands together. "That's settled then."

"If we're all to go to the village together," Emily said, "then there is something you have to do for me."

"What's that?" Alice asked.

"See if you can get some scissors and cut off my hair, too!"

Daisy ran down to the office, then came back with a big pair of scissors. Emily took the pins out of her roll of hair. She shook it out and it fell loose over her shoulders.

"You do it, Alice," Daisy said. "I'd be afraid I'd mess up."

"Are you sure about this, Emily?" Alice asked, glancing nervously at Daisy. "It's a big step to take. Daisy and me, we've got nothing to lose, but your family . . ."

"Absolutely," Emily said forcefully. "I'm not letting you two be modern women if I can't be one, too."

"Right then. Here we go." Alice picked up a length of Emily's hair and there was a satisfying snipping sound. The lock of hair tumbled to the floor. Emily sat still, holding her breath while hair piled up on the floor around her.

CHAPTER TWENTY-THREE

The end of their stint in the Women's Land Army came sooner than expected. A spate of bad weather set in, turning fields into lakes. It was clear no more planting could be done. Miss Foster-Blake assembled the women.

"His Majesty's government thanks you for your service," she said. "Most of you will not be needed again until next spring, and not even then if the war is over and the men have returned home. I am asking for volunteers to stay on and work with farmers who have animals throughout the winter. We have requests for milking assistance, plus one for pigs. You may be called upon to serve again next spring."

"You ain't catching me working with no pigs," Alice muttered to Emily, who was standing beside her. "And I wasn't too hot at milking either."

"I don't mind volunteering for the pigs," came a voice at the back, and they turned in surprise to see it was Mrs Anson.

She smiled at the horrified faces. "I am actually fascinated with pigs. Such intelligent creatures, and the piglets are adorable."

A couple of hands were raised for milking duties.

"Thank you," Miss Foster-Blake said. "And the rest of you, there will be some kind of transportation coming for you in the morning to take you into Tavistock."

Emily approached her as the others dispersed. "We plan to go back to Bucksley Cross," she said. "Do you think the bus or van could take us there tomorrow?"

When the older woman looked surprised, Emily said, "We are hoping to work up there and spend the winter."

"Do you have someone who will take you in?" Miss Foster-Blake asked, a worried expression on her face.

"I hope so. I think I've come up with a plan. If it doesn't work, then I will have to think again, but Alice has a place where she will be welcome, so she'll keep an eye on me. And Daisy will probably have a job, too."

Miss Foster-Blake put a tentative hand on Emily's arm. "Are you sure you are doing the right thing, my dear? It can be quite cold and bleak up near the moor like that. And far from a doctor, I should imagine. I'll give you my card, and you can always contact me if you change your mind about the home."

"You are very kind," Emily said. "But I am hopeful this will work out for me. One thing I am sure of—I'm not going to give up my child."

She joined the others packing up their belongings.

"I can't say I'll be sorry to leave this dump," Alice said. "It's getting ruddy cold in here now that winter's coming. And I won't be sorry to stop planting ruddy onions either."

"I feel the same," Daisy said. "Although I enjoyed having all of you to talk to. That part was fun, wasn't it? And I liked the apple picking. And when the three of us were working in Lady Charlton's garden."

"You can come and help me push the mower when we are back there, if you've a mind to, Daisy," Emily chuckled.

Daisy looked worried. "What if Lady Charlton doesn't want another maid? What if nobody wants me there?"

Alice put an arm around her bony shoulders. "Don't you worry, love. We're not going to leave you out in the cold. We'll find a place for you, I promise. But I think the old lady would need her head examined if she didn't take up your kind offer of being her maid. Anyone can see that house is in need of a good cleaning."

"You're all right, you lot," Maud said, entering their conversation. "You've got it figured out. I haven't. I could go home, but my mum is always bossing me around, and I've six brothers and sisters, and I have to share a bed, and there's no work for me to do."

"Make sure you give us your address, Maud," Alice said. "If we find something for you, we'll let you know."

"Will you really? You're so kind. You're a good lot, all of you."

Her round, placid face broke into a big smile.

The next morning, an old, rickety lorry took the other girls into Tavistock and then returned to drive Emily, Alice and Daisy up to Bucksley Cross. They were deposited, with their suitcases, at the bottom of the village green. Emily and Daisy let Alice go ahead into the pub. She seemed to be in there for quite a while, and then she came out, beaming.

"Nell Lacey nearly wept when I told her what we were suggesting. She said she had no idea how she was going to cope when her bloke came home and I must be an angel from heaven."

They waited for her to say more. She saw their faces, then added. "Oh, and I said you might be staying at the pub, depending on how things went. You can bring your things in for now, anyway."

There was a big fire now burning in the bar, and the room was deliciously warm. Nell poured them all a cup of tea, and they sat close to the fire. Emily hesitated for as long as she could, then said, "Well, I suppose I had better get it over with. At least, I want to know."

"Know what?" Mrs Lacey asked.

"She wants to move into the cottage."

Nell threw back her head and laughed. "I shouldn't think there would be a single reason to prevent you from doing that, my lovey. Who else would want to live there?"

"It's more complicated than that," Emily said. "But I hope you are right."

She buttoned her overcoat over the uniform that she'd be wearing for the last time and walked resolutely up the drive to Bucksley House. This time, she rang the front doorbell. Mrs Trelawney opened it, the suspicion showing in her face when she saw Emily.

"Oh, it's you again. What do you want?"

"I'd like to speak to Lady Charlton please," Emily said, as pleasantly as she could. "Is she available?"

"I'll go and see." The woman turned and walked away, leaving Emily standing on the front step. She returned, frowning. "Her Ladyship will see you. Wipe your feet."

Emily wiped her feet dutifully on the doormat, then followed Mrs Trelawney down the hall to the drawing room. The old lady was sitting by the fire, and she looked up with a smile of anticipation when Emily came in. "Well, this is a delightful surprise," she said. "I thought you had gone for good. I imagined you'd be on your way to Australia by now. In fact, I got out the atlas to see if I could trace your sea journey." She glanced up at Mrs Trelawney, who was hovering in the doorway. "We will have coffee served in here right away, Mrs Trelawney. And some of your gingerbread." She turned back to Emily. "Do sit down, my dear. Pull a chair up to the fire. The weather has turned quite cold."

Emily moved an upholstered chair closer to the fire and looked up to see Lady Charlton staring at her. "Have you decided to become a man?"

"A man?" Emily was confused. She had practised so many times what she wanted to say, and this had completely thrown her.

"Your hair, young lady. It makes you look like a man."

"Oh, my hair." Emily put her hand up to the unfamiliar bob. "I decided to be a modern woman, and it's so much easier than long hair."

Lady Charlton was still frowning. "I have to say that it suits you, although I have no wish to become a modern woman myself. So has the trip to Australia been postponed?"

Emily took a deep breath. "I won't be going to Australia any longer, Lady Charlton," she said. "You see, my young man was killed. His plane crashed."

"Oh, I'm so sorry. What a shock for you."

"Yes," Emily said, her voice breaking. "A great shock."

They both lapsed into awkward, sad silence, only broken by the slow tick of the grandfather clock and the crackle of the logs on the fire.

"So what will you do now?" Lady Charlton asked.

"Actually, that's why I came to see you," Emily said, remembering herself. "I have a proposition for you, Lady Charlton."

"A proposition?" Lady Charlton sounded amused.

"I would like to live in that little cottage, and in return, I'll continue to take care of your garden. I don't ask for any pay, just to take my midday meal at the house and for Mr Simpson to provide me with either wood or coal for the fire and stove."

Lady Charlton was frowning. "Now, why on earth would you want to do that?"

"To put it simply, because I have nowhere else to go. My parents and I do not see eye to eye . . ."

"You've quarrelled with your parents?"

"They didn't approve of my young man."

"I see. But breaking off contact with your family is a serious move, my dear. Something you might come to regret later."

Emily hesitated, then took a deep breath. "I have to be completely frank with you: I'm expecting a baby. Lieutenant Kerr and I were not able to marry before he died, although he had proposed and given me a ring. But in the eyes of the world, that makes me a social outcast. My parents have made it more than clear what they think of girls like me. So I can completely understand if you would not want to be tainted with someone in my condition."

Lady Charlton was still frowning. "I can't possibly allow you to work in my garden," she said.

Emily went to stand up. "I quite understand. I won't trouble you any further."

Lady Charlton waved a hand to stop Emily as she started to rise to her feet. "No, no, silly girl. What I meant was that you can't be expected to work in the garden in your condition."

"I really don't mind," Emily said. "I'm not an invalid. I don't think I can manage the lawnmower alone, but I can certainly weed and prune and take care of the kitchen garden."

"Maybe for another month or so, but the winters can be quite brutal here. But I have a proposition for you in return. I need someone to catalogue my husband's collections and books. I have kept meaning to do it, but old age has made me lazy. And I rather fear I may have to sell some of his things to keep this place afloat if the home farm is not able to spring back into operation soon."

"I can certainly help you with that," Emily said. "In fact, I'd enjoy it immensely."

"And there can be no question of your living at the cottage," Lady Charlton said. "We can find you a room in the house."

Emily shook her head. "No, thank you very much. But I'd rather have my own place. I don't want Mrs Trelawney to feel beholden to me, and I want to stand on my own feet."

The old lady looked at her long and hard, then she nodded. "I understand. You need space to work through your grief."

Emily returned her gaze. "Yes," she said. "That's it exactly. Since I heard the news, we've been working hard in the fields all day. At night, I've been sleeping in a room with five other women. And then the shock about the baby . . . I have locked my grief away."

"Just don't let it overwhelm you," Lady Charlton said. "You will get over it, you know. At this moment, you think you won't, but you will. In time, you will be able to look back upon your beloved as a fond memory."

"So I can move into the cottage?" Emily asked, finding this conversation almost more than she could bear. "And I can ask Simpson for some coal or firewood?"

"With my blessing," the old lady said. "But why don't you take your meals here at the house?"

"As tempting as that is, I have to learn to be independent. I have been coddled all my life. Now I shall be responsible for a child. I'd appreciate a midday meal if I'm out working in the garden, but other than that . . ."

"I hope I might persuade you to dine with me on occasion," Lady Charlton said. "I'd welcome the company. There is nothing more dreary than dining alone."

"Then I will be happy to join you, on occasion," Emily said.

"Well, that's settled then," the old lady said. "Work on the garden if you like. I can understand you don't want to be cooped up all day with an old woman. But when the weather is not conducive to outdoor activities, then you and I shall catalogue the collections." A wistful look came over her face. "This might prove helpful if I decide that I have to sell Bucksley House."

"You might have to sell?"

Lady Charlton gave a tired little smile. "My dear, this house is hardly the correct size for one old lady. I don't have the staff to run it properly. Poor old Ethel's joints creak so badly that she can hardly get up the stairs. It should have a family in it. Life and laughter. Happiness."

"What happens to your husband's title? Is there no heir to move in?"

"The title has died out, I'm afraid. There are no immediate relatives and only a couple of female cousins." She sighed. "No, there is no legitimate claim on the Charlton name." She paused, then chuckled. "Which is lucky, don't you think? Or I might have been turned out of here by now. Heirs have a habit of doing that to elderly dowagers."

Emily hesitated, then took a deep breath before saying, "One thing, if I may. I don't want the rest of the village to know about the baby and my situation. Not yet, at least."

"Don't worry, my dear. We'll just say that you're a war widow, like so many others. Nobody will question it these days. What did you say your young man's name was?"

"Flight Lieutenant Robert Kerr."

"Then you are Mrs Kerr—the war widow. The truth shall remain between the two of us."

Emily looked at Lady Charlton and felt tears coming to her eyes. She had never dared to hope that this remote and haughty old woman could be so kind. It felt like an answer to her prayers. "Thank you. You're very understanding," Emily said.

The door opened, and Mrs Trelawney came in with a tray bearing a silver coffee service. Emily wondered whether she had been listening outside and how much she had overheard.

"There wasn't much of that gingerbread left," she muttered as she put the tray down on a low table. "You ate the rest. So I brought some biscuits."

"Then please bake some more," Lady Charlton said testily. "You know how fond I am of it."

"I'm not a magician, am I," Mrs Trelawney said, equally testily. "We're still on rations, you know. And they are out of black treacle at the village shop."

She was about to make a grand exit when Lady Charlton called after her. "And please get Ethel to bring out some bedding for"—she paused—"Mrs Kerr. She has had the bad news that her husband has been killed in action."

"She'll be staying here?" Mrs Trelawney frowned.

"No, I'm going to be moving back into the cottage," Emily said. "So I won't be under your feet too much, Mrs Trelawney."

Mrs Trelawney gave an audible sniff as she went out. They heard her yelling. "Ethel? Where are you? Someone needs to go up to the linen closet and I have the luncheon to prepare."

Emily exchanged a grin with Lady Charlton. "I'm rather afraid Mrs Trelawney doesn't welcome my presence."

"Mrs Trelawney has grown extremely lazy with the years," Lady Charlton said. "I keep her on because she has been with me since I moved into this house thirty years ago and because I wouldn't want to start afresh with someone new." She paused, then gave a throaty chuckle. "And because she doesn't cost much." Then her face became sombre again. "And she is quite devoted to me in a dog-like way."

Emily sipped the coffee with relish. How long since she had drunk coffee from a bone china cup? She finished the cup reluctantly, and was about to make herself go and face the cottage when she remembered. "I think I have a way to ease the burden on Ethel and Mrs Trelawney," she said. "Do you remember the young girl, Daisy, who worked in the garden with me? She is a trained housemaid, and she is willing to come and work for you. I don't think she'll need paying too much."

"Have you asked her?"

"Oh yes. It was she who suggested it. She saw the house was in need of extra hands when we were here before. And she, too, has nowhere to go at the moment."

"She's not also in the family way?" Lady Charlton asked sharply.

Emily had to laugh. "No. She does not wish to return to the house where she was in service before. The master had wandering hands."

"I see." Lady Charlton nodded. "Well, you are full of surprises, Miss Bryce—or I should say Mrs Kerr. Of course I accept her kind offer. And I am sure Ethel will be more than grateful. Mrs Trelawney, too, only don't expect her to show it."

"Then I'll go and tell her now, once I've taken the bedding down to the cottage." Emily stood up to go, then held out her hand to the old lady. "I can't thank you enough. I don't know what I would have done if you'd said no."

"It's purely selfish on my part," the old woman said. "I enjoy your company. I'm tired of living on my own."

As Emily went through to the servants' quarters, Ethel appeared, her arms piled high with sheets and blankets. "Here you go, miss," she said. "Although why you'd want to live in that cottage is beyond me. They say it's haunted."

"Cursed, that's what it is." Mrs Trelawney appeared from the kitchen. "Bad things have happened to every woman who's lived there. Two murders, one woman hanged. So either the cottage is cursed or the women are cursed who come to live there. I'm not sure which." And she gave a malevolent little smile.

As Emily carried her pile of bedding down the hill, buffeted by the wind, she met Simpson, coming towards her with firewood in his arms.

"Well, little missy, what are you doing here again?" he asked.

"I'm coming to live in the cottage for a while, Simpson," Emily said. "I'm glad I bumped into you. When you have time, can you stock me up with coal or wood or whatever I need to keep the fire and the stove going?"

"Coming to live in the cottage? Well I never! Are you sure you want to do that?"

"Yes—for now, anyway. I'm going to keep working on the garden and also help Lady Charlton catalogue her husband's treasures."

"She'll be pleased about that, I don't doubt," he said, nodding with satisfaction, as if he, too, was pleased. "She became quite fond of you in that short while, and that's not like her. Usually, she doesn't take to people—quite snooty and standoffish, she's been, especially since her husband, son and grandson died. So you're bringing her out of her shell." He smiled. "I'll bring you both coal and wood, my dearie. It will be more wood than coal these days, what with the rationing and all. There are always plenty of downed branches on the estate, if I have the energy to cut them up. And I don't suppose you've had much experience in getting fires going, have you?"

"None at all. No experience in anything, except planting crops now. I'm quite good at that."

This made him laugh. "Don't you worry yourself then. I'll give you a hand."

Emily reached the lane and walked up the narrow front path between the overgrown bushes to the front door. *I should try to make time to tame this little wilderness, too,* she thought, pushing trailing branches out of the way. As she stepped into the tiny living room, she realized that she might have created a rose-tinted image of the cottage. She was now looking at a forlorn little room with the bare minimum of furniture and no adornments of any kind. She realized that it hadn't seemed so bleak when the three of them had sat on those chairs and laughed while the setting sun streamed in through the window. The cottage felt damp and cold, and a draught blew strongly down the chimney. She felt a moment's panic. Why did she want to be in this place when she could have a room in the big house and sit with Lady Charlton by the fire? But she answered her own question. Like a fox being chased by the hounds, she needed a bolthole in which to lick her wounds.

CHAPTER TWENTY-FOUR

Emily put her bags down in the narrow front hall and climbed the steep stairs to the attic bedroom where she had slept before, bending her head as she stepped inside. Without the sun shining, it was dark and gloomy and cold. The sloping ceiling felt oppressive, almost threatening. She decided she'd be warmer and somehow safer sleeping downstairs, and so she came down carefully. When she had finished making up the bed, she carried her bags into the room and was going to put her clothes into the rickety chest of draws in the corner, but remembered that Daisy would be waiting to hear from her. So instead, she headed straight for the Red Lion and found Alice and Daisy still sitting by the fire with big mugs of tea in their hands. Daisy seemed remarkably happy to hear that she would be working at Bucksley House.

"I don't know why you are looking so delighted at going back to being a maid and working under Mrs Trelawney every day," Emily said. "I don't think I've come across a more unpleasant woman."

"That's all right," Daisy said. "She'll be so glad that I'm taking over the work that she'll be nice to me."

"I hope so, for your sake," Emily said.

"At least I'll be close to you and Alice," Daisy said. "And far away from my dad and that other place."

"So all went well with Lady Charlton?" Alice said.

"Couldn't have gone better," Emily replied, accepting the mug of tea she was offered. "She didn't want to give me the cottage, she wanted me to stay at the big house."

"How nice for you. I hope you accepted," Alice said.

"No, I did not. I told her I'd rather have my own place, if she didn't mind."

"You'd rather have that damp and draughty place than a manor house? Are you daft, girl?" Alice asked.

Emily had to laugh at her expression. "No, you don't understand. I need to learn to live on my own. I have no skills at all. How am I going to take care of a baby if I can't even do the simplest tasks? And I need a place where I can have a good cry if I want to. I don't want to be brave all the time."

"Of course you don't," Alice said. "And don't you worry, love. I'll come over and teach you a bit about cooking if you want."

"And I'll come down from the big house and clean for you," Daisy said.

"You are both too kind." Emily looked from one to the other. "But I need to learn to do my own cleaning, Daisy. I've got to be completely independent, I see that."

"Well, I'll come up now and help you with getting the fire going and things," Alice said.

"And I'll take my bags up to the big house and get myself settled up there. Then I'll come down and report to you," Daisy said.

Alice and Emily walked together across the green and up the lane to the cottage.

Emily paused at the gate to the cottage. "Oh, and, Alice, you haven't told Nell Lacey about me, have you? About the baby and everything?"

"I haven't said a word, love."

"Because Lady Charlton said exactly what you suggested—that I call myself Mrs Kerr and say I'm a war widow. I don't like lying, but at least for now I think it might be so much easier."

"Of course it will. So mum's the word. Now, let's see what needs doing in here, shall we?" She went ahead of Emily, opening the front door and stepping into the living room. "Strewth, girl!" she exclaimed, as if seeing it for the first time. "It ain't Buckingham Palace, that's for sure. You've got yourself a big job ahead." Then, as Emily stared around her, she went on, "Well, don't just stand there. Let's get cracking, shall we? First things first, we need to get that stove going or there will be no hot water. And that kitchen floor and them windows need a good washing. And them curtains—they look like they're about to fall to pieces, and they won't be no good at keeping out the cold. You tell them at the big house that they need to find you some better curtains." She walked on through to the kitchen. "And some more pots and pans, too. There ain't no way you can cook yourself a decent meal with what you've got there."

"I won't need much in the way of cooking things," Emily said. "I'm planning on taking my midday meals up at the big house, so I'll only need breakfast and supper here. And supper can be bread and cheese, can't it? And breakfast can be toast or a boiled egg if we can get eggs."

Alice frowned. "You'll need to be eating properly," she said. "You're eating for two now, remember." As she spoke, she took down the saucepans from the shelf and filled the biggest one with water.

"Alice?" Emily asked. "You and Bill didn't have any children then?"

Alice stopped what she was doing. "We had a little girl," she said, almost in a whisper. "My little Rosie. Sweet little thing, she was. Good as gold. Hardly ever cried. And when she was just turned one, she caught diphtheria and died. And we weren't blessed with another one."

"I'm so sorry." Emily felt her own eyes welling with tears. "We've all lost so much. Why is life so full of suffering?"

"The blokes at church would tell us it's so we appreciate heaven more one day, I suppose," Alice said with a bitter laugh. "I don't think there's any answer myself. You're either lucky or you're not. And right now, most of us are ruddy unlucky. And we just have to make the best of it. Come on. Hand me the plates from that dresser and let's rinse them off or you'll be eating dust."

Emily looked out of the back window. "Oh, here comes Simpson with the firewood now. We can get the stove and a fire going."

"Here we are, little missy," Simpson said, setting the firewood down. "I'll be back with more wood and coal, too. Do you want me to get the fire going for you?"

"It's all right," Alice said. "I can show her. I've lit enough fires in my life."

"Well, that's good then. I'll leave you to it," he replied.

Between them, they got the fire and then the stove going. Then Emily swept while Alice scrubbed. They were red-faced and panting after an hour's work.

"I wonder if it's time for your dinner," Alice asked. "You need a clock here, don't you?"

"I brought my watch with me from home. It's in my suitcase. But I don't think it's wound," Emily said.

"A watch. How fancy," Alice said. "I wish you'd shoved a couple of nice rugs and a few cushions and pictures in that suitcase when you left home."

"I had to leave so many nice things," Emily said. "I could only carry the bare minimum without arousing suspicion. And so much of my clothes would be useless to me now."

"Here, don't let that fire go out now," Alice said. "Bring in some more wood and I'll show you how to bank it up. You'll need to do that at night so that the embers are still good in the morning."

At that moment, the church clock chimed twelve.

"There's your answer to the time, Alice," Emily said. "I won't go up to lunch until one. In fact, I'm not sure I should go up there at all today, since Mrs Trelawney wasn't expecting me. She wasn't at all pleased to see me, so I don't want to annoy her more than necessary."

"Then you come down to the Red Lion with me today, love," Alice said. "Nell Lacey's made a stew that's big enough for all of us."

Emily needed no second urging. After the meal, Alice and Nell helped her make a list of groceries she would need. The list soon became awfully long, as they kept thinking of more and more items. "And flour. And baking powder, currants and sultanas if you're ever going to make a cake. Not that you'll find what you need these days at the shop, with everything being in such short supply," Nell warned.

"Hold on a minute." Emily held up her hand. "I don't even know how many minutes it takes to boil an egg. I can't visualize myself baking a cake for a long while yet."

"Didn't your mum teach you how to cook then?" Nell looked concerned.

Emily blushed. "We had a cook at home. My mother didn't know how to cook either."

"My word," Nell said. "So you came from a real swanky type of house then? What on earth are you doing here?"

Emily took a deep breath. "My parents and I didn't see eye to eye about the man I wanted to marry," she said.

"I see. He wasn't good enough, is that it?"

"He was Australian. He didn't operate by their rules—polite etiquette and all that. But there was nothing wrong with him. He was a wonderful man."

She turned away, not wanting Nell to see her stricken face. Nell put a hand on her shoulder. "Sorry, my dearie. I should never have brought it up. Of course it brings you pain just to think of him. Half the women in this village are in your boat. No, half the women in England."

"I know," Emily said. "But that doesn't make it any easier."

She left them then, and went to the village shop with her grocery list in hand. They had whittled it down to the bare essentials, but she got a shock when she read out her needs to Mrs Upton.

"I don't stock milk, madam," the shopkeeper said.

"Is there a milk delivery route then?" Emily asked.

"Not what you'd call a proper route. You'd have to have a word with Mr Gurney from the home farm when he comes through early in the morning. If you put out a jug or a churn, he'll fill it for you. Twice a week, he comes through."

"And bread?" Emily asked.

"I'm not a bakery, my dear. The women around here bake their own. And I'm not a butcher either. You have to go into Tavistock or arrange with one of the farmers when you hear he's going to slaughter a sheep. And frankly, these days, it's hard enough to get your hands on any kind of meat. It goes straight to the government, doesn't it?"

Emily saw that fending for herself in the cottage was going to be harder than she had imagined. "So what can you let me have?"

"Did you bring your ration book?" Mrs Upton asked. "Because most of the things you want are on ration these days."

Emily hadn't thought of that. Her ration book was still at home with her parents. The government had fed her while she was a member of the Women's Land Army. And if she managed to acquire her ration book, it would still be in the name of Emily Bryce. It seemed as if there was to be one problem after another.

"It's still at my parents' house, I'm afraid," she said. "I'll have to write to them and ask them to send it to me."

"Well, I can't let you have anything without it, my dear," the woman said, looking more kindly now. "It would be more than my neck is worth. They have fines, even prison for those who abuse the system."

"I see. Thank you anyway." Emily came out into the bitter wind. How was she going to feed herself and her child with no ration book? But if she wrote to her parents and asked them to post it to her, then they'd know where she was living, and she didn't want that at all costs. She went back up the hill to Bucksley House, her footsteps dragging now.

"Mrs Trelawney," she said, "I don't know if Lady Charlton has told you that I'll be taking my midday meal here while I work on the garden."

"She might have mentioned something about it." The woman eyed her coldly.

"So I wondered if I might have a few staples from your kitchen so that I don't have to bother you for my other meals," Emily said. "A little flour and sugar and tea, butter . . . those sorts of things."

"Those things are on ration these days," Mrs Trelawney said. "Do you have your ration book?"

"I don't. It's at my parents' house," Emily said. "I'll have to send for it, but in the meantime . . ."

"I suppose we can spare enough to keep you going," she said grudgingly.

"And I wondered, if you bake bread for the house, if you could maybe bake an extra loaf for me," Emily dared to add.

"As if I don't have enough work around here," the woman snapped. "You think I'm your servant, too?"

"Of course not. It's just that I've never had to bake bread, but I'm willing to learn if you can show me."

"I don't want you under my feet. I'll bake you the loaf," she said.

Daisy came into the kitchen. "She can share my rations, Mrs Trelawney," she said, having overheard the last of this conversation. "I've got my book, and I don't eat much."

"I expect we'll manage then," the woman said with an exaggerated sigh. "Did you take up the clean clothes to Her Ladyship's bedroom?"

"I did," Daisy said. "What would you like me to do now?"

Emily looked at her with secret admiration. She seemed so naive and awkward, but she knew how to work with people like Mrs Trelawney.

The older woman was looking at Daisy almost fondly. "You're a good little worker, I'll say that for you," she said. Her expression hardened as she turned back to Emily. "So you'll probably be wanting your supper here tonight, seeing as how you've no provisions yet."

"If you don't mind," Emily said. "But after that, as I said, I'll just share my midday meal with you and manage for myself in the evenings. I can make do with something simple like bread and cheese."

"Bread and cheese?" The woman sniffed. "That will give you bad dreams, that will. But then you're probably going to get bad dreams anyway in that cursed place. I've only been in there a few times myself, and each time I felt it—that malevolent presence. You'll feel it if you haven't already, believe me."

She grudgingly packed a basket with tea, milk, sugar, bread, butter and jam. "They'll keep you going for now," she said. Emily thanked her, and carried them back to the cottage, where she unpacked her belongings, putting them away in the rickety chest of drawers. Then she went up to the attic, unpacked the books from the trunk and dragged it down the stairs, before going up again to retrieve the books. As she placed the books on top of the trunk, she fingered the leather-bound journal. *I suppose I can read it now,* she thought. *Daisy said it would bring me bad luck, and it already has, so my luck can't get much worse at this moment.* But still she hesitated. *Not now,* she thought, although after all the tales about the cottage she had heard, her curiosity was piqued. She put it down and went back to her chores. Then suddenly she was overcome with exhaustion. She lay on the bed and fell asleep. In her dream, she was hiding in the upstairs room. "They won't find me here," she was saying, and then she realized that she had long black hair flowing over her shoulders. She awoke with a start, her heart thumping, to find it was almost dark. The dream had quite unnerved her. Had she been dreaming about the witch who had once lived in the cottage? But she had actually been the witch in her dream. She tried to shake off the feeling of unreality as she splashed water on to her face. Mrs Trelawney would be waiting to serve supper, and would not take it kindly if Emily were late. She put on her mackintosh and hurried up the path. Daisy and Ethel were already seated at the kitchen table.

"Well, there she is, queen of the cottage," Mrs Trelawney said. "Thought you'd had a better offer, we did."

"I'm sorry," Emily muttered, taking her place at the table. A large bowl of something brown and spongy was put in front of her. With it came the overwhelming smell of onions.

"What is this?" she asked politely.

"Tripe and onions," the housekeeper said. "You have to take whatever meat they can give you these days."

Emily had never eaten tripe in her life. She wasn't quite sure what it was, but seemed to remember it being something to do with a cow's stomach. She tried a mouthful. It felt slimy and chewy as she fought to swallow it. She was all too aware that if she rejected it, she would be fed the worst scraps of everything from now on, if she was fed at all. She swallowed bravely, holding back the bile that rose in her throat. She washed it down with mug after mug of tea. As soon as she had eaten it, she got up.

"Would you excuse me? I'd like to finish cleaning the cottage tonight so that I can start work on the garden tomorrow." She didn't wait for an answer. As soon as she was clear of the house, she disappeared into the rhododendron bushes and vomited her meal on to the carpet of leaves. Her stomach still heaved as she made her way down to the cottage. It was pitch-black, and she stumbled several times. How was she going to find her way on dark winter nights? She certainly couldn't carry a candle in this wind. Then she realized she'd have to leave a lamp in the cottage window to guide her.

This time, the cottage felt warm, but the shadows from the flickering fire emphasized the bleakness and were somehow unnerving. She realized she had never slept in a house alone before, and wished she had accepted Lady Charlton's invitation for a room in the big house. *But I have to learn,* she thought. She took out pen, ink and paper, deciding it was time she wrote to Clarissa, but she couldn't make herself put the words down. She didn't think Clarissa would think badly of her, but she couldn't risk losing one of her only friends. So she did what Alice had shown her and banked up the fire, then she got undressed and climbed in between the cold sheets. Wind rattled at the windows and moaned down the chimney, filling the cottage with smoke. The grim reality that this was her future overwhelmed her.

"I want to go home," she whispered.

CHAPTER TWENTY-FIVE

The morning dawned bright and breezy. As Emily opened the back door to step out to the privy, she heard a small noise at her feet. A black cat sat there, looking up at her with anticipation.

"Mew?" it said.

"Hello." She bent to stroke it, and it purred, rubbing against her legs. When she went back into the house, it darted in front of her. "Well," she said, "I suppose you can stay. But you'll have to be a good hunter. I can hardly feed myself."

The cat settled itself in front of the fire. She looked at it fondly. At least she was no longer alone. "You'll have to have a name," she said. Blackie, Sooty, Satan . . . she toyed with several, then settled on Shadow. "My Shadow and I," she said. It felt quite satisfying.

After a couple of slices of bread and jam, she went out to work, starting on the kitchen garden, which was in serious need of weeding. The summer crops had died off, and she now knew that winter vegetables should be planted in their place. She weeded and dug out dead plants all morning, then picked the few remaining apples on the trees, carrying the basket up to Mrs Trelawney. The woman actually looked pleased.

"Well, fancy that. They'll come in handy. Now I can bake a couple of pies for the harvest festival on Sunday. I was wondering what to take this year, what with not having much in the garden. And I don't suppose there's a marrow left?"

"A couple of little ones," Emily said. "There's a good-looking pumpkin."

"There you are then." Mrs Trelawney nodded with satisfaction. "A pumpkin it will have to be. If you pick it and bring it up to the house, we'll take it on Sunday." She looked up from her baking. "It's not what it used to be, of course. Before the war, there was always a rivalry here. Mr Patterson at the school always grew the biggest marrow, and Dickson the carter, he always had the best-looking cabbages. And in those days, we had the three gardeners, so we had plenty of good-looking produce to carry up to the altar, although Her Ladyship has never been much for church herself. Won't set foot in the place here. But we servants go."

They had a hearty vegetable soup and cold pork pie for their midday meal, then Emily went back to work. She was interrupted by Simpson with a message from Her Ladyship. Would she take sherry and dine with her that evening? So she changed out of her work clothes and presented herself at six o'clock for sherry. The outdoor work seemed to have done her good, and she was feeling quite hungry when they sat down together by the big fire.

"So did you survive your first night in the cottage?" Lady Charlton asked. "Did you meet the ghosties and ghoulies and things that go bump in the night that Mrs Trelawney seems to think inhabit it?"

"Actually, I slept remarkably well," Emily answered. "And I have a room-mate. A small black cat."

Lady Charlton chuckled. "How appropriate for a witch's cottage."

"Was there really a witch here once?" Emily asked.

"Depends what you mean by 'witch,'" the lady said. "Long ago, a cow would die and the owner would claim that someone had cast a spell on it or had given it the evil eye. There have been several women who lived alone in that cottage, and that is always suspicious to the general population. Why is she living alone without a man? Surely that must mean she is up to no good."

"But I was told there were murders?"

Lady Charlton chuckled again. "You don't want to believe anything the villagers tell you. There was one woman who disappeared, and the rumour went about that the man she was betrothed to had killed and buried her. But her body was never found, and the man in question also disappeared from the neighbourhood soon after. If you want my opinion, what probably happened was that she ran off with a handsome gypsy who was camped nearby. Anyway, it was a long time ago."

"Before your time here?"

"Oh yes, before my time here," she said. "I've lived in this house for thirty of my eighty-three years. Less than half my life. I wasn't overjoyed to come here in the first place, but Henry inherited the title and property, so we had to give up a rather exciting way of life abroad and settle down here. Naturally, we hoped for more children after James, but sadly that didn't happen."

How ironic, Emily thought as she watched the flames flicker. Two women who had wanted more children in their marriage and had not been able to have them. And here she was, with one brief encounter with a man and a child growing in her belly. She put her hand to it now. In spite of her expanding waistline, it still didn't seem real.

They dined at one end of the table in the large, chilly dining room. There was a clear broth followed by lamb's liver in a rich gravy, and then rice pudding with sultanas. Emily found it extremely satisfying, but Lady Charlton apologized. "I'm sorry we have reverted to nursery food," she said. "In spite of living in the country and having a home farm, it becomes harder and harder to obtain decent meat."

They took coffee by the fire, and then Emily got up to leave.

"I do hope I can persuade you to join me for dinner every evening," Lady Charlton said. "It is extremely tiresome to dine alone, and I get the feeling that you enjoy an old woman's stories."

"Oh, I do," Emily said. "I love to hear about your experiences in different parts of the world."

"Well then, why the reluctance?"

Emily shifted uneasily. "I suppose I feel I should be learning to stand on my own two feet, not have someone else cook for me."

"Rubbish," Lady Charlton said. "What else does Mrs Trelawney have to do but to cook? And if she cooks for one, it is just as easy to cook for two. So I think we've closed that matter for me. And when can I expect you to join me in the house, sorting through my husband's collections? Is there really much to do in the garden at this time of year?"

"The rest of the roses need pruning, and the kitchen garden should be restocked with winter produce to keep us going," Emily said. "I'm going to speak to Simpson about onion sets and Brussels sprouts and the like. I know a little bit about planting those now."

Lady Charlton smiled. "Quite the little farmer."

As Emily made her way back down the hill, she allowed herself a small grin of satisfaction. She had acquired some skills. She was able to earn her keep.

Back in the cottage, she settled herself at the table, close to the fire, the cat at her feet, and took out her writing set.

> *My dear Clarissa,*
>
> *I am sorry I have ignored your last letter for so long, especially when you are going through such a harrowing time with the influenza cases. We have not seen any sign of it here yet, thank goodness. I hope it does not succeed in travelling across the Channel, although I suspect some of the returning soldiers will bring it with them.*
>
> *Again, my lack of response has not been through laziness. On the contrary, I have been extremely busy, planting onions, ploughing, picking apples . . . quite the little farm girl—that's what Lady Charlton said. You would have been amused to see me trying to wrestle the plough behind two giant horses!*

But my real reason for writing only now is that I did not know how to put into words all that has happened recently. My life has turned upside down, Clarissa. I wrote of my hopes and dreams, my marriage to Robbie and a life in Australia. All dashed, I regret to say. He was killed, Clarissa, being frightfully brave and piloting a doomed plane away from a village.

And that is not all. I hardly dare to write this, and I beg you not to show the letter to anyone else—most of all, do not mention it to my parents. I find myself in the family way. I am overcome with shame as I write the words, and yet in some way there is a joy in having Robbie's child. At least a small part of him still lives. But as you can imagine, I have no idea how I am going to face the future. Certainly not with my parents, who have made their views on the subject more than clear. For the moment, I have taken up residence in a cottage at the edge of an estate close to Dartmoor. The owner, Lady Charlton, has been surprisingly understanding. I will help her with her garden and with cataloguing her husband's collections in return for having a place to live. To the rest of the villagers, I'll be Mrs Kerr, war widow. I only hope that

She broke off, as there was a knock at the front door. She got up and opened it, expecting a visit from Alice, or maybe Simpson with more coal, and was surprised to see a strange man standing in front of her. His jacket was tied together with string. He wore an old, shapeless hat over shaggy hair, and his face was half-hidden by an untrimmed beard. Emily recoiled at the smell of him.

"Yes? Can I help you?" she asked, while the thought crossed her mind that she was a long way from any assistance. They would never hear her in the houses across the lane if she shouted for help.

"I've got a sore thumb." The man held it out to her. Emily looked. It was more than a sore thumb. It had a great, yellow blister on it, and the skin around it was angry, swollen and red.

"That looks awful. You should see a doctor," she said.

He frowned. "My sort don't deal with doctors." He paused. "That requires money. Besides, you're her, aren't you?"

"Her?"

"The wise woman. The herb wife. It says so on the gatepost."

Emily stared at him as if he were talking a foreign language. "On the gatepost?"

"That's right. We tramps have signs of our own—signs that other folks can't read, telling us where we'll be welcome. And your gatepost says that the wise woman lives here."

It was so improbable that Emily had to laugh. "I'm no wise woman," she said, "but that is certainly a nasty-looking thumb. Come inside, and I'll see what I can do for you."

He wiped his feet carefully before coming in. Emily made him sit by the fire, and she put the kettle on the stove. Then she went to find her nail set—a pretty little kit from Paris in a morocco leather box that had been one of her twenty-first presents. She poured boiling water over the scissors and tweezers. Then she cut off part of the clean tea towel Mrs Trelawney had given her. There would be hell to pay about that, she thought, but she had to clean up the man's hand or he'd die from infection.

Seen up close, the thumb looked even worse, and her insides heaved as she cleaned it with the boiled water.

"I think we had better open up this blister," she said.

He nodded.

She took a tentative little snip with the scissors and pus streamed out. She snipped more away until all the pus was gone. Then she held his hand close to the lamp, retrieved the tweezers and carefully lifted something out from the wound. "There," she said. "You had some kind of big splinter in your thumb."

"That's right. I did. I were climbing over a fence and this ruddy, great splinter went right in. I tried to pull it out and it broke off."

"Well, it's out now," she said. "I'm going to wash it again with the hot water, and then I'll bandage it up with this clean cloth. That's the best I can do. I don't have any disinfectant, I'm afraid. I've just moved in."

"You've done a grand job, little lady," he said. "I reckon you are the wise woman after all. Are you going to bring the place back to what it was? My fellows will be pleased to know that."

This suggestion alarmed Emily. She imagined a procession of tramps at her front door. Instead of answering, she asked, "Would you like a cup of tea? The water has just boiled."

"I'd prefer a swig of whisky," he replied.

She smiled. "I'm afraid I don't keep any alcohol here. But if you go down to the Red Lion, tell Mrs Lacey to give you a drink and that I'll pay for it."

He shook his head. "Respectable folk don't want no dirty tramps in their establishments. There are a few farmers that let us stay in their barns on raw nights in return for some wood chopping, but on the whole they'd just as soon set the dogs on us."

"I'm sorry," Emily said.

"You wouldn't understand, nice refined young girl like you," he said. He glanced down at his cleanly bandaged thumb. "But I thank you for your trouble, and I wish you all the best."

He got up and went towards the door. As she watched him walk away, Emily realized that they were two of a kind. She was an outcast, too.

CHAPTER TWENTY-SIX

The encounter with the tramp had left Emily quite shaken. She made herself a cup of tea and sat holding the mug of steaming liquid in her hands, feeling the warmth flow through her chilled body. The wise woman, he had said. Was that the same as the witch? But the wise woman had obviously been a healer, not a curser. And yet others had hinted that the women who had lived in the cottage were cursed. Her thoughts went to that journal. Did it contain the writings of the wise woman? But that was from long ago, from the eighteen fifties. Had there been other wise women since? Emily had to know more. She went through to the bedroom and brought the leather-bound volume back into the lamplight. The ink had faded to a pale brown, and she held up the page as she reread what she had only briefly scanned before.

From the Journal of Susan Olgilvy, July 10, 1858
In the Village of Bucksley Cross, Devonshire

> *I have done it. I am officially the schoolmistress of the vil-*
> *lage of Bucksley Cross, Devonshire, installed in my own*
> *little cottage at the edge of Dartmoor. There are thatched*
> *cottages on the other side of the green, a church with a tall,*

square tower and a public house that looks quite invit-
ing (although I am sure that ladies do not venture into
a public house, especially not spinster schoolmistresses).

Emily read on, skimming over the woman's description of the cottage (which hadn't changed at all since the eighteen fifties), until she came to words that made her heart jolt.

I try not to think that the whole cottage would fit nicely
inside our drawing room at Highcroft. Nor of my claw-
foot tub that Maggie, my maid, would have filled for me
with steaming water. I must accept this new position in
life, grateful at least that I shall be kept busy and that I
won't starve. Mother would be horrified if she saw me
now, but then I must not think of her either. She did not
try to intervene when Father told me I would no longer
be his child if I ran off to London to marry Finlay.
*   The very mention of Finlay's name is painful to me,*
and I break off from writing this.

Emily stared at the pages as if the words were shouting out to her. Susan Olgilvy had fled to marry the man she loved and something had gone wrong. She skimmed ahead hastily.

Perhaps the last occupant has married and moved away
to a husband and a home, although I find that hard to
believe, too, given that part of the schoolmistress's contract
stipulates no contact with the opposite sex. At least the par-
ish council won't have to worry about my improprieties.
There was only one man for me, and he lies buried in
Highgate Cemetery, crushed by falling cargo at the London
docks, where he was working to make a new life for me.

Emily let the book drop and stared into the fire, lost in thought. Miss Susan Olgilvy had been just like her: she had come from a tragedy and a loss, fleeing to a little-known part of the country to heal her wounds. No wonder Emily had felt a connection to the cottage from the start.

She had to read on now.

July 10 and then July 11

> *I was studying the garden beneath my window. It is composed of hopelessly overgrown bushes, some half-dead, others covered in a riot of convolvulus. I found myself thinking of the gardens at home—the immaculate lawns, the herbaceous borders, all looking so effortlessly manicured. I'd like to bring this garden back to order and beauty, but how will I know where to start? I was suddenly overcome with weariness and turned away, lest a tear escape from my eye.*
>
> *I took a long time to fall asleep, and was awoken by an alarming sound. A distant growl and then a loud, distinct thud near my bed. I was awake instantly, leaping out of bed. What could have made a noise like that? A creature landing on the floor maybe? My heart was racing as I felt around in the darkness for the lamp. It had still been daylight when I fell asleep, and I had not thought to test it out. As I leaned forwards, something struck me on the head, and I cried out in panic. Something was running down my face. Blood? I put my hand up and realized that my hair was now wet. Tentatively, I held out my hand and was hit by a cold drop of water.*

That was when I realized that it was raining outside. The growl I'd heard was now repeated as distant thunder, and it was clear that my roof was leaking! I made my way around the room until I located the basin, and I placed it beneath the drip. The noise was now even louder, a plink and splash every few seconds, but at least I had stopped the room from getting flooded. At last the rain stopped, and I fell asleep.

I awoke to brilliant sunlight streaming in through my window. Beyond the village green, the hills rose majestically. I heard the rattle of a harness as a wagon rumbled past. I opened my window, and sweet, herby smells wafted towards me: lavender and others that I couldn't identify. I love the smell of lavender—Nanny always kept lavender bags in my clothing drawers, and my clothes always had that sweet smell. For a second, I was taken back to the freshly scrubbed nursery with the big rocking horse and white bedspread, and Nanny saying, "Time to rise and shine, sleepyhead. Remember, it's the early bird that catches the worm."

I noticed the basin full of water on top of the chest of drawers. I looked up at the ceiling and the wet patch in it. I had to find out where the roof was leaking, otherwise I'd have the ceiling down on my head. I wondered if the parish council would be responsible for mending leaky roofs. I sincerely hoped so.

I realized I had to find a way up into the attic. I looked around, and found a square trapdoor in the hallway with a string attached. I pulled, the trapdoor opened and a ladder cascaded down. I found a bucket, hoisted my skirts, then gingerly climbed the ladder.

It was horribly dark up there, but I could see daylight coming in between the slates. I had located the leak in my roof. I felt an absurd sense of achievement as I placed the bucket beneath it. This would demonstrate to those school board members and the villagers of Bucksley Cross that I am not a pampered, upper-class girl, but as resilient as any hardened countryperson. With the bucket in place, I looked around to see if there was anything that might be useful. My first inspection was not encouraging. A chair with three legs. A picture frame with no picture in it. A wooden box full of old bottles. But in the corner was a hatstand—absolutely what I needed to hang my clothes. I dragged it to the opening and lowered it down. Then, I spotted an attractive wooden box. I opened it, and it contained a sewing kit. Again, very useful, as I will need to mend my clothing in the future. (Another skill I shall have to learn, I'm afraid. My sewing abilities have not progressed beyond embroidery, and I wasn't very good at that!) I carried the box down with me, reaching terra firma successfully.

I managed to shut the trapdoor, then moved my new-found treasures into the bedroom. The sewing box contained only a couple of spools of thread, a thimble and a card of darning needles. No great find. But then I realized this was only the top layer. I lifted it up and then gasped. Underneath was not more sewing equipment, but an ancient-looking, leather-bound book. Hoping for intimate details of a long-ago schoolmistress, I opened it. The writing is in a faint, spidery hand, and I had to take it over to the window to better read it:

Being the recipes for the creation of tinctures, salves, infusions and all manner of medicinals produced from the garden of the herb wife, Tabitha Ann Wise.

Underneath was written: Begun on this day, July 11, 1684.

I felt my hand tremble as I held the book. Today is July 11. I began to feel that I was meant to be here, meant to find this book. The herb wife! I looked out of the window at the neglected and overgrown bushes. Lavender, and was that rosemary? And were the others all herbs? I realized that I had landed in the middle of a healing garden.

Emily felt a strange rush of excitement as she stared at the page. So that was what the tramp had been talking about: the wise woman, the herb wife. The overgrown garden was a herb garden, and maybe somewhere in the cottage was that recipe book from long, long ago. For the first time in several weeks, she felt a small bubble of hope.

CHAPTER TWENTY-SEVEN

Emily awoke early the next morning with a new sense of excitement and purpose. Susan Olgilvy's journal had struck a chord with her. Their paths were too similar to be mere coincidence. They had both come from good homes, had run away to marry the men they loved, then had fled to this faraway corner after the deaths of the men they had hoped to marry. She looked out of her window at the overgrown and tangled garden and wondered if somehow she was destined to come here. It was, after all, a garden that had brought Robbie and her together, and fate had trained her as a land girl. Had all the women who came to this cottage been fleeing to a place of sanctuary? Had they all taken on the role of herb wife? The wise woman? It was a little overwhelming, but a challenge, too. She felt a strong sense that this was something she was meant to do—a way to bring some kind of meaning to a life in chaos.

She put on her dressing gown and opened the back door. The crisp, cold air made her gasp, and her breath came out like a dragon's smoke, but she set out along the narrow flagstone path. Her knowledge of plants was woefully inadequate, but that was lavender on her right, and under that tangle of dying bindweed was rosemary. The scents came to her as she brushed past each plant, some familiar, like mint and sage, others exotic and unknown. Some had no scent at all. But all were now dying off for the winter. If she was to make use of any of the plants, she would have to harvest them soon or wait until spring.

She jumped as something rubbed against her bare leg.

"Mew?" Shadow the cat looked up at her hopefully. She bent down to stroke it. "I have no food for you, my dear," she said. "I'm afraid you'll have to go off hunting for yourself."

It was almost as if the cat understood her. It stared at her with unblinking yellow eyes, then disappeared into the undergrowth. Emily shivered in the cold, and retreated to the warmth of the cottage.

The first task was to find the book of spells. She paused in wonder as that word passed through her head. *Recipes,* she thought to herself. *Not spells.* Was the wise woman also the one they had referred to as the witch? Surely she was looking for simple herbal cures such as her nanny had used for a sore throat: slippery elm, friar's balsam, oil of cloves for a toothache. She was about to go back into the cottage when she glanced up at the rising sweep of moor behind the estate. On the crown of the hill, a lone pony stood, silhouetted against the rising sun, his mane streaming out in the wind. He was so beautiful that Emily remained unmoving, watching him. Then he tossed his head and galloped off over the crest of the hill.

Somehow, she took this as a good sign—that the gods of nature had blessed her intention. She knew this was stupid. She had grown up in a boringly traditional household, one in which God or religion were rarely discussed. One went to church on Sundays because it was expected. Her mother insisted on sitting in the front pew to display her new hats. She was also on various committees that did charitable work around the parish. But Emily couldn't recall them ever praying at home. Apart from one highly religious nanny who had not lasted long, she had never felt any personal connection to religion. In fact, the only time she had prayed was when her brother went off to war. "Please keep him safe," she had pleaded. The memory of her brother's funeral came to her vividly: her mother sobbing behind a black veil, her father standing proud and erect. And that time, she had not prayed but railed against God. "Why did you let this happen to him? Why didn't you keep him safe?" But God had not answered then, and since that moment, she had avoided all contact with the Almighty.

Emily went back into the cottage, lit the stove to make tea and put on the large pan of water to wash with. Then she went looking for the book that Susan Olgilvy had mentioned. Tabitha Ann's book of herbal remedies. It was certainly not with the books in the trunk. She had been through them before. And there was nowhere to hide it amongst the few furnishings downstairs. She went up the steep stairs to the attic, glad that someone in the years between Susan Olgilvy and herself had put in a staircase and she hadn't had to climb a ladder that dropped from a trapdoor in the ceiling. Wind whistled through the attic as she picked her way through cast-offs from long ago. She came upon a box full of bottles and jars, some with faded labels on them, now too faint to read. These would be needed. She wondered if Susan Olgilvy had used them. She would have to read the rest of the journal to see if Susan had taken on the role of herb wife.

Emily put the box of bottles by the stairs and then went through the rest of the discarded items in the attic, but could find no pretty wooden sewing box. She had to conclude that Susan, or one of the subsequent women, had taken it with her. She felt an absurd sense of disappointment. There was no point in harvesting any of the herbs without the recipes. She left the box of bottles at the top of the stairs and made her way down again. Then she washed and dressed, and after a breakfast of bread and jam, she wound her scarf around her neck, put on her mackintosh and went out to work in the garden. As she came out of the back door, she almost stepped on an object. A dead mouse lay there. The cat sat beside it, looking rather smug.

"Why, thank you," Emily said, "but I'm afraid I don't eat mice. You'd better finish this yourself."

She resumed working in the kitchen garden. Simpson came past as she was cutting back a large bramble that was taking over a vegetable bed.

"Nasty things, brambles," he commented. "Watch yourself."

Emily nodded, then said, "Simpson, I notice we don't have winter vegetables planted. I'll clear the beds, but do you have seedlings started somewhere?"

"I don't," he said. "To tell the truth, I'm not up to all the bending and planting any more, and what with the work for Her Ladyship, there hasn't been time. I wasn't hired to be a gardener, you know. I was the groom and then the chauffeur, and now I've become jack of all trades."

"So what do we do about planting winter vegetables? Can we buy seedlings somewhere?"

He nodded. "Dawes nursery and feed store should have what we need, just outside Tavistock. I have to go that way this afternoon to see about a coal delivery. Do you want to come along with me and choose for yourself?"

"Thank you. I'd like that," she said. "I hope you don't mind my taking over your work in the kitchen garden?"

He gave a wheezy chuckle. "Of course I don't mind, my lovey. It's all a bit too much for me these days, what with my rheumatics and this cold wind. You just carry on with what you're doing and we'll all be grateful."

As he went to walk on, she called, "And, Simpson, what do you know about the herb garden?"

"Herb garden?"

"The one around the cottage. Was there a wise woman living there during your time here?"

He frowned. "There was a schoolteacher before Mr Patterson came. She tended the herbs, I seem to remember. But the local folk didn't like her much. She was bossy and interfering—told us the way things should be done. And tried to force her herbal remedies on people whether they wanted them or not, so I've been told."

"What happened to her?" Emily asked cautiously.

"She left, eventually. Got a place in a bigger school somewhere else, and the parish council built the new school building with the house attached, and they hired Mr Patterson. He's been here twenty years now. I can't say we're too fond of him either, but at least he keeps himself to himself."

Simpson went on his way and Emily resumed tackling the brambles. So it seemed there had been no herb wife for a long while, and yet the tramp had read the sign on the gatepost. Now she was curious: she wondered how long Susan had stayed as the schoolmistress and whether she had taken the precious book with her when she left. She couldn't wait to get back to the cottage to decipher more of Susan's elegant, faded script.

As she ate her lunch in the kitchen, she told Mrs Trelawney that she was going to make sure there were vegetables to keep them going for the winter.

"I wouldn't say no to that," the woman replied. "Cauliflower. Make sure you plant plenty of cauliflowers. Her Ladyship loves my cheese sauce."

"I'd like that, too," Emily said, glad that the woman was no longer treating her as the enemy.

They looked up as the bell rang.

"That will be Her Ladyship wanting her lunch, I expect," Mrs Trelawney said. "You go, Daisy. You've got young legs."

Daisy went and returned almost immediately. "Her Ladyship wanted to remind Emily that she is dining with her again tonight," she said. "And she asked you, Mrs Trelawney, to make something special. She said she had grown tired of nursery food."

"Nursery food, indeed." Mrs Trelawney sniffed. "Doesn't she realize there is a war on and we're all on rations? What does she think I'm going to do, wave my wand and conjure a nice joint of beef out of the air?"

"I have to go into Tavistock to buy seedlings," Emily said. "Which butcher do you use? I could see if they have any good meat today."

"We use Hamlin's in the market square," she replied. "They have our ration cards there, and I wouldn't say no to a nice pork chop, or some lamb chops. It's been a while since we've seen either. Or failing that, there's Dunn's, the fishmonger opposite, and Her Ladyship likes a fillet of plaice."

"All right." Emily nodded. "I'll see what I can do."

"Her Ladyship must think highly of you, letting you have the motor to go into Tavistock," Ethel commented, looking up from her macaroni pudding. "What with petrol being so hard to get."

"Simpson had to go to arrange for a coal delivery, so he suggested I go to the nursery for seedlings," Emily said hastily, noticing Mrs Trelawney's face. "We need to get the winter veg going if we are going to eat, don't we?"

Then she made a hurried exit. It was a pleasant drive towards Tavistock. They stopped first at the nursery, and with the help of the owner, Emily selected a tray of small plants, plus onion sets and seed potatoes. She came away well pleased, and they drove on into Tavistock.

"Take your time, my lovey," Simpson said. "I'm going to pop in on an old friend and see how he's doing. I hear he got this flu that's been going around."

A free afternoon—Emily couldn't remember when she had had any free time to herself. How often she had been bored at home when the hours had stretched out ahead of her with nothing to do. Recently, every moment had been occupied. She looked forward to having time to browse, but first she had a list of commissions from Lady Charlton and Mrs Trelawney. She started with the easy ones: cotton wool and corn plasters at the chemist's. While she was there, she remembered her tramp, and bought a bottle of antiseptic lotion and some cotton wool for herself. She posted two letters for Lady Charlton, as well as her own letter to Clarissa.

Then she went into the butcher's, but the man shook his head sadly. "I wish I could help Her Ladyship," he said, "but I haven't seen a chop in weeks. I can offer her kidneys or sausages or a neck of mutton, but that's about it." He paused, then added, "I could give you a nice rabbit if the old lady might like that for a change."

Emily decided to risk the rabbit. She also took the sausages, and then added a fillet of John Dory from the fishmonger. Having completed her commissions, she walked up the high street, her basket over her arm, enjoying looking in the shop windows. The toy shop, the dress shop and the shoe shop all looked sadly depleted. She bought darning wool for Mrs Trelawney and a small sewing kit for herself at the haberdasher's, then headed for the bookshop.

"Can I help you, miss?" the owner asked.

"Might you have any books on herbs?" Emily said.

"Herbs to use in cooking?" he asked.

"No, books on cultivating herbs and using them medicinally."

He frowned. "I do have a herbal dictionary that might be of use." He found it. "It gives the Latin names and drawings of the plants."

It was three and sixpence, a large expense for someone who had fifteen pounds to her name, but Emily wanted it. At least it would be a start in identifying what was growing in her herb garden. She paid for the book, and was going to leave the shop when she remembered Daisy and Alice. She had promised to teach them to read, and so far had not done much about it. With the winter coming and its long evenings, it would be an ideal time. So she wandered to the children's section to look at reading primers. She found what looked like a helpful book and was coming back to the counter when she heard an imperious voice saying, "I am looking for a novel by Baroness Orczy. A friend has particularly recommended it. I'm not sure of the title, but it is about . . ."

Emily froze, then stepped back between the shelves. It was her mother's friend Mrs Warren-Smythe, mother of Aubrey, with whom her parents had hoped she would make a match. What she was doing as far afield as Tavistock Emily couldn't imagine, but it was imperative this woman did not see her. She waited in the shadows, holding her breath until the shopkeeper came back with three Baroness Orczy books and put them on the counter in front of Mrs Warren-Smythe.

"These are the ones I have at the moment, madam. If you'd care to take a look and see which one was your friend's recommendation?"

As Mrs Warren-Smythe bent over the books, Emily put down the primer with regret, then sidled towards the exit, moving as silently as possible. Once outside, she looked around, making sure that Mr Warren-Smythe was not lurking outside waiting for his wife, then she walked away as quickly as possible. All the way home, her heart was beating fast. The almost-encounter had unnerved her. She hadn't considered before that Devon society was small and that her father was a well-known figure. The chances of being recognized were high. Then she told herself that she was overreacting. If she had actually encountered Mrs Warren-Smythe, all she'd have had to say was that she was still working with the Women's Land Army. It wasn't as if anyone could tell she was expecting yet. Her hand strayed to her stomach. *But soon,* she thought. *Soon it will be obvious.* Then she would have to stay put in the village.

CHAPTER TWENTY-EIGHT

The rabbit, fish and sausages were all deemed acceptable by Mrs Trelawney, and Emily carried her new book on herbs back to the cottage. The drawings were old-fashioned woodcuts, but they were good enough for her to be able to identify many of the plants. She drew a plan of the garden, then went outside and started to write down names. Some plants had died off this late in the year, and she would have to wait until spring to identify them, but others still had enough leaves to make them recognizable.

What's the point? she wondered as she came back into the cottage. *If I don't know what to do with them, then I'm wasting my time.*

She sat down and picked up the journal from the table. She felt a reluctance to go on reading, Daisy's words still whispering a warning in her head. "It's bad luck to read someone else's diary." But this wasn't a living person. She'd had the bad luck already, and anyway, she was an educated woman of the twentieth century. Surely she didn't believe in folk superstitions?

The next entries were frustrating because they referred to the recipes she hadn't been able to find. But they told her that Susan had also felt compelled to take on the role of herb wife, and had thrown herself into the task with enthusiasm. Emily skimmed over the domestic details, like making new curtains, harvesting herbs and hanging them to dry in the attic. Then visiting her classroom, meeting her pupils. At least there were a few valuable details here and there that she could use. But then she read a sentence that made her pay attention again. *"I hope Tabitha won't mind my using her book, but I left home in too much of a hurry to think about bringing a journal with me. And now I have no money to spend on such frivolities, even if the local shop stocked ladies' diaries, which I'm sure it doesn't."*

Using her book? Emily frowned. Then she gave an excited little laugh and turned the leather-bound volume over. The front and back covers were identical. And there, on the front page at the other end of the book, were the words *"Being the recipes for the creation of tinctures, salves, infusions and all manner of medicinals produced from the garden of the herb wife, Tabitha Ann Wise."*

Eagerly, Emily turned the page. The writing was badly faded and the script so old-fashioned that it was hard to read, but there were drawings and a list of plants.

> *Necessities for all manner of healing in the herb garden: Hyssop, Wormwood, Rue, Coriander, Pasqueflower, Rosemary, St John's Wort, Costmary, Lady's Mantle, Lady's Bedstraw, Angelica, Heartsease, Lily of the Valley, Marigold, Milk Thistle, Thyme, Sweet Woodruff.*
>
> *To these I plan to add, as time permits: Wood Betony, Comfrey, Coltsfoot, Cowslip, Hawthorn, Lavender, Lemon Balm, Meadowsweet, Sage, Valerian, Yarrow and Winter Savory.*

Emily had no idea what most of these plants looked like and whether they were actually all growing in the herb garden. She turned the page to what were indeed recipes. She translated from the ancient spelling as she went along:

For the easing of a chesty cough: Coltsfoot syrup.

Place two ounces (a goodly handful) of coltsfoot in two gills of water. Place a saucepan on the hob and cover with a lid. Simmer for twenty minutes then strain off the liquid and discard the herbs. Reduce by one third. Dissolve six ounces of sugar or honey into the liquid. Allow to cool.

Administer one spoonful three times a day.

She realized something else, too. Local people had spoken of the wise woman, and Emily had taken this to be an attribute of hers. But the writer's name was Wise. A doubly wise woman. She looked up with reluctance when the church clock chimed the hour and she realized she should go up for her evening meal.

"I am going to start working on the herb garden around the cottage," she said casually to Lady Charlton.

"Are you really? I am impressed with this enthusiasm for gardening."

"I just thought Mrs Trelawney might appreciate herbs for cooking," she said, not wanting to say anything about the recipes and the role of herb wife until she could prove that she was capable of making some of the remedies.

"Don't tire yourself out too much," Lady Charlton said. "I think you will find that the herbs can wait until spring. Most of them have probably died back for the winter anyway."

"Yes, you're right," she agreed.

Lady Charlton looked up from her sherry. "Did you have an agreeable visit to Tavistock this afternoon? I never thanked you for bringing my items from the chemist."

"It made a change to look in shop windows," she said. "It's something I haven't had time to do for ages."

"I don't go out much any more," Lady Charlton said. "I find it so depressing. One realizes how dreary everything has become since the war started—shabby, outdated clothing, tired-looking people and no young men on the streets. When the war ends, I wonder if we will have the energy to recover."

"I'm sure we will," Emily said, more brightly than she felt. "We are a resilient nation, after all."

Lady Charlton nodded. "It is young people like you who give me hope. You have been through the fire, and yet you choose to believe in the future."

"I have no choice," Emily replied. "I am responsible for a child now, so I can't give up or give in."

"Quite right."

Lady Charlton looked up as Mrs Trelawney came in with the main course. "The young lady managed to find you a bit of John Dory," Mrs Trelawney said. "And there's a rabbit, too. It will make a rabbit pie for tomorrow and a stew after that."

"You seem to be a worker of wonders," Lady Charlton said. "How long since I've had a decent piece of fish, Mrs Trelawney? And rabbit? What a treat."

Mrs Trelawney gave Emily a sharp, hostile glance as she went away.

Emily hurried back to the cottage, anxious to read more of Tabitha Ann Wise's book. She had just started making notes for herself when there was a tap at her front door. She opened it cautiously, half-expecting to see another tramp there, but instead Alice barged in.

"Well, there you are," Alice said. "I hear you've gone all hoity-toity on us. Dining with Her Ladyship every night!" She put on a false upper-class voice. "And not enough time to visit your old mates any more."

"It wasn't my idea to dine with Lady Charlton," Emily said. "I tried to tell her I needed to learn to be independent, but she wouldn't hear of it. She's starved for company, and I'm not saying no to a good meal."

"And what about your poor, old friend?" Alice asked.

Emily laughed. "You're not starved for company. You've got Nell Lacey and anyone who comes to the pub. How are you getting on there?"

"We get on like a house on fire, Nell and me. We're always laughing and joking. Of course, it's not all tea and crumpets, you know. We got a new barrel of beer delivered today and we had to get it down the steps between us. I don't know how she managed before I arrived."

"Any news on her husband?" Emily asked.

Alice shook her head. "Still much the same. I wonder if he'll ever leave that hospital. So what have you been doing with yourself?"

"Working in the garden. I went into Tavistock to buy seedlings for winter vegetables." She took a deep breath. "And I've found out that there is a herb garden around the cottage. I'm planning to see if I can make herbal remedies. You know they said a witch lived here once? Well, I think it was a woman who made healing potions. I'm going to try some."

"You want to be careful," Alice said. "You might end up killing us all. And from what they say, the women who lived here all came to bad ends." Then she grinned. "Anyway, how are you feeling?"

"A lot better," Emily said. "The sickness is improving—apart from after having to eat tripe and onions, that is."

"Tripe and onions? That's enough to make anyone throw up." They exchanged a grin.

"Would you like a cup of tea?" Emily asked.

"No thanks, love. I'm looking forward to my nightly gin. But this place is looking better already. More homely, somehow. And Daisy's getting on all right?"

"She's taken on all the hard work, so they all adore her. I don't think she minds. She enjoys being appreciated."

"I expect we'll see you on Sunday then, if you don't come down to the pub before that," Alice said. "The harvest festival at the church. You'll be coming?"

"Oh yes. I think so. Mrs Trelawney was talking about what vegetables to bring. Apparently, it's something of an ongoing competition. And she's baking apple pies for the supper afterwards."

"What's that?" Alice jumped as Shadow appeared and sidled up to her.

"It's my cat," Emily said. "He's adopted me, apparently. Actually, I'm not sure what sex it is, but he seems like a male. I'm calling him Shadow. I leave the scullery window open and he comes and goes as he pleases."

"Don't let the locals know you've got a black cat or they'll start saying you're the new witch. They'll be on the lookout for you riding past on your broomstick." Alice laughed.

"I must say, I enjoy his company," Emily replied. "He's quite undemanding, and he brought me a mouse this morning as a present." She bent to stroke him. "Do you know, I've never had a pet before. Mummy had an aversion to animals. They thought they made the place dirty."

Alice gave her a long, hard look. "I don't know how you turned out so well. That mother of yours sounds like a right old grouch, if you don't mind me saying so."

"I don't mind, and I have to agree with you." Emily laughed.

CHAPTER TWENTY-NINE

Emily rose extra early the next day and started on the task of harvesting some of the herbs. She tied together stems of lavender, rosemary, thyme and sage, as well as others she had not yet identified, and hung them in the attic to dry. Then she set to work preparing the bed in the kitchen garden and planting out her seedlings. Simpson came to watch and advised her to use mulch to keep out the frost. Then he came back with a roll of bird netting.

"You'll need this over them little plants, my lovey," he said, "or you'll find the rabbits will get them all." He helped her stake out the netting over the bed. By the time darkness fell, she looked with satisfaction at the neatly planted beds. *If my parents could see me now, they'd be amazed,* she thought. Then a picture of Robbie came to her. "My word, you're turning into quite a farmer," he'd say, smiling at her. "And I thought the farm in Australia would be too much for you. But I can see you're going to do splendidly."

"Oh Robbie," she whispered, staring out into the night sky. Was there a heaven, she wondered, and was he there, looking down on her? It was all too painful to contemplate. She brushed away a tear and started picking up her garden tools.

That evening, she wanted to begin transcribing the remedies, but Lady Charlton lingered over dinner.

"Shall you be coming to the harvest festival at church on Sunday?" Emily asked.

The old lady shook her head. "I don't think so. I'm too old to be jostled by crowds, and frankly, I am not particularly popular with the villagers."

"Why is that?" Emily was surprised to hear herself asking this.

The old lady sat, her face having taken on that haughty expression Emily had first encountered. "I suppose it was my own fault. After the business with my grandson—who was extremely well liked locally, I might say—and then the death of my son, I virtually shut myself away. I had no wish to be polite to anybody. So I reverted to acting the grand lady of the manor."

"You should come with me," Emily said. "I think we all need each other these days. There isn't one family around here that hasn't lost a husband or a son. We're all hurting."

The old lady sighed. "I suppose you are right, but not this time. You can tell them the cold wind is not good for my aged joints."

"I don't think there is anything wrong with your aged joints," Emily said, giving her a critical frown. "You need to get out more. Come and talk to me when I'm working in the garden. It would do you good."

"If I thought you were going to be my new governess and order me around, I'd never have invited you for sherry in the first place," Lady Charlton said, but she smiled.

On Sunday, Emily, under Mrs Trelawney's supervision, picked the basket of vegetables to be placed at the altar.

"It's not like the old days," Mrs Trelawney remarked critically. "But the pumpkin's not bad. And nobody will be able to find fault with my apple pies, that's for sure."

Emily carried the vegetables and Daisy and Mrs Trelawney took the apple pies down to the church hall. The altar steps were already piled with fruit and vegetable offerings, and Emily noticed there was one large marrow. Mrs Trelawney would not be pleased about that, she thought.

The harvest service of thanksgiving was conducted with lusty singing of "Come Ye Thankful People, Come." The vicar preached a sermon saying that, in the toughest times, God still revealed his bounty to us. Afterwards, everyone assembled in the parish hall, where the tables were now covered in a fine array of food.

"It's not like the old days, is it?" Emily heard someone repeat Mrs Trelawney's words. "We always used to have a pig roasting on a spit."

"The war will be over soon, so they say. Those Huns are running for their lives, and we've killed so many of them they'll have to come to terms," was the reply. "I'd say we've taught them a lesson."

"But at what cost, Mrs Upton? At what cost, eh?"

There might not have been a pig roast, but there were egg and bacon pies, sausage pies, all manner of sandwiches and pickles and then jellies, blancmanges, rock cakes and fruit pies. Emily joined Alice and Daisy at a table beside Nell Lacey. Mrs Soper from the forge came to sit beside them.

"It's all very well for them to be saying the war will be over soon and everything will go back to normal," Mrs Soper said angrily. "It won't go back to normal for me, will it? How am I supposed to cope with the blacksmithy, I'd like to know? We're doing our best, but my husband's father is now ninety. He knows the trade all right, but the strength is not there. And frankly, I'm not up to it either. I don't see how we'll get the place up and running again after the war ends. Not unless some willing young men come home, which I can't see happening."

A sudden thought struck Emily. She leaned across to Alice and whispered in her ear. Alice grinned and nodded. Emily turned to Mrs Soper. "We think we might know someone who can help you," she said. "One of the land girls who worked with us was really big and strong. We think she could do the work of a man. She's not the brightest, but if you showed her what to do, I think she might work out for you."

"Really?" Mrs Soper looked hopeful. "Do you think she'd want to come to an out-of-the-way place like this?"

"I think she would. I don't think there was anything for her at home, and she enjoyed our company. Should I write to her for you?"

"I'd be most grateful if you would, my dear," Mrs Soper said. "I could certainly use any kind of help. You ladies coming here was a godsend."

Emily noticed Mr Patterson, the schoolmaster, sitting alone at the end of one of the long tables. He was a slim, effete-looking man with a receding hairline, smartly dressed in suit and cravat, and he was eating a pasty in a fastidious way, dabbing at the corners of his mouth with his napkin. Emily felt sorry for him, and at the same time had an idea. She got up and went over to him. "We haven't met yet, but I'm Emily Kerr." The lie was still hard to say out loud, and she felt herself blushing as she said it. "I've come to live in the estate cottage, as you have probably heard," she said. "I wondered if I might ask a favour of you. The two women who have come with me have very poor reading skills. I wondered if I might borrow a beginning reading primer from the school so I could work with them in the evenings."

The man rose to his feet and held out his hand to her. "How do you do, Mrs Kerr? Yes, my pupils have informed me that we have visitors in the village. I am most pleased to make your acquaintance. Perhaps you will be good enough to share a glass of my parsnip wine one evening. I am rather proud of my home-made wines, and the parsnip is particularly fine, I believe."

Emily began to think that her evenings would never be her own, but the man had a guardedly eager look on his face. "I've never tried parsnip wine," she said, "but I'd be delighted to sample it."

"Splendid," he said. "Shall we say tomorrow then?"

"If you like."

"I will be happy to show you what reading materials I use for the children, as well as some stories that are suitable for a beginning reader."

"Thank you. That will be perfect."

"I commend you for wanting to help your fellow travellers."

"Oh, I think it's vital to be able to read," Emily said. "I don't know what I would do without books. I've been starved for them these past few months while I've been working with the Women's Land Army. We've been so exhausted after dinner that we've fallen asleep straight away, and when we haven't, there have been five other women in the room, all chattering."

"So now you'll finally have some peace and quiet, I'd imagine. I also have a good library of my own. You'd be welcome to inspect it and borrow anything that takes your fancy."

Emily glanced up to see the vicar's wife, Mrs Bingley, watching her critically. *Perhaps she does not approve of my talking to an unmarried man,* Emily thought, and tried not to smile. But she didn't want the villagers to think of her as flighty. "I should go back to my friends," she said. "Tomorrow evening then."

As she walked away, Mrs Bingley stepped out to intercept her. "A word with you, Mrs Kerr," she said. There was a strange, triumphant look in her eyes that Emily couldn't quite interpret.

"Of course." Emily gave her a friendly smile.

The vicar's wife drew her aside. "I happen to know that you are not what you seem," she said.

"I beg your pardon?"

"I've been watching you ingratiating yourself with all and sundry. I wonder how they would feel if they knew the truth. You are not a war widow, at all. You are an unmarried girl who has got herself into unfortunate circumstances and has fled to hide her shame."

Mrs Trelawney, Emily thought. She had been eavesdropping, and had been delighted to spread the news. She fought back rising anger. "For your information, Mrs Bingley, under normal circumstances, I would have been married by now. My fiancé was sent back to the front and died a hero."

"All the same, you are still a sinner in the eyes of the church."

"Are we not all sinners, Mrs Bingley? I believe my nanny taught me something about the one without sin who may cast the first stone."

"Jesus also had plenty to say about hypocrites," Mrs Bingley snapped, "about those who claim to be what they are not."

"It was suggested to me that it would be simpler if I claimed to be a war widow," Emily said. "But I really don't mind if you spread the news around the village. I think you'll find that everyone else appreciates my plight and the difficult situation in which I find myself. And if they don't, then I have enough friends here and enough places where I am welcome."

"I trust you will not dare to show your face at the church, or anything that I am running."

"Doesn't Jesus welcome the repentant sinner?" Emily asked. "Only actually, I'm not repentant. I'm very glad that my young man went back to the front, and ultimately to his death, knowing how much he was loved." It was Emily's turn to look triumphant.

"And what about Lady Charlton? What if she knows?" Mrs Bingley asked.

"She does know. I couldn't accept her hospitality under false pretences," Emily said. "And I can see now why she is not keen to attend any function at the church. Now please excuse me. I must return to my friends." She gave a polite little bow and went back to Alice.

"What was that all about? Was she asking you to join her altar guild or teach Sunday school?" Alice asked.

"No, quite the opposite. She was telling me I wasn't welcome at her church because she's found out the truth about me."

"Spiteful old biddy," Alice said. "Don't mind her, love. You've already got enough friends here. I think you'll do just fine."

Yes, Emily thought as she walked home. *I think I will do just fine here.*

CHAPTER THIRTY

In a way, Emily wished she had turned down Mr Patterson's invitation to parsnip wine. She was now keen to decipher the herbal remedies and see if she could make any of them. From the little she had read of Susan Olgilvy's diary, Emily had learned that she had thrown herself into the role with enthusiasm and had commented on the success or failure of each recipe. But it would have been unforgivably rude to cancel on Mr Patterson, especially when she had heard what a recluse he was.

All the same, she hesitated as she went through the school playground to his front door. If Mrs Bingley had already told him the truth, then perhaps he would no longer wish to be associated with her. His face, when he opened the door, showed that he was indeed pleased to see her. His tiny sitting room was meticulously neat. A white-lace-trimmed tray held a crystal decanter and two glasses. A fire blazed in the hearth, and two leather armchairs faced each other. The walls were lined with books.

"Do take a seat, Mrs Kerr," he said. "The evenings are already getting chilly, don't you think?"

Emily agreed that they were.

"And I have found some reading material that might be suitable for your friends," he said, handing her a pile of books. "Are they able to read at all?"

"One has rudimentary reading skills but could benefit from practice," Emily said. "But the other never learned to read at all. However, I think she is bright and willing."

Mr Patterson nodded. "If you feel that this task is not agreeable to you, then I would volunteer to teach the young lady myself in the evenings."

"That's very kind of you, but I think she may feel intimidated by a strange man. She is embarrassed that she has never learned to read."

Conversation proceeded along conventional lines. The weather. The hopefully swift ending to hostilities. Emily admired his books, and they discussed favourite authors. The parsnip wine was surprisingly potent, and Emily gave a little gasp as she took a sip.

"Yes, it does have a kick to it, doesn't it?" Mr Patterson looked pleased. "My nettle wine was, alas, rather a failure this year. The elderberry wine was not bad at all, but the parsnip is my pièce de résistance, as they say."

He did not ask any personal questions, and Emily hesitated to do so, as if this might be crossing a line. But when she asked how long he had been in the village, he replied, "Twenty years."

"You have not grown tired of it?"

He shook his head. "I came here as a young man after I managed to survive a bout of consumption. I was given up for lost many times, but I recovered. And it was suggested that I should live far from the smoke of the city because of my damaged lungs. I had inherited a small amount from my father, and at that time I had the deluded notion that I should write a great novel. So I came here. The teaching is not exacting. I enjoy the fresh innocence of my pupils, but alas the great novel has not materialized. I have had a couple of pieces of poetry published, but that is the extent of my literary success."

"Surely many writers do not meet with success until they are older than you," Emily said tactfully.

He smiled again, the frown lines disappearing from his face. "Kind of you, Mrs Kerr. But I have to admit that I lack talent. When I have tried a story, I can see it is but a rehash of a novel by a master."

"But you should not stop trying," Emily said.

"Indeed, I will not."

After what she considered was an appropriate amount of time, Emily got up to leave.

"Just a minute." Mr Patterson held up his hand. He darted into the kitchen, then returned holding a small jar. "Please accept some of my honey. I keep bees up on the hillside, and the heather makes such an agreeable flavour."

"How very kind. Now I have something to look forward to with my breakfast," Emily said.

"I do hope we can do this again," he said as he accompanied her to the door. "I found our conversation most agreeable. That is what one lacks in a village. Stimulating conversation is, I am afraid, at a minimum."

"I look forward to it," Emily said. "And if I can ever turn my little cottage into a civilized place, I shall return the favour."

"You don't mind living there?" he asked, the frown returning. "One hears such awful rumours about the place . . . Why nobody has lived there in so long and what befell former residents. Old wives' tales, I'm sure, but nonetheless . . ."

"I feel quite at home there, Mr Patterson," she replied. "What's more, I am working to bring the herb garden back to life."

"That's right." He broke into a smile again. "There used to be a herb garden. I remember hearing about it. One can do so many wonderful things with herbs—teas and salves."

"I aim to try some of them. If I am successful, I will let you know."

"Then I wish you *bonne chance*," he said.

Emily felt the warm glow of the parsnip wine as she walked back along the lane. She had worried that she would be all alone in the world, but already she had found friends. Mr Patterson was, like herself, a fugitive from the outside world.

After she had undressed, she brought Susan's diary into the bedroom and pulled the covers up around her while she read by candlelight. Shadow appeared as silently and mysteriously as ever, and without waiting to be invited, he jumped up on to the bed beside her. She felt the warmth of his slim body against her and the vibration of his purring. The diary continued in matter-of-fact fashion: new remedies tried, small encounters with problem pupils. It seemed that the Lord Charlton of that time was a bachelor who chose to spend most of his time in London. Susan thought it a pity because she greatly admired the grounds of Bucksley House, which were kept in immaculate condition.

Emily mused that Susan had shared nothing of her own loss and distress after those first pages. One would never know how lonely she was, whether she wished for her former privileged life, even how she managed to fend for herself in the cottage. She got on with it. *Which is what I am doing,* Emily decided.

A breakthrough came when one of Susan's pupils developed whooping cough and was suffering with wrenching bouts of coughing. Susan made a batch of Tabitha Ann Wise's cough syrup, and the result was more successful than she had dreamed. The child's spasms lessened, and he became more comfortable immediately. Thereafter, other members of the community started coming to her with various maladies.

Then came another long entry:

> *Interesting encounter today. A Mr T. appeared on my doorstep. He was concerned about his wife, and hoped I could do something for her. They had recently returned from India, and were leasing a house about three miles away. His wife had not been able to endure the Indian*

climate, and was in poor health. Would I at least come and see her, and perhaps be able to concoct a tonic for her to restore her to health?

I pointed out to him that I was no physician. I could make teas and infusions that eased simple ailments: rheumatism, gout, colds and influenza. But if her problems were more serious, then she needed the help of a doctor.

"What she needs, if you really want to know," he said, "is a woman friend. Someone who is concerned about her health and is helping her to get better. I truly think the tonic could contain sugar water and she would improve, if she really believed in it."

With some reluctance, I agreed that I would come. He came for me in a trap with a sprightly little grey on the following Saturday. On the way there, he told me that he had been in the army, the Bengal Lancers, and had enjoyed the excitement of military life, but he had resigned his commission out of concern for his wife's health. He wasn't sure what he wanted to do next or where he wanted to settle. Maria favoured living somewhere like Bath, but he couldn't stomach city life and the daily round of polite society. He was born to be a man of action, he said.

The house was a good solid stone one, such as we had at home in the north, set amid extensive grounds, but quite remote from any village. Maria T. was lounging on a daybed, a coverlet tucked around her, even though the day was a pleasant one. She was pretty in a pale, Nordic sort of way, with almost white-blonde hair and skin as translucent as the china dolls I had played with as a child. She held out a languid hand to me. The hand was like ice, and I cradled it between my own.

"I felt the heat so dreadfully in India," she said. "And now I am afraid I feel the cold. I do nothing but shiver and require the servants to fill hot-water bottles for me."

We talked for a long while. She told me about India, which she had found a horrifying, brutal place. Beggars with sores all over them, small children deformed by their parents to earn money begging. Flies everywhere. Snakes. She had once thought that one of her black stockings lay in a chair. She went to pick it up and it was cobra.

"It was fine for Henry," she said. "He was off with the other officers playing polo or pig sticking when they weren't keeping the natives in check."

"You presumably had other wives whose company you enjoyed?" I asked.

"Too much of their company, which I did not particularly enjoy." She sighed. "We lived in each other's pockets. They gossiped and talked endlessly about their children. Flirting with other officers was a sport for them. And they didn't seem to mind the heat and the filth. I felt drained and indisposed the whole time."

I promised to help her regain her health and said I would make a tonic for her. Her husband was pathetically grateful. I went home, studied the herb book and came up with a tonic that would raise her mood, as well as stimulate the blood flow in her body. I hope it will do her some good.

The candle flickered and was burning low. Reluctantly, Emily closed the journal, blew out the candle and pulled the covers up around her. The cat curled up next to her, showing no indication of wanting to spend the night outside.

CHAPTER THIRTY-ONE

A few days later, Maud arrived. Emily and Alice took her to meet Mrs Soper. She didn't seem at all daunted when she was shown the forge and the tasks she'd have to perform.

"I've never had to shoe a horse before," she said, "and my experience with milking cows wasn't too good, but I reckon I'll get the hang of it."

"We're quite a little community now," Alice remarked as they walked back together along the village green. "If my Bill could see me pulling the pints, he wouldn't half laugh. 'You've got muscles on you, girl,' he'd say."

"I was picturing Robbie doing the same," Emily said, and realized she could mention his name without a violent stab of pain. Maybe there was hope that she was starting to heal. That evening, she went over the notes she had taken from the two journals and decided to try some of the recipes using the herbs she had harvested. She had identified and collected a good dozen plants. Some of the recipes called for the flowers, which were not obtainable at this time of year, others for the bark or the roots. A tea with balsam and lavender worked as it was supposed to, making her drowsy. Creating a tincture looked a little daunting, so she left that for later. Then she went back to Susan's journal, anxious to know if the tonic was successful for her languid Mrs T.

I have been to see Mrs T. on several occasions now. She claims my tonic is doing her good, but she still has no energy and her skin is still so frightfully pale, as if she has no blood flowing through her veins. And she shows so little interest in anything. I have tried reading the newspaper to her, talking about fashions and food, but I get no flicker of response. I suggested that she see a doctor, but she claims she has seen countless doctors who have yet to find anything wrong with her. The last one advised brisk walks in the fresh air and suggested she would be more healthy if she had children. The poor woman broke down in distress as she told me this. Apparently, she is incapable of having a normal physical relationship with her husband, who has endured this patiently over ten years. It seems to me more and more that the problems are emotional, not physical. She is afraid of everything, and thus excludes herself from most of what life has to offer.

More entries followed:

It was a gorgeous spring day, and I offered to take Mrs T. to see the daffodils that are blooming in profusion on a nearby hillside. She claimed the wind was too chilly for her. I wish I knew what to do to break her out of this cycle. It is clear she welcomes my visits, but I think that I am her only caller.

Mr T. and I had a lively discussion on the way home about the Irish question. Words became quite heated, and he apologized as we pulled up in front of the cottage. I told him I enjoyed a good debate and invited him in for

a cup of tea. He examined my small herbal laboratory
I have set up in the former scullery and was impressed.

Emily read on. Susan said nothing, but Emily could tell that a connection was growing between herself and Mr T.

A strange and wonderful but also frightening event happened today. I can hardly bear to write down the words, but I want to remember every detail, lest I forget it. We were driving back to the cottage as usual. Mrs T. seemed a little worse on account of the spate of bad weather, which affects her head, giving her constant headaches. I agreed to try the remedy for headaches I have read but have yet to make. It involves wood betony, skullcap and the bark of the willow, which conveniently grows beside our rushing stream.

Anyway, on the way home, the heavens opened and we were drenched within seconds. Then there was a flash of lightning and almost simultaneously a great crash of thunder. The poor little mare took off, running away with us at full tilt. Mr T. tried in vain to stop her, but to no avail. We came down a steep hill with a narrow bridge going over the stream at the bottom. I thought we should surely tip over at any moment, and I clung to Mr T. and the side of the trap as it lurched from side to side.

Without warning, a large branch came down across the road in front of us. It was an act of God. The horse reared and stopped dead in its tracks. We were safe. Mr T. jumped down and calmed the terrified animal. Then he climbed up beside me again.

"I'm so sorry, Miss Olgilvy. Are you unharmed?"
Mr T. asked me.

"A little shaken, I must confess." I started to laugh nervously. "I thought I enjoyed speed, but that was a little too fast for my taste."

"My dear girl, you are a marvel," he said. "Any other woman would have had a fit of the vapours by now."

"I am not prone to vapours, Mr T.," I said, still laughing.

"No, of course you aren't. You are . . . just perfect." Then he took my chin in his hand, drew me towards him and kissed me. And I am sorry to say that, in the heat of the moment, I returned his kiss. Afterwards, we were both overcome with guilt and swore that this should not happen again.

Emily looked up from the book. *Poor Susan,* she thought. She had found a man who was right for her, and yet their love could never be. And the second thought that came to her was that Robbie and she had made love in a similar storm. It seemed as if their entire lives were progressing along parallel lines. She read the next entry.

I lay awake in turmoil all night, so bitterly ashamed of myself that I had betrayed the woman who had come to trust me. I realized then what I had refused to admit to myself before: that a connection had been growing between Mr T. and myself. And I could not blame him for that reckless moment. He was a healthy man who had been denied the intimacy a husband can expect. And I had to admit that I was also attracted to his lively mind and his rugged appearance. I had thought that I could never love another man after Finlay. How ironic that the man I could love is married to someone else. At least this proves that the heart can heal.

By morning, I had come to a decision. I should have to break off all contact with Maria T., lest I be tempted again. I would write her a note, telling her that I had been neglecting my duties as a schoolmistress and could no longer find the time to visit her personally. I would send over supplies of her tonic, if she felt it was doing any good, and wish her a speedy recovery.

It was with a heavy heart that I put that letter in the pillar box. I was never to see him again.

Emily closed the diary, feeling tears welling in her eyes. Susan had nobly renounced her own chance at happiness. But now she was curious. Did Susan then remain the spinster schoolmistress for the rest of her days, living a solitary life like Mr Patterson? And what happened to Maria T.? She flicked through the pages of the journal. There were not many more entries, and then sheets of plain paper. So either Susan had abandoned writing her journal soon after or she had bought herself another book and started afresh. Perhaps she had moved on to a new life and had found happiness elsewhere . . . Emily realized she couldn't stop reading now.

It has been a month since I last visited Maria T. Her husband came to see me, saying that his wife was in a terrible state after having received my letter, and he begged me to reconsider. I told him the truth—that I acknowledged an attraction between us and that we should not put ourselves in the way of temptation again. I could tell he was bitterly disappointed, and he clearly looked forward to my visits as much as his wife did. But he is also an honourable man. "I have grown immensely fond of you," he agreed. "I find myself thinking about you, going over every detail of our last moments together. But as you point out, I am married to another. I took her for better or worse, and I must abide by my promise."

When he got up to leave, he took my hands in his. "May I kiss you one last time?" he asked.

I couldn't speak, but nodded. I felt the jolt of desire as his lips fastened on to mine. When we broke apart, we stood there, holding hands, looking into each other's faces as if trying to remember every detail. Then he said, "You should go away from here. You deserve a good life amongst bright and lively people. You deserve to make a good marriage and be happy and have children around you."

I felt like saying, "So do you, but you will not have what you want," but I wisely kept silent. "You should go," I said. "People will talk if they see you lingering too long in my cottage."

He smiled then. His whole face lit up when he smiled. "I love you," he said simply. Then he walked away.

There were only three more entries. *So she took his advice and moved away,* Emily thought. *She found happiness elsewhere.* She turned the page. There was something different about the writing. Until then, the penmanship had been perfect. Now it seemed scratchy and jagged, and there was a blot on the page.

Today, I had a visit from two policemen, who came with terrible, shocking news. Maria T. has died. I was asked a lot of questions pertaining to the tonic I prescribed for her. I showed them the recipe and pointed out that the ingredients were all simple herbs, quite harmless. I thought they went away satisfied, but I was left very shaken. They can't have thought . . .

November 21, 1858

The policemen returned, and with them was a man from Scotland Yard in London. It seemed that tests had been done on Maria's body, and they had found traces of arsenic. More questions were asked about the tonic. Then they moved on to my relationship with Mr T. I replied haughtily that there was no relationship with Mr T. He merely drove me to and from his house. One of the policemen was grinning in a most unnerving way. It seemed I had been seen kissing Mr T. "Locked in a passionate embrace," was how he put it.

"And what better way to get rid of an inconvenient wife than with a tonic that was supposed to cure her," he said.

I replied most indignantly that I had done nothing wrong. The passionate embrace they had mentioned was nothing more than a friendly hug from a man who wished to cheer me up. As for the tonic, I showed them the recipe.

"And how easy to add a little arsenic to it," the policeman said. "You are to remain here until further notice. Do not think of running away, because that would only make it worse for you."

I am all a-tremble. I cannot think where or why Maria T. obtained arsenic. I can only think that she planned to end her own life, and mixed the arsenic with the tonic to swallow it. Or . . . and my blood now runs cold . . . she had realized the truth that her husband and I were falling in love. She decided to end her own life and punish the two of us at the same time. I saw how that was all too possible. But then a third thought, most disturbing of all, came to me. Surely it wasn't possible that Mr T. had administered the arsenic to his wife so that he could be together with me? This I could not believe. He was a man of honour, I would swear to it.

But whatever the circumstances, the outlook is bleak for me. I am so tempted to write to my father and beg for his help. He is a man of influence, but far away in the north of England. And he may be of the opinion that anything that befalls me since disobeying him and eloping with an unsuitable man is my own fault, and I must face the consequences. But he would not let his only daughter hang, would he?

As I write the word "hang," I feel a chill running down my spine. Is my life to be ended because of a vengeful woman? A woman whose mental state was clearly not stable?

And there was one more entry.

To anyone who reads this: I am innocent. Will nobody come to my aid? The black carriage has drawn up outside. They have come with a warrant for my arrest . . . on a charge of the wilful murder of Maria Tinsley. May God have mercy on my soul.

CHAPTER THIRTY-TWO

Emily could not sleep that night. She still felt guilty that she had read Susan's diary, and yet the last page showed that Susan wanted it to be read. She wanted someone to come to her rescue. But who could have done so? Mr T. would presumably also have been a suspect regarding his wife's death. He could not have vouched for Susan's innocence. Then the awful truth struck her. The villagers had said there were two murders. One was the woman whom Lady Charlton thought had not died, but had run off with a gypsy. And the other . . . the witch who was hanged.

"It's my own fault," she said out loud. "I should never have read her diary. Now I'll never be able to get her out of my mind."

The next morning, she looked at her notes and the dried herbs on the table. *I should stop this nonsense right away,* she thought. *Maybe the villagers are right and the cottage is cursed.* She dressed hurriedly, wrapped a shawl around herself and went outside. Then she wielded the pruning shears and cut back all the plants in her little garden until there were just bare stalks showing. "No more," she said. She didn't know why she had been so attracted by the stupid notion of taking over as the herb wife, the wise woman. And the notion that she was somehow fated to come here and fulfil the role now terrified her. Those women had all met bad ends. That was what they said in the village. She was tempted to take Lady Charlton up on her offer and move into the big house right away, but the thought of Mrs Trelawney shadowing her, looking at her with those spiteful little eyes, was not appealing.

As she re-entered the cottage through the back door, she heard a letter land on the front doormat. Shadow rushed to examine it, decided it wasn't edible and walked away again. Emily picked it up and saw the armed forces postage stamp on it. From Clarissa!

> *My dear, dear friend,*
>
> *I was so shocked and sorry to read your sad news. And even more shocked at the callous and cruel behaviour of your parents. To reject their only daughter like that when you were in such dire need of love and nurturing. Well, rest assured that I shall not turn you away in your hour of need. As soon as I come home—and it should be only a matter of weeks now, they are saying—I aim to find a job nursing in a proper hospital. I may have to do some studying or an apprenticeship, but I feel that I am well qualified, and they would be lucky to get me! (You see, I never did lack confidence, did I?)*
>
> *And when I am settled, I shall rent a little house nearby, and you shall come to live with me, and together we will raise little Humphrey or Hortense or whatever you choose to call him/her. Won't that be fun? An adoring auntie on hand!*

Emily put down the letter, as she felt herself about to cry. Finally, a door had opened for her—someone did care about her. She could look forward to plans for her future. She did not have to stay in this place. She was surprised at the swift pang of regret that she felt. She liked it here. She enjoyed the company of Lady Charlton and the women in the village. At least, she had liked it here, until she had discovered the truth about Susan Olgilvy.

"No more herbal nonsense," she said out loud, making the cat look up from washing himself in front of the fire. She went out to check on her newly planted vegetables, making sure the rabbits had not found a way under the bird netting, then she went on up to the house. Lady Charlton had just come downstairs after breakfast in bed and looked surprised to see her.

"To what do we owe this honour?" she said.

Emily smiled. "I think I've done all I can in the kitchen garden. I've come to see if you want to work on that cataloguing you spoke about."

The old woman's face broke into a smile. "Splendid. Let's get started, shall we? Should we tackle the library or the artefacts first?"

"Whichever you prefer."

"Then I think the library presents an easier task. At least we can work our way along shelves. Let me find paper in my husband's study . . ." Emily followed her along the hallway. She noticed the house felt cold and damp apart from in that one sitting room.

"Are you sure you want to do this now?" she asked. "It's awfully cold for you. May I bring you a shawl?"

"My dear, I am made of sterner stuff," the old lady said. "One does not live on the edge of Dartmoor for over thirty years without acquiring some resilience. Anyway, you can go and ask Mrs Trelawney to light the fire in the library for us."

Emily went off in the direction of the kitchen.

"Light the fire in the library?" Mrs Trelawney demanded. "What next? Does she think coal grows on trees?"

"No, but she thinks wood does," Emily replied, grinning.

Daisy chuckled. Mrs Trelawney frowned. "That's as maybe. Don't blame me if she catches cold. Daisy, you'd better get that fire lit as quick as possible."

"Don't worry, Mrs Trelawney. I'll do it," Daisy said, getting up from her seat at the kitchen table where she had been peeling potatoes.

Emily went to find Lady Charlton. She was standing in a dark room that was shrouded in dust sheets, staring at a portrait on the wall. It showed a handsome man in military uniform.

"Your son?" Emily asked.

"My husband. He was a good-looking fellow, was he not? I still miss him every day, as I'm sure you miss your brave lieutenant."

"Yes," Emily said.

"Well, let's not stand here dilly-dallying. Let's get to work." Lady Charlton opened a desk drawer and took out sheets of paper. She handed them to Emily, then picked up a fountain pen. "My husband's pride and joy, this pen," she said. "Such a sensible invention. No more blots."

Daisy was already on her hands and knees in front of the fireplace in the library when they entered. "I'll soon have it going, Lady Charlton," she called out.

"What an amenable creature she is," Lady Charlton commented as Daisy left, the fire crackling away.

Emily drew up a plan of the library and numbered the shelves, and then they started on the books: title, author, publisher, year published and brief synopsis. Emily put some of them back on their shelves with regret. "If I had this library, I'd never leave it," she said.

"I have told you that you are welcome to borrow any book at any time," the old lady replied.

"You're most kind. I don't seem to have had much time for reading, but now I intend to start. A good book at bedtime every night."

"Do you like Jane Austen?"

"Oh yes, very much. But I don't think I've read them all."

"Have you read *Northanger Abbey*?" Lady Charlton handed it to her. "It is one of my favourites. So funny. So insightful about devious young ladies. An absolute spoof on gothic novels. You'd enjoy it."

Emily smiled as she put the book to one side.

"But won't this spoil our cataloguing if I have removed a book?" she asked, teasing now.

"Jane Austen is from my personal collection, not my husband's, who found them too silly. They would not be for sale."

They worked all morning, had luncheon, then worked until it started getting dark. They had an early dinner, then Emily went back to the cottage, clutching *Northanger Abbey*. She had just started on it when there was a knock at her door. Alice stood there, with Maud behind her.

"Let us in. It's starting to rain," Alice complained. She came inside. Maud hesitated before following her.

"Nice little place you've got here," Maud said. "Warm and cosy."

"Can I make you a cup of tea?" Emily asked.

"No, thanks. We're here on an urgent visit. Maud's burned herself at that ruddy forge. Go on, Maud, show her."

Maud pulled back her sleeve and showed a big ugly red and blistered mark on her forearm.

"Ow. That looks painful," Emily said.

"It is." Maud nodded vehemently. "I reckon I hadn't quite realized how hot that fire was. But Alice said you'd know how to make it better."

"Those herbs of yours," Alice interjected. "You said you'd found a book and were trying out some of the remedies. Have you got anything for burns?"

"Mrs Soper put butter on it," Maud said, "but that didn't seem to help much."

Emily hesitated. She had only just sworn off any more association with the herb garden, and yet she couldn't leave poor Maud's arm untreated.

"Sit down," she said. "Alice, you can put the kettle on for tea while I see if there is a remedy for burns that I could possibly make."

She went through to the bedroom where the book lay on her bedside table, along with all the notes she had made. Comfrey, also known as knitbone, was good for treating wounds. St John's wort worked on burns. Chickweed, marsh mallow and witch hazel were all recommended in the recipe. She thought she had most of these, especially the roots. She retrieved the dried plants from where they were hanging, poured boiling water over them, then let them sit. When it had cooled, she soaked a piece of linen in the mixture and laid it over the burn.

"I think it's working already!" Maud exclaimed after a few minutes. "Not burning so much."

"Then let me fill a bottle for you to take with you. You can repeat this whenever you need." Emily took a clean bottle from the rack in the kitchen and carefully poured some of the mixture into it. "It would be better if it was a salve, but I don't have any grease. I'll have to think about that."

They chatted for a while. Emily told them about Clarissa's letter.

"So you'll go and live with her then?" Alice asked. There was disappointment in her voice.

"I think so. I can't rely on Lady Charlton's charity for ever."

"It's not charity. You're doing a lot for her, aren't you? Stocking up her garden and helping her in the library."

"I suppose so, but I still feel as if I don't belong here. Do you feel you'd like to stay?"

"I do," Alice said. "Obviously, I can't go on living with Nell Lacey forever, but if a cottage becomes vacant, I may take it over. When the war ends, people will come back to this part of the world, that's what Nell says. Ramblers and sightseers. We could start a little tea shop. Make sandwiches for the ramblers." She looked up from her cup of tea. "You could stay on here with me. Help me run my tea shop. What shall we call it? The Copper Kettle? How about the Black Cat?"

Emily didn't know what to say because truly she was torn. But Maud answered for her. "She wants to be back with her own kind, doesn't she? She's had her fill of common folk like us."

"It's not that at all," Emily said hastily. "Of course I'd like to stay here with you."

"It's all right, duck," Alice said. "I understand. You want what's best for your baby. In the long run, right?"

"I really don't know, Alice," Emily said. "I can't decide right now. Clarissa is my oldest, dearest friend, but you have become a dear friend, too."

"That Mr Patterson is posh like her," Maud said, giving Alice a nudge. "She went to visit him the other night, and Mrs Soper's boy said the teacher has looked pleased with himself ever since and hasn't used the cane once."

"Oh, please!" Emily didn't know whether to laugh or be angry. "That's just village gossip! I went to visit him to collect some primers to help Daisy with her reading. You, too, Alice, if you want some practice."

After they had gone, Emily thought about Mr Patterson. It had struck her that he kept bees. He could supply her with beeswax, which would be perfect if she wanted to make a salve. But then she realized something else. If she went to his house again, it would be noticed. She had seen for herself how dangerous village gossip could be. She was essentially living in a fishbowl, and she would have to tread with caution.

CHAPTER THIRTY-THREE

The next morning, Emily walked up to the forge to see how Maud's burn was doing. She was glad to see Mr Patterson was out in the school playground as his pupils lined up to enter the school. It allowed her to speak to him without creating more rumours. He gave her a little nod of recognition. "I hope the books and the honey proved satisfactory, Mrs Kerr."

"Most satisfactory, thank you. I look forward to starting lessons with Daisy as soon as possible. And may I ask you for another favour? Do you think you could spare some beeswax? My friend Maud has burned herself, and I think I could make a salve to help her."

"Most certainly," he said. "I have some in the house. If you come to see me as soon as school is dismissed, I shall be happy to give it to you." He turned away, frowning. "William Jackson! Are you out of line? Ring the bell please, Katie, and then proceed in an orderly fashion. No pushing, Sammy Soper." He gave Emily an exasperated smile, then followed his pupils into the building.

Emily continued on her way to the forge. Maud and Mrs Soper were sitting at the kitchen table.

"It's getting better, look!" Maud took off the bandage. The burn did look less angry.

"I told her it's part of our trade. I've had more burns than I could count since I tried to take on the forge," Mrs Soper said. "But I've never heard of putting that stuff on them. But now I can see it works, I'll give it a try, too. We always used butter. Where did you get the idea for it?"

"There are herbs growing in my cottage garden, and I bought a herb book the other day," Emily said, not wanting to say more.

"Then perhaps there is a remedy for me in that book," Mrs Soper said. "I've had trouble sleeping ever since my husband went away, and it got even worse when the telegram came to say he'd been killed. I don't think I've had a proper night's sleep for two years now. Do you think you could make me something to help me sleep?"

Emily shifted uneasily. It was one thing to make a simple herb poultice to put over burns, but a concoction to put someone to sleep? Balsam and lavender to make her drowsy was one thing, but she wasn't so sure about toying with more dangerous herbs.

"I'd be ever so grateful," Mrs Soper went on. "You don't know what it's like, lying in that big cold bed, staring at the ceiling every night and praying for morning to come."

"I do know," Emily said. "I've felt the same since my Robbie was killed."

"Well then, we both need it. You can make it for both of us. For all the women in this village, I reckon. There's not one of us who hasn't lost somebody."

"I suppose I could try," Emily said, wanting to refuse, but seeing the tired lines of desperation on the woman's face. She knew exactly what it was like, lying in bed, worrying about her man, and then getting the worst news of all—that he wasn't coming home. And this woman had the added worry of having two sons who were approaching enlistment age. "I think I did read a recipe that might help somewhere, Mrs Soper."

"God bless you, my dear," Mrs Soper said. "I've been to the doctors, and they just give me something that knocks me out, but then I'm all groggy the next morning, and you have to have your wits about you when operating a forge, as young Maud here has just found out, eh, Maud?"

Maud grinned sheepishly. "I won't make that same mistake again, Mrs Soper," she said.

That evening, Emily studied the old texts. In Tabitha Ann Wise's book, she had written down a remedy that seemed useful.

> *For anxiety and the uncalm spirit, for a peaceful sleepe without evil dreames.*
>
> *Make an infusion of hoppes, skullcap, vervain, vale-rian, wild lettuce and passion flower. To these can be added lavender, lemon balm and chamomile to sweeten the potion and to infuse the air with calming sweetness.*

Emily was pretty sure there were no hops growing in the garden, and she had no idea what a passion flower looked like, nor wild lettuce. But she thought she had identified the others, with the exception of skullcap, which sounded rather alarming. She decided to omit that one for now. Further study revealed that the valerian should be a maceration of the chopped root, which was lucky, as the plant itself was almost dead due to the coming winter. She chopped the various ingredients, adding fresh lavender and lemon balm for their scent, and she tried the infusion herself before going to bed. It was a little too bitter, so she decided to add some honey next time. However, she did fall asleep quickly, and she awoke without troubling dreams. Success!

Emily took round a packet of the mixed herbs in the morning and suggested adding honey. Not only was Mrs Soper delighted, but apparently she had told everyone else in the village, so Emily had more requests for her magic brew. Except, that was, from Mrs Bingley. She accosted Emily as she returned from the forge.

"I hear you are brewing up concoctions for people in this village." She gave Emily a cold stare. Emily said nothing. "You do realize that this is tantamount to practising medicine without a licence—a criminal offence."

"I hardly think a few sprigs of lavender and other herbs constitutes practising medicine. These are old folk remedies."

"The people in these parts are still very naive and easily influenced," Mrs Bingley said. "I wouldn't want to see them taken advantage of."

Emily fought to keep calm. "You don't think I am charging them for these, do you? Look, Mrs Bingley, I was doing a favour for a woman who hasn't been able to sleep since her husband died. If a few herbs can help her to feel drowsy, then I'm sure there is nobody in the world who could object, except you." Emboldened now, she went on, "I get the feeling that you are jealous because my friends and I have settled in so well here. Maybe if you were a little more pleasant, you might get along better with your neighbours."

Emily gave a curt nod and left the woman standing there. She felt rather pleased with herself as she went up to the big house. On the way, she paused to examine the seedlings. The net had held in place, but some of the tender plants had been flattened in the last rain. As she bent to straighten them, she experienced a strange sensation that caused her to stand up again. Her hand went to her stomach. It was more than a twinge—it was a sharp jolt. Her brain went to appendicitis, but then it came again, right under her hand, and she realized with astonishment what it was. The baby was kicking her. She stood still for some time, her hand covering the side of her stomach, waiting to feel it again. Since the sickness had subsided, she had almost forgotten about the baby. Now here was proof that it was alive and growing inside her. She felt scared, but a little excited, too.

As she went on up to the house, she decided she would write to Clarissa and accept her kind offer. It would be good to be with a friend, especially a friend with medical knowledge. She was happy here, but it was rather remote. So that night she wrote a letter, telling Clarissa how grateful she was and how she looked forward to their being together again. She felt a pang of regret that she'd be letting down Alice, Daisy and Lady Charlton, but this had only been a temporary solution, after all. However, she decided to say nothing to Lady Charlton—not until the time came for her to make her move.

The next day, they were together in the library going through a shelf of travel books. The cataloguing was taking longer than it should have because they were studying the pictures together, and Lady Charlton was reminiscing about her adventures at the Pyramids and with the Bedouins in Morocco. Suddenly, a sound floated to them on the breeze. They both stopped and looked up.

"What's that?" Lady Charlton asked.

"It's church bells," Emily replied. "Church bells are ringing."

And, to their astonishment, the bells of Bucksley Church joined them. They went outside. It was a misty November day, and the air resonated with the sound of bells.

Daisy appeared at the door. "Is it an invasion, do you think?" she asked nervously.

Simpson came running up the drive as fast as his old legs could carry him. "It's all over!" he shouted. "The war is over. They just signed the armistice. Eleven o'clock this morning, on the eleventh day of the eleventh month."

"Thank God," Lady Charlton said.

There was great excitement in the village. A party was planned in the church hall for the next Sunday. The schoolchildren were put to making decorations and planning a concert. Ration restrictions were being eased, and it was agreed that there would be a pig roast. Even Mrs Trelawney was in high spirits, making pork pies and agreeing to use the last of her pickled cabbage. The village hall was festooned with paper chains. Nell and Alice had supplied beer from the pub, and Mr Patterson had donated six bottles of his home-made wine. There was lemonade for the children.

Even Lady Charlton agreed to attend this time. She was dressed in a very grand, black Victorian dress, with a cape trimmed with sable. Emily had had a little trouble with deciding what to wear. Her waistline had expanded beyond the two good frocks she had brought with her. Her skirts were now held together with elastic. She had to make do with draping her good shawl artfully across herself. As the church hall was always chilly, this was quite acceptable. The day started with a thanksgiving service, then they processed across to the hall to where the tables were laid for the feast. Mr Patterson played the piano, and two of the older pupils accompanied him on violin and recorder. To begin with, everyone was in high spirits. The pig had been roasting on a spit outside all night, and the aroma wafting in through the door was mouth-watering.

Grace was said. The pig was carved, and for a while the hall fell silent as everyone ate.

"I can't believe it's over," Nell Lacey said. "After so long."

"I don't know exactly why we're celebrating," Mrs Soper replied. "What is there to celebrate? That's what I want to know. We've all lost someone. Life will never be the same."

"We're celebrating that at least no more sons will be lost," Nell said. "Your boys will grow up without you having to fret that they'll be sent to the front."

"My boys will have to grow up without their father," Mrs Soper said bitterly. "Who will teach them the trade properly? Granddad here knows his stuff, but his eyesight is so poor that he's not much help. We women are muddling through right now, but how long can we keep going? And if we have to close the forge, then where will folks get their horses shod?"

"Maybe we'll all take to motor cars instead," one of the younger women suggested, "and motor tractors. I saw one working in a field the other day. Going ever so fast, it was."

"If you ask me, this village will start dying," Mrs Soper said. "Who will be coming back to work at the home farm? And if nobody is working, who will buy from the shop? Or who will visit the Red Lion? We might as well call it at day and move to the nearest town."

"There's no way you'd find me living in a town," Nell Lacey said hotly.

"Nor me," Mrs Upton from the shop replied.

Emily had been sitting at one end of a long table, next to Lady Charlton, who had been afforded the place of honour.

"Then I say it's up to us women now," Lady Charlton said. There was silence as they turned to her. "Maybe we give up the smithy, but there are other things we can do. Market gardening at the farm instead of livestock. Chickens instead of cows. People will always need to eat. This young lady has got my winter vegetables going, and we can all do the same. We can survive . . ."

"And some of the boys will be coming back," one of the young wives from the cottages said. "My Joe is alive and well, last I heard. His ship will be coming back from foreign waters, and he'll go back to the farm."

"And my Johnny," Fanny Hodgson, another of the younger women, spoke up. "He's alive still. He wrote to me just two weeks ago. He'll be—"

She had a squirming toddler on her lap and a young boy running around with the other children. Suddenly, this boy let out a scream.

"It's Dad!" he yelled. "He's coming now!"

Women jumped up from the tables and raced across to the windows. A young man in a soldier's uniform was walking up from the bridge, his kitbag over his shoulder. Fanny Hodgson gave a little cry, handed her toddler to another woman and pushed her way through the crowd, running down the path to meet him, arms wide open.

The whole crowd stood in silent awe as the couple came into each other's arms, embracing with abandon. Emily blinked away tears—tears of joy for this couple, and tears of regret that she would never have a reunion like this.

CHAPTER THIRTY-FOUR

The days after Johnny Hodgson came home were ones of hope for Emily. Two more men returned—labourers on the home farm. There was optimism in the air, and she found herself thinking about the future. Maud had been right. She did miss her own kind. She did miss having someone to share thoughts and worries with. Lady Charlton was being extremely kind, Emily knew. And she had come to look upon Emily as a young relative. Alice and Daisy were also great pals, but somehow it wasn't the same. Even though Daisy was making strides with her reading, Emily realized she would probably never tackle Dickens or read poetry. And the more she thought about it, the more she realized that she wanted to move out of the cottage before the curse could strike her. She told herself over and over that she was a modern woman and she did not believe in curses, but she couldn't put Susan Olgilvy out of her mind. Had she been hanged? She wanted to know more, and yet she was afraid to learn the truth.

There is nothing I can do about it anyway, she told herself. *Best to forget I ever read that diary.* And yet it seemed she was destined to take over Susan's role in the community. Several more women had approached her to ask for the sleeping potion she had given Mrs Soper. She found herself walking through the herb garden and wondering what plants might shoot up again in the spring. She had noticed some remedies to "appease the torments of childebirthe," and considered making a batch in order to be ready.

One bright morning, she was walking up from the cottage, pleased to notice that her little cabbages and cauliflowers had turned into sturdy young plants and that the saucers of beer that Simpson had put out had taken care of the slugs, when she sensed someone watching her. A man was standing on the hillside above the garden, hands in his pockets and staring at her. At first, she took him for another tramp, but then she saw that he was clean-shaven, with short blond hair. He kept staring for a moment, then started to come down towards her. He was young, but his face was thin to the point of looking haggard, and his eyes were sunken as if he had been ill. The lower half of his face was hidden under a big blue woollen scarf and he was wearing a tweed jacket. She, in turn, walked up to the drystone wall that surrounded the property.

"Hello. Can I help you?" she asked.

"Are you the new owner or a servant here?" His voice was distinctly aristocratic, with that authoritative tone the upper class use when addressing inferiors.

"I'm neither. There is no new owner, and I am currently staying in the cottage."

"So the old lady is still alive then?" he asked.

"Yes. Hale and hearty."

"Good to hear." He didn't sound too enthusiastic. He was still frowning at her. "You're not a relative, are you? I didn't think . . ."

"You seem remarkably interested in pigeonholing me," she replied, feeling slightly annoyed by his questioning gaze now. "I am merely a friend who is helping Lady Charlton catalogue her library."

"I didn't think she had any friends, and it's not like her to want help," he replied, almost bitterly.

"You are acquainted with her then?"

"Oh yes. Well acquainted. Too well acquainted."

"Would you like to come in and say hello? I believe she should be up and about by now. You could climb over the wall right here."

"No, thank you," he said briskly. "I don't think that would be wise. I should be going. I just wanted to have a look at the old place again. Just to see . . ." He gave an embarrassed little cough. "I've taken up enough of your time. I should be getting on my way."

As Emily watched him turn away, an impossible thought came to her. "Excuse me," she called after him. He stopped and looked back.

"You are not—you can't be her grandson, Justin, can you?" she asked.

He flashed her a look of surprise and wariness. "Oh, so you know of me then? I'm still famous in the neighbourhood. That's nice to know." Another bitter laugh.

"But they all think you are dead!" she exclaimed. "They understood you'd been blown to pieces."

The arrogant look on his face faltered. "Then they don't know? They didn't hear?"

"Didn't hear what?"

"My dear lady," he said, "I have just returned from a German prisoner-of-war camp."

"How awful. I am so sorry." She went to reach across the wall to touch him, but withdrew her hand at the last moment. "Nobody knew. Please, come up to the house now. Your grandmother will be overjoyed to see you. Everyone will. They'll think it's a miracle."

Still he hesitated. "You really think my grandmother will be overjoyed to see me?"

"Why wouldn't she be?"

He frowned. "I'm the coward. The disgrace to the family. Hasn't she told you that?"

"She said some heated words were exchanged because of your beliefs."

He gave a derisive snort. "It was she and my father who told me I was letting down my country when I said that I didn't believe in fighting and was going to register as a conscientious objector. They called me a coward and no member of their family. My grandmother said everyone knew that war was wrong in principle, but if someone else starts it, they have to be stopped, and everyone has to do his duty. Actually, I was planning to volunteer as an ambulance driver, but my father got the enlistment board to refuse my request to register as a conscientious objector. I was drafted into the Devonshire regiment and sent straight to the front. That's what they did with people like me. Get them killed off as quickly as possible."

"Your family only heard that your body was never found," Emily said. "Your grandmother told me you'd either been blown to pieces or you'd deserted."

"Is that what they thought of me?" He gave a brittle laugh. "Knowing her, she would probably rather I'd been blown to pieces than a deserter."

Since this was exactly what the old woman had hinted, Emily said nothing. "But I'm sure she will be so happy to know you are alive."

"What about my father?" he asked. "Is he at home, too?"

"Your father was killed at the front. You didn't know that?"

"No. I didn't know." For a second, the supercilious stare vanished, and he looked like a vulnerable boy. "I've known nothing for two years. I've been in a private hell." A spasm of pain crossed his face. Then he collected himself. "He's dead, you say? So the stupid, old fool re-enlisted and went off to fight." He shook his head. "All this for-King-and-country nonsense that's been ingrained in my family. He was too old, you know. He could have stayed quietly home and grown cabbages."

"So you are all that your grandmother has," she said. "The one surviving relative. Won't you please come in and see her?"

She could see the agony of hesitation on his face. "Nobody even bothered to write all the while I was there," he said. "No letters. No packages. Nothing."

"Nobody knew where you were," she said, her patience now wearing thin. "So what happened to you? Why didn't anyone hear news about you?"

He shrugged. "Actually, I was captured by the Germans on our first offensive. I ran too far ahead of the others when we were told to go over the top, I suppose. I was a little more agile than the other men. It's such chaos, explosions all around, men being blown up. You don't have time to think. And suddenly I found myself amongst Germans. This bloke was coming at me with a bayonet when there was an explosion, and that's the last thing I remember for some time. When I woke up, I was a prisoner. I had a bad head wound, amongst other things. And I suffered from amnesia for a while. I couldn't even remember my own name. My identity tags had been blown off me. I had no idea who I was. I was going to be shot as a spy, but then I was shipped off to Germany and spent two miserable years in a prison camp. You have no idea how bad it was. Daily beatings, and singling out men to be killed if we did anything wrong. It was pretty much like hell. And not one word from my family."

"They would have written if they'd known," she said. "Of course they would."

"Do you think so?" Again, for a second, he sounded hopeful. Then he shrugged, stuffing his hands deeper into his pockets. The wind whipped at the scarf around his neck, sending it streaming out behind him. "You people have no idea what it was like," he said bitterly. "The front. The prison camp. And you sit at home, eating strawberries and cream."

"It hasn't been easy for many of us," she retorted, feeling the colour rising in her cheeks. "Almost every woman in this village has lost a husband or son. I lost the man I loved and am having a child he'll never see. I have nothing and nobody, so don't think it was all strawberries and cream."

"I'm sorry." He looked at her with understanding for the first time. "That's rough," he said.

"We all have to get through it somehow." She found his gaze somehow unnerving. "Please come and see your grandmother. She thinks she has lost a husband, a son and a grandson. Seeing you would lift her spirits so much. She's very lonely. And she has probably suffered with guilt all these years for driving you to what she thought was your death."

"If you really think that," he said, giving her a withering look.

"I do. I believe your grandmother has changed. When I first met her, she was cold and haughty, but she has been so kind to me—made me so welcome. I have come to be very fond of her."

He stood like a statue, his hands resting on the top of the drystone wall, staring down at the house below them. Emily could sense the battle being waged inside him. He wanted to go home, but he was afraid he wouldn't be welcome.

"Well, what have I got to lose?" he said at last. "I suppose it's the right thing to do, to let her know that I'm still alive. But I'm not raising my hopes too high . . ." And he started to climb over the wall.

"So what are you doing here?" he asked as they walked up the path together. "Did she advertise for a companion or something?"

"No, I came here as a member of the Women's Land Army to help with her garden. Then when . . ." She had been going to say, "the man I was going to marry," but couldn't do it. "When the man I loved was shot down, I needed a place to be right away. I needed somewhere to adjust to life with a child, but no husband. Your grandmother took me in, and I've been trying to help her wherever I can."

"May one know your name?"

"It's . . ." She hesitated before going on. "It's Mrs Kerr." Instantly, she regretted lying to someone as haughty yet vulnerable as Justin Charlton.

"It's not easy being a war widow, I'm sure," he said.

"Most of the women in this village are."

"Really?"

"Three men have come home so far. All labourers on the home farm. Mr Soper was killed."

"Really? Old Soper? He was as tough as nails. What about Ben Lacey?"

"He's still alive, but he's in no fit state to leave the hospital."

"My God. How does she run the pub without him?"

"One of my fellow land girls is helping her out. And another is learning to operate the forge."

"So you've provided a band of visiting angels, I see." There was what she took for sarcasm in his voice.

"We've all tried to do what we can," she retorted angrily. "We are all hurting. It's somehow easier when we all band together."

"Sorry," he said. "I'm sure you're doing a splendid job. Anyone who can stomach my grandmother for more than a few weeks must be headed for sainthood."

"I've found her extremely kind," Emily said. "And she's hurting, too. She thinks she's lost everyone. You'll make her so happy."

"That remains to be seen." He was staring ahead, frowning. "But I'm willing to give it a try. It might be nice to see the old place, my old room . . ."

Again, she noted the wistfulness in his voice. *Of course she'll welcome him home,* Emily thought. *Who wouldn't? He seems so wounded. So much in need of his family.*

They reached the house, and Emily pushed open the front door. Again, Justin hesitated.

"I'll go and see if she's in the sitting room, shall I?" she said. "Maybe prepare her a little?"

"That would be wise." He nodded, and followed her into the foyer. "Nothing has changed," he said, looking around.

"I think you'll find a lot has changed," Emily replied. "We are down to Mrs Trelawney and two other servants. Most of the rooms are shut off, covered in dust sheets. The only fire is in the drawing room. Coal is rationed, as is everything else, but that should get better now. Wait there."

Emily had only taken a few steps towards the sitting room door when Ethel came around the corner. She took one look at Justin and let out a scream. "A ghost! It's a ghost! Mrs Trelawney, I've just seen a ghost!"

"What is that abominable noise?" Lady Charlton appeared at the sitting room door.

"It was Ethel. I'm afraid she saw—" Emily started to say, but Lady Charlton had spotted Justin. She stood, as if turned to stone.

"It can't be," she said. "Is it really you?"

"Hello, Grandmother," Justin said. "The wanderer returns."

"But it's not possible." She put her hand to her heart. "We all thought . . ."

"Here, hold on to me." Emily rushed forwards, as the old woman looked as if she might faint.

"I'm perfectly all right, Emily. Don't fuss." The old lady brushed her hand away. "It was a bit of a shock, that's all."

She continued to stand, staring at her grandson.

"How about inviting me in?" Justin said. "And how about some coffee? I've walked from the main road, and it's freezing cold out there."

Lady Charlton nodded abruptly. "Emily, dear, please tell Mrs Trelawney that we would like . . ." There was no need to finish the sentence. Mrs Trelawney and Ethel had both come out of the kitchen and were clinging on to each other, staring, mouths open.

"Well, don't just stand there, woman," Lady Charlton said. "Go and get us some coffee. Mr Justin needs warming up."

Lady Charlton took Emily's arm this time and allowed Emily to ease her into her favourite chair. Still Justin hesitated, standing and looking about him, before following them into the sitting room. "I used to dream about this place."

"Where were you? What happened to you? Why did we hear nothing?" Her voice was sharp.

"He was in a German prisoner-of-war camp, Lady Charlton," Emily said.

"So that was it, was it?" Her voice was still haughty and cold. "You gave yourself up. Surrendered to them?"

"Is that what you think?" he asked quietly.

"You made it quite clear that you did not want to fight."

"No, I did not surrender. I went over the top with the rest of my unit, bayonets drawn as we charged against the tanks and the big guns. It was suicide. Chaps around me being blown up with every step."

"So how did you manage to survive then?" Again, there was a note of harsh suspicion in her voice.

"I am a fast runner. I outran the rest of them and found myself amongst Germans. A chap was coming at me with a bayonet, and then a shell exploded right next to us, and when I woke up, I was in a German prison cell."

"Then why did we hear nothing? All this time?"

He is still standing at attention, the prisoner being interrogated, Emily thought. She wanted to intervene for him, to tell the old lady to stop acting like this, to get up and hug him.

"I had a bad head wound and suffered from amnesia. I couldn't remember who I was, where I came from. And my identity tags had been destroyed. I was going to be shot, but then they had to move out in a hurry, and so they changed their minds and I was sent to a camp. My memory gradually returned, and I gave them my name, but I could never remember my serial number. I did tell them the name of my regiment, but I suppose they couldn't be bothered to pass it along."

The old lady was still frowning. "An interesting tale."

"You don't believe me?" he demanded.

She shrugged. "You always were a good storyteller. I remember as a child you fabricated the most amazing tales to get yourself out of trouble."

"Then what do you think happened to me such that you heard nothing for two whole years?"

"Frankly, I wondered if you'd deserted. When your body wasn't found, I thought you'd managed to slip away and hide out in France. You do speak good French, after all."

"If you think so poorly of me"—his voice was bitter—"then there is nothing more to be said. I suspected it would be a mistake to come back here." He started towards the door.

"Wait. This is now officially your house, I suppose. You realize you have inherited the title. You are now Viscount Charlton. You have every right to stay here."

Justin shook his head. "Viscount Charlton? How ridiculous. And how could I stay where I am not wanted? Goodbye, Grandmother. You don't have to worry that I'll turn you out of my house. I'd rather be with people who enjoy my company." He strode out of the room.

Emily stood watching the drama play out. She glared at the old woman. "Don't let him go!" she shouted. "Say something." She ran after him and grabbed at his sleeve as he reached the front door. "Please don't go. She didn't mean those things."

"Of course she did. She hasn't changed one bit. She and my father happily sent me to my death, and now she's rather annoyed that I've turned up alive."

"But this is your home."

"Apparently not."

"She just said you had inherited it."

He gave her a withering look. "Obviously, I'm not going to turn her out, and there is no way I'd want to live under the same roof as her."

"Where will you go?" she asked. "What will you do?"

"I wasn't planning to come back here anyway," he said. "I'm staying with some pals in London. I'm going to write. About the war. To let people know what it was like." He managed a little smile. "You shouldn't stay here. You're too good for her. Too kind. She'll let you down in the end, too."

Then he ran down the steps and along the drive.

Emily stood watching him, feeling sick and scared. She fought the urge to run after him, to beg him to stay. Then she turned and went back into the sitting room. The old lady hadn't moved.

"I can't believe you said those things," Emily blurted out. "That was your grandson. He'd come from a prison camp. Did you see how thin and gaunt he looked? He has suffered, and now you've driven him away."

"You are forgetting yourself, Miss Bryce," Lady Charlton said stiffly. "You have no right to speak to me like that."

"I have the right to stand up to injustice. Justin hesitated to come in to see you because he thought he'd get this kind of reception. I persuaded him because I thought that you'd be overjoyed. Instead of that, you didn't even believe him. And now he's gone, and it's your own fault."

"I said you were forgetting yourself," Lady Charlton snapped. "May I remind you that you are here at my grace and favour?"

Emily took a deep breath. "In that case, if you no longer welcome my company, I'll leave right away."

"Where would you go? You have nowhere."

"Actually, my friend Clarissa has invited me to live with her as soon as she returns from nursing in France. And until then, I'm sure Nell Lacey will let me stay at the Red Lion. I've enough money saved to pay my way."

She didn't wait any longer, afraid that the old lady would see the distress on her face. Instead, she ran from the room, all the way down to the cottage.

Emily shut the cottage door behind her and stood, catching her breath. She was still in shock about what had just happened, and looked around her at the little room that had now become a haven. There were jars of herbs on the table, the recipe book open beside them. Shadow the cat came over to rub against her leg. And now she'd have to leave it all and start over.

"I was going to move in with Clarissa anyway," she told herself. "At least now I don't have to do it with regret and guilt about leaving the old lady alone."

But her gaze still lingered on the herbs. She had just started to do something worthwhile. She had been looking forward to the spring, when new plants would shoot up and new flowers would bloom. Now she would never know what effective cures she could make. The healing garden would go dormant again. The cottage would become empty and unloved. And Susan Olgilvy's legacy would be forgotten.

CHAPTER THIRTY-FIVE

"I should pack up my belongings," Emily said to the cat. "I'd like to take you with me, but I don't think you'd want to move away from here."

She went up to the attic to retrieve her suitcases and lugged them down the stairs with some difficulty. Her growing waistline had affected her balance, she noticed, and she came down the steep steps with extreme caution. Once inside her bedroom, she started to fold items of clothing, stacking them on the bed before packing them into the suitcases. Her heart was beating very fast now. What if Nell Lacey said no? What if there was no room for her at the pub? Then she told herself that Alice would not let her be turned out into the cold. She'd offer to share her room and her bed if necessary. And Clarissa would be home any day now, if she wasn't back in England already.

Emily looked up when she heard a knock on the front door. She just prayed it wasn't another woman wanting her sleeping draught. She didn't feel up to spreading the news that she was leaving the cottage and soon leaving the village. She went to the front door, and recoiled when she saw Lady Charlton standing there, leaning on her stick and breathing heavily.

"I'm sorry," the old woman gasped. "I was wrong. I don't want you to go."

"You said some terrible things. You drove your grandson away."

"I know. I was stupid." She paused. "May I come in? I am not used to hurrying any more." She put her hand to her heart.

Emily stood aside to let her come in. She pulled out a chair and aided the old lady into it.

"You shouldn't have walked all this way," she said. "I'll make you some mint tea. It's very restorative."

She went through to the kitchen where a kettle was on the stove and poured hot water on to a sprig of mint picked from a plant that was growing in a pot by the sink. She stirred honey into it, then came back through and handed the mug to the old woman. "You're right," Lady Charlton said after taking a sip. "Very restorative. I'd forgotten." She paused, then reached out to Emily, taking her hand. "You won't leave, will you? I've come to depend on you. I enjoy your company."

"You could have had your grandson's company if you hadn't rejected him."

Lady Charlton took another sip of the hot tea. "I know. I don't know why I behaved that way. The shock of seeing him, I suppose. He and I often butted heads, and he did tell monstrous lies when he was a little boy . . . like how an owl flew into the room and knocked over my favourite vase. He had a great imagination."

"Do you really believe anyone would make up a prison camp?" Emily asked.

"I suppose not. And he did look dreadfully thin."

"So what are you going to do now?" Emily asked. "Are you going to risk losing your only grandson forever?"

"What do you think I should do? Write to him and apologize?"

"That would be a start," Emily agreed.

"But I wouldn't know where to find him."

"His regiment might help. And I know that he is living with a group of friends in London. A group of writers."

"Writers!" The old woman gave a snort of disgust. "If his father could hear that, he'd turn in his grave."

"Not everyone has to follow the same path in life," Emily said. "Justin can't be his father and grandfather. If he needs to write to express the horrors he has lived through, then why should you begrudge him that?"

"Why do you always have to be so insightful and so right?" the old woman snapped. Then she held out a bony hand to Emily. "You will stay, won't you? And help me find him and bring him home?"

"I will stay for now," Emily said, wincing as she thought of leaving Lady Charlton when Clarissa returned. "And I will help you find him."

A letter was written to the army, but they had no forwarding address; in fact, they had him listed as killed in action. So Justin had been right. The administrators at the prison camp had never contacted his regiment. Emily felt such incredible sympathy for him. She had seen the unbearable hurt on his face when his grandmother had talked to him with such scorn. To have endured those conditions in which every day could have brought torture or death and then be rejected by his own family member was so harsh. Then she realized that they were two of a kind. She, too, had been rejected by her family. If she had any way of making this right for Justin, she would do it. But she had no way of tracking him down in London. She could hardly go to the city and wander around the neighbourhoods where writers might live. They could be anywhere.

Right after the letter had arrived from Justin's regimental commander, she received a letter of her own from Clarissa. She opened it with excitement, only to read:

> *I'm back on British soil. I can't tell you how good it is to get a proper cup of tea and scones and jam and a hot bath. Bliss. However, I'm not being released from duty just yet. I've been sent to a hospital in the East End to*

help with the influenza crisis. Apparently, the flu has crossed the Channel, and in the crowded conditions of the city, it is spreading rapidly. They do not have enough hospital beds and are sending nurses like me out into the homes to do what we can. Frankly, there isn't much we can do. When the disease strikes, some people are dead in a couple of days. And it's not always the frail and elderly. In France, I watched strapping young men just fade away as if the life had been sucked out of them.

I'm glad you're safely tucked away in the country. Take care of yourself. I won't risk coming to see you in case I bring the disease with me. In the meantime, I'm going to write to hospitals around the country to see who might offer me a position. Not in the East End, I think. I have had enough of squalor!

Emily put down the letter. In a way, she was glad that she didn't yet have to break the news to Lady Charlton that she was leaving. Christmas was approaching, and there was food in the shops again. Mrs Trelawney went into Tavistock and returned with the news that she had reserved a turkey at the butcher's. She had also bought fruit to make the Christmas pudding. Emily found herself thinking of Christmas at home. Before the war, there had been so much food, a tall Christmas tree with glass ornaments on it and presents. There had been Christmas parties with parlour games and much laughter. An image came into her head of her brother, Freddie, being very silly as he played charades. How he had loved life. So had Robbie. If he had returned from France, they would have been married by now and on their way to Australia.

Instead, here she was, thinking about what she could give her new friends as Christmas presents. She certainly had no spare money to buy anything. A shilling bottle of Woolworth's Ashes of Roses would hardly be the sort of gift she could give Lady Charlton. She also wanted to give

Alice something, and Daisy, which probably also meant giving something to Mrs Trelawney and Ethel. And Mr Patterson, too. He had been very kind to her, and she enjoyed their occasional visits and discussions about books. It was when she was with him that an idea came to her. He was telling her that he planned to build more hives, and maybe sell his honey at the village shop as he used to do before the war.

"If you do that, will you have more beeswax?" she asked. "Because any wax that you have to spare I can use to make my ointments and salves."

"I have some now, if you'd like," he said. "One of my colonies has abandoned me, I'm afraid, so I have the comb that they've left behind."

Emily took it home excitedly and experimented with making a hand cream. She knew it would be better with fresh flowers, but the lavender and sage still retained their sweet smells. And she had a recipe that Susan had written.

> *Marigold hand cream.*
> *Take one ounce of marigold petals and add one pint of good-quality oil. Place in a bain-marie. Simmer gently for two hours. Strain off the oil and pour into a saucepan. Add one ounce of beeswax and stir until well absorbed. Pour into clean jars.*

It was not the season for marigolds, but she did have lavender, rosemary and sage. She experimented with almond oil from the chemist. When she had produced what she felt was a satisfying consistency, she scooped it into the smallest jars and cut ribbon from the good dress she had brought with her to tie around them. She was quite satisfied with the result.

When she came across Christmas cards in the village shop, she found herself thinking again of her parents. Would they be worried about not having heard from her? Even if they thought she was still with the land girls, wouldn't they be expecting her to come home for Christmas? She picked up a card. Should she send them one to let them know she was all right? But then they'd see the postmark and come to find her, and that could not happen. Instead, she bought a card and addressed it to Miss Foster-Blake. Inside, she wrote that she was well and had been invited to live with a friend, so her future was secure.

"You will be spending Christmas Day here, I hope," Lady Charlton said.

"I will certainly be happy to have Christmas dinner with you," she said, "but I don't want Alice to feel left out. Mrs Lacey has gone up to London to have Christmas with her husband in hospital, and Alice has been left alone running the Red Lion for her."

"Then invite her, too. The more the merrier," Lady Charlton said. "I presume the public house will be closed on Christmas Day and Boxing Day."

"Are you sure?" Emily asked. "She is a working-class woman from London."

Lady Charlton shrugged. "The war is over, and I expect we'll find a good many things will change. Since I have no family to share my feast . . ."

"I have tried to find Justin," Emily said, "but it's hopeless. How does one start in London? My friend Clarissa has been sent to work in the East End, but I doubt she'll have time to do any investigating for me. Do you think you should hire a private investigator to track him down?"

Lady Charlton sighed. "I think we have to accept that Justin wants no communication with me at the present. When I die, he will take over this house anyway and can do what he likes with it. Until then . . ."

"Don't talk about dying." Emily reached out instinctively to her. "You've a lot of life in you yet."

"One never knows." She sighed again. "If you'd met my husband, you would have thought him a vibrant, lively man—one who loved life. And yet he sickened and died so rapidly."

"Just like those with influenza are doing now in London."

"So one hears. We must pray it doesn't come to us."

"I think we're too remote for anything to find us, including influenza," Emily said, smiling.

Emily went to see Alice at the Red Lion and extended the invitation to her. Alice gave her a look of horror. "Oh, no thanks, duck. I mean, ta all the same, and it was nice of you to think of me, but I couldn't see myself sitting at a dinner table with a titled lady. I'd be scared every time I opened my mouth that I'd put my foot in it." She chuckled. "Anyway, some of us have been invited to Mrs Soper's to celebrate. Not that we'll feel that much like celebrating—even those whose men have come home." She drew closer to Emily and said in a low voice, "You remember Johnny Hodgson who came home, and how happy his wife was to see him? She came to the pub with him the other evening, and she told me quietly that she's worried sick about him. He wakes up at night screaming and in a cold sweat. He has these awful nightmares, you see. He hears the guns. It frightens the children."

"How sad," Emily said. "I don't suppose anyone gets over being in the trenches in a hurry. But, Alice, I wanted to spend Christmas Day with you, really. But I couldn't say no to Lady Charlton."

Alice put a comforting hand on her shoulder. "Don't give it a second thought. And I tell you what—you come down to the Lion on Christmas Eve. We're all going to have a bit of a party, a good old sing-song with sausages and hot toddy."

"All right," Emily agreed. "I'd like to do that. I'll bring Daisy with me. Ethel, too, if she wants to come."

Ethel let it be known that she never went near public houses, and neither did Mrs Trelawney. So on Christmas Eve, Daisy and Emily set off together. It was an almost exclusively female gathering, apart from the two old men and one of the labourers who had returned. Emily noticed he drank a lot and didn't say much. But the gathering was a merry one.

Alice took Emily aside and gave her a gift of balls of white wool, needles and knitting patterns. "I reckon we all better get started on the knitting if this poor kid is going to have anything to wear," she said.

"Oh dear, I don't even know how to knit," Emily said. "My nanny tried to teach me once, but I was hopeless."

"I'll help," Daisy said. "I'm a good knitter."

They opened their presents from Emily and were impressed with the hand cream.

"It smells really nice. And my hands still haven't recovered from all that digging potatoes," Alice said.

Emily was pleased.

"I don't have anything for you." Daisy looked worried. "But I'm going to help you look after the baby when it comes. I would have liked to train as a nursery maid."

They walked back up the hill together in companionable silence, their footsteps echoing on the frosty ground.

Christmas Day dawned, bright and frosty. It had snowed on the moor, and the uplands sparkled white as Emily walked with the others to church. Whether Mrs Bingley welcomed her or not, she was going to attend on this day. They sang the old carols lustily while Mr Patterson hammered out the tunes on the organ: "God Rest Ye Merry Gentlemen," "Once in Royal David's City," "It Came upon the Midnight Clear."

Afterwards, Emily and Lady Charlton took sherry before Christmas lunch. Emily handed the old lady her present and was surprised that Lady Charlton seemed so touched. "What a delightful gift. Handmade. The best," she said. "And I have something for you. Come with me." She led Emily upstairs and along the corridor to the far end, where she opened a door to a bright room. It was the former nursery, with a rocking horse in the window, a shelf of toys and books and, in the middle, a basinet draped with lace.

"This is now yours," she said. "I hope you will move into the house before the baby arrives, and we shall acquire a nursemaid for him."

"How lovely." Emily could hardly say the words, knowing that by the time the baby arrived she would probably be with Clarissa.

When they came downstairs again, Lady Charlton took her not into the sitting room, but along the hall to the library. "I want you to choose something," she said. "Anything you like."

"Oh, I couldn't," Emily stammered.

"Please. It would give me pleasure to know that some of our prized possessions were going to you instead of an auction, or being disposed of by my grandson one day."

"But didn't you say it's really his house now? I couldn't take anything belonging to him."

"These artefacts are all mine. Collected by my own hand on my travels around the world, and I want you to have one."

Emily hesitated. She was loath to take a book, but the artefacts were equally precious.

Lady Charlton went to one of the display tables. "You seemed particularly interested in Egypt," she said, and opened the glass top. "I think you'd enjoy this scarab. It is a symbol of good health and good luck." She handed Emily a golden scarab encrusted with semi-precious stones.

"Oh, I couldn't possibly," Emily stammered. "It's much too valuable."

"I insist you must have it. I want to give it to you, and you wouldn't deny an old woman some pleasure, would you?" She pressed it into Emily's hand. "My husband gave it to me in Cairo. It had come from a pharaoh's tomb, so one gathers."

The object felt heavy and cold in Emily's hand. She stood staring at it.

"I don't know what to say."

"You could try 'thank you.'"

"Oh yes. Thank you." And impulsively she hugged the old lady, who turned quite pink.

They celebrated with a huge traditional Christmas dinner: turkey, chestnut stuffing, roast potatoes and root vegetables, followed by the Christmas pudding carried flaming to the table with a sprig of holly in it. When Emily went back to the cottage that night, she thought about her parents. This was their first Christmas without her. Were they missing her? Thinking about her with regret? She felt a great longing for them, for her home and for security. "But I can't go back," she told herself. "I can never go back."

And she thought of Robbie's parents, facing Christmas without their son. Again, she was tempted to write to them. *When the baby is born,* she decided. *I'll send them a photograph, so that they know.* Her hand moved to her belly, and the baby responded with a sharp kick.

CHAPTER THIRTY-SIX

Christmas was followed by the first serious snowstorm of the season. Emily slid and floundered as she made her way up from the cottage to the big house, hardly able to see in the wind-driven snow. She was gasping for breath as she entered the front hall. Lady Charlton came down the staircase and saw her.

"My dear girl, what possessed you to come out in this storm?" she demanded.

"I thought you wanted to start on the Indian artefacts this morning," Emily said.

"Such devotion to duty, but foolhardy. What if you had lost your way in the blizzard? Or slipped and frozen to death?"

"I'm really quite hardy." Emily grinned. "And it isn't too far from the cottage to the house. I could see the shape of it, even in a blizzard."

"You have no idea how difficult the weather can be here in winter. Almost arctic," Lady Charlton said. She went ahead into the sitting room and jerked violently on the bell. Daisy appeared almost instantly.

"A cup of something hot for Miss Emily. She has braved the storm to come here. And, Daisy, please put sheets on the bed in the blue bedroom and light a fire. There is no way she is attempting to go back to the cottage until this storm abates."

"But my cat!" Emily blurted out. "I can't leave him alone."

"Oh yes, the witch's cat." Lady Charlton looked amused. "But trust me, my dear, cats can fend for themselves in any weather. Is it shut inside?"

"No, I leave the scullery window open a sliver and he goes in and out that way."

"Then I assure you he will be fine. And we can send Simpson down later to have a look when the snow stops."

"Lady Charlton, Simpson is almost as old as you. It's a wonder he can do half the work you give him."

"Nonsense. Keeps him young," she replied.

Lady Charlton would not allow Emily to go home that night, or the next. She had to admit to herself that it was rather nice to sleep in a big warm bedroom with a silk eiderdown over her and someone to bring her a cup of tea in the morning. It reminded her of her old life. It was so tempting to give in and tell Lady Charlton that she would move up to the house. But the cottage nagged at the corners of her brain. "I should go back," she told herself. "I am supposed to be there."

When the storm had abated and the sun sparkled on fresh snow, she made her way back down the hill. The cottage looked like a scene from a fairy tale. The roof was softened by a blanket of white and the herb bushes were now gentle humps and bumps. As she came up to the front door, she saw that someone had been there. Footsteps led to her front door, then went away again. Two sets of footsteps, or rather the same footprints had come twice. She suspected it was Alice, coming to see if she was all right after the blizzard. But as she traced the steps away from the cottage, they did not lead down the lane and across the green to the Red Lion, but rather up the lane. Intrigued by this, she followed them, and found that they ended at the furthest of the thatched cottages where the farm labourers lived. The cottage of the Hodgsons, the young family whose father had returned from the war. The father who cried out at night.

Someone at that cottage had come to see her twice. She went around to the front door and knocked. The wife, Fanny Hodgson, opened it, relief flooding her face as she saw Emily.

"Oh, thank God. You're here. I was afraid you'd gone away."

"What's the matter, Fanny?" Emily asked. The young woman looked distraught, as if she hadn't slept in days. "Is it your husband?"

"No, it's Timmy, my boy," she said. "He's come down with the influenza, and there are snow drifts blocking the road. No doctor could get through, even if we could get to the telephone box for one. But the phone lines are down, too."

"Influenza? Are you sure?"

She nodded. "It has to be. I've read descriptions in the newspaper, and that's exactly how it's affecting our Tim. High fever, tossing and turning, and he can't breathe. You have to help him, Mrs Kerr."

"Me?" Emily took a step backwards. "I'm not a doctor, Mrs Hodgson."

"But you're her. The herb woman. Your sleeping potion worked a treat. You have to make something for Timmy before he dies." She clutched at Emily's arm, like a drowning person. From inside the cottage, Emily heard moaning.

Emily's brain was racing. Had she seen any recipe that might be of any use for a disease that killed healthy men in days? And yet the woman was desperate. "I'll try," she said. "But you know how serious this disease is, don't you? I'm not a miracle worker, but I'll do my best."

"Anything. Anything at all at this stage. I feel so helpless watching him suffering and knowing I can't do any more than put a cold compress on his forehead and bathe away his sweat."

"All right. I'll get working on it then," Emily said.

She saw relief on the woman's face. "God bless you, my dear."

Emily found it hard to breathe as she stepped into her cottage. It was icy cold, the fire having gone out some time ago, and the cat met her with an accusing mew, staring up at her with unblinking yellow eyes. She put down a saucer of bread and milk, then got the fire and stove going. She noted with satisfaction how easy these tasks had now become. Then she sat with her quilt wrapped around her, studying Tabitha Ann Wise's original recipe book and her own notes.

Knitbone was recommended to promote sweating, but the part to be used was the flower, which she didn't have. *Combine with yarrow, elderflower, peppermint, angelica and mulberry leaf to combat a fever.* She had yarrow, angelica root and peppermint, but not the other ingredients. Catnip was also recommended, and she was pretty sure she had some of that, judging from Shadow's attraction to a certain small plant.

Then she read that cowslip root, thyme and elecampane were lung restoratives. Cowslip was a spring flower, so no chance of that, and she had no idea what elecampane might be. But willow bark was reputed to reduce a fever, and she knew where there was a willow tree by the stream. It was hard going, ploughing through the snow, but she returned triumphant with willow bark. The recipe recommended finely chopping or grinding the bark. She took down the kitchen mincer and did her best.

"I have no idea how much I should be using," she worried, "or whether too much is dangerous, but I suppose at this stage anything is worth trying."

The final concoction she made included the ground willow bark, dried catnip, peppermint, angelica root, thyme, sage and yarrow, to which she added ground ginger and purple echinacea root, since Susan had mentioned that it possessed marvellous anti-inflammatory properties. She poured boiling water over the mixture and allowed it to steep. When it had cooled, she poured off the liquid into a jug and carried it up to Timmy Hodgson.

"I'm not sure whether it can help," she said as she handed it to Timmy's mother. "But it can't hurt. All of these herbs are beneficial."

"I won't ask you to come in and see him for yourself," the woman said, "knowing how the disease is so catching. I'm keeping the other kids in the kitchen, and my man is not feeling too well, so he's staying in bed, but we can just hope, can't we?"

Emily went back home, trying to swallow down the sick feeling. She had never been called upon to save someone's life before. If the child died, would she be blamed?

Realizing that Lady Charlton would be worried about her, she trudged back to the house. The old lady looked relieved to see her. "Thank God you've returned. I sent Simpson to see if you had fallen into a snow drift. He said he saw smoke coming from your cottage chimney, so I was hoping you were not stupid enough to want to stay in the cottage."

"I think I had better stay down there, if you don't mind," Emily said. "A crisis has developed in the village. Young Timmy Hodgson has come down with influenza."

"Then given your delicate condition, you should stay well away." Lady Charlton wagged a warning finger.

"Oh, don't worry, I didn't go in to check on the child," Emily said. "But I have tried to make a brew to see if we can bring down his fever and ease his lungs."

"Have you? What do you think might work against something as virulent as influenza?"

"I don't know if anything can," Emily replied. "But I'm trying willow bark because it's supposed to be effective against fever, and several other things to ease the lungs and excessive phlegm."

Lady Charlton nodded. "That sounds like a sensible plan. Let's just pray that it works. They have just got their father back safely. They don't need to lose a child now."

Emily insisted on going back to the cottage. She made another batch of the remedy, in case more was needed. First thing the next morning, she went back to see how Timmy was doing, almost dreading to hear the worst. But the news was good.

"He seems a bit better, you know. The fever broke overnight, but now I think our Lizzie is coming down with it."

Emily supplied more of the remedy, and then heard that Mrs Soper's older son, Sammy, had also developed influenza. Emily treated him, then his brother went down with it, and then Maud and Mrs Soper herself. Emily couldn't believe that someone as robust as Maud could be so stricken. She had made a vow not to go near the infected people, but in the Sopers' house, there was nobody to take care of them. Only the old grandfather seemed to be immune. "You can't die, Maud!" she shouted as Maud moaned and tossed in her fever and Emily attempted to force some of her mixture past her dry and cracked lips.

Alice came up to the Sopers and found Emily there.

"You want to watch yourself, love," Alice said, looking at her with concern. "You should be thinking of yourself. If you get it, then what might happen to the baby?"

"I can't let anyone die, Alice," Emily replied. "If my herbs can do any good at all, then I have to keep going."

"Well, I suppose it wouldn't be the worst thing in the world if something happened to the baby," Alice said. "It would actually be the best solution for your future, but—"

"No!" Emily exclaimed. "Nothing is going to happen to my baby! I won't let it."

"Then let me do the actual nursing," Alice insisted. "It don't matter if I get it. Nobody's going to miss me." And she laughed.

"I'd miss you," Emily said. "You're the big sister I never had."

"Go on with you!" Alice poked her in the side, but Emily could tell she was moved.

She had just reached her front door, looking forward to putting her feet up by the fire, when she saw the vicar slipping and sliding down the lane towards her. He waved and shouted. "You have to come right now," he called, gasping for breath as he reached her. "It's my wife. She's very bad. I don't think she's going to survive."

Emily hesitated. Mrs Bingley's unkind words echoed in her head. How easy it would be to refuse. But instead she went inside, poured more of the infusion into her jug and set off again.

By the end of the week, three quarters of the inhabitants of Bucksley Cross had contracted influenza. Emily stayed well away from the big house, hoping that the disease would not reach the old lady. She brewed more and more of her mixture, and she and Alice went from house to house. By the end of the month, the disease had run its course and nobody had died.

"Quite astonishing," the doctor proclaimed when he could finally make it through the snow to visit his patients. "It must be so cold and bleak up here that even the influenza didn't want to stick around."

Emily felt the warm glow of accomplishment. *I helped with that,* she thought. *They are alive because of me.* It was an amazing feeling, and the irony struck her. She had wanted to join Clarissa and be a nurse, but had been turned down. Now it was her medical skills that had saved a village. Clarissa would be impressed. She got out her writing paper and wrote her a letter.

> *I know it wasn't anything like as terrible here as your conditions in London, but I am sure some of these people would have died without my remedy. I'm enclosing the recipe, just in case someone in the medical profession at your hospital would like to take a look at it and see if it could be of any help to you.*

At the end of the week, she received a letter with a London post-mark, but written in a strange hand.

> *Dear Madam,*
> *I am not sure of your last name, as you only sign yourself as Emily. I am the matron of the Royal London Hospital,*

and I am sorry to inform you that Nurse Clarissa Hamilton succumbed to complications of influenza two weeks ago and passed away. She was a brave young woman who worked tirelessly in the worst conditions of the East End and gave her life for others. I am enclosing her family's address in case you would like to write a letter of condolence.

Emily sat staring at the piece of paper, as if willing the words to change. "Not Clarissa!" she wailed out loud. "That's not possible. It's not fair!"

Clarissa, the fearless, strong one. The one who had taken the risks at school, sneaking out of the dorm window, smoking in the old bell tower. Who had risked her life every day at the front in France. To have perished now, in her own country, when the war was over, seemed the ultimate cruelty.

"I still can't believe I won't see her again," Emily said to Lady Charlton, trying desperately not to cry in front of the old woman.

"I felt the same when Henry died, then my son, James," Lady Charlton said. "There is nothing to say except that life is unfair. You will get over it, just as you will get over the death of your beloved lieutenant, but only time will heal your wounds, and then not completely. We just have to make do with what we have left and treasure those around us who are still alive."

"But I have nobody," Emily wanted to say, but didn't. She also now had no alternative—she was stuck there in the little cottage in the village of Bucksley Cross, whether she liked it or not.

Later that evening, she was sitting alone in the cottage, not wanting to engage in polite conversation, when there was a tap at her door. *Please, no,* she prayed. *Not another case of influenza.* She opened it, and was startled to see several people standing in the darkness. One carried a lantern. They looked as if they were a band of carol singers, only it wasn't Christmas.

Mrs Soper revealed herself in the lamplight as she stepped forwards. "We've come to say thank you, Emily," she said. "We may call you by your first name, may we not? Because you are one of us now."

Emily looked around the group. "I was glad to help," she said, "and so glad that my remedy actually worked so well."

"You took a big risk for strangers," Mrs Soper said. "I know my family and me wouldn't have made it without you, and so I wanted to say we know there's a little one on the way. We're all going to be making the layette. Anything you need for the baby, you shall have it."

"And I've got the pram I used for our Lizzie," Mrs Hodgson added, coming through the group. "I don't know how to thank you enough. Your coming here was a miracle."

"I don't know what to say." Emily's eyes were welling with tears. "Would you like to come in? There's not much room, but I can make you a cup of tea."

"Cup of tea?" Nell Lacey's voice came from the back of the crowd. "We've brought a bottle of whisky with us. We're going to have a toast to beating that ruddy influenza."

That night, Emily lay in bed with Shadow curled up beside her. *I do have a place where I belong after all,* she thought.

CHAPTER THIRTY-SEVEN

Spring came to Bucksley Cross. First, the snowdrops appeared on the hillside, then the crocuses, and at last the whole of the grounds of Bucksley House were filled with daffodils. And in the herb garden, there were new leaves and the first flowers. Emily did more identifying from the herb book, and picked, dried and carefully labelled the new herbs. She had now started attending the meetings of the Women's Institute, and they were being given a lecture on how to make jam with local wild berries when one of the farm wives said, "It's all very well and good, knowing how to make jam, but how do we pay for the sugar? That's what I want to know."

"That's right," someone else said. "My husband isn't coming home, is he? How am I supposed to exist on my widow's pension?"

"We should have young Emily make her miracle potion and sell it in case the flu ever comes back," Mrs Soper suggested. "I bet it will work on other things, too—chicken pox and the like."

"I couldn't do that, Mrs Soper," Emily said. "I'm not a qualified doctor. I'm sure that selling medicines is against the law."

"Well then, what about that hand cream?" Alice asked. "It worked wonders on my chapped hands."

"Yes, why not?" Nell Lacey agreed. "I tried it, too. Lovely, it was. Smelled nice, too."

"We'd have to have enough beeswax and have small tins made to put it in," Emily said, but she could sense her own growing excitement. "And I'm not sure if my small garden will produce enough lavender."

"I've got lavender bushes behind the house," one of the wives said. "And Lady Charlton has every flower you could ever think of growing in that big garden of hers. Lovely roses. I reckon this is something we could all do. You just show us, Emily, and we'll all help. We'll have our Bucksley Dartmoor cream in all the posh shops."

Emily felt their enthusiasm and saw their hopeful faces. "We can give it a try," she said. "And if it goes well, perhaps we can work on a face cream and lotion, too, now that the flowers are coming out."

Mr Patterson was also enthusiastic about the idea. "You've given me the incentive to put in more hives," he said. He and Emily were meeting again once a week, and nobody seemed to want to gossip about it any more. Emily enjoyed her evenings with him, discussing books and her herbal remedies. One evening, when she was getting ready to leave, she could sense that he was nervous, and wondered what she had done. He cleared his throat.

"My dear Emily," he said. "I know that a little one is expected soon, and I know the truth of your circumstances. Mrs Bingley told me some time ago, meaning to spoil our friendship, I've no doubt. But I do know that you are not a widow." He paused. *He's going to tell me he doesn't want to associate with me any more,* Emily thought. Then he cleared his throat again. "I have been a confirmed bachelor for many years, and I am a good deal older than you, but I wondered if you might consider marrying me, to ensure that the child is born with a legitimate name. I know how hard it will be for a child with no father and no name. I am not what they would call a good catch." He gave a little smile. "But I am not without funds, and I think you can see that the schoolhouse is a snug enough little dwelling. And I would take good care of you both. I think you enjoy our little village, and you are well liked here, well respected. I do not think you would be unhappy with such a life."

There was a silence, then Emily said, "I am lost for words, Mr Patterson."

"Reginald, please."

"Reginald, I always knew that you were a kind man, but this goes beyond kindness. To give up your solitude and your way of life for someone you hardly know is a great sacrifice."

"Hardly a sacrifice, Emily. I have come to look forward to our little chats, and I enjoy your lively mind. I think we would be quite compatible, quite good companions, eh?"

"Yes, I believe we would," Emily said. "I, too, enjoy our little chats. But this is so sudden, so unexpected—I don't know what to say."

"Then say nothing right now. I do not demand an immediate answer. Think about it. Consider it. Consider your future and what might lie ahead if you have no male protector and no solid means of employment."

"What you say is true, Reginald," Emily agreed. "But marriage? That is such a big step."

"You do not find me too repulsive, do you?" he asked.

"Not at all. I find you an altogether pleasant man, one that I should be happy to call my friend for years to come. But marriage should include love, should it not?"

"I think you'll find that many marriages are matters of expediency rather than romance, my dear. You would not be the first woman who married for financial security. But I repeat—take your time. Think it over."

Emily walked back to the cottage with her head reeling. It would indeed be the answer to many of her worries. She would be taken care of, and so would her child. *But I'm twenty-one years old,* she thought. *I have a whole life ahead of me. Do I really want to be stuck in the back of beyond for the rest of my days?* And then another thought followed. *He's a nice enough man, and I'm sure he'd treat me well, but I think of him as an uncle, an older friend of the family. Could I possibly learn to love him?* It was one thing enjoying fireside chats, but what if he wanted to claim the rights of a husband? She tried to imagine him kissing her, taking her into his arms . . .

And the moment she considered this, an image of Robbie came into her mind. Robbie's bright, suntanned face and unruly, red-blond hair. The way his eyes sparkled when he looked at her. And how she felt when he had made love to her. How could anyone replace him? How could she ever love again?

She didn't mention Mr Patterson's proposal to anyone, not even Lady Charlton. They had almost finished cataloguing all the books and artefacts, and Emily felt that she should be turning her attention to the spring garden, but Lady Charlton resisted this strongly. "A woman in your condition? Unheard of."

"I'm sure women work in the fields in places like Africa and China until their babies are born," Emily pointed out.

"This is not Africa or China, nor are you a peasant woman," Lady Charlton said. "The men are back on the farm, aren't they? We'll ask the farm manager to send over one of them to dig up the beds, then you can decide what should be planted . . ."

Her voice trailed away at the end of this speech. Emily looked at her with concern. "Are you all right?" She pulled up a chair. "Here. Sit down. You look very pale."

"There's nothing wrong with me but old age," Lady Charlton said, but she sat, gratefully. "Actually, I am rather tired these days. I don't think my heart is working as well as it should."

When Emily went back to the cottage, she studied recipes for a weak heart. Hawthorn blossoms were recommended as a cardiac tonic, along with yarrow and wood betony. Other notes included using periwinkle and something called heartsease, which turned out to be *Viola tricolor*, the little pansy-like violet that was now springing up in her front garden. She went out and picked plenty of hawthorn blossoms from the hedgerows, and the next day, when she went up to the house, she brought a bottle of the tonic with her.

"I've made something for your heart," she said.

The old woman took a sip. "It tastes disgusting. Have you put hemlock in it?"

"Of course not! You can add honey or sugar if you like." Emily smiled. "But it should do you good."

"I think you've inherited the powers of the witch," Lady Charlton said, a few days later. "I do feel a lot more sprightly. I'd like to know what is in your tonic."

Emily wrote down the ingredients for her, and Lady Charlton nodded. "An interesting mixture. Well done."

Then Emily turned her attention to experimenting with creams and lotions. The beeswax felt too sticky for a face cream, so she sent away for glycerine, and also asked if lanolin could be procured from the local farms. It was too early in the year for the first lavender, but she tried other spring flowers, as well as the last of the lavender she had dried the year before.

"Try this," she said to Nell and Alice at the pub. They both agreed that it smelled nice and made their hands feel soft. "Then let's get started, shall we?" she suggested. "Let's try a sample batch."

The cottage was too small to work in efficiently, so they took over the back room at the Red Lion. The local women threw themselves into the task with enthusiasm. Small tins were ordered. Various mixtures were tried, and Emily also found a recipe for soothing lotions—good against bruises, sprains and rashes, so the recipe said. Rose water, borage juice, witch hazel and chickweed. It was too early in the year for roses, but she bought rose oil at the chemist and added a few drops to the liquid. This seemed to be a big success. The women said it felt lovely when they patted it on their faces, and it also helped with bruises. So bottles were ordered, and Mrs Soper's oldest boy, who possessed artistic talent, designed labels. It seemed their commercial enterprise was getting well underway. Local chemists agreed to stock a few bottles and tins, then ordered more.

"I reckon we're going to be all right here after all," Nell Lacey said.

Mrs Soper glanced at Maud. "I reckon we are."

"Now we need to start making plans," Alice laughed. "We want the front counter in Selfridges department store."

"Hark at you, with your big ideas!" Nell Lacey gave her a friendly shove. "You'll be wanting to sell it in Paris next."

"And why not?" Alice replied amid laughter.

At the same time, visitors started venturing out again, and Alice and Nell began offering cream teas at the pub. Mrs Upton started selling bottles of pop and sandwiches at the shop. Emily had been so busy and so preoccupied with getting their business going that she had put thoughts of the baby to one side. So she was taken by surprise when, as she was planting runner beans, broad beans and peas, she felt a sharp pain in her stomach.

I've pulled a muscle, was her first thought as she straightened up. But then the pain came again, this time wringing her whole middle section so violently that it took her breath away. Then realization dawned. It was happening. She was having the baby. She put her tools away in the shed methodically, then went up to the big house.

"Emily, is that you?" Lady Charlton called. "Where have you been?" She came out of the sitting room and saw Emily's mud-spattered apron. "You've been working in that garden, you naughty girl, after I told you . . ." She stopped. "What's the matter?"

"I think I'm having the baby," Emily gasped, holding on to the banister to steady herself.

Lady Charlton went over to the bell and pulled it urgently. Daisy appeared and was ordered to get Emily up to bed and to send Simpson to fetch the doctor. Ethel was to boil water and find towels. Emily allowed herself to be undressed and put to bed, then lay there, feeling scared. She knew so little about what was about to happen, but she had heard women whisper about childbirth when she had still been at home. It was an awful ordeal, she knew. The worst pains ever. Women died. She stifled a cry as her body was overcome with pain. How long would it take before the doctor arrived? Would he be able to do anything to stop the pain? She wasn't sure how long she lay there with the cycles of pain rising and receding, but then someone put a cold compress on her forehead.

"It's all right, love. I'm here now," said a voice, and Emily opened her eyes to see Alice sitting beside her. "Daisy came and got me," she said. "You don't want to go through this alone."

Another wave of pain came, and Emily clenched her teeth.

"You squeeze my hand, and yell if you want to," Alice said.

"Oh, Alice," Emily gasped as the pain subsided. "Am I going to die?"

"Don't talk such bloody rubbish," Alice said. "You're as strong as an ox. Not long now and it will all be over."

Emily grasped Alice's hand, her forehead bathed in sweat as the contractions came and went. Suddenly, there was a strange and new sensation. "Alice. I think it's coming," Emily said.

Alice pulled back the sheets and lifted Emily's nightgown. "Bloody 'ell," she muttered. "I think you're right. I can see something."

And as she finished speaking, the small, red bundle slithered out and lay between Emily's legs. Alice grabbed a towel and lifted the baby. Little arms flailed, and the bundle let out a lusty and angry cry. Alice and Emily looked at each other in amazement.

"A little girl," Alice exclaimed. "You've got a little girl."

There was a tap on the door and the doctor came in. "Well," he said, "I see you've managed everything perfectly well without my help. Well done."

That evening, Emily sat up in bed with her daughter in her arms. The child had a light down of hair and stared up at Emily as if she was trying to make sense of things. Emily thought she was the most perfect thing she had ever seen.

"So what are you going to call her?" Lady Charlton asked.

"I was going to call her Robert if she had been a boy," Emily said.

"Then call her Roberta."

"Roberta." Emily tried out the name. "It's a bit austere for a little baby, isn't it?"

"You'll no doubt come up with a baby name for her."

So Roberta she became.

The village women came to visit. Mr Patterson came, too.

"I'm afraid it's now too late to give her a legitimate name," he said when they were alone, "but my offer still stands. And I am prepared to adopt her legally if you wish."

Emily took his hand. "I am so grateful, Reginald. You are such a good man. But it's too soon for me. I loved someone so much, and he's gone. I think it will take a while before anyone could take his place."

"I do understand." He nodded. "I also loved deeply once. I met her when I was suffering from consumption. She was in the same hospital. But she died. It was very painful. You and I have more in common than you imagine." He bent to give her a light kiss on her forehead before he tiptoed out of the room.

CHAPTER THIRTY-EIGHT

Roberta, now known as Bobbie, was three weeks old, and Emily's strength and energy had returned. The first batches of lotion and creams had sold out, and the women were waiting for Emily to make more. The first roses and many of the herbs were ready to be picked and dried. Emily refused to stay in bed any longer and escaped with the baby down to the cottage. For several days, she was so fully occupied that she hardly saw anything of Lady Charlton.

She was disturbed one evening, when she arrived for dinner with baby Bobbie in her arms, to find that Lady Charlton had not left her bed that day. She deposited Bobbie in the nursery and went to visit the old lady.

"There's really nothing wrong with me," Lady Charlton said, waving her away. "I just feel rather weak, that's all. As if all the strength has been drained out of me."

"I'll go down and have Mrs Trelawney make you a good, nourishing broth," Emily said. "And some calf's foot jelly, perhaps."

The old lady nodded and gave a weak smile. Emily's heart was beating fast. Lady Charlton couldn't die. Not now. Not after everything else. She ate hurriedly, left Bobbie in the nursery with Daisy in charge and went back to the cottage. She should make more of the heart tonic, maybe brewing a little stronger this time. She studied the list of ingredients: hawthorn blossoms, preferably freshly picked. Yarrow, wood betony, periwinkle and heartsease. All of them were recommended for stimulating a failing heart, which was what she suspected was wrong with Lady Charlton. Then there was a side note that foxglove was a powerful stimulant for a failing heart. The next day, she picked the flowers. Luckily, hawthorn was blooming in profusion along the hedgerows, and the little *Viola tricolor* known as heartsease. Violets were also in various front gardens. She laid out the ingredients, looking at them. When she came to the foxglove flowers, she hesitated. Tabitha Ann Wise had written words of warning. *Use this with great caution. The wrong dose can kill.* She put it aside, not wanting to take any risks. Then she put the other ingredients in a pan and boiled them until she had a concentrated brew. Then she carried it up to Lady Charlton.

"I've made you another tonic," she said. "A little stronger this time. It should be good for the heart."

She poured a little into a glass. Lady Charlton took a sip, then made a face. "This one tastes worse than the last," she said. "Are you trying to poison me?"

"It will do you good. I'll add some honey."

She went down to the kitchen and requested some hot water with honey in it from Mrs Trelawney. "I've made her a tonic, but it's too bitter to drink," she said.

She carried it back upstairs, mixed the tonic with the sweet water and then handed it back to Lady Charlton. Lady Charlton took a sip or two, then lay back on the pillows. "Is there anything I can do for you?" Emily asked. "Would you like me to read to you?"

The old woman had closed her eyes, and she shook her head. Then, as Emily was about to tiptoe out, she sat up suddenly, put her hand to her heart and fainted. Emily rushed downstairs and summoned the servants. Simpson was sent to fetch the doctor. Luckily, he was on his rounds not far away. He took one look at Lady Charlton and sent for an ambulance.

"It's her heart, right enough," he agreed. "It's been failing for some time."

The ambulance men carried her down, and they set off for the Royal Devon and Exeter Hospital. Emily really wanted to go with them, but she couldn't leave the baby. She stood watching the ambulance take Lady Charlton away, wondering if she'd ever see her again.

The next day, she arranged to take Daisy with her to help with the baby, and Simpson drove them to the hospital in Exeter. *Father's chambers are in Exeter,* she thought. She asked to see Lady Charlton, but was refused because she wasn't a family member. "Besides," she was told, "she's not fully conscious. It may just be a matter of time. You should notify family members."

She joined Daisy and the baby outside the hospital. They drove through the city centre as they headed back to Bucksley Cross. The motor car had to halt as they passed the great cathedral rising from its gardens on the high street. She peered out of the window, awed by its majesty. Was there a god that made humans create buildings like that? Did that god really know what all those little people down below were doing and thinking and feeling? She swallowed back the great despair that threatened to engulf her. Then, as Simpson began to drive on, she saw something that caught her attention. "Stop!" she cried.

On the railings that bordered the cathedral grounds, someone had posted a notice. The words "War Poets Today" were splashed diagonally across a poster that read: "The group of young men known as the War Poets will be reading from their work on Tuesday at 2 p.m."

"We have to stay," she said. "They may know where we can find Justin Charlton."

They found a place to park the motor car. Simpson decided to visit a nearby pub while Emily and Daisy went in search of lunch. They ate beans on toast in a little cafe, and then found a secluded corner of the garden behind the church where Emily could feed the baby. Then they went into the cathedral. Emily had been taken inside the building as a child, but had never been struck before by its beauty and magnificence. The fan-vaulted ceiling stretched all the way to the great stained-glass east window. Pools of coloured light danced on the stone floor. Attendance was sparse, or seemed sparse in so great a space, and Emily slid into one of the back pews as a member of the clergy talked about documenting the suffering of war, then introduced the young men who had put their own stories of the war into powerful poetry. They came out and took their places at the altar steps. Emily gasped. Justin was one of them. She waited impatiently as they began to read from their work. The poems were brilliant and moving, but she couldn't really concentrate all through the reading, and then through the questions that followed. It was only when tea and biscuits were being served afterwards in a small side room that she was able to corner Justin.

He looked up in surprise when he saw her approaching him.

"Viscount Charlton. I'm so glad. I've been trying to find you," she said.

He winced. "Oh God. No Viscount Charlton, please. Titles are meaningless. I'm plain Mister, or Justin if you like. So you came to hear our poems?"

"Yes, but it's really a miracle that you were here today. Your grandmother is in the Royal Devon and Exeter Hospital here. She's dying. They told me to contact family members. I really think you should go to see her."

He looked at her uncertainly. "She's dying, you say? You want me to make my peace with her? After what she said to me?"

"Justin, she bitterly regretted the way she spoke to you. We've been trying to locate you through your regiment, but they had you listed as killed in action. I would have gone up to London to look for you, but I've just a baby, and I was in no condition to travel. Won't you please come to see her? I beg of you. I tried to visit her, but they wouldn't let me in because I'm not family."

She could see the indecision on his face. "I suppose I could do so," he said. "I should do so. After all the dying that I have seen, I would not want her to die alone."

"Thank you." Instinctively, she reached out towards him. "You don't know how much this means to me."

He looked at her long and hard. "You really care about the old woman, don't you?" he asked.

"Yes. Yes, I do. My family has rejected me, and she took me in. She has been kindness itself, and she means a lot to me."

He was still studying her with interest. "Your family rejected you?"

"They did." She wanted to tell him the truth, but couldn't, not in this public space. And, she also realized, she didn't want him to think badly of her. "They did not approve of my choice of husband."

"Then we are two of a kind, aren't we?" he said. "Both of us are outcasts. Come on then. We'd better go straight to my grandmother."

"I have her motor car waiting," Emily said.

"Jolly good. I'll just tell the fellows."

"And I have to find my baby and the nursemaid." She hurried off.

"Here we are then," Justin said as the motor car pulled up outside the large red-brick hospital building.

Emily shook her head. "They won't let me see her. Only family, they said."

"Don't be silly. Come on. You're Cousin Emily. Nobody will dispute that." He grabbed her hand. "You want to see her, don't you? To say goodbye?"

"I'd really appreciate that."

"Then let's go." He yanked her from the motor car.

The old lady was lying in a narrow white bed, her face as white and still as a statue's. But her eyes fluttered open when the nurse said, "You've got visitors, my lady."

"Justin?" she asked.

"Hello, Grandmother," he said softly. "How are you?"

"Not dead yet," she said. Her eyes opened wider. "And Emily. How lovely to see you. You found Justin for me. You really are a miracle worker."

"It was pure chance," Emily said. "He was one of a group of war poets reading their work at the cathedral."

"War poets—what in heaven's name are those?" Already the critical note had come into her voice.

"We need to talk about our experiences," Justin said, "and the only way some of us can do it and let people experience what we went through is with poetry."

"Do you have a book of these poems?"

"We're not published yet," he said. "We are touring the country, giving readings."

She gave a snort. "I don't know what your father would say." Then her expression softened. "Still, I suppose to each his own. I can't force you into being someone you are not."

"Thank you," he said. He reached out and covered her bony hand with his own.

They left her soon afterwards when she drifted back to sleep. Neither said anything as they walked down the hospital corridor. As they came down the stairs, Justin said, "Let's get a cup of tea, shall we? I expect it will be foul, but at least it's warm and wet, and my throat is parched after reading out loud."

"Yes. Good idea." They followed the signs to the cafeteria. Justin bought them two cups of tea and teacakes and sat beside her.

"I think she might pull through, don't you?" Emily said tentatively.

"Probably, just to make sure I don't have to claim my inheritance too soon," he said.

She slapped his hand. "What a horrid thing to say. Justin, you have to give her a chance. You have too many unhappy memories. You must let them go. Think of the future. Be happy you are still alive when so many are not."

He managed a little smile. "How come you are so bloody wise? How old are you?"

"Almost twenty-two."

"I'm twenty-four. And we've both lost what should have been the best years of our lives."

"You never know. They may still be ahead," she said, wondering as she said it how she could possibly look forward to anything again.

"So how did you like my poems?" he asked, clearly trying to break the sombre tone of their conversation.

"Your poems were really good. They all were. So moving. Almost the whole audience was in tears."

"Good. That is what we hope for—to make people realize the futility and horror and waste of war."

There was another pause. Then he asked, "You say your family rejected you because they did not approve of the man you wanted to marry."

She nodded.

"And you say he was killed. You keep telling me to make my peace and put the past behind me. Can you not let bygones be bygones and go back to them?"

"I didn't tell you the whole story." She toyed with the spoon in her saucer. "He died before we could marry. I have just had a child, and my parents made it very clear what they thought of girls who disgraced their family in that way."

"I see." He nodded. "You've been through a tough time."

"But your grandmother made it easier for me. She took me in, even after I told her the whole truth. And the whole village has welcomed me—apart from the vicar's wife."

"Oh, she's poison," he said, and they both laughed.

"Will you be in the area for long?" she asked. "You said you are on a tour with your poet friends."

"Yes. We're in Plymouth tomorrow, then we're staying with one of the chap's families nearby for a couple of days before we go on to Bristol and then into Wales."

"I see," she said. "You couldn't find a way to stay close to your grandmother in case she passes away, could you?"

He thought about this. "I suppose I should stick around, shouldn't I? Yes. I'd like to stay with her. I'll tell the chaps I'll skip the Plymouth reading and meet them again when I can."

"Will you let us know?" she asked. "Will you send a telegram to the house if . . . ?" She broke off, unable to utter the words.

"Of course." He got up. "I'd better go and set things straight with the chaps, and maybe find a boarding house near the hospital."

They walked together through the hospital and lingered on the steps at the entrance.

"I've enjoyed talking to you," Justin said. "I'm sorry, I don't know your first name."

"Emily," she said. "Emily Bryce. Not really Mrs Kerr. That was your grandmother's suggestion."

"There was a Freddie Bryce at school with me at Taunton," he said.

"My brother."

"Really? Good chap. A couple of years older than me. He was my prefect."

"He died at the beginning of the war. Only lasted a couple of weeks in the trenches."

"I'm sorry."

"I am, too. But I'm finally coming to terms with it."

He stood for a moment, just looking at her. Emily detected a wail from the motor car parked across the road. "It sounds as if my baby has woken up. I'd better go, and so had you."

"What did you have—a boy or a girl?"

"A little girl."

"That's good, isn't it? She won't be called upon to fight."

"Oh, Justin. This is the war to end all wars. Let's hope nobody will be called upon to fight again."

"I pray that you're right." He continued looking at her. She realized that he had grey eyes and a sweet smile. "I think I'll go back up to the old lady for a little while. Just to sit with her, you know."

Emily nodded. He held out his hand. "Goodbye, Emily."

His hand lingered holding hers. She was unprepared for the current that she felt, and she blushed.

"Goodbye, Justin," she said, a little breathlessly.

She felt him watching her as she ran down the steps to the waiting motor car.

CHAPTER THIRTY-NINE

When Simpson deposited Emily outside the cottage, she was intrigued to see a big black car waiting nearby in the lane. When she had reached her front door, she heard footsteps behind her. She turned and saw two men coming towards her.

"Can I help you?" she asked.

"Are you the woman who lives here?" the older of the two men called. He was a hefty chap, middle-aged, with sagging jowls that gave him a bulldog look.

"I am."

"The one who calls herself Mrs Kerr?"

Emily frowned. "Yes. What is this about?"

"We're from the Devon County Constabulary," the older one said. "Detective Inspector Payne and Sergeant Lipscombe."

"Is it bad news?" she asked, holding baby Bobbie tightly to her.

"May we come in? We really don't want to be discussing this where everyone can see."

"All right." Emily opened the cottage door and let them in.

Inspector Payne looked around. "Nice little place you've got here. Well-furnished."

"Thank you," Emily replied. "Now, if you'll just tell me why you are here. Has there been a robbery?"

"Maybe." He smirked then. Emily found it strangely unnerving.

He sat in her one armchair without being invited. Emily continued to stand, the baby in her arms. "I'll just put the baby down in her cradle," she said, and went through to the next room. When she came back, the two policemen were standing together and examining the objects on her mantelpiece.

"Some interesting things you've got here," said Inspector Payne. "That compass—pretty impressive."

"Yes. It came from Lady Charlton," she replied. "Those are all things she picked up on her travels."

"I bet they are," the man replied.

Emily had had enough. She was tired from making the trip to Exeter and worried about Lady Charlton. "I'm not sure what you are implying, but I'd like to know why you are here and what you want."

The big man sat again, while the sergeant continued to stand. "Let's start with your full name. I take it it's not really Mrs Kerr?"

"It's Emily Bryce."

"Miss Emily Bryce?"

"That is correct."

"So not a war widow then?"

"Why should this be of interest to anyone?" Emily demanded. "I have not tried to obtain anything under false pretences. I have collected no widow's pension. My fiancé was killed in France before we could marry, and I find myself with a child. It was Lady Charlton who suggested I call myself by his name. I see no harm in it. So would you like to tell me why you are here?"

"We've had a report of a most serious nature," he said, "concerning you and Lady Charlton."

"What sort of report?" She pulled up a chair and sat facing him.

"Yesterday, Lady Charlton fainted and was rushed to hospital, correct?"

"Yes."

"This happened, so I am told, right after you forced her to drink some kind of concoction you had made."

"It was a herbal tonic to help her heart," Emily said. "And I didn't force her to drink it."

"She was heard protesting that she didn't want it, and you were heard saying it was good for her."

"Yes, that's because it was too bitter. I went down to the kitchen and brought up some honey water to mix with it in order to make it more palatable."

"And then she drank it, and immediately clutched her heart and fainted."

"Yes, she did."

He smirked again, looking rather pleased with himself. "Most fortuitous, wouldn't you say?"

Emily was staring at him with disbelief. "Are you insinuating that I deliberately tried to harm Lady Charlton?"

"That's what it looks like to me."

"That's utterly ridiculous, Inspector. I don't know who told you this, but I can assure you that what I gave her was a perfectly harmless tonic with herbs that are restorative for the heart. A tried and true remedy from several old books. It contained hawthorn blossom, periwinkle, *Viola tricolor* . . . herbs from my garden."

"And the foxglove? Did you forget to mention the foxglove?"

"There was no foxglove in the mixture."

"And yet you were seen picking foxgloves that very morning. And lily of the valley . . . known to be quite poisonous."

"Yes, I did. A lot of flowers are blooming right now. I picked several plants to dry them for later use. Lily of the valley can be efficacious in some herbal remedies when used with caution, but I did not include it in this mixture. I can make another batch to replicate it, if you like."

"Leaving out the items that would have overstimulated an ageing heart this time, naturally."

"I have just told you what I put in that mixture. And if you don't believe me, there might still be some left in the glass on the bedside table, if the maid has not cleared it away."

He was still smiling. "But you threw that away yourself, remember? As soon as the old lady fainted and you sent for help, you waited until everyone was running in all directions, and then you poured the rest of the mixture down the sink in her bedroom. You were seen."

"That is completely untrue!" Emily shouted now. She heard Bobbie whimper in the next room. "Inspector, I don't know where these lies come from, but I can guess. A certain member of Lady Charlton's household has always resented my coming here. I suspect it is she who has fabricated these things." She paused, taking a breath to calm herself. "Besides, what possible reason would I have for wanting Lady Charlton dead? She has welcomed me into her household and I have become very fond of her."

"You must admit it's all rather fortuitous, isn't it?" he went on, glancing up at the sergeant for confirmation. "You arrive out of nowhere, as a gardener, so they say. Then you ingratiate yourself with the old woman and start helping her in the house, and suddenly things start going missing. Valuable objects that have miraculously turned up here in your cottage. I suppose you thought the old lady wouldn't notice, being short-sighted and forgetful."

"She is neither short-sighted nor forgetful," Emily snapped, "and every object here was given to me by Lady Charlton as a present."

"She gives a gardener quite valuable gifts then." Another smirk. "Is that usual?"

"I helped her catalogue her books and artefacts," Emily said calmly, "and I take no pay. The objects were small thank-you gifts."

"Not very small gifts, if my eyes don't deceive me. Quite expensive gifts. As I see it, this is how it all happened. You find yourself in the family way. You hear about a lonely, old widow . . . a rich, old widow. You turn up here, claiming to be a gardener. You start to help her in the house. You quietly help yourself to objects that take your fancy. And maybe she discovers your little game and wants to get rid of you. So you get rid of her instead."

"This is beyond belief, Inspector." Emily tried to sound assured and indignant as she fought down the knot of panic growing inside her. "And you couldn't be further from the truth."

"Or maybe you now have an even bigger motive," he said, rubbing his hands together as if this whole conversation was giving him great pleasure. "The old lady had changed her will, hadn't she? Including you in it."

Emily went pale. "Changed her will? I had no knowledge of that. And even if she had, the house and estate were not hers to leave. There is an heir, her grandson, Justin."

"But her personal possessions she can will if she wants to, right? I'm told she was leaving you the contents of her library . . . books and items that she and her husband collected during their travels. A nice, little haul."

"I had no idea of this," Emily stammered. "Who told you of it?"

"One of the people who reported this to me had been called upon to witness the changes to the will. I'm afraid you are in big trouble, Miss Emily Bryce. If Lady Charlton dies, which seems very likely at this moment, then you might very well find yourself accused of murder."

"This is ridiculous," Emily said forcefully, but her insides were churning. She could see all too clearly how each of the things he had said made sense . . . would make sense to a jury.

"We'll wait and see, shall we?" The inspector stood up. "Attempted murder would be a lesser charge, but probably easier to prove, since it's not a hanging offence. Either way, I'm afraid you'll have to come with us to the police station."

"You can't do that," Emily protested. "I have a three-week-old baby, and I'm not going to be separated from her."

She stood with her chin out, staring at him defiantly. "You can't subject a tiny baby to separation from her mother, Inspector. Even you couldn't be that cruel. Besides, I haven't been charged with anything yet."

A tiny whimper from the next room made him look across, then he turned back to her.

"Then I'll be merciful and allow you to stay put until they send the big guns down from Scotland Yard. But you are not to leave this place. I'm putting a guard on your door."

"I'm not likely to try to go anywhere with a young child, am I?" she retorted. "And let's hope that the big guns from Scotland Yard, as you put it, are able to see that this is nonsense."

She wanted to mention her father, but realized that this might not be helpful. If her family had rejected her, then that would be another reason to doubt her good character, making it seem even more likely that she had wanted to take advantage of Lady Charlton.

"We'll be back, Miss Bryce," said the inspector while pausing in the doorway, before ducking his head as he went under the low lintel.

Emily watched the black motor car drive away, feeling sick and scared. As she looked around the cottage, it came to her suddenly that she was fulfilling her role in the curse. She had become the wise woman, and the wise woman always came to a bad end. That's what everyone had said, hadn't they? Susan Olgilvy had been innocent, but that hadn't mattered. Was she now destined to suffer the same fate?

She went through to the bedroom and sat beside her sleeping infant. How peaceful and lovely she looked, like a little cherub. Who would look after her if she really was taken to prison? At that moment, there was a tap on her front door and Daisy came in.

"What's going on, Emily?" she asked. "Mrs Trelawney's strutting around the kitchen looking like the cat with all the cream. And she said something to Ethel that she knew from day one that that girl would mean trouble, and now she's getting what she deserves. And I saw a strange motor car driving off."

"Oh, Daisy." Emily reached out and took her hand. "Two policemen were here." And she went on to recount the entire episode.

"Why, that spiteful, old cow!" Daisy exclaimed. "I knew she didn't like you. She's said some pretty horrible things about you. But to go to that trouble . . . to make up those stories."

"The problem is that I can't really disprove them, can I? I did make a herbal tonic, and she did refuse to drink it at first, and then she sat up, clutched her heart and fainted. Maybe I did make a mistake and one of the things I put in it was too much for her heart. I'm not an expert. I don't really know what I'm doing . . . But all those ingredients were supposed to be heart restoratives, I swear." She put her hand up to her mouth as she swallowed back a sob. "And all those nice things she has given me. If she dies, how can I ever prove they were gifts? She always gave them to me when we were alone together in the library, so nobody ever could have witnessed it."

"What's going to happen now?" Daisy asked.

"A man is coming down from Scotland Yard. And then . . . then I suppose they'll take me to prison, and I'll stand trial, and if the jurors don't believe me, I'll hang."

"Didn't you say your dad was a judge?"

"Yes, he is. But—"

"Then, for heaven's sake, write to him. Tell him everything. He will make it right for you."

"He might not." Emily looked away.

"He certainly won't let his daughter hang, will he?"

"I don't think so," she said hesitantly. "But how does he know I'm innocent? I'm sure judges' daughters commit crimes."

"Has he ever had cause to think you don't tell the truth?"

"Well, no."

"There you are then. Sit down. Write him a letter, and we'll make sure he gets it."

Emily stood, then shook her head. "I can't, Daisy. If he loved me, he'd have wanted my happiness, wouldn't he? He wouldn't have banished his only daughter, whatever she had done."

"I still think you should give it a try," Daisy said.

"I'll think about it," Emily said.

"I don't suppose you'll want to come up to the big house for dinner, will you?"

"I'm supposed to be a prisoner here," Emily replied. "Besides, I'm not going anywhere near that poisonous woman again."

"Then I'll bring you down some food."

"Don't," Emily said. "I wouldn't put it past her to try to poison me—literally, I mean." She attempted a laugh, but it failed miserably. "Oh, Daisy, I'm so scared. I don't think I could eat anything."

Daisy left her then. The baby awoke, and Emily picked her up mechanically and put her to the breast. "What's going to happen to you?" she said softly, staring down at that perfect, tiny face.

There were footsteps outside, then a knock at the front door. Emily was in the process of covering herself and putting down the child when whoever it was came in.

"Emily, it's Alice," the voice called. "Daisy's just told me. I've brought you some soup from the pub. And a glass of brandy. I thought you'd need it." She came through to the bedroom and stood looking down at Emily with pity.

"Oh, love, what an awful shock," she said. "How could that woman ever have said those things?"

"I don't know, Alice," Emily replied. "Maybe she really does think I poisoned her mistress. Maybe she really thinks I stole from the house. It's her word against mine, isn't it?"

"Lady Charlton's not dead yet, is she?"

Emily shook her head. "No. I went to see her with her grandson. He promised to give me any news."

"Her grandson? He came back then?"

"It was pure chance. He was reading from his poetry with a group of friends at Exeter Cathedral. I went to tell him about his grandmother, and he agreed to go and see her. At least I've done one thing right."

"You've done a lot that's right," Alice retorted. "Don't you dare say that."

Emily placed the baby back in the cradle and started to change her nappy as she stared up at her with big serious eyes. "I'm worried, Alice. Have I been really stupid and naive, making my herbal remedies when I really know nothing? Everything is based on someone else's knowledge. What if they got things wrong? What if they poisoned someone by mistake?"

"You saved this village from the flu," Alice said. "Don't ever forget that."

Emily shook her head, but could find nothing to say.

"Now," Alice said. "Have you written to your father yet? Daisy said you didn't want to."

"He may not want to help me," Emily replied. "He didn't earlier. He didn't seem keen to welcome me home after Robbie died. And then he made it quite clear . . ."

"When you told him you were expecting?"

Emily nodded, not looking up from changing her daughter.

"What exactly did he say?"

Emily hesitated. "Well, I didn't tell them I was expecting. I wanted to, but then my mother launched into a tirade about a neighbour's girl who had brought disgrace on her family and had to be sent away, and my father agreed with her. So I kept quiet."

"Emily Bryce, are you saying to me that you never actually told them?"

"How could I? I'd just heard that they would have banished that girl forever. I assumed they'd say the same to me. I didn't want to hear the words coming from their mouths."

"Oh, Emily, love." Alice put a hand on her shoulder. "People say a lot of things about other people. They enjoy passing judgement to feel superior. But when it's their own child . . . well, then it's different, isn't it? You write him a letter immediately, and I'll take it to him in the morning. I'll bet you ten to one that he'll want to come to your aid."

Emily looked up now. "Well, I suppose I've got nothing to lose at this point, have I? I've already lost the man I love, my reputation, and now I'm about to lose my life. All right. I'll do it. And I thank you for being so kind, Alice. You're a good friend. I don't know what I would have done without you."

"Oh, get along with you." Alice gave her an embarrassed slap. "You'd have done just fine."

CHAPTER FORTY

The night seemed endless. Emily stared at the ceiling, wondering what it would be like in prison, whether it hurt much when you were hanged. Had Susan Olgilvy felt the same? Had she lain there in the same bed, trying to come to terms with the cold truth that her life was over? As she lay there, she felt a gentle brush against her cheek. For a second, she wondered if it was Robbie's ghost, coming to say he loved her and was watching over her. But then she realized it was Shadow, not out hunting as usual, but realizing in that uncanny way of his that she needed his company. He curled up against her, purring gently.

"And who is going to look after you, old thing?" she said softly, stroking him.

As the cold light of dawn silhouetted the upland of the moor, she got up, lit the stove and put on the kettle. Bobbie still slept in peaceful bliss in her cradle. There was no sign of Shadow. She wrapped her shawl around her and went out into the garden. Everything was blooming, and sweet scents surrounded her. The first of Mr Patterson's bees were visiting the flowers. *If only I hadn't been stubborn and had married him, this would never have happened,* she thought. Could he be someone she could ask for help now?

When she came in to make a cup of tea, she glanced outside the front window and saw that a policeman was now stationed there. She turned away, the sick feeling returning. She went about her morning chores, put the baby outside in her pram to get her daily dose of fresh air, then wondered if she should pack up all of Lady Charlton's gifts to be returned to the big house. "But she did give them to me," she said out loud. "She wanted to make me happy." Now who would believe that?

Around mid-morning, the big motor car Emily had seen the day before pulled up outside. The original detective inspector was accompanied by another man, as well as his sergeant. Emily let them in. The newcomer was the inspector from Scotland Yard. He was less aggressive in manner than the Devon detective, but Emily sensed his questions were more dangerous. No, she was not qualified or experienced in herbal medicine. She had taken her recipes from old books. She thought that what she was doing was harmless and beneficial. So it was possible that she had, in fact, done harm to the old lady?

"I suppose it is possible," Emily said, "but I can give you a list of every ingredient and make another batch of the tonic for you to test."

"You were seen picking foxgloves—a potent heart stimulant."

"Yes, but I didn't use them," Emily said.

"Then why pick them?"

Emily hesitated. "I read that they were efficacious in cases of heart failure, but also dangerous," she said. "I considered using foxglove, but then decided against it."

He nodded, stared thoughtfully at the ground, then looked up suddenly. "Why did you come here, Miss Bryce? What made you seek out Lady Charlton? Was she a prior acquaintance of your family?"

"No," Emily said, warily now. "I was a member of the Women's Land Army. We were sent here to help with her garden. She and I got along well, and we stayed in this cottage, which hadn't been used for years. When I needed a place to go after we were released from service,

I wondered if she'd let me use this cottage in return for continuing to work in her garden."

"Why not return home to your family? Do you not have a family?"

"Yes, but . . . ," Emily began. She was interrupted by a loud knocking on the front door. Before she could move, the sergeant went to answer it.

"Is this the residence of Miss Emily Bryce?" a man's voice demanded.

"That's right, but . . . ," the sergeant replied.

"I'm her father, Judge Harold Bryce." And he pushed past the sergeant into the room.

Emily stared at him in amazement. How could Alice possibly have delivered a letter to him by now? Judge Bryce's gaze swept around the room, then focused on his daughter. "Emily, what on earth are you doing here? What has been going on?"

Emily stood up and took a step towards her father. She fought against her desire to fling herself into his arms. "Daddy, you got my letter."

"Letter? I received no letter. In fact, your mother and I have heard nothing from you these past months. Your mother has been worried sick. When we heard nothing from you at Christmas, we contacted the woman in charge of your land army girls and learned that you had all been dismissed for the winter. She said something about you going to live with a friend, so we had no idea where the devil you were. That woman didn't know. Nobody knew. What in God's name made you come here?"

"It's a long story, Daddy, and I'd like to tell you, but these are policemen who think that I tried to kill Lady Charlton when I was only trying to help her."

"That's what I heard. The commissioner came to my chambers first thing this morning and said he'd heard talk of an Emily Bryce being arrested for attempted murder. He didn't think there would be more than one Emily Bryce in the county, so he was sure I'd know about it.

Naturally, I didn't like to admit that we'd not seen hide nor hair of you in months. I got the address and came straight away."

"You're the girl's father?" the Scotland Yard inspector asked. "A judge?"

"I most certainly am. A judge of the Devon assizes. What exactly is my daughter supposed to have done?"

"There are several allegations—she prepared a potion that caused the old woman to have a heart attack. She has been accused of stealing from her, and it has even been suggested that she wanted the old woman dead because she is now mentioned in her will."

"All nonsense, Daddy. I am incredibly fond of Lady Charlton, as she is of me. Those things they say I stole, they were all gifts from her as thanks for helping her catalogue her collections. And I knew nothing of her will."

"And this potion?" her father asked.

"I have inherited a herb garden and books on herbal medicine. I have been trying to educate myself. I made what I thought would be a good heart tonic. There was nothing harmful in it, I'm sure. In fact, I have the recipe here, if the gentlemen would care to see it, and I would be happy to make up another batch from the same ingredients."

Her father was frowning. "Making herbal remedies? I suppose that could be construed as practising medicine without a licence."

"I was only trying to help," Emily said. "She said she was getting weaker."

Judge Bryce turned from his daughter to the two policemen. "Gentlemen, my daughter might be stubborn and inconsiderate, but I have never had an occasion to question her veracity. Nor have I ever seen any sign of avarice or of kleptomania. If she says the items were gifts, then I believe her. Besides, she comes from a comfortable home. Why would she need to steal from an old woman? Why would she care about being mentioned in her will? She will inherit a goodly amount from me one day." He paused to let this be digested, then continued.

"If she says she was trying to help, we must believe her. If she is guilty of anything, it is of ignorance and naiveté in dealing with unfamiliar herbs. Murder, as you very well know, must demonstrate intent."

"All the same, Judge," the Scotland Yard man said, "if the old lady dies, then it would not be unreasonable to bring the charge of manslaughter."

"Only if it is proven that the herb mixture really did contain an ingredient that could have precipitated her death," Emily's father replied. "And if she is guilty of manslaughter, then I would say that any doctor whose patient dies after his best intentions should be similarly hauled before the courts."

"You have a point there, sir," Inspector Payne muttered. "Of course, you are very well known amongst the Devon County Constabulary—known to be a fair man. We had no idea the young lady was your daughter. Why did you not tell us?" He glared at Emily.

"You didn't give me any time to explain anything," Emily said.

The Scotland Yard inspector got to his feet. "Well, I think we've done all that we came for today. If you will be good enough to make up another dose of that tonic, then at least we can have it tested and see if it might have contributed to the lady's heart attack. But as for the attempted murder charge, then I would say, Miss Bryce, that someone has a grudge against you."

"That may be true," Emily agreed. "It may also be that the person genuinely felt that I wished her mistress harm. She is not the brightest woman in the world, and is very possessive of her employer."

"Generous of you." The inspector nodded. "Perhaps you'll be good enough to bring in this herbal mixture when you return to Exeter," he said to Emily's father.

"I'd be happy to." He glanced across at his daughter.

When the policemen had gone and the motor car doors had slammed, Emily took hesitant steps towards her father.

"Daddy, you were wonderful," she said. "I don't know how to thank you."

He turned to her, smiling now. "I could always put forward a good argument. But in this case, I meant what I said. You have never lied to me that I know of." He took a deep breath. "Now, if you would tell me what in God's name you are doing in this hovel. And why you were hiding out from your worried parents all this time. Your mother feared you had committed suicide in grief after your young man was killed, and she blamed herself terribly."

"I'll show you why." Emily walked through the kitchen to the back door, opened it and led her father outside. "That's why," she said, and pointed at the pram.

"A baby?" he asked incredulously. "Yours? You have a baby?"

She nodded. "A little girl. She's three weeks old."

"That was why you came here? Why on earth didn't you tell us?"

"Daddy, you made it very clear what you thought of the Morrisons' daughter when she found herself in my condition. I assumed I would get the same reception. I thought you'd send me away and make me give up my baby, and I didn't want to bring shame on you."

"My dear girl," he said, staring at her now. "Your mother sometimes spouts off with things she doesn't really mean. She is quick to judge others, as you well know. And the Morrisons' daughter did have a reputation for being a little too fond of the boys. But you—our only daughter—did you think we would not have come to your aid?"

"Yes, I did. I really did. When you came to take me home when I was working in the fields, and expected me to give up Robbie Kerr, you told me quite clearly that I need not come home again if I chose to disobey you."

He nodded. "It was hot-headed of me. I think we wanted to frighten you into obeying. We'd never seen you so headstrong before."

"Because I loved Robbie, and I was going to marry him. He was a good man, Daddy. Frightfully brave. He must have been special, because I was prepared to go all the way to Australia with him."

"And this is his daughter." He peered into the pram. "She's beautiful."

"Yes. I've called her Roberta after him. But right now she's Bobbie."

"You must come home right away," he said. "We'll get a proper nursemaid for her."

Emily shook her head. "I don't want to embarrass you both. Mummy would be worried about what people say."

"We can say you're a war widow. Half the women in England are, these days. You ran off to marry an airman and he was killed. No one will question that."

"Then I'd like to come and visit you, but I'm going to stay on here," Emily said.

"Why would you want to do that? You have a comfortable home waiting for you."

She looked around the garden to the cottage and out to the lane beyond. "Because I'm needed here. I'm useful."

"Not making more of your damned herbal potions, I hope."

"Not exactly. At least not heart tonics for the time being." She smiled, and he returned her smile. She bent to pick up the child and carried her inside. As they came back into the cottage, she glanced through the front window. "Oh goodness," she said. "What on earth is this?"

A group of people was coming up the lane towards the cottage. At its head was Alice, closely followed by Mr Patterson and Mrs Soper. Emily opened the door.

"Where is he?" Alice demanded. "Where is this policeman? We've got a bone to pick with him." She pushed past Emily into the cottage and stepped up to Emily's father.

"We've come about Emily here," Alice said. "We're not going to let you arrest her. Anyone who could believe she was capable of harming anyone needs his ruddy head examining, if you ask me. Anyway, we've got signatures here from everyone in the village thanking Emily for all she's done for them. She saved them all, you know. Not a single person died of the flu because of the medicine she made for them. They all recovered, and you can't say that for most places, can you?"

"Indeed you can't," Emily's father said, looking at Alice as if she were a dangerous dog that might bite at any second. "But I have to inform you that I am not with the police. I am Emily's father."

"You are? Blimey," Alice said. "I've just got back from delivering a letter to you. Someone saw that motor car come into the village, so we thought you were the police come to take her away, and we weren't going to let you."

Mr Patterson stepped forwards to join Alice. "We consider Mrs Kerr a great asset to our community," he added. "And we are all prepared to testify on her behalf in court, if it comes to that."

Emily's father turned to her. "Well, you've certainly enough character references, young lady."

"It seems so," Emily replied, smiling.

CHAPTER FORTY-ONE

The police did not return, and she heard no more about the mixture she had sent for testing. But at the end of the week, Justin Charlton appeared at her front door.

"My grandmother has rallied against all odds," he said. "I always knew she was a tough old bird. She is making good progress and keeps asking for you. I have borrowed a friend's motor car, if you have time to come with me now."

"I'd love to," Emily said. "I'm so happy to hear this news. Just let me fetch Daisy to look after the baby."

She hurried up the path to the house. The first person she saw was Mrs Trelawney, who looked at her with surprise. "You're still here?" she asked.

"Yes, why not?" Emily replied calmly.

"But I thought that potion you gave the old lady . . ."

"Was quite harmless. And she's rallying. She'll be home in no time at all. So make sure the house is shipshape for her."

Emily concealed her sense of triumph as she left. During the drive into Exeter, she told Justin about what had just transpired with the police.

"Lucky the old lady pulled through then," he said. "That old witch, Trelawney, will have to go. I never liked her. Always sneaky, you know."

He grinned. "I've an idea. We'll send her to live in the cottage and you move to the big house."

Emily grinned. "Actually, I like my cottage. It feels like home now."

"But you won't want to stay there forever?"

"Probably not, but at this moment, it's my safe haven. And your grandmother likes having me around. She's lonely, Justin. Will you consider moving back home some day? It is your house now, you know. Lord of the manor and all that."

He chuckled. "It's hard to picture myself as lord of the manor. Viscount Charlton. Ridiculous. The war made nonsense of all that stuff we used to take seriously. Lords and blacksmiths died side by side in those trenches. But if my grandmother really needs me . . ." He didn't finish the sentence.

As they approached the hospital, Emily hesitated. "Justin, does your grandmother know about that incident with the police? I wouldn't like to worry her unnecessarily, nor to hint that Mrs Trelawney tried to accuse me of murder."

"You're too kind. She did try to accuse you of murder. And I'm sure she was dancing around happily, thinking of you swinging on the gallows. She's a horrid old bat. She was the one who took great delight in informing my grandmother of my misdeeds—which took place quite often, I'm sorry to say."

"I agree she's not very nice," Emily said. "And I think she did want to get rid of me because she was jealous. But she's been loyal to your grandmother, and I don't want to be the cause of concern to her now."

"Very well. I won't say anything to Grandmama at this moment. As for Trelawney . . . we'll see."

Lady Charlton was sitting up in bed, a cup of tea in her hand. She looked very pale and fragile, but her eyes lit up when she saw Emily come into the room. "I'm so glad to see you, my dear," she said, holding out a white hand on which the blue veins stood out.

"I wanted to come sooner, but I've been rather busy," Emily said. She bent to give the old woman a kiss on the cheek. "With the baby," she added.

"I have to say this dear boy has been most attentive." She looked up to smile at Justin, who hovered in the doorway. "He read me some of his poetry. It's quite good."

"Quite good, Grandmama? It's brilliant." Justin grinned.

"I'm so glad to see you're recovering so well," Emily said. "We were so worried."

"I just made up my mind I didn't want to die yet," Lady Charlton said. "Mind over matter, you know. I want to see the estate back to what it was before the war. Speaking of which, how are you progressing with your cottage industry?"

"Cottage industry?" Justin asked.

Emily smiled. "The ladies of the village have joined me in making salves and lotions using the herbs from the garden. We've had modest success, and the first reorders from local chemist shops."

"You need endorsements from people who matter," Justin said.

"All very well to say that," Emily replied. "I'm stuck here with a young baby."

"Give me samples. I can show them to influential people when I next go to London. And at the very least you can say that Viscount Charlton uses your cream on his boils."

"Justin, you are a hopeless case," Lady Charlton said, but she was laughing. They were interrupted by a stern sister, who ousted them from the room.

"Do you feel like a cup of tea?" Justin asked Emily. "Not in the awful hospital cafeteria. There is a cafe across the street."

As they sat drinking tea, an idea came to Emily. "You know what I'd like to do while we are here?" she said. "Do you think the assizes court keeps archives of old cases?"

"I'm sure they must."

"Then could I possibly pay a quick visit to my father's chambers?"

"Why the interest in old court cases?" Justin asked.

"I wanted to find out about a woman who lived in my cottage many years ago. She was arrested for murder, and I wanted to find out if she was really hanged. Our lives moved on such similar paths . . ."

"That's right. A woman who lived in your cottage was hanged. It's village lore," he said.

"Oh." She sat silent for a while. So Susan hadn't been so lucky. She'd had no father to defend her.

"But it was an awfully long time ago," Justin went on. "In those days, they hanged people for the least reason, didn't they? Like if someone looked at a cow, and then the cow died. And then there was the ducking stool, the hot pokers . . ."

"Ducking stool? That was centuries ago."

"Well, so was this. The woman they hanged as a witch. She was back in the seventeenth century. Tabitha Something."

"Tabitha Ann Wise," she said. She felt a huge flood of relief. The witch hadn't been Susan after all.

At the assizes, Emily was told Judge Bryce was in court, but she could leave him a message. She wrote briefly about Susan Olgivy and asked if he could find details of the court case.

They drove back to the cottage.

"I expect you'll be going to join your friends now that your grandmother is getting better," Emily said. She was embarrassed that there was a note of wistfulness in her voice.

"Yes, I can't leave them alone too long to read their inferior drivel when the world could be enjoying my brilliant poetry," he said, chuckling. Then the smile faded. He turned to look at her. "But I had a long talk with my grandmother the other evening. She wants to get the home farm back on its feet. I told her I'm no farmer, but she's concerned it's not producing income and the land is going to waste."

"So she wants you to come back and run the farm?" Again, she was surprised at the hope she felt.

He nodded. "It used to have a prosperous dairy herd when my grandfather was alive."

"I probably wouldn't advise dairy now," Emily said. "You need too much manpower, and there just aren't many men."

"Oh, I forgot—you're the expert!" He laughed, but she realized he was not making fun. "What do you suggest?"

"Sheep would be easy," Emily said. "They look after themselves until lambing season and shearing. And it might be a good idea to plant a cash crop, too. Again, one that doesn't need much manpower. What is the quality of the soil like?"

"How on earth would I know?" He laughed again. "You'd better come and talk to the farm manager. He knows his stuff, but he's getting old."

They reached the cottage. "You'll take good care of Grandmama until I return?" he asked.

"Of course I will."

"That's good." He paused. "And you will stick around? If I'm going to turn into a farmer, I'll need help."

"I won't be going anywhere, as long as you let me live in the cottage," she said. "Apart from an occasional visit to my parents."

"As official owner of Bucksley House, I can promise you the cottage is yours for as long as you want it."

"That's so good of you." She felt tears coming to her eyes. "Thank you."

"Purely selfish on my part, I promise you." He paused, looking as if he was going to say more, then added, "Who else will advise me on what cash crops I need to plant?" He reached out and touched her arm gently. "I'll see you soon then."

Emily found herself smiling, too, as she went back into the cottage. As Susan had written in her diary—the heart can begin to heal.

Rhys Bowen

Two days later, a letter arrived from her father's office. It contained a transcript of the trial of Susan Olgilvy, November 1858.

The counsel for the defence showed that Mrs Maria Tinsley used a face powder that contained arsenic, and that she'd had a deformed heart that had caused her lingering illness and precipitated her death.

A verdict of "not guilty" was delivered by the jury.

"She lived!" Emily exclaimed, dancing around the kitchen and waving the letter in triumph. "Susan lived."

Lady Charlton was brought home in the motor car by Simpson at the beginning of June. Emily and Simpson had worked hard on the garden so that the roses along the drive were magnificent and the borders in full bloom. The old lady smiled as she looked around her home. "It's good to be back," she said. "And I'm looking forward to some decent food again. No more of that hospital slop. A good, hearty steak and kidney pie. Where is Mrs Trelawney?"

"I'm sorry to tell you that she has left, Lady Charlton," Emily said. "She went to be with her invalid sister."

She didn't say that Justin had arrived out of the blue one day and dismissed Mrs Trelawney.

"I decided to use my powers as Viscount Charlton for good," he had said, laughing at Emily's expression when he told her this. "You should have seen her face."

Emily had stared at him with delight. "So now we'll have to hire a new cook. Will you help me choose one who won't poison us? And we need servants."

"You could make Daisy head housemaid," Emily had suggested. "She's really good."

"And Grandmama likes her?"

"She does."

"Then consider it done."

"You see, you can be the lord of the manor after all," Emily had said.

"We've no idea what we can do until we try." His eyes had held hers. "I've been able to look forward to the future without dread for the first time. How about you?"

"Yes," she had agreed. "I think I can."

Emily looked forward to telling Lady Charlton about the changes Justin was planning. "Now that you are back," Emily said as she settled Lady Charlton in her favourite chair, "we must arrange for Bobbie's christening. I wanted to ask you to be her godmother. Alice is going to be the other godmother. Mr Patterson is going to be her godfather."

"I don't normally like going near that church," Lady Charlton said. "But in your case, I'll make an exception. What names are you giving her?"

"Well, Roberta, and then Alice, and I'd like to give her your name, too."

"It's Susan," the old woman said, and she gave Emily a knowing smile.

Emily opened her mouth to say something, but the old woman added, "A very common name, especially in these parts." And her face said, "Don't ask me any more."

Is it possible? Emily wondered. And she remembered that the old woman had known about the trunk in the attic and hadn't been surprised that Emily had taken over the herb garden. And she had been away from the village for many years, coming back suntanned and middle-aged. The villagers would not have associated the new lady of the manor with the former schoolmistress.

It was all meant to be, she thought, and a feeling of contentment swept through her. She had been told that the house was cursed, but instead it had turned out to be her destiny. She let her thoughts go a little further. Susan had married the man who had then become Viscount Charlton.

The christening was held on a bright, sunny Sunday in June. Roberta Alice Susan wore the christening robes of the Charlton family.

The whole village was in their finery, and a feast had been set up on the green outside the church for after the ceremony. To her surprise, Emily's parents arrived, her mother looking tense and suspicious, but her haughty look melted when she saw the baby.

"She looks just like you at the same age," she said. "You were always such a pretty child."

Justin had been away with his fellow poets, still on their tour of Britain, so Emily was surprised to see him striding towards the green as they sat talking long into the evening and swallows flitted through the pink twilight.

"Well, here you all are," he said. He gave Emily a little smile.

"To what do we owe this honour?" Lady Charlton asked.

"I've come to claim my rights!" he said dramatically, then laughed at her face. "No, silly. I didn't want to miss the big celebration. Where is the young star of the proceedings?"

"Sleeping in her perambulator," Emily said. "Too much excitement for one day."

Justin approached the pram and stared down at Roberta Alice Susan, now sleeping blissfully amid the layers of her antique lace christening gown. He stared at her for a long while as Emily watched him. Then he looked up. "She's beautiful. Absolutely perfect. Of course, I would have expected no less." And his gaze moved to Emily, sending the colour rushing to her cheeks.

"So you left your tour to come back for this?" she asked.

He looked pleased with himself. "The tour is over—a great success. A publisher has approached us, so you'll have another book to add to your library, Grandmama. And so I've come home. I thought we'd better get started on improving that farm of ours while it's still summer."

"You've come home." Lady Charlton's voice cracked a little. "That is good news." She paused. "That farm has been suffering from neglect for too long now."

Justin pulled up a chair next to Emily. "Also, I have good news for you. I gave your lotion to a friend of mine who is a chemist at Imperial College in London. He tested it, and he found it pretty good. It turns out his uncle has a factory, and he might be interested in manufacturing it commercially. What do you say?"

Emily looked around the long tables at the women who had become her friends, her sisters. "I'd have to confer with my partners first," she replied.

ABOUT THE AUTHOR

Photo © 2016 John Quin-Harkin

Rhys Bowen is the *New York Times* bestselling author of more than thirty mystery novels, including *The Tuscan Child* and her World War II novel *In Farleigh Field*, the winner of the Left Coast Crime Award for Best Historical Mystery Novel and the Agatha Award for Best Historical Novel. Bowen's work has won sixteen honors to date, including multiple Agatha, Anthony, and Macavity awards. Her books have been translated into many languages, and she has fans around the world, including seventeen thousand Facebook followers. A transplanted Brit, Bowen divides her time between California and Arizona.